the Res.
An American Novel

GUY M. MADISON

Published by:
M² Publishers
6025 Lois Madison Drive
Marysville, WA 98271
(360) 651-0967
FAX: 651-0960
Email: M2write@aol.com

Printed by:
Snohomish Publishing Co.
114 Avenue C
Snohomish, WA 98290
(360) 568-1242

First Print: April 1998

Copyright: Guy M. Madison 1998
Copyright: M² Publishers 1998
All rights reserved

Cover Illustration Copyright:
Richard L. Madison 1998
All rights reserved

Publishers Note:
This is a work of fiction.
Names, characters, and incidents either are the product of the author's imagination or are used fictitiously, and any resemblance to actual persons, living or dead, and or events is entirely coincidental.

ISBN: 0-9657032-9-0
Printed in the United States of America
First Edition

Foreword

The Res is Madison's first book in an epic "coming of age" trilogy. This book begins the story with a time in American history that was not particularly pretty: civil unrest, out-of-control racism, despairing poverty, Vietnam. Madison is a Native American. You can see it, hear it, and feel it, especially in his dialogue. The male and female characters, from two generations and three races who live on the Reservation, struggle to find their own paths as their Tribe and the nation do the same. While the turbulent '60's and '70's in America are studied by everyone from social historians to media magicians, Madison's approach is fresh, enlightening, and insightful.

This is a story of life on an American Indian Reservation, told from the inside out, and set in a time period both comfortable and intriguing. Madison has followed the first rule of writing – "write about what you know best" – to produce a novel with broad appeal. Everyone will be able to draw something from the three main characters: Jonny, Caj and Nicki-D. I soon realized how skillfully Madison points out the common bonds between all races that often highlight their differences.

Madison's attention to descriptive detail, to the day-to-day processes of living, to the inner thoughts behind the *seemingly* illogical actions of his characters, all contribute to the reader's enjoyable journey to another time and place. Read it on a bright sunny day, and feel a little excitement as you look forward to the next book in the trilogy. And let Little Mouse from the Old Storyteller's tale be your guide.

Lori Zue McNeil
Former editor, *Finesse Magazine*
President, Whitehorse Marketing, Inc.

ACKNOWLEDGEMENTS AND THANKS TO:

*My Editor and Publisher; Floreda Mary,
My brother, artist Richard Madison, for his creative
support and art work,
Lori Daniels for her continuous inspiration,
Brenda Werner for her uplifting presence,
Bob Bryce for all his support,
Copy Editor; Kimbra Owen, for her dedication to detail,
Rich Ives for being there in the beginning,
Kris Kane for her encouragement,
Seven Arrows and the Coast Salish and
Western Washington Indians, Book II,
for their meaningful words.*

DEDICATION

To My Family:

*My Loving Parents who brought me life, and made me who I am today:
Frank Freeman Madison and Lois Evelyn Madison*

*And to my Brothers and Sisters, whom I love very much:
Carol Mae,
Sandra Lynn,
Frank Steven,
Michele Renee,
Richard Lee,
Karen Gaye,
Marguerite Anne,
Kimberly Kaye,
Ellene Lisa*

the Res.
An American Novel

GUY M. MADISON

TABLE OF CONTENTS

1. THE RES 15
2. TIGER LADY 25
3. EAGLE 35
4. BEST FRIENDS 45
5. THE PARTY 61
6. REJECTION 71
7. GINNY 81
8. LOIS 91
9. TWO WOMEN 103
10. POEM 109
11. DUMP 119
12. SCHOOL 131
13. LOST INNOCENCE 141
14. HANFORD 153
15. CHRISTIAN 157
16. SPIRITS 167
17. DROWNING 179
18. GOOD BYE 191
19. CAMPUS 205
20. AWAKENING 215
21. ROTC 231
22. GIFT 245
23. DREAMS 261
24. JONNY 269
25. SHADOW 273
26. COFFEE 277
27. VIETNAM 287
28. THE ENEMY 299
29. HOME 313
30. TOGETHER 323
31. FEELING 341
32. MOTHER 351

Story-Teller

Children clustered around the Story-Teller with anticipation. He lit his Pipe and began:
Once there was a Mouse.
Squinting his eyes, he touched his nose to the nose of a little girl near him.
He was a Busy Mouse, Searching Everywhere, Touching his Whiskers to the Grass, and Looking. He was Busy as all Mice are, Busy with Mice things. But Once in a while he would Hear an odd Sound. He would Lift his Head, Squinting hard to See, his Whiskers Wiggling in the Air, and he would Wonder. One Day he Scurried up to a fellow Mouse and asked him, "Do you Hear a Roaring in your Ears, my Brother?"
"No, no," answered the Other Mouse, not Lifting his Busy Nose from the Ground. "I Hear Nothing. I am Busy now. Talk to me Later."
He asked Another Mouse the same Question and the Mouse Looked at him Strangely. "Are you Foolish in your Head? What Sound?" he asked and Slipped into a Hole in a Fallen Cottonwood Tree.
The little Mouse shrugged his Whiskers and Busied himself again, Determined to Forget the Whole matter. But there was that Roaring again. It was faint, very faint, but it was there! One Day, he Decided to investigate the Sound just a little. Leaving the Other Busy Mice, he Scurried a little Way away and Listened again. There It was! He was Listening hard when suddenly, Someone said Hello.
"Hello, little Brother," the Voice said, and Mouse almost Jumped right Out of his Skin. He Arched his Back and Tail and was about to Run.

"Hello," again said the Voice. "It is I, Brother Raccoon." And sure enough, It was! "What are you Doing Here all by yourself, little Brother?" asked the Raccoon. The Mouse blushed, and put his Nose almost to the Ground. "I Hear a Roaring in my Ears and I am Investigating it," He answered timidly.

"A Roaring in your Ears?" replied the Raccoon as he Sat Down with him. "What you Hear, little Brother, is the River."

"The River?" Mouse asked curiously. "What is a River?"

"Walk with me and I will Show you the River," Raccoon said.

Little Mouse was terribly Afraid, but he was Determined to Find Out Once and for All about the Roaring. "I can Return to my Work," he thought, "after this thing is Settled, and possibly this thing may Aid me in All my Busy Examining and Collecting. And my Brothers all said it was Nothing. I will Show them. I will Ask Raccoon to Return with me and I will have Proof.

All right Raccoon, my Brother," Said Mouse. "Lead on to the River. I will Walk with you."

"Get me another brand from the fire, my son," the Story-Teller said. "And we will talk more about this Mouse."

Lighting his Pipe, the Chief looked up at the little girl nearest him. "And what will happen to little Mouse?" he asked, grabbing the end of her nose. She blushed and looked down at her hands.

1

THE RES.

Dok-a-bles, the Changer, had come down from the sky. He wandered the earth where the first humans lived. The Changer came to talk to them. He knew their spirits. Some he turned to rocks and some to plants, some animals and then ... there were the humans.

The Res. swallowed up people. It is a place where most people would never go if they had a choice. Its evergreen trees concealed most people that lived there. It was a place where you went on your own or you were planted there. Most white people came on their own.

The Indians were planted there.

The whites who settled on the Res. usually wanted a change in their life. The land was free and clear and nobody bothered you. The waters of Puget Sound were cold and dark; the winds made it ideal for sailing. Rich white people bought their land on the bluffs of the Res. They built their big houses facing the beautiful bay so they could see across it and watch the sun come up and go down. Most were second homes, used only in the summer. They filled the waters with their big sailboats or fast speed boats with no consideration for others. They treated those below their economic status with contempt and indifference. They wouldn't know an Indian if you put one in their face. They could afford not to.

There were other white people on the Res. who were outcasts and couldn't make it on the outside. Living in little cabins between the trees they were loggers and forest people paid to watch the trees and the wildlife die off, or trappers and hunters who stayed after the last animal fell to their traps and guns. They became land owners at the Indians expense. The government leased them Indian land at twenty-five dollars a year with a lease of ninety-nine years and an option for another ninety-nine. There was so much land at the time, and so few people that nobody noticed; except the Indian land owners, of course. These white people had to mingle and deal with the Indians on a daily basis. They never could understand the Indian way. It was too foreign for them. They lived side by side the best they could.

It was under these conditions that all the people must live. The Res. had its boundaries, its customs, and its traditions. You lived by its rules or you left; it was as simple as that.

If you lived under its rules, you received all the benefits of living within the Reservation. Rewards and compensation came from the peaceful communal lives of its inhabitants. The only thing was; you had to recognize what those rules were.

The Res. never changed. Franc Esque wasn't happy about that. He was on the leading edge of progress. Change was slow and to an outsider it would appear nonexistent, but Franc saw it. He sensed a strength emanating from some of his people. The people were the reservation's future. The future was now.

Franc thought of Shaman Tom and his words: "A dream within a dream." Shaman Tom would always repeat this statement wherever he went. "We are the dream and we are the dreamer." How Shaman Tom found logic in this illogical saying was beyond Franc.

To Franc, this statement meant confinement. He reinterpreted it as a box within a box; boundaries of no escape. Franc was a literal man who talked of spiritual ways, but the box confined him.

The night was dark; darker than Franc had ever seen it. He was a little drunk. He looked up into the cold, dark sky and watched the bright stars in a cold December night. They twinkled and blinked back at him, letting him know that they were watching.

Standing on his old dilapidated porch he could barely see the harsh water out in the night. It was a black desert that swallowed up all light as it moved away from land. Franc's eyes adjusted as much as they could, but still couldn't make out anything farther than five feet away. He stood there, in the night, in deep thought.

Lois Esque was inside her warm house located on Totem Beach. She watched her husband, Franc, as he stood on the porch. He was a big man – about six feet tall, with a slim build. He said it came from his Alaskan side. Her penetrating, light-blue eyes took in the night. Her ears listened to the howling wind coming in from the frozen north. Fear grabbed her as she thought she could see a shape in the night. It came from the sky. No, that was wrong; it came from the darkness; a huge shape of a bird. It was the Thunderbird of the Indians. Her eyes widened as she watched the shape grow as it came closer. It was coming in to attack. Her heart started beating faster. It was so large. She closed her eyes.

The wind hit the window pane with a whoosh. It splattered little bits of debris over its pane. Lois opened her eyes and peered out. The wind was blowing hard against Franc. The tip of his cigarette glowed in the night. Why did Franc have to teach his boys on a night like this? Was it some male challenge or something? She could never understand the male psyche. She peered into the darkness, still fearful of what was out there. She would never go out on a night like this.

Grandma Delia sat in the corner of the house on the couch. She was with Big Ed, a large white man, who was her husband. Lois didn't like either one of them when it came to their drinking, but she tolerated them. They both had a quart bottle of beer in front of them. They showed up and Franc drank from that point on. What could Lois do? Delia was Franc's mother. She pointed at Lois in her drunken way and spoke: "Evil spirits. Evil spirits." She laughed.

Lois wrapped her two little boys in the warmest clothing she could find. Lois wasn't about to send them out in the cold night unless she knew they were protected.

"Morgan-Mckenzi, bring me your mittens. I want Jonny to wear them." Morgan Mckenzi, the silent one, came running into the room with her mittens.

"What if he loses them?" she asked with wide-eyed fear.

"Then he does."

"But what about me? I won't have anything to wear then." Morgan-Mckenzi wailed against the injustice of having to give them up to her brother.

"Morgan-Mckenzi, he wouldn't lose your mittens. Now give them to me and go back in the kitchen where its warm. " Lois took the gloves and put them on her little boy. The shabby surroundings of her house didn't bother her at all. She felt warm and safe in her house and she thought that, of the eight houses on Totem Beach, she had the best view. She loved her home. Lois looked down at her little boys wrapped up in all the clothes she could find. Their eyes peered out from bundles of clothes. She bent down.

"Now listen, Caj, I want you to hang on to your brother's hand and not let go. You're his big brother. Look out for him. You know your father will be there all of the time. So don't get scared, Okay?" Lois was nodding her head up and down and looking at Caj until he began to nod his head along with her. Jonny, the youngest boy, was so small - even at this age. Her heart melted at the thought of Jonny walking in the cold night. Jonny stared back at her with little understanding. His eyes were devoid of any thought of harm. Lois almost laughed at him, but caught herself. She grabbed him and hugged him against her.

"You two stay with your father and don't wander too far from him, you hear?"

They both nodded at her. There wasn't much else to say. She had to send them out eventually. Their father was expecting them and, being a woman, she had to let them go with him. Lois opened the door. Franc was still smoking a cigarette and looking out across the bay. It was so dark. Why did he pick a night like this to bring the boys with him? She wanted to tell them all to come back inside where it was warm and safe. She held her tongue. The porch light flooded over Franc.

Franc looked down at his boys. He almost laughed. Two little bundles of clothes stared back at him. He sighed, thinking of their mother and how she tried to protect them. A strong wind rushed through the porch, causing Franc's neck hairs to stand up. Evil spirits, he thought. He better get started. He grabbed his sons. Like all Tulalips, he thought of his sons as his future. "Let's go."

It was a big adventure for the boys. Their daddy was home and they were going with him.

All three of them stepped into the darkness. The light from the house was there, but not there, as the dark night crept into their vision. Caj and Jonny could feel their daddy's big hands holding them and they felt no fear. He took a step and then waited for them to take their small steps. Then he took another step and they would take their small steps. Franc began a rhythm that they followed. It was the rhythm of the earth.

The houses on Totem Beach all had their lights on and the boys could see them. They were old homes, spaced about one hundred yards from each other. Caj and Jonny peered out with little eyes and tried to see the waves rushing onto the beach; but it was too dark. They already knew that the wind would kick up white caps. Only on the harshest days did the wind blow over the islands and bring in the roaring white caps. Tonight was one of those days.

Franc began to talk. The boys didn't understand what he was saying; they only knew that he was talking to them and they should listen.

"I'm going to tell you a story of our people. We are the Sdo-hobsh Tribe of the salt waters. We also are from the Jimicum village, from the Sdoqualmie Tribe. We have been put here to live by the white man. This is our reservation. This is our home. Do you understand?"

Caj understood a little bit, but not much. He was still too young; Jonny didn't have a clue.

A dog from the Henry place started to howl. The two boys stopped for a second. Franc stopped too. He didn't know if the dog howled because he knew a bad wind was coming or if he knew Franc and his boys were walking and getting too close. It didn't matter; the dog wasn't going to do anything to them. It scared the boys.

"Are you scared? The world is made up of many strange and frightening things. Are you scared of that dog? He is only a dog. He has his ways and he only follows those ways. There are some mean dogs and some good dogs, but it don't matter as long as you know that they are the same. It is the spirit that makes us what we are. There are good spirits and bad spirits, witches and others that act different but come from the same place. That is what you have to watch for, because someday you will have to deal with your own spirit. There is no getting away from this."

Franc moved on. He walked a little further. He noticed the old Catholic church on the tip of Totem Beach. Many of the Tulalips were Catholic. He was. The bell on top of the tower of the white building would wake them every Sunday morning, bringing them all together to ask for help for their sins. Franc never understood this concept. It was a world where it seemed like those that called you to repent your sin were the ones who sinned the most ... and mostly against the Indians. To ask for their forgiveness seemed wrong and he never could bring himself to do that.

He was beginning his walk. His mind thought of the reservation today; the families that lived on it. His family were the Esques; part French and part Indian. He was part Tulalip and part Alaskan. His cousins, the Madisons, were Jimicums from the Monroe village; they were also Alaskan Indians, with tall bodies and light brown skin. The Henrys were short, dark, stocky Indians, with their off-shoot families of Josephs and Gonzales. The Jones so numerous in number that they broke off into three family groups. The Frybergs and Williams made up another group of tall dark Indians. They owned Hermosa point, just north of Totem Beach. They were the big families of the Rez.; families connected through marriage and agreements and coalitions. Politics came mostly through family ties.

The Moses, were part of the short, dark Sdo-hobsh people. All the families belonged to the Sdo-hobsh tribes. The Moses were part Jones, and they voted with them. Another family of short people were the Gobins. The Gobins were short and light-skinned, with round bellies. All of the families blood lines were thinning out from constant marriages to non-Indians. Franc Esque knew all the families and now he was going to pass on to his sons the stories of how the families came to be. He thought of all the constant battles and make-ups between the families. Everyone was related through marriage and their children. Because of this arrangement, the families had to learn how to get along. A culture of avoidance developed from the ashes of the reservation system.

Confrontation was avoided, and this lead to larger fights and blow-ups and animosity, at times. Franc thought of this as Caj left his side and ran in front of him. He watched Jonny, who held on to him tightly. When Franc stopped, his youngest son stopped and waited for him to go again. Franc knew that Jonny was still too young to let go, but the more walks in the dark they took and the older Jonny got, the less he would have to hang on to him. This was his first walk.

Franc thought of the old ones; the people of the tribe who lived in different times – a time when he was a boy. The reservation was so different then. People were so different. The old ones watched Franc's generation's very souls being ripped from them. He remembered some of the women who would beat the children. Why they were so mean he didn't understand. He only knew that, along with his generation, their generation was lost. They drank and didn't know how to act. The white man put them in schools and told them how to act. The elders could only watch as their children were torn from their hearts.

The Elders cried and tried to maintain the old ways that no longer helped their children in the New World. They told their children that they must learn; that they must work in the white man's world. Then they condemned the children for learning the white man's way and not keeping to the old ways. Franc remembered more and more.

Franc remembered the old ones' stories of how it used to be. It was a dream to him; it was life to them. He thought of the stories of the animals: like the tricksters, Coyote and Raven; stories of the Salmon

Prince; and of our brothers, the black fish, who herded salmon into the bay for the humans. He remembered how the children not sent to the boarding school at Tulalip talked about the stories given to them by their grandmothers and grandfathers. They would talk of Dok-a-bles, the Changer, who came down from the sky and changed the First Ones. The First Ones were humans who called themselves by Grizzly Bear, and Blue Bird. When the Changer came down, he turned them into what their spirit was like. Franc remembered this from his childhood.

"I want to talk to you about how you came to be here." Franc looked at his two boys. They watched him with interest, probably happy that he was paying attention to them. Caj was fidgety and looked at the world through small, curious eyes. Jonny stood next to his father as his strong, low voice reached his ears. He would remember this night as one of the first memories of his life.

"You have come from two worlds; The Indian world and the White world. Some would deny you this, but it will be up to you to one day decide what world you will follow. For now, I will tell you about your Indian side - about the old people; your grandmother and her grandmother. I will talk about the villages and how I grew up. I will tell you this because I want you to be proud of who you are. You can't be proud if you don't know where you came from and who your family is. You must learn what I say."

Franc watched Caj fidget some more. Jonny stood there waiting for more words. He knew that his two boys had already made up their minds as to which world each would go. He sighed and moved on. It was cold out tonight. They would walk some more on another day. He smiled. "For now, maybe we better go back in where it is warm."

Lois watched from the window. Even though she knew it would be a short walk tonight, she worried. Children were always getting some dreadful disease and dying. She didn't want that happening to her boys. She had wanted Franc to wait for another night, but he said no. She was just happy he wasn't drunk, as he had been with Gray, her oldest boy. She wouldn't let Franc take them unless she knew that she could protect them. It was always that way. She controlled what went on in the house when it came to the kids.

"Mom! Are you coming in to help us bake the bread?" Morgan-Mckenzi stuck her head out from the kitchen. Lois saw Clair, her second-oldest daughter, beating the bread dough. Lois smiled at them. It seemed right that her daughters would be in the kitchen with her while the boys were with their father.

"Mom, how come I don't get to go out with the boys?" Morgan-Mckenzi wanted very much to be part of everything. If she could, she would be in the kitchen and outside with the boys.

"Because you're my girls." Lois looked out into the darkness. Small dots of light hit her eye and she squinted to see. It was just too dark. The boys needed to be looked after. The girls already made their own decisions. It was a mother's responsibility to take care of her boys. Lois didn't know why, but it was different. With her girls, she never worried as much as she did for her boys. That was how it was when she grew up and, as far as she could tell, some things hadn't changed and they might never change. Lois was determined to make all of her children strong.

"Evil spirits. Ha-ha." Grandma Delia was drunk. Lois gave her a stern look and went back to looking for her children. She sighed and got up and went into the warm kitchen to join her daughters in their bread-making.

Franc sighed. The night was so dark. He knew some of his stories were made up from his own life. It was all sad. His life; their life; his mother's life. It was all hard. Life in America was what you made it. He tried to make it, but never could quite reach his potential. Something always interfered. The war immediately entered his mind. It was America and its lie; the lie that you could get ahead if you worked hard and played by the rules. He had done that: played by the rules and even gone overseas and fought for his country. A lot of good that did. He was bitter. His life was hard, thoughts of the war troubled his mind, and he was drinking too much. Life was never good for him in America and he wondered if it would change much for his kids.

Caj was already at the front porch of the pink house. Franc had a hold on Jonny; his youngest son. He was three years old and both Franc and Lois knew there was something wrong with him. His speech was labored and he stuttered. Lois thought he would grow out of it, but Franc wasn't sure. Caj would do well. He was strong and athletic and full of life. While Jonny was introverted and withdrawn, Caj was gregarious and outgoing. They were two opposites that occupied the same space. Franc was already calculating that one of them would break the chains of poverty that bound the reservation. Franc already put his money on Caj. He would be the one to lead. He would be the one who would bring respect to the Esque family. Today they both learned about their families and their duties. Today, Franc could see the future.

Lois slammed the dough down on the bread board. She threw some more flour on the dough and took her rolling pin and began a back-and-forth roll over the dough. She flattened out the dough until it was thin enough, then pulled it back up and molded it again.

"Mom, let me do it." Dani was impatient with her mother. She was the oldest of the children and was used to getting her own way. She chose to be the bread-maker tonight. Claire was sitting in the corner with Morgan-Mckenzi, telling her a story. The children were accustomed to stories. Clair was telling about the Ste-tots, and ghosts, and witches, and the Changer.

"The Changer came from the east and found all these people here near the waters of the Northwest. There were so many who spoke different languages that he decided to make them into tribes. We are the saltwater people by the bay. Sdo-ho-bsh. The white people call us the Snohomish; like the county we live in. It was named after our tribe."

Morgan-Mckenzi listened to her sister, but fidgeted a little. "Where did we go?"

Clair looked perplexed for a second. "I don't know."

She thought about it some more, but with no satisfactory answer she dismissed it and moved on.

"The White man put us on this reservation. They say they gave us this land to live on but Dad says that we already owned this land and they gave us nothing. He says the White man changed history to make them look good. But we used to own all the lands to the Cascade mountains and we gave them the land. Dad says..."

"That's enough Clair. Come over here and help us put the bread in the stove."

Lois was thinking about the changes of life. She had ten kids: seven girls and three boys. Franc relied on the boys to bring change within the tribe. Lois knew it was the girls who might bring about real change. Each of her girls was the smartest of the family. She could see it in their eyes.

Lois used to think that it was too bad that, with their brains, they were born girls. The world and the reservation worked against girls. Heck, even the girls' own hormones worked against them when it came to children. It was hard for them. It was hard for Lois and her sister when they grew up. Women were second-class citizens who, most of the time, had to simply accept their station in life.

Now, she thought, the world will change and women will have a bigger role in it. It wasn't something she thought of as good or bad; it was just reality. Lois was a spiritual person living in a real world. Franc may want to tell his boys stories of the old people and how they lived, but Lois wanted to teach them that they had to live in today's world. Franc was a dreamer. As far as Lois was concerned, her kids had to survive to dream.

Today, they were cooking food for a funeral tomorrow. One of the Jone's little boys died from crib death. Funerals were a reality of the reservation. Lois wasn't about to let that happen to her kids. She would fight hard to keep them safe and able to survive. This was how their lives broke down: Franc and Lois Esque; two sides of the same coin. Lois would concentrate on survival, teaching her kids the basic ingredients of life – a life of hardship that was certain to follow them.

Franc will teach them how to dream. No; that wasn't even true. Lois would teach her girls how to dream and Franc would teach his boys their dreams; then they would switch, with Franc teaching the girls about life and Lois, the boys. It was hard to understand the gender gap. Lois and Franc didn't; they just lived it.

Lois heard the front door open. She could see shadows moving around in her house. Franc was back. That was good. Now everyone was safe under her roof That is all she worried about. The world was right again.

"Clair, bring your father some coffee."

Grandma Delia sat in the corner of the room. "Evil spirits. Evil spirits. Ha-ha."

2

TIGER LADY

Nikki-D sat in the back of the new '56 Chevrolet that belonged to her father. He was driving. Her mother sat upright in the passenger seat. Her eyes straight ahead, they watched nothing but the road in front of her. They had been traveling for some time; the plane flight, then the car ride, was tedious and tiring. Nikki-D moved a little because her rear was stiff from sitting. The car ride alone was over an hour. She watched out of the windows, looking from one window to the other, trying to see what she could. Even that was getting tiring after a while. She settled down and just sat there, but her excitement still ran wild.

Nikki-D watched the brown and gold leaves swirl up as the wind kicked at them. They had turned left off highway 99, into the Tulalip Indian Reservation. She felt her mother stiffen. It made her do the same. Her father didn't notice. As usual, he was too intent on the road ahead to see what was going on around him. The trees were tall and green. Some small trees; most of them having lost their leaves, leaving them bare and ugly, stood at the bottom of the Evergreens. The road twisted right, then left, as they drove into the heart of the reservation.

Nikki-D sat back and remembered the last few days.

There was frantic movement all around her as the movers carried everything from the house. Their furniture was stacked out on the lawn, ready to be stuffed into the big moving truck. "Rotor Movers" was painted on the side of the truck. Nikki-D sat on the porch, watching her world being carted away. All her friendships, all her plans, were crumbling in front of her. She knew it was almost time for them to go. The pressure was building inside her. The tears came to her eyes. She sat there trying to maintain herself. Men picked up the heavy furniture and lifted it onto the truck. It was almost full, and the lawn was becoming bare. When the last of the furniture was loaded, they would be off.

The moving truck would leave before them. They would stay at her Aunt's place until they flew out next week. Nikki-D saw her father talking to one of the men in white overalls. He signed a piece of paper that was handed to him and the man jumped in the truck. The engine roared and the truck began to move, an inch at a time. Nikki-D watched the truck as it moved down the road. She watched until it disappeared.

She didn't want to move. She wanted to stay and she knew her mother was unhappy, too. It wasn't fair. They were going to a new state: Washington.

They passed a small store on the side of the old Tulalip road. "Priest Point Groceries" was the name on the sign. There were some men standing outside by the doors. Their long, black hair looked like hers. She moved over to the passenger window, her coal-black eyes taking in everything in front of them. The men looked scruffy and haggard, hair down to their shoulders. They were laughing at something or someone.

It was the first time Nikki-D saw anyone like them. Their faces looked old and tired, but they laughed as if they were young. These were her first Indians. Her black eyes darted back and forth, taking in all the strange sights.

"Don't stare," her mother said. Ginny was frightened. She was scared to look, afraid that it would antagonize *those* people. She hated the dirty way they dressed and their long, shaggy hair. Their clothes showed her their poorness.

Nikki-D moved back to the center of the seat. She could barely see over the bottom of the windows. She sat back and watched the terrain go by. She wondered when they would get there.

"And quit fidgeting!"

The car moved down the old Tulalip road until they turned left at Totem Beach Road. Nikki-D had her face against the window. There was a cemetery, and more Indians. Lots more. She could see them standing by a grave. Two people were being buried side by side. They all seemed sad. When they saw her car, everyone looked up. None of them said anything, they just watched, their faces etched in time. Most of them wore black. Nikki-D saw their eyes as they watched. She would never forget them. Today was her first memory of Indians. Rain began to pelt the window as droplets floated from the sky; sprinkles of water that cleansed the earth. The people didn't seem to notice it. They just stood there, watching, as the car went by.

"I told you not to stare." Nikki-D could hear the fear in her mother's voice. "Now sit up straight and act like a lady."

Nikki-D did what she was told. She tried to see out of the corner of her eyes. She wanted to see the strange people by the graves. The car turned onto the road that went to the top of Mission Heights. She was about to see her new home.

The wind blew over Mission Bluff. The big house stood at the top of Mission Heights; hidden. A high, contemptuous fence followed a path from the road, all the way to the deep bluffs of Mission Hill. It was the highest of the high, lording over the other homes running up and down the bluffs. Its dark wood blended with the forest around it; it was a dark house. A shingled roof slanted down to let the water run off. Two large bay windows faced the water. At night, people on the water of Puget Sound guided themselves by the lights of the house. It was a great house; everyone looked up to it.

Big evergreen trees formed a natural boundary for the home. The forest was dark and deep on the hill, running for five miles to the main road. Secret pathways ran through the woods. Deer wandered through the woods; other animals, too.

Two hundred feet of trimmed grass surrounded the house. From the road the driveway had flowers on each side that when in bloom, took on every color of the spectrum. Bright red roses, white and yellow gardenias; the gardener cut and holed each plant making sure they were arranged right. The garden wound around the edge of the house and lead up to the doorway. It left its invitation like a taunt for the uninvited.

Ginny Thomas walked with discipline, showing her aristocratic background. She walked straight and direct, always in control. She was poised and in command, Or, at least, she acted as though she was.

She noticed the couple in the house just below hers. A man and a woman watched them as they walked into the house. Then they closed their curtains.

The house was filled with boxes that she had packed weeks ago. The moving men had came and gone. Now it was up to her to unpack and get the house ready. Right now all she wanted was to get some sleep. It had been a long trip. Nikki-D ran through the house, but she would be asleep soon, too. It all could wait until tomorrow.

Officer Pete Livingston stood at the window as the Thomas's walked up to their new home. Anger built up inside him as he watched them survey the surroundings and then enter their home.

"Shit. Just what we need - some chinks living next door to us."

Nora and the kids stayed at the window, watching the new family. Tammy her daughter, was about the same age as the little Asian girl. Tammy watched her with intense interest. Her older brother, Jimmy, looked at the little girl, too, but his thoughts were of something completely different. Desire grew in his eyes. She seemed so exotic.

"Nora, get those kids away from the window. Jesus Christ, its only some damn white man who don't know his place. Just because he has money, he thinks he can bring his chink wife here. That's all we need is Chinks and Indians on the Rez."

Nora moved away from the window with Tammy hanging on her. She feared Pete when he got angry. He had his uniform on and would be off to work soon. Nora made his lunch and pressed his clothes. He looked so handsome to her.

"They have money; you can tell that. Did you see the furniture they brought last week? The moving men said they came from the other side of America. You shouldn't talk like that in front of the kids. She looks like a mixture anyway."

"I don't give a shit. Is my lunch ready? I got to go."

"Yes, its on the counter. Don't forget your keys."

"I don't want any of you to go over there, either. There has been another death for the Indians and we'll be hearing those damn drums for the next week. Why can't they bury their people like normal human beings?"

"Tammy, honey, go and kiss your father good-bye." Nora pushed her little girl to her father. They were all scared of him. Tammy stood, tentatively with her head down in front of her father. Officer Pete bent down and hugged his little girl; it was one of his long hugs, with his hands roaming down her backside. He smiled down at her and then he was gone.

Jimmy watched the little girl. She was the best thing he had ever seen in his life. Feelings of want and need rushed through his groin. It wasn't a new feeling, only now it was connected to this little girl, with her beautiful eyes and long black hair. She would fill Jimmy's dreams and desires from now on.

Tammy ran back to her mother and they returned to the window to watch the new family move in. She wanted to see the little girl, too. They were the same age.

Nora sat down in their living room. It was a confessional room that neither stood out nor brought attention to itself. Everything in the house was clean. Her husband demanded that of her and her children. She wasn't a pretty woman, and she thought she was lucky to have married her husband.

Having this house on the bay was what most women would kill for. She knew her husband had bad bouts, but she overlooked them to keep her life simple and happy.

Officer Pete drove down Mission Heights, burning. He couldn't understand the fact that a Chink lived in the upper house. He hated having the second-best home on the Heights. Here comes another uppity rich person coming in to show him their wealth, and underscoring his status as a Police officer who just happened to inherit his home on the bluff. It wasn't fair.

He drove by the funeral that was going on at the Indian cemetery. Wait until they see what happens in the next couple of days. I wonder how they will like their nice home then. He smiled at the thought and drove on by the raggedy Indians standing next to the graves.

Ginny worked from morning to night and still wasn't done. She surveyed the house that would be her family home. Ginny Thomas wasn't happy about the move but would make it work. Her work ethic was one of her strengths. She could do something with this ... in time. She stood there for a long time with her coffee in her hand. The boxes were in a state of being unpacked. Her long, black hair was in a bun, hairs never out of place. Her head was throbbing from the drums. Boom-boom-boom; night after night it went on. It never seemed to end. She wore her light-pink sweater and blue jeans; comfortable clothes to finish unpacking.

She walked into the bright living room. Nick Thomas was standing by the fireplace, a drink in his hand. A tall man, he slumped when he stood. It was something she had been trying to change most of their married life. She sighed; apparently with no success. His blond hair was getting long. It added to his look of dishevelment. She remembered when he was a dashing young officer in the Air Force stationed in Hawaii. Even then, she could see his slump; like a lost puppy trying to find someone to take him home.

Ginny looked around the living room. Boxes were still standing in the corners, some in a state of being unpacked, others empty. She brought all that she could. When you move, there were some things that you wouldn't take; you gave them to the Salvation Army or some other needy cause.

She hated this. Every time they moved she would have to go through all their things. It was like going back over their lives. When she had to let something go, it was a small part of her life that she gave up; a little memory no longer needed.

Nick looked up as she walked in. She became the center of attention the dominate figure in the room. It was her home the big house on the hill. She never wanted to come here and live, but now that they had, she was going to make sure it belonged to her.

She bought the best furniture to fill the rooms. The living room she stood in was spotless, with everything in place. There was an overstuffed sofa in the sunken living room, and a fire burning in the fireplace. She pulled out a scroll from one of the boxes. It would hang from the wall, one for each of them. The scrolls had serene mountains and Confucius settings of houses on a cliff. A waterfall flowing beside a house. People fishing from their boats. She could tell them apart because of the Chinese lettering and the signature stamp at the bottom. Nicole's scroll was different; in hers, there was the same waterfall, but at the top a tiger peered through bamboo shoots at the people below. This was her favorite. Ginny smiled. Yes, this was her home. She was in control.

Ginny Thomas's head hurt. The drum beat became louder and louder. She closed her eyes and rubbed her temples. Boom-boom-boom; they never stopped for a second. For three days now, it continued. She tried everything to stop it, but it kept coming.

Boom-boom-boom. She looked down at the end table with its stack of unopened letters.

Irritation crossed her brow, but she never picked them up. She was waiting for the aspirin to kick in and take away her headache.

Ginny walked to the two big bay windows. Night was coming.

The fires across the bay reflected off Nikki-D's coal-black eyes. She kept watching, as though in a trance. Nicole-Dane Thomas was a pretty little girl with long black hair and coal-black eyes, set on a small, light body. Exotic, she would grow up to be a beautiful woman. Part Chinese and part white, she inherited the best of both races.

Born under the Chinese sign of the Tiger, she was aggressive, sensitive, and intelligent. She raised her small hand to the window and tried to touch the fire. All she could touch was the cold window. The huge fire across the bay rose up high in the night sky. Nicole-Dane Thomas thought it was coming to touch her. The hypnotic rhythm of the drums called to her.

She could see the shadow people dance to their beat. Shadow people sang their songs; their voices traveled across the bay. The moonlight beamed through the cloudless night. The water was still and silent. Their songs and voices stirred deep within her. Nicole could barely understand what it was about, but she knew it was calling to her. She knew the voices were speaking to her; voices beckoning to her to come and join them. She put her other hand against the window trying to reach out to the drums.

"Nicole, get away from that window," her mother yelled. Nicole didn't listen. She didn't move; defiant and unconcerned, she maintained her vigil. Ginny, a small Chinese-American woman with long, thin limbs moved toward Nikki; anger came over her. "I said get away from that window." Ginny Thomas ran over and grabbed her by the arm, jerking her from the window. It surprised Nicole, who wasn't ready. Nicole regained herself, and yanked back. Freeing herself from her mother, she ran back to the window.

"Did you see what she did?" She aimed her anger at her husband, Nick Thomas. The drums beating in the night frightened her. Boom-boom-boom. She hated it. Her small stature stood in front of her husband, daring him to say something.

He was a failure and a drunk. He was a Virginian, born and raised. He started drinking one night long ago when the family was vacationing at Chesapeake Bay. He never stopped. He could never find anything worth a damn within himself, so he drank. He knew it was self-pity but never really needed an excuse to drink. It was the one thing he was good at.

Nick stood there, towering over her. The drink in his hand began to feel heavy. His blond hair hung on his forehead; his blue eyes showed no emotion.

"Leave Nikki-D alone, she just likes the drums. "When he said this, he knew it was the wrong thing to say. Her back began to rise, like some she-cat getting ready to strike. His hands began to tremble and he lifted his glass of scotch to his lips, taking a long drink.

It was just like him to talk against her. Ginny hated him for that. She was trying to make a good home for them, but he always had to ruin it with his drinking. Couldn't he see how hard she was working to keep things together, how she tried to maintain control? What would happen if she wasn't around to clean up after they wrecked what ever control she had? No restraint; these two will never understand. Nikki-D was just like her father. Ginny could see that right off. She was a dreamer. Well, Ginny would teach her different. She would make her understand. Nikki-D may be influenced by her father, but she would be guided by her mother: that, Ginny knew.

Nikki-D was still at the window. Her daddy had been calling her Nikki-D since she was a small baby. She could feel the tension between her parents. It was because of her. She didn't like her parents to fight. They were always fighting. Mommy didn't want to move here. She made that known from the first day.

She was too young to understand. The world was exciting. Everything was new and wonderful. No matter how much her mother wanted to go back, Nikki-D knew this was going to be her home for a long time.

Their house was one of the colonial houses that sat on Mission Hill. A dark brown house that sat near the woods, its front faced the bay. From their front porch, they could see all the islands that made up the sound. Just around the corner there was the Indian cemetery. At night, when the wind blew, it was like a hundred voices crying in the night.

"I hate this place." Ginny thrust her hand out and took Nick's drink from his hand. Her quickness caught him by surprise.

"That's enough!" Nick's anger exploded. He had a hangover that he was trying to cure with his drink. The new job wasn't going well. He wanted to be happy. He wanted his wife to be happy. She never was. Her demons were beyond him. Now all he could do was survive.

"You yell at me and you let your daughter talk back to her mother." Boom-boom boom; Ginny's head throbbed. "This is why I hate it here. Everything is falling apart."

"I keep telling you it was this or nothing. Can't you understand that?"

She understood, all right. The anger churned in her belly, created by the fear. It came from her being Chinese-American. That was all. All she knew was America. A dark cloud moved over her heart ... to others it was how you looked or how you acted that made you.

She looked at her husband, her eyes piercing through him. "I understand that you are the boss of a small bank while your brother is the

President of one of the largest banks..."

Nick's back straightened like a rod. Always the same old jabs, the same comeback that tore him down and left him floundering. He moved toward her. This was their pattern. They verbally punched and shoved each other, neither giving ground. They always tried their best to hurt each other. Their anger grew to a point of no return.

"Hey you bit..."

He couldn't finish his sentence. Nikki-D had wedged between them and was holding them apart.

"Don't fight." She was crying. Her small arms tried to keep them apart. "Please don't fight."

They looked at each other for one second and the hate and fear disappeared. Nikki-D was there for them. That was part of their pattern, too.

She sat at the big window in the living room, staring across the bay. The drums pounded in the night. Nikki-D, no longer aware of her surroundings, watched the flames rise in the night sky. The shadows danced around the flames. The drum's beating, boom boom-boom, riding the air waves across the water to her ears. The moon was high in the night sky, its beam lighting the water beneath it, like a beacon in the night. Nikki-D watched the smooth ripples of the water as the wind blew by. The sound of the east wind tickled her inner ear, talking to her. She was home.

3

EAGLE

The sun beat down on the white sand of Mission Hill Bluff. It was a warm, lazy summer day and a cool breeze coming off the water of the bay. The beach seines were lined up and down the beach. Each seine-boat waited in turn to set out their nets. Crews of dark men stood around the bullwinches, waiting to start pulling the handles down, bringing in the net a winch at a time. The water sparkled in the sunlight. Speed boats flew by farther out from the beach, pulling water-skiers behind them. Hat Island glared back at them. Just south was the city of Everett. The big marina was home to most of the boats in the region. Sails bobbed in front of the place, lazily moving with the wind. There were so many of them that they looked like a flock of birds on the water. From Mission Hill, you could see the whole of Puget Sound.

He was part way up the bluff. It was hard to climb higher because of the loose sand. Jonny put his hand over his eyes and looked up to the edge of the cliffs. Above them was a deep blue sky dotted with small white clouds. Jonny brought his head down; the dizziness rushed through his body and he leaned against the sand. Finally, his head quit spinning and he looked down.

Jonny's people were all up and down the beach. Each family had their own spot to fish on the beach. They burned their fires between the logs on the beach. One boater was bringing his net around, while another was just letting his out. Everyone took turns, one after the other, until night came and they all loaded up and went in to sell their catch.

Jonny heard some laughter near one of the winches. The men were all calling to each other, making jokes and challenging the others to catch as many fish as them. There was always competition and laughter on the beach. These were memories that Jonny would carry with him all of his life.

Jonny looked up at the white bluffs. He was playing in the hot sand. A lizard was trying to run from him, but the sand was too loose for it to get a foothold. Jonny would throw some more sand at the lizard and watch it slide back down. A shout came and he looked up.

He could see his brother running along the beach and up the sandy hill. Cajun was a bundle of energy and vigor. He was always wanting to try something new. Life was great for him. He already had strong opinions on how things should be and stated them to anyone who would listen. Most of the time, it was to Jonny.

Jonny wanted to be like his older brother. He was too shy and withdrawn. Caj liked to fish and work with his hands, while Jonny liked books and reading. Caj was fearless and brave and took risks in everything.

Jonny watched as his brother came up the hill. His smile was as wide as always, like the world was his oyster and he was going to enjoy every minute of it. Caj was crawling on all fours as he dug into the soft sand to bring himself up.

Caj had deep black eyes that penetrated you when he stared. His dark, tanned skin was almost black from the sun. With curly black hair falling down to his shoulders, he looked like a wild Indian.

"What are you doing?" his older brother asked, standing over Jonny and looking up at the people on the bluff.

"Nothing." The sand was getting hotter, and the sun wasn't even all the way up yet. He didn't move his feet, dug deep into the white-hot sand. His toes wiggled in the cool dirt beneath, as he watched the lizard scurry away.

Caj was looking up the bluff; cliffs that rose straight up. He put his hand over his eyes so he could see better in the sun. The cloudless sky, bright and deep blue, had a couple of small puff-clouds going by.

Caj was interested in those homes at the top of the bluff.

"I wonder what those people do? They just stay on their porches and look down on us."

Jonny knew something was going to happen. Caj didn't ask questions unless he wanted to get some answers. Jonny looked up at the homes. They were the biggest houses he had ever seen. Their long, flat porches jutted out from the homes, stairs running down the white cliffs, all the way down to the small docks that held new speed boats. Jonny had never seen anyone actually walk down the steps, but they had to get down somehow. He looked down the beach; there were about twenty homes and each one had stairs. Like spider webs hanging down. The

Pah-studs (whites) didn't like Indians to use their stairs.

"We should go up and see what its like to look over the bluffs." Caj eyed the sand falling down the bluff; the ravine formed were the bluff must have fallen. It was a place where you could climb the cliff without the help of stairs, but it would take much climbing.

"I think we could make it."

Jonny wasn't too sure. They were pretty small and the hill looked bigger each time he looked up. "I don't think so." Jonny wanted to let him know that he wasn't going up something like that. If Caj wanted to go, it would have to be alone.

"Fraidy Cat." Cajun stood over Jonny, staring at him. There it was; the challenge. It was how his older brother got him to do anything.

He hated to let his brother get the best of him.

"I'm not either." He looked up with determination in his eyes. But he was scared.

"Come on. I'll take care of you. It'll be fun." Caj grabbed Jonny by the shoulder and pulled him up with him. Caj took the lead, moving crab-like, using his arms and legs at the same time. After he climbed a few feet up, he looked back down at Jonny.

"You coming?" He had that "are you really scared or not" look on his face.

Jonny sat there for a second. He watched his family fishing on the beach. That's where he really wanted to go. Back down to them. Caj wouldn't let him rest until he came with him. Jonny knew he was caught again. He was a quarter of the way up the hill. It took a struggle for him to get this far. He didn't think he could make it. He didn't want to let his brother know that. He began to climb.

Caj was pulling away from him.

"Wait up." Jonny could feel the sweat from climbing and the noon sun. It was hot. They were way up there now and he could feel a rushing in his head. He'd never been this high. A knot formed in his stomach. The sand was still loose, causing his feet to slide with it, but it no longer burned his feet and he pushed them hard against the loose grains. The people down on the beach were still fishing. No one had noticed them yet. If they did, he was sure they would be in some deep trouble. Trouble never bothered Caj. He just took it and went on with life. All the people of the Tribe liked him. Jonny wanted to be like him, too.

Caj turned around and made sure Jonny was behind him. They were halfway up by now. "Come on. You can do it." Caj looked out to the sea. White seagulls floated a foot or two above the water. The nets were pulled in by the men of the families. Women were helping and kids were running on the beach. Caj felt alive. The world was there for him and all he had to do was grab it. Then he saw the dark figure in the sky. Like a shadow, it hovered above the seagulls. Its white head held two huge eyes that saw everything below it. It was a sign.

Jonny made it up to Caj. He looked at Caj and could tell that he never even broke a sweat to get here. His long legs and big arms helped him dig into the sand and push off. He was always a big boy. Jonny was small. It was another thing Jonny hoped would change.

"You all right?" Caj asked.

Jonny couldn't think because of the roaring in his head. He was scared. He was too tired to say anything.

Caj saw the tired look on his face. "Its all right. Just don't look down." Jonny was too scared to not look down. Caj pointed up to the sky.

"Look at that. Its an eagle."

Jonny looked up to where he was pointing. There he saw the biggest bird in his life.

"It must be the biggest eagle in the world," Caj said, excited. He started pulling himself up, climbing to get to the highest point and see the eagle eye-to-eye.

"I'm scared." Jonny couldn't go any further. He was too small and too scared.

People on the beach were looking up at them. Jonny was clinging to the side of the hill, while Caj went on. Jonny looked over his shoulder to the people below. He could see safety down there, where his family and people were. Going higher was too frightening for him. He was stuck halfway up. He knew he couldn't go any further.

To Caj, the heights didn't matter. It was exhilarating to get this high. He made sure Jonny was OK and then moved on. Now he was sweating. The sun was very hot. He could see the porches of the white people. He had only a quarter of the way to go. He was going to make it. He could feel the rushing in his head. It wasn't from fear, like Jonny. His heart was pounding from the thrill of being so high. He stopped for a second and looked out to the sky and sea. The seagulls were below him. Like the eagle, he could see them from the top. He knew what it was like for the eagle to swoop down on them from above. Then he located the eagle again. It was still higher than he was. The only way to get as high was to get to the top. Yes, he could feel the rushing in his head. It wasn't from fear, but it was from life. Jonny heard his brother laugh loudly. He knew his brother was going to make it to the top. It made him sad. Mentally, he was kicking himself for being afraid. He wanted to be up there with Caj. He knew he belonged below: on the beach.

Roy Henry was on the beach watching his family setting out the net. The day had been good. His family was way ahead as far as catching the most fish. Competition was rampant between the families on the beach. Most of the time, it was good-natured ribbing and hollering. When someone didn't adhere to the rules of the beach, it could get tough.

Today there were no problems. The mornings catch promised a good afternoon. Roy knew he would keep the crew out until dark. They would grumble, but they knew they had to stay until the fish were gone. Days like these were good. The men would make money and the families would eat well at the end of the week. If the week stayed good, the men would have a poker game ready for those poor souls who dared put up their money.

The sun was out, its heat beating down on the people on the beach. He was sweating now and he walked closer to the water.

"Get that net out. Slow down the Goddamn boat or you'll swamp the splash boy." He shouted his orders as he walked. His skipper was his oldest son. He knew what he was doing, so Roy didn't worry too much.

"Where are those two boys?" He brought his nephews out so they could make some extra money. They were the splash boys for him today. He had to watch out for them. He looked up and down the beach, but couldn't see them anywhere.

"Anybody see the boys?"

Everyone looked around, but nobody knew where they were.

"Hanford, get out there in the splash boat." Hanford was his youngest son. He watched as the boy grudgingly went out in the boat.

Roy walked up to the women on the logs. The fire was hot, roaring around the big black pot in the middle. The girls were putting in crabs from the last set. He never could understand how they could stay around a hot fire during the hottest part of the day. It was something he couldn't do. "Have any of you seen the Esque boys?" They looked at each other, then one of his men pointed up to the hill.

Roy followed the pointed finger. His eyes spotted the lone, dark speck on the side of the hill. About halfway up, he could see one of the boys just hanging there, not moving up or down. It looked like Jonny.

"Shit."

He started running to the hill. It was more like a hobble because of his bad leg. He was moving faster than he had in a long time. The boy was still hanging there, flat against the wall. Now he could see that he was crying, from fright. He grabbed the man from the winch.

"Get up there and get him." The man looked to where Roy was pointing and then started running up the hill. "Make sure he's all right." Then Roy looked up higher. Three quarters of the way up, he saw the other boy. Caj was moving higher. Roy couldn't believe it. He smiled as he watched the boy climbing higher and higher. Caj reached his hand up and grabbed hold of some more dirt. The sand was becoming harder the higher he climbed. The heat was unbearable to him. His muscles ached. Lactic acid ran through his shoulders, causing them to tighten up. He could barely lift his arms. His legs remained straight, not bending at the knees anymore. He stopped for a rest.

Resting, Caj looked down. He could see Jonny just hanging there; not moving. He looked so small from up here. Sweat ran down Caj's forehead and into his eyes. He couldn't let go to wipe it, so he had to move his head to his arms and rub it against his shirt. That helped a little. Facing sideways, he could see above Hat Island, off in the distance. It was too bad Jonny couldn't see this.

Jonny was crying. He couldn't move. He moved his head from side, to side trying to figure a way out. His fingers and toes were getting tired from hanging in the sand. He wanted to go back down. He thought he was going to fall. He was frightened to death. Then he looked to the side of the ravine and almost let go. He let out a yelp.

"Aaaahhh," he cried.

The men and women on the beach were yelling at him to keep calm. Jonny could hear them calling to him. He looked over. The fear shot straight through to his head.

"Help me."

Then he looked over and saw it. Fear grabbed his heart. He watched as the small, light-gray pup crawled toward him. Its gray eyes stared at him. This is what frightened Jonny so much. It was a ghost. It was coming to get him. His fingers were too tired to hang on anymore. There was nothing he could do. Too tired, he let go.

The big arms of Pete Henry wrapped around Jonny.

"Whoa there – I got you."

Jonny could feel arms around him. The tears ran down his face as he continued to cry. Adrenaline was pumping through his heart. He was safe. The climb down was uneventful. Jonny stayed in the arms of the man that rescued him. He rested and his tears went away. The only thing he did was sneak a look at the spot where he saw the gray pup. Nothing was there. He was glad.

They made it all the way down to the beach before Pete put him down. The women came and brought him over to the fire and told him to sit on one of the logs. His face was streaked with dirt where the tears had ran down his cheeks. He sat there with his arms and hands together between his knees, his head turning while people came up to look at him. A big shadow came over him as Uncle Roy came up to make sure he was all right.

"Are you all right?" Roy's voice traveled over the beach. The other families knew by his voice that he was concerned. They all watched as he leaned down to Jonny. "No bones broken?"

Jonny shook his head: no. He was scared of Roy. His big voice and big body made him shake. He could see the others going back to their work. The men began whinching in the net. He could see his cousin, Hanford, out in the splash boat, his oars going up and down, smacking against the water.

"I want you to stay right here." Roy's big, baritone voice drove Jonny back. "You hear what I say?"

"Yes." The tears came back to Jonny's eyes. He couldn't stop them. Roy's voice softened. "Listen-I just don't want you to get hurt. Your mother would kill me. So stay here and have something to eat. And don't wander off anymore. Okay?"

Jonny moved his head up and down. Then he looked at the ground. He was too scared to look up.

"Your dumb-shit brother is still climbing. He ain't got enough brains to stop and come down."

"I saw a gray puppy." Jonny's voice just barely squeaked out.

"What?" The women moved closer. Their ears were always open.

"I saw a gray pup-dog. It was gray all over. Like a ghost." Jonny was embarrassed. He should have never brought it up. His face was red.

"A gray pup? Like a ghost?" Roy's eyes weren't so sure now. "You saw a spirit – is that what you're saying?"

Jonny was very scared now. Was it a spirit? He couldn't be sure. He wished he was back home. Everyone was listening now. The men all watched him.

"I don't know. It was gray ... and small. Like a little dog ... crawling toward me. On the ledge." Then Jonny stopped talking as everyone began nodding to each other. He didn't know what was going on, but he knew they did.

"You women take care of him." Roy took one more look up the cliff. "Your brother's a real dumb shit." He stormed off to help pull in the net.

Jonny looked up the cliff. He could barely see Caj climbing the cliff; he was so high. A woman came over and handed him some pop. The bottle was cold, from sitting in the water. She also gave him some food to eat. He watched Caj as he climbed higher and higher. The sand was dark dirt now.

Caj didn't believe he could move another muscle. He was so tired. People on the beach watched as he moved an inch at a time. The sweat from his body was dry. The muscle tissue was squeezing each ounce of lactic acid it could, out of every pore of his body. It hurt so bad. His eyes were red from pressure. He was stuck. He looked up at the edge. It looped over and out, a lip that was almost perpendicular to the ground below. Another twenty feet and he would be there. Frustrated, he felt like crying. No; that wasn't like him. He would not give in. He had come too far.

Caj reached his hand up and grabbed some more roots, his fingers gripping and tightening around anything they could. He brought his foot up and pushed. The lip was above him. He reached over the lip with his right arm and grabbed some grass. He would have to find something to hang onto that would support his weight as he climbed over. He felt around some more. His arms were bone-tired now and he didn't think he would last too much longer. If he fell, it would be two hundred feet before he would hit anything. He looked down. Dizziness came over him and he quickly turned his head back. The pain was numbing his arms. His back hurt from keeping his toes in the dirt and clinging. He didn't think he would make it.

Caj's feet slipped out from under him. Instinct took over and he grabbed whatever he could. His right arm and hand still had hold of the grass on top. He dangled from the lip of the ledge. There was only one way he could go. He had to make it up and it had to be now.

Tension covered every inch of his body. He was struggling, his feet kicking out as he tried to get his leg over the lip. His ankle caught the edge the first time, but he didn't have enough of his leg over to pull himself up. With a slip, he went swinging back and forth in the air. Sweat washed over his body as he thought he was going to fall.

Then the Eagle flew by. It was so close Caj thought he could touch it. It was the biggest Eagle he had ever seen. It was watching him. They were eye-to-eye. It floated there in front of him, as though it was waiting for him. Caj could feel strength flow through him and an exhilaration passed over him, bringing adrenaline with it. It was his time. He would not fail. He knew he would not fall.

With every ounce of strength he had left, he pulled and swung his body up and over the lip. He got both hands full of tall grass. His hands tightened their grip, refusing to let go. His left leg was halfway over. He got a good hold. His last bit of strength drained from him. He pulled with his arms and legs and, finally, rolled his body over the lip. He lay there on his back, sweat pouring out of him. He had nothing left. He looked up to the sky. He made it. Caj lay there for some time, waiting for his strength to came back. When he felt all right, he got up and looked out over the panoramic view. Yes, the excitement was coming over him again. He could see. Caj walked over to the edge of the lip. Peering down, he could see all of his people and more. He could see the islands and the rivers. He could see as far as the sky and the mountains. He laughed. He had made it. Looking down the fear began to creep into his veins. Caj was too scared to go back down. He was amazed that he made it all the way up here. But to go back the same way he came - he could never do that. He looked around. The homes were large and expensive. People were sitting on their porch; most looked bored. How could they be? Stiff and bored: Caj didn't understand that. Not when there was life flowing through him. They didn't move or anything; just sat there alone on the bluff. At the end of the clearing was a road. It was the only way out for Caj. Taking one last look down the hill, he knew it was the road he had to take. There was no going back.

With the sun in the sky, it shined down on one lone figure walking down the narrow road.

4

BEST FRIENDS

    The light, feathery wind blew over the bluff. Its delicate touch flowed through Nikki-D's hair. She sat, subdued, at the edge of her yard. It was 1959, the last year of the decade. She would remember this year. It was her tenth birthday. The gentle breeze rolled over her like a soft reminder of the Fifties. It was a decade of smooth transition. The summers were warm, not hot. She watched the parking area at the bottom of the hill. Small dust devils twirled round and round, not causing any great stir, each one about the same height and shape. Nikki-D could feel the lazy afternoon and didn't want to move. It was like her to sit for long periods of time, just thinking. Her long, black hair was braided down her back. At the end was a pink bow. Her mother made her wear it. She wanted her to be ladylike. Better not to think about that now. She wanted to think good thoughts. A strap on her overalls kept falling on her arm and she would pull it back over her shoulder and put it back in place. Her clothes were always pressed and clean. Her black shoes, each with a single strap, covered her feet. They shone in the day's sun. The trees around the house didn't move. She watched the waves below, as they moved rhythmically, gently crawling up the beach. Everything seemed to move in slow motion. That was like the Fifties... slow.

    She carried her books with her. Reading was one of her passions. She went through her fence to the bluff. The walking trail ran down the edge of the bluff. From the top of the hill where her home was, down to where Missions Heights flattened out, there were three houses besides her own. She looked down the trail and saw green trees standing tall between the houses. Nikki-D looked up at the top of the trees. There was no movement. She shifted her books in her arms and she set off to her favorite place to read. It was down the hill a bit. Her black satin shoes caused dust to kick up as she walked. She passed the first house. It was the Livingstons; Jimmy lived there. She didn't like him. Neither did Tammy, her friend. Their house was a little smaller, but looked nice. Nikki-D could barely see it from the bluff. It was back about one hundred feet, hidden from sight by trees and bushes. She moved on.

Her thoughts were taking up her time as she walked. She was a special student and her mom talked about putting her in special classes for the gifted. Her dad wanted her to grow up normally. It was hard on her.

"I cannot forgive a scholar his homeless despondency."

She spoke the quotation out loud. She remembered things like that. It was easy for her to quote some author or person, especially when it was about a subject that was close to her. Her mind, even at ten, wondered about the world. She tried to find answers to her questions that came from reading books and listening to people, mostly grown ups talk, as they sat around the patio in front of the house. She was naturally curious, and bright enough to follow it up with research. Nikki-D couldn't remember a day when she wasn't reading a book or two. As she said, it was one of her passions.

The trail led down to the next house. Barry and Colleen Hollowpeter lived there. Their daughter, Tez, played with Nikki-D and they were in the same classes. They played the same sports. Nikki-D loved sports, even thought her mom hated it. She said her daughter was a tomboy, and little girls shouldn't act like boys. Nikki-D could hear her mother saying this to her, over and over. She always begged to go out and play. Girl's baseball was in now. She would practice after school. She played second base and was one of the best players on the team. Just thinking about it made her adrenaline flow. The season was almost over. That made her sad.

Her books were heavy and she shifted them again. Looking at Tammy's house, she wished her friend was here. They went to her grandmother's house down the coast. She would be back for Nikki-D's birthday.

Nikki-D's mother was planning it for her. She would invite all the kids that she thought Nikki should know. None of them were her real friends; in fact, aside from Tammy, she didn't think she had any friends. That's why she missed her so much. She watched the house for a few more seconds, just standing there. Then she moved on.

The trail, interwoven with grass and dirt, was long and narrow. It used to be an old deer trail until the homes were built. Nikki-D walked it all the time. Most of the others would only walk on the road in front of the houses, but she was an adventurer. Her curiosity was always getting the best of her, so she would seek out new things to discover. She stopped and bent over to look at the little wild blackberries on the side of the trail. They grew at the edge of the bluff. Nobody picked them, so they got big and long and juicy. Nikki-D picked the biggest one. It had a shiny blackness to it; with a flick, she tossed it in her mouth. The sweetness engulfed her tongue and the roof of her mouth. The taste was exquisite. She began to pick more and put them in a small bucket she had brought. Every once in a while, she would toss another one in her mouth. Finally, she had picked enough to enjoy while she read her books. She was happy at the thought. She picked up her things and moved on down the trail.

She came to her favorite place on the hill. The trail moved off toward the left to a spot right next to the bluff. It was a beautiful spot here and she would often come to get away and think, or read. She was about halfway down the hill. From here she could see the houses going out to the end of the spit. Those homes were houses crammed together side by side. Their porches ran right out on the edge of the bluff. She never looked at them much. They held no interest for her. She would look at the ravine that divided the houses on the spit from the houses on the hill. At the top of the ravine was a flat, square area. People would park there and look out over the sound. They would look down at the people on the beach. The Indians. They would watch them, make comments about them, and then move on. That was in the beginning of the summer months. Later on, like now, there would hardly be anyone here. It was a slow, lazy time of the year. 1959 seemed dull and boring; she wished something would happen. She always wished something would happen. She just wasn't the type that could keep still very long. She set her books down and lay beside them. She covered her eyes with her hand and looked up to the sky. She picked a blade of grass, put it between each thumb and blew. The sound carried over the quiet of the day. She picked a long stem and put it in her mouth, chewing it. She was becoming drowsy and lethargic, her eyes grew heavy. The world became dreamy and out of place. In a few minutes, she would be asleep. The world was so quiet.

"Eeee ... Eeee." The sound came from high in the sky breaking the silence of the day. Nikki-D opened her eyes. The eagle was the largest she had ever seen. It sat on top of the tree. She could see its white head moving back and forth. Something was causing it concern and the eagle was shouting its unhappiness. Suddenly, it spread its huge wings and began to flap them. The only thing keeping it from flying were its talons hanging onto the limb of the tree. When it let go, it soared up and away from whatever was disturbing it. Nikki-D sat up and watched the bird fly away. She could see the strong muscles of its shoulders push against the light air. Each flap of the eagle's wings carried it higher. It flew further and further away until it was gone.

Nikki-D stood up and looked around. The day was still lazy, but it wasn't so quiet. She could hear words and scuffling down the trail a bit. She looked over the top of the grass. She could see the small dust devils twirling in the parking area.

Her black, almond-shaped eyes watched as two boys grabbed a smaller boy. The little boy didn't say anything, but he tried to fight them off. He was one of the Indians that lived down by the bay. He was a small, dark-skinned boy with light-brown hair. She moved down the hill a little at a time.

At first, she wondered what he was doing up here. Usually only white kids were up here. She never saw Indians unless she drove by their homes in the car and saw the Indian kids playing by their broken-down homes. They were always laughing and playing games. She wished it was like that where she lived. The people at Mission Heights kept to themselves and never mixed well together. It took a long time for her to make friends. Mostly, she stayed around the house. Playing by herself, she moved a little farther from her home, exploring, just as she was doing now. Her curiosity kept her moving in different directions. She always wanted to know what was going on around the corner. Her mother warned her against going too far. She never listened to her. She had to know.

The bigger boys held the little boy's arms. He kicked out with his legs but they were too short to reach the bullies. She could hear their derisive laughter. Still the little Indian boy didn't say anything. She knew who the bullies were. One of them was Jimmy Livingston, and the other boy was named Brad. She could identify Jimmy by his blond crewcut hair. The boys were bigger than the Indian boy. Their laughter was getting louder as they teased him. Then, the boy broke free. Instead of running, he went up and punched Jimmy right in the nose. Nikki-D could see Jimmy covering up his face with his hands and she heard him wail. The Indian boy tried to hit Brad, but he was too big for him and Brad threw him down on the ground. What was play was fast turning into something ugly.

Jimmy moved over the boy as Brad held him down.

Moving down the trail, Nikki-D was close enough to hear what was going on. Jimmy grabbed the boy's arm and they lifted him up. "We're going to throw you over the Cliff."

Jimmy's eyes had a mean look to them – a look that Nikki-D didn't like. She was tense, trying to think of what to do. She watched the boy as he was pulled to the edge of the cliff.

He was going to fight them to the end. Still, he never said anything. Jimmy wanted the boy to break down and cry, beg them to stop. Nikki-D knew that wasn't going to happen. She could feel it.

His little legs were digging into the ground. His torn tennis shoes were slipping on the dirt and rock. At the same time, he was trying to twist free. The boys were too big for him. They were getting close to the edge. He fell to his knees, becoming dead weight. It was all he could do. Jimmy and Brad both were sweating from the exertion of getting him to the edge. They just wanted to scare him, but the more he fought back, the madder they became. He was a tough little kid, but, finally, they got him to the edge of the bluff.

"Now we're going to throw you over." Jimmy was smiling as he talked. He wanted the boy to know that he was crazy enough to do it.

The boy didn't say anything. His determined eyes never gave in.

"OK Brad, on three. One. Twooo." They were swinging him. One more swing. And ..."

"Stop it, Jimmy Livingston."

It was a girl's voice. Jimmy knew immediately that it was Nikki-D. Both he and Brad looked over to her.

"You better let him go or I'm going to tell my father."

He could see her standing in her new coveralls. She was so pretty. Jimmy felt trapped. Where did she come from? How much did she see? Thoughts were rushing through his head. Brad stood there, waiting for him to say something back to her. He had a stupid look on his face. Jimmy knew Brad didn't care one way or the other. He was from one of the houses on the spit, so he wanted Jimmy's friendship and would do anything Jimmy asked of him.

The soft wind was kicking up the dust devils. Small dust clouds swirled around them.

"And what if we don't?" He was bluffing; a bravado that he didn't feel.

"You better let him go." Nikki-D wasn't going to back down. She had a stubborn streak in her that kept her from backing down from anything she felt was wrong. Her mother always told her it would get her in trouble someday, but that was the way she was.

"You don't scare me, Jimmy Livingston. You better not hurt him or you're going to be in big trouble. Same with you, Brad."

Her eyes narrowed, showing them that she meant business. She didn't back down an inch, and she wasn't going to. She knew Jimmy from school. She didn't like him. He always treated her nice, but he was a bully to everyone else. He let them know that he lived on top of the hill. That gave him special status. He couldn't say that to Nikki-D, though; she lived above him.

Besides, he never hid his interest in her. He told everyone that would listen that she was his girlfriend and they should stay clear. Nikki-D couldn't stand him.

Brad kept watching Jimmy to see what to do. Jimmy knew he had to say something. "This Indian shouldn't be up here. You know that. They belong down below. We're not going to let them come up here without a fight. We got to teach them who's boss around here." Jimmy had the boy's arm twisted around his back and he gave a yank to prove his point.

Nikki-D could see the boy wince. She knew his arm must hurt, but he still didn't say anything. He must be a tough kid. She knew he was no match for the boys, who held him tightly. They would keep hurting him until they got tired unless she did something to stop it.

She saw the rock at her feet. It was about the size of her hand; the right size to throw. She bent over and picked it up raising it above her head. Her arm was cocked to throw it.

"If you don't let him go, I'll hit you with this. I mean it."

Brad was the first one to say something this time.

"Go ahead. You're just a girl."

Nikki-D threw it with all her might. The rock left her hand and sailed through the air. She used all the power she had in her arm and legs to throw it. She could see Brad's stupid face as the rock hit. Right on the side of the temple. The stunned look was almost comical to her. Then the blood came. Brad dropped the boy's arm and raised his hands to the side of his head. She could see the blood squeeze through his fingers. It scared her.

Fear was also in their eyes. Brad let out a wail, his mouth as wide as his jaws would let it. Tears came out of his clenched eyes. He opened them and looked at his hands. The blood he saw scared him even more and he let out another wail. Jimmy still held on to the boy. He looked at Nikki-D and then he twisted the arm again. He heard some air escape from the boy's lips. He smiled. He would get satisfaction if he had to break the arm off. Jimmy couldn't stand it when somebody stood up to him. His father was a policeman and was strict, with strong opinions. Jimmy was the same way. Anger rose in him as he thought about it. No Indians came up here. They knew where they belonged. The only time he saw them was when they went to the cemetery across the road. His dad said they should dig it all up and move it away. That way we would never see them. Now they're starting to come over here as if they own the hill. It was something that concerned everyone. The anger came again. He twisted the arm.

"You better stop it or I'll break his arm."

Brad was still crying. He was getting louder.

"Shut-up, Brad. It can't hurt that much."

Brad looked at Jimmy. "I'm going to get her." He turned to go after Nikki-D.

She could see she was in trouble. Brad was too big and dumb not to hurt her just because she was a girl. She turned to ran, when someone in a cloud of dust and dirt came running by her. She couldn't see who it was because the dirt got in her eyes. She closed them against the pain. Her two little fists rubbed her eyes, trying to get the dirt out. They were watering and the tears flowed down her cheeks.

Each time she tried to open her eyes, the dust would get into them again. She was caught up in the big dust devils caused by the boys running through the dirt. The wind came over the bluff, pushing the dust higher and higher. The intensity was swirling around her. She heard loud voices. There must have been three of them, but one louder voice replaced all of them. Nikki-D opened her eyes.

Another boy stood there, over Brad, who was lying on the ground. He was talking to Jimmy. His lean, dark frame was tense and ready. She could see the long, curly black hair that fell to his shoulders. It was the boy that came over the edge of the bluff. She could see his strong, broad shoulders and muscular arms and imagined him climbing the cliff. He turned toward her briefly. She saw his fiery black eyes as he yelled at Jimmy.

"You touch my little brother again and I'll come and break both of your arms."

Jimmy couldn't say anything, because there were two other Indians holding him down. They were bigger boys; older than Nikki-D and the little boy. Jimmy was sitting in the corner of the lot, holding his shoulder. She knew his arm must hurt badly. He still didn't say anything.

"And you! You big punk. You want to pick on girls? Instead of finishing, he hit Brad across the mouth. Brad covered up and tried not to get hit. Jimmy didn't move.

"Let them go, Caj."

It was the little boy. Nikki-D couldn't believe it. His voice was so quiet, and low.

She liked it. The big, intense boy – Caj, looked at his younger brother as if he was crazy.

"What do you mean, let him go? He was going to break your arm. This stupid white boy needs to learn some manners."

Nikki-D agreed with Caj. What was wrong with this kid? Now she was getting angry.

"I'm all right."

Caj looked at his cousins, Hanford and BJ. They were having fun with the two white kids. They also were intense and wanted to fight. The excitement was what all three of them were about. Caj loved the feeling; it was life to him.

Then he looked at the little girl. She was Asian. Or a mix. He didn't know. She was pretty, though. Her almond eyes reminded him of his own people. She could pass for an Indian if she wasn't so light-skinned.

"What about your girlfriend?"

Nikki-D's hair on her back rose. "I'm not his girlfriend." She wanted to make that clear right now. Caj looked at her and smiled. His smile covered his whole face. It showed a row of white teeth; a beaming smile. Then he turned back to his brother.

"If any of those guys come back, you let us know. We'll come back and make sure they leave you and your girlfriend alone. You hear me; Jonny?"

The boy nodded his head yes. He seemed all right now. There was still some blood on his knees, mostly scrapes that would scab over later. The boy was so quiet ... and calm.

Nikki-D was mad. The boy, Caj, was making fun of her and she knew it. It was because he was older.

It was just like boys to act like that. She watched as the older boy looked over at the smaller brother. He laughed; an infectious laugh. Nikki-D's heart gave a jump. Her face flushed. Then the boy and his cousins left. They laughed and shoved each other as they walked down the road. They kidded each other about the fight with the bullies. Putting each other down. Just like boys.

Nikki-D turned her attention to the boy she had helped. He stood there still staring at the ground. He was so quiet. "My name's Nikki-D. I live up on top of the hill." She pointed to her house. It was the biggest one on the hill. "That was Jimmy Livingston and Brad. Jimmy lives right below us." Her eyes were intent on reaching him. He kept his head down. Boy, he must be shy.

"What's your name?"

He moved a bit. His face was dirty and smudged from the sweat. He finally looked up at her. It was the first time she looked at his face. Nikki-D couldn't believe the sad, deep-brown eyes that looked back at her. Because of his dark skin, the eyes were more pronounced. Even further and deeper she could see the sadness. For some reason, she felt anger boil up inside her.

He had light-brown hair, cut short. His short body was lean and wiry. She figured him to be her size and maybe the same age. That would make him ten years old. She looked out on the water. The summer day was lazy. She remembered this bluff because of the boy climbing over it. It was some time ago. But it wasn't this boy. The other boy was much bigger and stronger looking; wilder, too.

"What's your name?" She asked.

"MM ... mm Jonny."

She barely heard his voice, it was so low. Like a whisper. Nikki-D would find out that it was the way he always talked.

"What?"

She watched his lips as he talked. Nikki-D wanted to make sure she got it.

"Mm ... mm Jonny."

His voice was still a whisper. He wouldn't look at her. This made Nikki-D mad. Why did he look at the ground all the time? She remembered her mother and father talking about it once. She couldn't remember what they said. Something about the Indian way of not looking you in the eye. "Why don't you speak up? I can't hear you when you talk." She wanted him to look at her. She stared right at him.

He began to run his foot back and forth against the ground. She could tell he was thinking. It took so long for him to answer her. She remembered her mother saying that Indians were all lazy and probably stupid too. Her mother always did that; calling people one thing or another. Nikki-D didn't know why, but it upset her to hear her mother talk like that.

"Why are you taking so long? Why don't you answer?"

"MM ... mm. I don't know."

"Well it is long. I want you to talk faster." She moved closer to him. She looked him up and down. His knees were bleeding from scrapes, but he seemed fine otherwise. Still looking down, Jonny began to speak. "This is Scy-you Point. Ghost Point. My people used to bury their dead in the trees."

Nikki-D's interest perked up. She had never heard this before. School never focused on the people of the reservation. The only time she heard about the Indians was when someone was making a remark or joke. Most of the time, you never even saw them. She remembered when she came here. She remembered all the old, broken-down homes on the side of the road. She remembered her father saying it was where the Indians lived. She asked him where they were. He said he didn't know, but he was sure they were around.

When they had settled in their home, she forgot them; except when they had their funerals. Then you heard their drums. Every once in a while, she would see them, like when the older boy, Caj, climbed over this very spot. It was the only spot on Mission Heights that had no trees. It was a clearing for parking and for people to look out over the bay. It was graveled from the road to the logs that marked the edge of the bluff. Then another three feet of tall grass grew to the end of the bluff. From there, the cliff wall went straight down.

"I saw a spirit. Down there; halfway up the hill. I was trying to climb the hill. I couldn't make it. I was real scared. So scared that I thought I would never make it down again. I began to cry. Like a baby. My arms were getting tired. But I couldn't move. I thought I was going to fall and die."

He looked at her, his eyes big as he remembered the scene he was describing.

"Then I turned my head and I saw something crawling toward me. It was a little pup. Crawling on its stomach. It scared me so bad that I let go. But someone was there to catch me. So I didn't die." He looked again at the place where he saw the spirit. He was transfixed by the spot. Nikki-D didn't know if he was kidding.

"There's no such thing as spirits. Are you making fun of me? Because if you are, then I'm going to leave and the next time that Jimmy and Brad want to beat you up, I won't do anything. I'll just let them. So if you're making fun of me, you better stop." She stood there with her arms crossed, her black hair braided down her back. She was wearing overalls, blue, with black shoes.

He just looked at her, not saying anything; not moving. The breeze blew his hair from his forehead. His deep brown eyes watched her.

"Mm ... mm. I'm not making fun of you. It was a spirit. It scared me. So I come back here to see it again ... but I never did."

She knew he was telling her the truth. She relaxed. Her interest increased. This boy was so different: the way he talked, with his low voice; the things he talked about. She wanted to get to know him better. She wanted him to be her friend.

"You're going to be my best friend," she blurted out.

"Mmm ... mm. What??" He backed away from her.

Well, this was going to be harder than she thought. Nikki-D waited for him to stop. He was moving away, and it looked as if he was going to leave. She didn't want him to leave. "I watched someone climb over the bluff once. It was a big boy. I was standing over there." She pointed over to the bushes. "He didn't see me. I watched him until he left."

She could see that she hit something. The boy was getting excited and looked like he was going to speak.

"Mm ... mm. That was my brother, Caj," the boy said. "I was climbing with him that day. That's when I saw the spirit-pup."

He moved closer to her.

"Mm ... mm. Did you see it?"

"No, but I saw an eagle."

"That's what my brother saw. He wanted to be as high as the eagle, so he could see down on everybody. He says that's what the whites do to us when we are fishing. Looking down on us."

"Well, where else would they look?"

He lowered his head. "I don't know." He stood there silently.

She waited until he was through. He was not like his brother. Actually, he seemed the opposite of the older boy. This boy contemplated before he spoke. His words were honest, but there was no elaboration. Nikki-D was used to conversation that required comment or commentary. Her mother wanted that. She would go on and on about any subject. She was well-read, just as everyone in the family was. Discussion began when they woke and ended when they went to sleep. She thought of her father, whose embellishment would bring out her laughter. A frown crossed her face. He wasn't embellishing much lately. It was the drinking... and the work. She wished he would quit both.

"What kind of spirit? You mean like the Holy Ghost?"

Clearly he was embarrassed. "Mm ... mm. I don't know what the Holy Ghost is."

"The Holy Ghost. You know." Everyone knew about the Holy Ghost.

He shook his head. "Mm ... mm. It was my spirit. A little pup. Crawling toward me. It scared me and made me lose my hold on the cliff. I almost fell, but my uncle was there to catch me. I told everyone about the pup, but they didn't say anything back to me. Except they say it was my spirit." With that, he was done. He crossed his arms.

Nikki-D listened to the explosion of words out of the boy's mouth. He was talking fast, trying to get all the words out at once. His voice was low, not like his brother, whose laughter she still heard. "You saw it where?"

He moved toward the edge of the cliff. She followed. They walked side by side until they got to the edge. She looked over and down. It was straight down. The beach was bare and the tide rolled up over the sand. She couldn't believe that the bigger boy, Caj, had climbed the face of the cliff. Jonny was next to her. He pointed to a spot halfway down the cliff. Nikki-D could see why he thought he might fall. Even at that point he must have been a hundred and fifty feet from the beach. She looked more closely at him. He was about her height and weight.

"Do you think it was a real spirit?"

"I don't know. Why would they lie to me?"

She thought about that. Her parents were very religious. They went to church every Sunday. She never questioned her own belief or what they taught at church. It was just part of her. They made her pray every night. She never had seen the Holy Ghost or any other spirit. That didn't make her believe they weren't there, but she was becoming confused about the issue. It was something she had begun to work on in her mind. Still, she believed.

"Maybe it will come back?" She said this more for herself than for him.

His eyes darted over the face of the cliff, still not seeing anything.

"Maybe."

"I'm having a party at my house. Its my birthday. My mom's having all kinds of kids over." She grew reflective. "Most of them I don't really know. My best friend, Tammy, is coming home and she will be there. I can't wait for her to get back. The summer has been so boring. Don't you think?"

He was looking at the ground again. Before he could answer, she went on.

"I think so. Nothing happened all summer until today. Unless you count seeing your brother climb up the cliff. How old is your brother, anyway? Does he go to the middle school? He sure has a nice smile. Don't you think?"

"Mm ... mm. You talk a lot."

"I'm just trying to get to know you. Do you live down there with the rest of the Indians? How many of you are there?" She knew she was talking fast and asking many questions. She wanted to get to know him. She could feel inside her that they were going to be best friends. Not like Tammy, who was similar to Nikki-D, this was different. She could see a new world opening up to her if she could get him to become her friend. He seemed a little slow. Her mother said that they were all slow and had their own ways that nobody knew except them. It was better to stay away and leave them alone.

"Mm ... mm. My family lives down in the Totem village. Most all of the families live in one of the villages."

"Why do you call them villages? My mom calls them projects. My dad says they're ghettos."

"Mm ... mm. My mom says that all you have your noses stuck up in the air and hide behind your walls and gates. She doesn't think any of you are happy."

Nikki-D thought about this for a second and decided to change the subject.

"Do you catch the bus to go to school? I never seen you there. It would be neat if we both went to the same school. Don't you think?"

The sun was beginning to lose its heat. He was looking down the cliff again. She could see the bottom, the beaches and the waves. Then she looked at the spider webs going down the side of the cliff, the stairs that kept everyone on top. She knew about those stairs because her family had some going down the front of her house. They would walk down the long stairs to the water. They had a dock at the bottom where they kept their pleasure boat. They would go directly from the house down to the dock and get into the boat never once touching the beach. Looking down now, she wished she could be there; on the beach, with the waves rolling over her feet. She wished...

Jonny moved away from the edge. She watched as he began to walk home. He didn't say anything.

"Where you going?" She heard his feet scrape against the ground. Every once in a while, he would kick a rock.

"Hey..." she yelled.

"Mm ... mm. I got to go home." He kept walking.

"Hey. You want to come to my party?"

She watched him stop.

"What?"

She moved toward him. "I want you to come to my party."

"When?"

She became excited. She knew he was going to come. This made her feel happy.

"Tomorrow night, at five."

Without saying anything, he moved on walking down the road by the cemetery.

"Well? Are you coming?" She had to yell now.

Then she heard his answer. It floated back to where she stood.

"Mm ... mm. Maybe...

"He will fall into the river," she answered in a voice almost too small to be heard.

"Aai ya hey!" the Chief said, gripping his Pipe. "Did Seven Arrows visit you and whisper the Story in your ear?"

"No," She giggled. "Grandfather told me the beginning."

"That is exactly what will happen," the Chief smiled. "But let us talk about it before we continue."

"As you already know," began the Chief, "we were discussing the riddle of men. Men are like little Mouse. They are so busy with the things of this world that they are unable to perceive things at any distance. They scrutinize some things very carefully, and only brush others over lightly with their whiskers. But all of these things must be close to them. The roaring that they hear in their ears is life, the river. This great sound in their ears is the sound of the Spirit. The lesson is timely, because the cries of mankind now are everywhere, but men are too busy with their little Mouse lives to hear. Some deny the presence of these sounds, others do not hear them at all, and still others, my son, hear them so clearly that it is a screaming in their hearts. Little Mouse heard the sounds and went a short distance from the world of Mice to investigate them."

"And met Raccoon," the little boy added. "Is the Raccoon the Great Spirit?"

"In a manner of speaking he is, little brother, but he is also the things that man will discover, if he seeks them, that will lead him to the Great River. The Raccoon can also be a man, or men."

"Men?" another said? "What kind of men?"

"Men," continued the Chief, "who know of the Medicine River. Men who have experienced and are familiar with life. The Raccoon washes his food in this Medicine. These types of men are unique, my children."

"Now, let us continue the Story," the Chief began again, glancing quickly at the little boy. "That is, if you wish."

The little boy turned his eyes back to the Teacher. "Yes, please continue," he said, settling himself in place.

The man turned his smiling face to the mountains, clapped his hands together, and began.

Little Mouse Walked with Raccoon. His little Heart was Pounding in his Breast. The Raccoon was Taking him upon Strange Paths and little Mouse Smelled the Scent of many things that had Gone by this Way. Many times he became so Frightened he almost Turned Back. Finally, they Came to the River! It was Huge and Breathtaking, Deep and Clear in Places, and Murky in Others. Little Mouse was unable to See Across it because it was so Great. It Roared, Sang, Cried, and Thundered on its Course. Little Mouse Saw Great and Little pieces of the World Carried Along on its Surface.

5

THE PARTY

Jonny sat at the table in the dark living room. The candles burned brightly. Jonny had a towel wrapped around his shoulders and his mother was rubbing his head dry with another towel. His older sisters, Dani and Clair, were arguing over who did the dishes last. He heard his mother's voice from behind. Its, soft delicate waves seemed far away even as she stood behind him. Jonny loved his mother's voice. He could listen to her most of the night. It was a voice that was gentle, but strong. It was effortless but convincing, resolute and unwavering as she talked. Her kids always listened for it. They followed her command without question. It was their early warning system.

"Clair, its your turn to wash the dishes."

Clair, the second oldest of the children, had a look of horror on her face. It was something that became common when she fought her older sister and her mother took the wrong side. She couldn't believe it.

"Why me? You always stick up for Dani. Why do I end up doing all the work when she gets off every time?" Even as she said this, she walked off to the kitchen to do the dishes. Dani, the oldest of the kids, smiled.

Jonny heard his mother again. "I wouldn't smile if I was you. I want you to sweep the floor and then mop it."

Anger showed on Dani's face. "Why?" Then she looked at the candles and the shadows in the house. "Its not like anyone would be able to see how clean the house is." He heard the easy voice of his mother again. It was more forceful this time. "It doesn't matter if anyone can see it. We have to live here. You don't have to see a clean place to live in a clean place. Go get the broom."

It was words like that which made Jonny listen. She would always come up with words that made his life make sense. She could take the pain away with understanding. She made it so that the only time he felt poor was when he went outside.

Jonny felt fear. It was people that made him uneasy. The girl, Nikki-D, really made him nervous. He could still hear her voice. It was a deep voice for such a small girl. It was a voice that Jonny couldn't forget. He wanted to talk more to her, but the lump in his throat got bigger and bigger. It was all he could do just to answer her questions. He moved in the chair. He was becoming skittish. The time for him to leave was near.

"Stop moving."

His mother set him up straight and continued to comb his wet hair. She trimmed it up so he would look good at the party. His eyes were going from side to side, trying to see what everyone was doing. His sister was sweeping the floor. The windows let the last light of the day in and he could see that the floor was already clean. Why his mother made Dani sweep it again, he didn't know.

Caj came into the room; his big smile, as always on his face.

"Jonny's got a girlfriend," he said. The harassment made Jonny uncomfortable. He gave Caj a mean look. He wanted desperately for him to leave him alone.

"Ahh, is Jonny nervous?"

Obviously, he wasn't going to back off. Jonny moved again. Both his hands were on the seat of the chair. He knew better than to say anything to Caj. If he did, Caj would just ride him harder. Besides, he knew that his older brother never said anything to really hurt him. He wasn't like that. Its just he treated everything and everyone as if it was a game. Sometimes his kidding went too far.

"Its the little chink girl, isn't it?"

"What was that word." Lois asked. Her anger was apparent. Her words showed how upset she was. "I don't ever want to hear those words in this house again. Do you hear me?"

Jonny watched his mother and Caj square off. It was funny, because Caj, even at twelve, was taller than his mother. He was starting to fill out. But when she talked, he would always back down. All the kids had respect for her but, to Caj, there was more. It was a deep love. Jonny never understood this.

"OK. OK. I'm sorry." He laughed and went back into the kitchen.

Jonny could tell by his mother's face that she was still mad. She had a round face that matched her round body. She stood about five-foot-four, with kind blue eyes and light-brown hair. She had led a hard life, yet she seemed to weather it well -with dignity.

"I don't want any of you to talk like that."

Dani immediately looked over to the couch where the younger sisters were sitting. There were three of them: Kate, Alexcia, and Shawn. They were always together playing and having fun. Shawn was the youngest. Jonny was finally able to see his mother without a baby on her side. It seemed odd, as if she wasn't all there without the little one hanging from her. Now the girls were all old enough to go to school. Things were changing. Jonny could see their little dark eyes staring at their mother, waiting to see if they should run and hide. It was the first thing that they all learned as they grew up. All she wanted was for them to listen to her. When she talked ... they listened.

Now she was talking to Jonny.

"You go to the party. It doesn't matter who the person is on the outside; its the inside that counts. Don't be scared because they have money and live in a big house. They're just like you and me. No different. This girl must like you if she invited you to her party. You go and have a good time."

Her voice was subdued to Jonny. It must have been something she felt very deeply. He always listened to the way people talked. It was his way of knowing what they really wanted you to know. Most of the time, words just got in the way. This time he couldn't see her but he could feel the words she was saying. It made him want to respond.

"Mm ... mm. I know, Mom. When I hear them call me names and things, I can feel the anger in them. The sadness. I don't know why they don't like me. They say things like Caj, but its not like him. They say we're different, he says we're different. Its confusing."

She wrapped her arms around him and gave him a big hug.

"That's why you're special." She put his head in her hands and kissed him. "Go up and get dressed. You don't have much time." She blew the remaining hair from his neck and took the sheet from around him. Jonny stood up and looked back. His sisters all took turns looking at him and telling him how good he looked. It made him feel better, but he was still nervous. He walked through the blanket they used as the kitchen door; a dark gray blanket that they got from the tribal thrift shop. Blankets were used for most of the doors in the house, except for the bedrooms. The blankets kept in most of the heat in the winter, and the cool air in the summer.

Caj was sitting by the cast iron stove. The portable radio was on. Not loud. Nothing was ever loud in the house. Their mother wouldn't let them get loud in the house; there was enough noise when they had to run and hide from their father and his friends. Most of the kids didn't mind just having some peace and quiet whenever possible. Even Caj followed this rule. He was sitting, waiting for the iron to get hot. Caj ironed his clothes all the time. He was immaculate. All of his clothes had to be clean and spotless. He would iron them first then put them on hangers. That's all he spent his money on: clothes. Their father was the same way.

"Hey, squirt." He grabbed the iron from the stove and walked around the ironing board. A shirt was lying there. He put the iron down and began to push back and forth. Jonny could see the wrinkles of the shirt smooth out. There were more shirts on hangers behind him. Each one had creases that could cut bread.

"Hey..." Jonny stood there.

"Is she still mad at me?" Caj kept ironing. He looked up at Jonny's face.

Jonny could see the worry lines on his forehead. It always baffled him about his brother. He was always humble when it came to their mother.

"No, I don't think so."

The big smile came back to Caj's face. Jonny could see the energy flow out from him. He turned back to his ironing. His arm moved faster as his other hand held down the edge of the shirt. He was happy again.

"Hey I didn't mean anything about the girl."

"I know."

"It was the one yesterday, wasn't it? The girl that helped stop those two white boys."

"Uh-huh."

"I thought so. Hey, she's going to be good-looking when she grows up. I think you got a find there."

"She asked about you."

Jonny didn't want to tell him this. Sometimes he got jealous because everyone liked Caj. Most of the time, it didn't matter. The girls always liked him. For some reason, Jonny didn't want this girl to like Caj. He looked at his brother and found him staring right back at him. He blushed.

Jonny ran upstairs. He was ashamed that he was jealous. He made it to his room. Actually, it belonged to both him and Caj. They had always stayed in the same room. There was one big bed, which they shared. It had many blankets on it for the cold nights. Jonny never knew what it was like to sleep alone. His sisters were in the next room. Five of them slept in there, so Jonny didn't complain much.

On the wall hung a guitar. It was Caj's. He had a good voice and could play the guitar like a pro. Caj would learn something and then move on. He always grew bored. Jonny went over to his aquarium. He picked up the food for his turtle. It was his pet. Jonny would sit there for hours and watch the turtle, just thinking.

All he was thinking of now was getting dressed. He went to the dresser and opened the drawer. There were some socks and underwear placed neatly inside. Jonny took out a pair of each and put them on the bed, then he opened the next drawer and took out his only good pair of jeans. They were his school jeans. Clean and pressed by his mother, he could see a shine to them from so many washes. It wouldn't be until the next school season that he got another pair. Every year, all the kids would get at least one set of new clothes. It was the most exciting part of going back to school.

Jonny took off the clothes that he had on. The shirt was covered with hairs. He brushed the back of his neck. It had been itching, so it was a relief to get his shirt off. He put on the clean underwear and socks. They were white gym socks. He sat on the bed and pulled his jeans over his legs and then jumped up and snapped the front. Reaching down he pulled up the zipper. He took out the belt from the old pants and pulled it through each loop around his waist. He went over to the dresser and looked at the right corner of the drawer. He only had one clean shirt left. It was his striped tee shirt. He picked it up and pulled it over his head, then he stuffed the bottom into his pants. He was done.

The old, cracked mirror was skinny but full-length. He took a look at himself. His hair was slicked back from the water and cuts. His mother had parted it on the right side. He looked clean and fresh. He walked over to the aquarium one last time. He looked down into the tank. He felt alone and afraid. He thought of the girl and who she was. It was time to go. Downstairs, he ran into Caj again.

"Whoa. Hey, is that what you're going to wear?"

Jonny looked at himself, a little embarrassed. "Yes."

Caj lifted up the shirt that he was ironing. The shirt was smooth. It fit Caj. He kept looking over the shirt, looking for any defects. "Take off your shirt."

"What?"

"Take off your shirt." Then he walked over and put his shirt in front of Jonny, trying to see what kind of fit it would be.

Jonny took off his tee shirt.

"Wear this. Its a little big, but I think it will look good on you." It was a blue and white, long-sleeved shirt. It felt like silk to Jonny. It was his big brother's shirt. Caj' never let Jonny touch his clothes, let alone wear any.

Jonny reached out and took the shirt and put it on. It was big. The shoulders hung over his arms and the tail went to his knees.

Jonny heard his brother's big laugh.

"Take it off. I think its a little too big." Caj went to the other shirts and rifled through them. He pulled out a light-blue silk shirt. It was one of his best. He told Jonny about how he got it tailored when he bought it. It was slimmer than the others. "Here, try this. "

Jonny couldn't believe it. It was Caj's best shirt. He was going to let Jonny wear it. After Jonny put it on, he could feel the shirt against his skin. It was silk and the cloth seemed to barely touch his skin. It fit snugly.

Caj was there looking at him. Then he gave the thumbs-up sign. "Yea. That's it."

"Thanks." It was all Jonny could say.

"Hey, no problem. Can't let you go up with those rich kids without you looking

right."

Jonny just stood there smiling. He felt good.

"Too bad you ain't got a present to bring." Then he grabbed his shirts and went up stairs to put them away.

Jonny walked back through the blanket-door to the kitchen. His family was all there to see him off. They oouuhed and aaahed at him and told him that he was good-looking. His little sisters were following the older ones, trying to get in on the excitement.

Jonny stood in front of his mother. She looked at the blue shirt and Jonny saw a sparkle in her eyes. She knew Caj let him wear the shirt. She understood these things.

"You mind your manners when you get up there. Behave yourself and don't get into trouble."

Jonny nodded his head up and down for yes. He would watch his manners. His mind was racing, trying to imagine what it would be like at the party. He could see a whole room full of kids. Rich kids. That scared him.

"I know you will have a good time. When you leave, be sure to thank them for inviting you. You hear?" is mother had been talking all of this time. He nodded his head again. "Mm ... mm. I got to go, Mom."

"OK. OK. I wish we had a camera to take a picture with." She looked around the house as if she might see one sitting there, waiting for her to pick it up. There was no camera.

"Next time," she said wistfully.

"I got to go, Mom." Jonny wanted to get going. His stomach wasn't feeling too good.

His mother bent down and gave him a hug. "Everything will be fine."

When Jonny heard these words from her he began to feel better. It was as if she knew what he was thinking and feeling. It eased his panic a little.

It was time to go. His mother stood back up and looked at him one more time. Jonny knew that they didn't need a camera.

Lois opened the front door for him and Jonny walked out of the house. The air hit his face. It was fresh with the smell of the sea. He stepped off the porch and looked back. His mother and all of his sisters were standing on the porch, waving good-bye. He gave a last wave and started off to the party.

Nikki-D stood in front of the window that looked down on the road below. The gate was open, but it didn't matter since she was on the second floor and could see the street below, anyway. Kids and their parents were still arriving. She was glad because she was waiting for him to show up. She was nervous all day. Her mother noticed it but didn't say anything. She was so busy talking to the parents dropping off their kids that she didn't have time to talk to her daughter.

Nikki-D's thoughts were scattered. All the kids were from Mission Heights or some other rich neighborhood. Nikki-D didn't know half of them and the other half she didn't like. She had an imperial outlook when it came to her friends. The ones she liked, she talked to. The ones she didn't, she couldn't care less about.

She looked down and lifted the hem of her dress. It was pink. She had a pink bow in her hair. She wore pink socks with her black patent-leather shoes. Her mother made her wear this outfit. She hated it. The dress she wanted to wear was the white one she saw hanging in the store when they went shopping. Her mother always bought her new clothes for a party. It was like a tradition for them. Each time, the clothes that Nikki-D liked were turned down and her mother would buy the outfit that she thought would make her daughter stand out.

Nikki-D stood out, all right. It almost made her cry. She hated it. She heard the voice behind her. It was Tammy, talking in her fast, staccato way, giggling as she went on. Tammy was back, and she was telling Nikki all the things that happened to her over the summer. Nikki-D rolled her eyes. Tammy could go on...

"My grandmother is getting so old." She giggled. "She wants us to come back again. And Mother says we are going back, although Daddy doesn't want to. "I could tell he was mad when mother said it." She giggled. "Daddy just stopped talking and smiled. Then he went out and sat on the porch. What could he say? Mother already said we were coming back."

Nikki-D tried to get back into the conversation but she was too far behind. Better to let Tammy get it all out first. She wanted so much to tell her about the new friend she made and how she invited him to the party. She wanted to talk so badly that if she didn't get it out soon, she would bust, but it was better to let Tammy finish. Nikki-D tuned her out again as she looked at the lonely street below.

Jonny walked up the street. He was almost there. The fear was getting to him. He felt like turning around and going back home. He could imagine his older brother teasing him until he died. He kept going. The houses were well-lit, their lights shining out to the road. It was dusk. The day was almost gone and he had to get to the house. He began to walk faster. His ears picked up the strange sounds of the night. The cemetery was to the left of him and he could see all the lonely white stones standing in the grass. It made him uneasy.

The sun was at the edge of the earth. He could see half of the orange ball in the sky. It was at the edge of night, and going down fast. Orange clouds hung in the light blue sky. The clouds got their last bit of warmth from the sun for the day.

Jonny stopped at the front gate. It was a big gate, with hardwood doors. Bushes crawled over and around the fence as it disappeared into the woods on the right and went around the house on the left.

He was too small to see inside. He would have to go through the gate to do that.

He felt movement in his pocket. His nerves were about to give out. He looked at his clothes to make sure they were still clean. The truth was he wanted to make sure that he wouldn't be embarrassed by them. He felt good. He looked good. He was glad his brother gave him his shirt to wear. It was a hundred times better than the tee shirt that he was going to wear. This was the best he looked in his life. He was going in.

They were all playing games in the spacious living room. Most of the kids were sitting and talking to each other as they eyed the huge cake on the table. Their presents were placed on both sides of the cake. Only one or two of them had actually picked out the present; most really didn't care what their parents got. Nikki-D knew this because that was they way they all did it when they went to a birthday party. Well, she wouldn't let it ruin her day. She had a real friend coming this time. She told Tammy about him, upstairs in her bedroom. It only took about an hour for her to stop talking so Nikki-D could finally talk. When she did let it out, they both squealed at her secret. Tammy was for her all the way. It was good to have a friend who would keep a secret. She had to tell someone. She watched the window. It was getting late. The sun was almost down. Apprehensive, she waited for the doorbell to ring. Time was going by so slowly.

Nikki-D could see her mother ordering the kids and their parents around, telling them where to go, what games to play, and who should match up with whom. Then she saw her mother coming toward her. Nikki-D knew she was in trouble for not mingling with her guests. Now she was going to hear about it. She could see the anger in her mother's eyes.

Her mother went right by her, grabbing Nikki's arm as she walked into the kitchen. Once they were in the kitchen, she let Nikki-D go.

"Well..." Her mother was incensed. It was the most upset that Nikki had seen her in some time.

"Well! I want to know. What's this about inviting someone's boy without my permission."

Nikki-D was stunned. How did her mother find out? She tried to speak, but it was impossible. Her mind was running over who could have told her mother. It must have been Tammy. She was the only one that knew. She couldn't believe it. Tammy, her best friend, would tell her mother. Especially her mother. Cold anger entered Nikki-Ds veins. It had to be someone else. But who?

"I want to know if its true that you invited some boy to come to your birthday party""

"Who? Who told you?" was all Nikki-D could mutter.

"It doesn't matter who told me. You are not going to have just anyone to your party. I worked so hard to make this a nice occasion for you. Then you do something like this. I will not allow it. Do you understand?" Her face moved closer to Nikki-D's face to make her point.

Nikki-D could feel the tears coming to her eyes. She tried to stop them, but they began to overflow. She felt as if she was drowning inside. The tears kept rising, like a flood of water ready to engulf her. Her legs were wooden, like sloshing around in a swamp. She was drowning again.

"He's my friend and I invited him to my party," she cried.

Her mother stood there her arms crossed and eyes narrowing to show her displeasure.

6

REJECTION

It was dusk. Jonny watched the orange clouds in the sky. This was the best part of the reservation to him. He stood in front of Nikki-D's house watching the kids having fun. He saw the other parents with their kids and wished he could have parents like that. He knew that his mother was too busy watching the other kids and his father ... well it was probably better that his father didn't show up.

He was seeking the courage. He looked up to the sky, hoping to catch a glimpse of the eagle. It would be a sign. He hoped the courage would flow through him like it did to Caj. Dani never had any problems with meeting new people, and in that way, Caj and she were alike. Jonny wished he could be like them. He always thought this way, but it never made any difference; he would never be like them. Courage ... Courage ... Courage.

His little friend crawled around in his pocket. His jeans were too big for him, so Jonny could grow into them and wear them next year for school. That's how his mother bought clothes, for him and the little kids. Caj and the older ones found money to buy their own clothes so they looked like the rest of the kids at school. Jonny never did wear clothes like the other students unless they were Indians. Then he fit right in... Sort of.

Jonny watched kids running around in the light of the big windows. He saw that creep, Jimmy Whoever, laughing and moving across the room with his big goon friend following behind him. Jonny's eyes scanned the house and he saw colorful and neatly wrapped presents sitting on one of the tables. Every once in a while a small child would walk up to the presents and looked at them with longing. Jonny's little friend moved in his pocket again.

Lois sat waiting. She was worried about Jonny going to this party.

It belonged to the rich people on the hill and she didn't want him to get his feelings hurt. She knew deep down inside that something would happen to him tonight and she was preparing herself. "Mom, I'm going out to Judy's place." It was Dani. She was leaving before her father and his hoods came in drunk. She couldn't stand some of the men he brought home from the tavern. Their eyes never left her body. It made her sick.

"All right, dear." Lois wanted Dani gone before he got home. She was growing up fast and the men watched her when she walked around. This made Lois uncomfortable.

"Clair, your dad will be home soon and when he gets here, I want you to take the kids upstairs. Keep them in the room and play. I don't want you coming down, either. Your father is drinking wine again, so stay up there."

"OK, Mom."

It was all Lois could do: Hide her kids. She looked out in the evening sky. Dusk was so peaceful here. The orange clouds followed the sun into the horizon. She always waited for the peace and quiet of each day. She would soak it up and rest in it. Lois knew it wouldn't be long until the bad things took over.

She heard them before she saw them. They walked down the road, laughing and making crude jokes. Four men. Franc brought them home to drink. They carried their apple-wine bottles with them. Lois hated that wine. It made them all mean and angry. She hated it when he came home like this. Tension rushed through her and she felt the stress rise.

"Hey, Lois, bring me some water, could you?" Dick was the only white man with the group. Eddie and Franc were fighting over the last drop of wine and Dick had just gotten back with another bottle. It was all they could afford.

"OK. I'll get you some water."

"Youuuuu ... filthy mother! Franc had the bottle raised above his head, ready to hit Eddie with it. They fought the whole night. They were loud and crazy.

"I'll kick your ass. Don't push me, Franc. I'll kick your ass." Eddie had his hands in front of him, ready to defend himself

Lois raised her eyes in disgust. She would be frightened if it wasn't so funny watching two drunk men stagger and slobber all over each other. Their eyes were red and almost closed. She was used to Indian drunkenness. It was a total drunkenness that no white man could ever match. Like Dick: He acted all right, even though he was probably as drunk as the others. It was amazing because you thought they would pass out; then another bottle came up and they would drink some more. At the end of the night, it would be the Indians who were the last ones standing.

"Hey you guys, I got more here."

Franc and Eddie stopped threatening each other and looked at the bottle of wine.

"Hey, bring it right over here." Franc could barely see, but moved the empty dishes of food that Lois had made them and put his glass out to be filled.

Just then, Clair came in the room with the glass of water that Lois filled for Dick. She waited for Dick to take it. Her hand trembled and some water spilled.

"Hey! You're spilling it." Franc stared at his daughter until she moved back. Hate rushed though him so hard that he didn't know what to do. "Get back in there and bring out another glass."

"That's all right, Franc. Who is this - your daughter?"

Franc didn't say anything and looked away. "Filthy pigs."

Clair went back into the kitchen, glad to be away from the men. She didn't like the way that Dick looked at her.

"Can't you tell them to get out?"

"Just go back upstairs."

Lois hated it when things went bad so early in the day.

It was getting late and Jonny had to decide what he was going to do. He still watched the lighted windows. Then he saw her. It was Nikki-D and her mother, walking out to the party. Jonny watched her. She was in a party dress. It was odd to see her like that; so different from earlier in the day. He liked it. She was kind of cute.

Jonny felt the courage come to him. It would be all right. He would just go up and knock on the door. That's all he had to do.

Nikki-D watched the door. She didn't want her mother to answer it if Jonny showed up. She wanted to talk to Tammy and looked for her in the room full of kids. She was standing in the corner with some other little girls. Nikki-D went over to talk to her.

"Did you tell my mother about Jonny?"

"No. Why? Did she find out?"

"Yesss. And she said he can't come to my party. Its my party. I don't see why I can't invite who I want."

"I know. Do you think he will come?"

"I don't know. He didn't say he would. I hope so."

"Maybe he will."

"I wonder who told?"

Then she saw him walking across the room: Jimmy, with his toady friend following behind. Nikki-D didn't have to ask any more; she knew who it was.

"Hi, Nikki-D. Nice party. Glad we got invited to come. Hey-hey." Jimmy had a strange laugh.

She hated him. He gave her the creeps. "I didn't think youuu... would come. I don't know why you did." Nikki-D wanted to let him know exactly how she felt.

"I know who won't be coming."

"Who?"

"You know."

"Jimmy Livingston, you don't know anything. Why don't you just go away?"

"Hey-hey, let's get some pop. Jimmy and his toady went over to the punch table, leaving Nikki-D almost in tears again. She hated him because he was the one who told her mother. Now she knew that Jonny wouldn't be attending her party.

Jonny moved to the door. His heart was pounding. Standing there, he thought of running home but knew he couldn't do that. He reached up and tapped on the door. Then he waited. There was no answer.

The party was going fine as far as Ginny was concerned. She kept her eye on the door, as well as on Nikki-D. She knew her daughter. She worked hard to throw this party and wasn't going to let her daughter ruin it. She invited only the right parents and their kids. It was important to her to do things right. That meant bringing in the right people. It started with this party.

They were the rich and famous people who owned the land around the bluff. They kept to themselves until they met at their meetings and homes. Their kids played with each other and learned together. That was what Ginny wanted. She would not let her daughter be taken down because of who she was or what she looked like. Ginny was sure of that.

The room was full of balloons and streamers made by her and bought by her. It was festive and the kids were having a good time playing Pin the Tail on the Donkey. There were screams of delight as they spun a little girl around and around and she tried to find the Donkey. Laughter came from some of the mothers, too, as they tried to get the best for their own kids. Fathers never came to these parties. It was unmanly.

Just as she thought this, she noticed Nick. He always wanted to be here with Nikki-D. Ginny resented this sometimes because she wanted him to be like the other husbands, even though she was glad he took an interest in his daughter.

Ginny saw Nora Livingston and her son talking with the other parents. She was a busybody. Ginny liked her little girl – what was her name ... Tammy – she was so different from the rest of them. A little sweetie. Her son was awful, though. When he came up and told her that Nikki-D invited one of those Indians, Ginny didn't know who she was more angry at: her daughter or the Livingston boy. Or herself.

She was so intent on watching things going on that she didn't hear the tapping on the door. She saw Jimmy coming over to her. Then she saw Nikki-D heading for the door. Panic hit her.

"Mrs. Thomas, I think there's someone at the door."

Ginny moved to the door. Nikki-D was too far away and stopped when she saw her mother. Ginny saw the grief already on her face. It was for her own good. They lived here on the Res. for five years now and never had anything to do with the Indians. Ginny and her group didn't mingle with those people. Most of the time, she didn't even see them. She had to drive by their homes some of the time and wondered how they could live like that. She saw their filth and broken-down homes, with beat-up yards, and rusted old cars sitting in some of the yards. The only real time Ginny saw Indians was when she heard the drums beating. Then she would watch as they gathered around and buried one of their own.

"Tap-tap-tap." Now Ginny heard the knocking at the door. The anger came back at her. Nikki-D knew better than to invite someone without telling her. She also knew Ginny would have said no. Now Ginny had to play the bad guy again.

"Tap-tap-tap.

Jonny didn't want to knock harder because he didn't want to offend the people inside. Usually when he came up this far to Mission Heights, he would have to fight to get back. The white kids would throw rocks at him and whoever was with him. Jonny and his friends would throw rocks back but they always ran back down the hill. There were too many of them. Now he was invited to one of their parties. He was still scared.

He thought he would knock one more time and then he would go. Jonny wasn't going to press his luck; besides, he could tell everyone that he tried. That would take care of any jokes made about him. He knew that anger would replace their humor once they heard that nobody answered the door.

'Tap-tap...

The door flew open. Light streamed out, blinding Jonny for a second and making him jump with a jolt. His heart beat faster and he began to sweat. He stood there in fear.

"Yes." Ginny looked down at the ragamuffin little boy trembling in her doorway. He wore clothes that must have been three sizes too big for him. She looked further down and saw some worn tennis shoes with shoe strings tied together at various places where they must have broken. He was a brown-skinned boy with odd eyes.

"See, I told you someone was at the door. **That's** one of the boys who beat me up. They all attacked me at the bottom of the hill." Jimmy Livingston stood behind Ginny with his mother, who had her hands on his shoulders.

Ginny looked at the little boy again. Jimmy must be a couple of years older than this boy, so she doubted that he was going to beat him up. She would have to get to the bottom of this later.

"I think we should call the police." Nora brought her son closer to her as she said this.

"Nora, why don't you take the kids back into the party. I'll take care of this." Ginny wasn't about to let things get out of hand. She knew how these parents' fear got the better of them. Some of her anger left.

"Well!" Her eyes bore into Jonny.

He didn't know what to say, so he hung his head down. His heart sped up even more. He felt this woman's anger against him and it ran deep. He kept his head down.

"Mm ... mm. Mm ... mm."

"I think you have the wrong address, young man."

Jonny's heart stopped. "mm ... mm."

"Well!"

Jonny stepped back. She didn't want him here. He was too nervous to say anything, so he just stood with his head down. Finally he looked up and caught a glimpse of Nikki-D in the background. She was crying and a big man was hugging her. Jonny made a mistake in coming; he could see that now.

"I think you should go home young man."

The door was shut in his face. Jonny stood there, not really knowing what to do. He stood in the silence of dusk.

Jonny sat on the log watching the house. He didn't understand why adults never liked him. All he knew was that it always hurt to be rejected by them. Inside was where it always hurt. Jonny thought of his father; he always knew that he didn't want Jonny around him, either. Other people never liked to talk to him because of how he spoke. It made him so mad and he vowed to talk right the next time. He was so stupid.

The tears began to run down his face. Jonny felt lost and alone. He was always alone at times like this. His heart hurt and his face was hot as the tears coursed down it. If he could find out what was wrong with him, he would fix it. But the woman tonight didn't even say anything. She wasn't white, so it must not be because he was Indian. What was it?

Jonny tried to wipe the tears away but they kept coming even faster. He couldn't stop them. He began to hiccup as he started to cry harder. This was his life: Always alone; always wondering why.

Jonny wondered what Caj would do. He wanted to be like his older brother, so he tried to think like him at times like this. As he thought of Caj, Jonny could see him getting angry and storming up to the door and saying what he wanted to the lady. Caj was like that. Jonny felt his courage coming back to him. He felt the little movement in his pocket and knew what he was going to do.

The last of the kids left with their parents. Jimmy and Nora were the last to leave. They came up to Ginny.

"Thank you, Ginny, for the party. It was the best. Hey-hey."

"Thank you for coming." Ginny remembered Tammy was going to stay over with Nikki-D, and they stood behind Nora and Jimmy.

"Thank you, Mrs. Thomas, for inviting me. I had a good time and hope Nikki-D liked my present." Jimmy gave her a big, fake smile. He was glad to be here but only to be near his desire.

"You're welcome, young man, and I'm sure she loved your present. I hope..."

'Tap-tap-tap.

It was the front door. Somebody must have left something. Ginny went to the door and opened it.

Jonny stood in his rumpled clothes as the woman looked down at him once again. No matter how he tried, he felt the fear inside of him. He worked on the words he wanted to say. The woman waited.

"What are you doing here again?" A note of impatience crept into her voice.

"Mm ... mm. I brought this for Nikki-D." Jonny held out his hand, with his little friend in his palm. The small turtle never moved and had his head in its shell. Jonny had his head down while he waited for the woman to take his gift.

"I don't think she can take..."

Before Ginny could finish her sentence, Nikki-D rushed up and snatched the little turtle out of the boy's hand.

"Nikki-D! Give that back to him. You can't take a present from him."

"No. I'm keeping it. Jonny said it was my birthday present. Its mine."

Ginny saw the stubbornness in her daughter and knew it wouldn't do her any good to demand it be given back tonight. She saw Nora and Jimmy waiting to see what she would do. The party went well tonight, so she let it go. "Then come here and thank him properly."

Jonny waited in the entrance as Nikki-D came up to the door. He finally looked up at her. She was smiling at him.

"Thanks, Jonny. Sorry about the party."

"Mm ... mm. That's OK. I hope you like my gift."

"I do."

Ginny put her hands on her daughter's shoulders and pulled her back a little. "That's enough. I think you should go home, young man. Its getting too late for you to be out. Is your mother coming to get you?"

"Mm ... mm. No."

"I think you better hurry, then. Its late."

She shut the door on Jonny. He stood alone again in front of the big, rich house, but it was different now. He turned around with a smile on his face. He did it. He got to see Nikki-D take his gift. He knew she liked it. The fear left him. The walk home would only take a second. Jonny felt joy from the night. It was one of the best he ever had, yet he didn't know why. That was all right. Everything was all right now.

The night sky was clear and the stars were out. It was a good time to have a friend.

"It is Powerful!" little Mouse said, Fumbling for Words.

"It is a Great thing," answered the Raccoon, "but here, let me Introduce you to a Friend."

In a Smoother, Shallower Place was a Lily Pad, Bright and Green. Sitting upon it was a Frog, almost as Green as the Pad it sat on. The Frog's White Belly stood out Clearly.

"Hello, little Brother," Said the Frog. "Welcome to the River."

"I must Leave you Now," cut in Raccoon, "but do not Fear, little Brother, for Frog will Care for you Now." And Raccoon Left, Looking along the river Bank for food that he might Wash and Eat.

Little Mouse Approached the Water and Looked into it. He saw a Frightened Mouse Reflected there.

"Who are you?" little Mouse asked the Reflection. "Are you not Afraid being that Far out into the Great River?"

"No," answered the Frog, "I am not Afraid. I have been Given the Gift from Birth to Live both Above and Within the River. When Winter Man comes and Freezes this Medicine, I cannot be Seen. But all the while Thunderbird Flies, I am here. To Visit me, One must Come when the World is Green. I, my Brother, am the Keeper of the Water."

"Amazing!" little Mouse said at last, again Fumbling for Words.

"Would you like to have some Medicine Power?" Frog asked.

"Medicine Power? Me?" asked little Mouse. "Yes, yes! If it is Possible."

"Then Crouch as Low as you Can, and then Jump as High as you are Able! You will have your Medicine!" Frog said.

Little Mouse did as he was Instructed. He Crouched as Low as he Could and Jumped. And when he did, his Eyes Saw the Sacred Mountains.

"Like those over there," the Chief said, pointing to the distant mountains. Then he went on.

Little Mouse could hardly Believe his Eyes. But there They were! But then he Fell back to Earth, and he Landed in the River!

The Chief laughed and looked at the little girl.

Little Mouse became Frightened and Scrambled back to the Bank. He was Wet and Frightened nearly to Death.

"You have Tricked me," little Mouse Screamed at the Frog!

"Wait," said the Frog. "You are not Harmed. Do not let your Fear and Anger Blind you. What did you See?"

"I," Mouse stammered, "I, I Saw the Sacred Mountains!"

"And you have a New Name!" Frog said. " It is Jumping Mouse."

"Thank you. Thank you," Jumping Mouse said, and Thanked him again. "I want to Return to my People and Tell them of this thing that has Happened to me."

"Go. Go then," Frog said. " Return to your People. It is Easy to find them. Keep the Sound of the Medicine River to the Back of your Head. Go Opposite to the Sound and you will Find your Brother Mice."

7

GINNY

"I told you I don't want her going around those people!" With that, Ginny walked away from her husband. He was left in the kitchen by himself , Ginny had no intention of letting Nikki-D's father in the middle of this. She wasn't going to let it happen; not with her daughter.

The party was a disaster nearly from the beginning. She had tried to make it perfect; she wanted it to be perfect. It wasn't. Her little girl had seen to that.

"Why can't she see that I want the best for her? If she only knew what I knew, she would see that I'm looking out for her own good."

Ginny began washing the morning dishes. Her husband, Nick, walked out the front door. There was no kiss for him. The fight was hard on them both. He wanted what was best for Nikki-D. To him, that meant she should do anything she wanted; play with whomever she wanted. Well, it was up to Ginny to put a stop to that notion. She forbid Nikki-D to see that little boy ever again ... or any of the other scruffy-looking Indians. Even thinking about them made her feel dirty. She rubbed her hands on her apron as she remembered the argument with Nick.

"You wouldn't be able to stop her. If she wants to find her own friends then she will. Some of those people seem like nice people. I watch them down on the beach. I'm sure the boy is nice." He was looking at his watch all the time he was talking. He really had to get to work. The bank audit was coming up and he wanted to make sure his files were all perfect. He put most of his time and energy into his work. It was where he was the most efficient. His wife was the same way at home. Even more so. She made it clear that appearance was the most important thing. Nothing else mattered. The main rooms were always spotless, except for little things here and there – mostly small messes from Nick and his daughter. She was just like him about that. And about people.

"I told you: I don't want any of our friends talking about us because of who our daughter is seeing. And they will talk. That's all they do in a small place like this."

"Come on, we don't even associate with people that live on the point. What do they care who our daughter is or what she's doing?"

"They care."

Ginny finished the dishes. She walked over to the coffee pot and filled her cup. She looked out of the kitchen window. The clouds were out today; some light, some dark, all floating by on the air currents. The wind would be rough tonight. She could already hear it howling. She could feel the goose-bumps rise on her arms. Ginny went over to the table and sat down. Her thoughts were deep. Small voices were speaking: they became louder. She took a drink of her coffee. She had no control over the voices in her head. They were voices from her past. She remembered her mother.

"You lazy! Lazy girl. Just like all Americans. Why I had you I don't know. People see you. They always watch. They care only how bad you do; nothing more. You make mother look bad. That how they know mother is no good." It was her mother, Empress. That's what everyone called her because that's what she was in China. Empress was from the Qing family. For most of her life, she was pampered and cared for by other people. When the Boxer Rebellion ran out the last dynasty in China, Empress and her husband Eddie had to flee. Both belonged to China's aristocracy. Ginny stood in the kitchen of the old restaurant: The China Garden. Her parents started it with the money they managed to smuggle out with them. It meant a whole new lifestyle that they were not accustomed to.

Every day, they would search the papers for news of China, a place Ginny had only heard of from their lips; a place she hated.

Her mother cocked her head, as if she had a secret. She looked at her daughter. "Good news today. The General is moving forward with the new government. Soon we will go back. Soon..." With that, her mother moved off to meet new customers. Ginny was afraid. China was so foreign to her. Her mother and father could only read the Chinese papers. Ginny read them all. She was a bright girl; excellent in school. Ginny had already read her news in the regular papers. She couldn't read the Chinese as well as the English papers. The information was the same. It scared her.

Why her parents would want to go to a place of starvation and squalor, Ginny didn't know. It seemed like a lost dream for them. The General her mother was talking about was Chiang Kai-shek, who had just formed the Nationalist government in Nanjing. Wherever that was. She would have to look at the map. Even greater than her fear of her parents was her fear of moving to China.

Ginny couldn't remember a day when she didn't work. Besides her school work, she had to come home and work in the restaurant. It had been the same routine for most of her young life. Menial labor wasn't new to her. The drudgery was overwhelming; she washed mountains of dishes, and swept and mopped the floors. The only way she escaped was through her dreams.

"A chimera. Dreams of wealth and plenty, like my parents when they lived in China, but different. I will stay here, in Hawaii. I will travel. I will not have to wash another dish or scrub another floor. I will be the Empress."

The hand rose behind her. She didn't notice. It came down and smacked her across the head.

"Lazy girl. Always daydreaming. No work. Only daydream. You make parents look bad. Look ... see all the dishes? They wait for you, but you only daydream." Her mother's hand went up again. Ginny cringed, but there was no pity. The hand struck her again. "Wash dishes! Wash dishes!"

Ginny began to scrub faster for mother's benefit. The side of her face hurt and a red, raised hand-print had formed on her cheek.

Her mother was a tyrant to everyone that worked for her. To Empress, it was no different from her former life, when all the people worked for her. It was her place to treat them with contempt and hatred, or they would get out of line. Like in China.

Ginny's mother dominated everyone in her realm. Ginny was the one that she began with in the morning and ended with at night. Her mother never wanted Ginny. She knew that for sure. She couldn't understand why she had her. She tried to do things right, but she never knew what her mother wanted. Or she never worked hard enough. Or she was always daydreaming.

School was the only pleasure in her hard life. It was her escape. It was lucky that her parents needed to show everyone that they could afford to send their only daughter to the best school in the neighborhood. The law required it. It was also her passion. Long, deep books took her away from the hardships of daily life. She was a dreamer. It was the only way to survive.

Ginny sighed. It was time to get to work. The rooms needed cleaning, the beds must be made and she needed to go shopping to get the food for tonight. The day didn't seem to have enough hours. It never did. She was worried about her. It hurt her to fight with Nikki-D. She was everything to her. She wanted her daughter to have every chance that life offered, but Nikki-D would always fight her. She said she was happy the way she was. Nikki-D took the easy way out. Never pushed herself. Not that she had to; she was a very smart little girl. Ginny felt it was a gift from her. All those hours of reading must have gone through her into her daughter. Ginny smiled. What would her mother say to that? She quickly shook her head: "Can't think about that now." She still felt the glow of that thought. As if she had won.

She was afraid that Nikki-D would squander what she had. She wanted to put her into a special class, but her husband stepped in when Nikki-D cried. At least, until now, she had the right friends. Now that had changed. Ginny could hear the other mothers talking, especially that Mrs. Livingston. She couldn't keep her mouth shut for anything. She was a real busybody. That's why Ginny watched her. Mrs. Livingston was a danger to Ginny's family and Ginny was determined to fight her off.

The anger still came over her when she remembered the little Indian boy at her door, looking so pathetic in those oversized clothes. It was clear he must have borrowed them, unless the boy's mother had no sense of fashion. How could Nikki-D have invited him on one of her most important nights? She ruined everything.

Ring ... ring!

It was the doorbell. It was early in the morning, too early for anyone except...

Ring ... ring!

Ginny's head began to throb. She hated that sound. She got up and went to the kitchen door. It swung as she went through it. She turned her head to the big bay windows. The water was jumping: the waves riding high. Hat Island lay in her view. It was a magnificent view. She could just sit in the morning and watch the world outside her window.

Ginny noticed that the wind was rustling the leaves on the tree tops. It would blow tonight. One thing about this part of the country: there was a lot of wind. Well, a lot of rain, too. It wasn't bad weather; not compared to the extreme weather on the East Coast. That was something she did not miss.

Ring ... ring!
I'm going to break that damn bell.

She opened the door. Nora Livingston stood in front of her. Her mousy-brown hair hanging to her shoulders. She had a big bright smile on her face. Ginny dreaded having her in her house so early; especially when she hadn't even cleaned yet.

"Hi. I came to see if I could borrow some sugar. I'm afraid I ran out. Need some for my coffee." She held a cup in her hands, lifting it up to Ginny.

Ginny knew this was a hint that she wanted to come in for coffee and chit-chat. "Nora. Yes. Yes. Come in. I have some in the kitchen. Would you like some coffee? I just made a fresh pot."

Ginny stepped away from the door. She opened the door farther for her next-door neighbor. Nora walked in like she owned the place. Of course, she'd been there many times before.

In the kitchen. Ginny poured Nora a cup of coffee. Then she poured one for herself and went to the kitchen table.

"I can't help thinking that our reservation is going up in smoke." She caught the double entendre and began to laugh. Heh-ha-heh-ha.

Ginny couldn't stand that laugh. It was like a donkey braying.

"Anyway – having that Indian boy come to the party! All of the parents applauded you when you turned him away." Her high, misty voice grew in volume as she began to warm up to the speech she had obviously prepared.

Ginny watched the woman that raised such a deep-seated sense of hatred in her. Her mother. It always came back to that.

"Who do they think they are? Coming up to this side of the reservation! Why, you never see them unless they have a funeral. And then they come out like flies. Where they come from, I don't know. It frightens me to think that they are all around us. You never know what might happen." Nora gently put her lips to the edge of the cup and took a sip of her coffee. Using both hands, she kept her pinkies up.

"Yes. I know what you mean." Ginny said little. She never had to with Nora, who was the busy-body of the hill. Her nose was in everyone's business. That was Nora.

"Like my little baby. He was beaten up by those heathens just the other day. Five of those Indian boys jumped him from behind. He took a terrible beating. He and his little friend fought back. And the Indians ran away. Isn't that just like them? My poor baby."

Ginny had never heard of this. None of the parents mentioned it at the party. She felt the hairs rise on her neck. She thought of Nikki-D running around with people like that. A real fear entered her. She would have to do something. Ginny thought for a moment.

I will have a talk with her father this evening. He will have to listen to me when I tell him about the beatings. Ginny felt a smug glow come over her. She would get her way in the end.

She wished they didn't fight over Nikki-D. It was the one area where they both thought they did it right. Nick wanted her to have the life he never had, a normal life. In a way, that's what Ginny wanted, too. He couldn't say that living in a house in the middle of a reservation could be considered normal. Nikki-D needed the schools that could help her become the woman that Ginny knew she could become. She could be anything. Now Ginny had to worry about her girl being beaten up by those Indians. It wasn't fair.

Nora was weeping. She just finished talking about the black-and-blue marks on Jimmy's face and body. Her husband had wanted to go right down to the Indian village and whip the boys that did it, but Jimmy wouldn't let him. Pete was mad, wanting the neighbors to stick together on this. After all, if it happened to their boy, it could happen to the others. Besides, the Indians should stay where they belong: Down in the projects, not up here on the hill.

Nora looked at her watch and through the tears, "Oh my goodness! Look at the time. Ginny, you're such a dear for listening to me. Sometimes I just need someone to talk to. You've been a saving grace ever since you moved here with your family." Nora walked over and put the empty cup and saucer in the sink. She turned around and faced Ginny.

"I hope we can count on you to keep this secret. We don't want to start trouble, but I hope all of us can stick together. You know ... all of us on the hill."

Ginny didn't answer right away. She got up and took Nora by the arm. They walked to the door. "Listen, Nora I won't tell a soul. I'll keep this between the two of us. You have my word."

"Thank you, Ginny. Things are so hard with the world changing everyday, nothing the same, people fighting ... what's going on with America? I just don't know!"

Ginny stood on the porch watching her neighbor walk down the road. She was concerned. Nora's boy was a brat, but if he was getting beat up, by the Indians then things were changing.

She went back into the house. In the kitchen, she put on her apron and cleaning gloves; it was time to get to work. She had to think about what she was going to say to Nick and their daughter. She thought better when she worked. She was always working and cleaning.

Ginny started her dusting in the spacious living room. She looked around at the corners of the room where her vases stood. She went up to the first vase. It was made of proto-porcelain, from the Han period, around 206 BC. One of her oldest pieces. She could picture the man or men who sat around the pottery wheel, forming it with their hands, and waiting for the right temperature so they could fire the pottery. Their judgment and experience were the only things telling them that the time was right. She dusted lightly around it. There was no design like the others had. The yellow color set it apart from the others; it was her baby.

She still kept the interests that her mother had tried to stop. Ginny read a new book every week, depending on what interested her at the time. She could never be like the other housewives on the hill, happy in their own little world. Although she took care of her duties as a housewife, she would never let that be the sum total of her life. Her husband and Nikki-D were a full-time job, but she always worked and that wasn't enough. She sought fulfillment.

Moving on, she dusted as she went. The fireplace had to be cleaned out. The ashes and wood were making a mess. Nick wanted to keep the wood by the fireplace, stacked by his own hands. He seemed proud of this. Why? Ginny didn't know. Hmm, must be a man thing. Never can tell what goes through their heads. She took the fire shovel, the small broom and swept the ashes, chips and papers. She swept until every corner of the fireplace was clean. She would continue until she was satisfied. It didn't bother her, because her mind was in another place another time.

Ginny finished cleaning the floors and the dishes. The kitchen was spotless. Anxiety was gripping her. The last of the customers were gone. She peeked through the doors to see her parents at the cash register counting their money. All the workers had gone home. Her mother never wanted the help to see the money made during the day. She paid them the smallest amount possible. Most of them couldn't say anything for fear of being sent back to China. There would always be slave labor for her mother to hire.

Ginny saw her mother look up. Her parents smiled at each other. It must have been a good day. Then her mother looked at the kitchen. Ginny stepped back. Hurriedly, she looked around the room. It all seemed spotless. She crossed her fingers.

The doors to the kitchen swung open. Her mother stood there looking down at Ginny. Ginny bowed her head. It was like this every night. She wanted it to end. Her studies. The pots and pans were shining as they hung from their hooks. The plates were clean and dried and put neatly in the cupboards. Her mother eyed each end of the kitchen. It was time for her to do her walk-through. Ginny never moved. She had learned how to hide her anxiety. She could feel the long, slanted black eyes on her. She burned inside, but nothing showed on the outside. She was expecting the worst. It was always bad, no matter how hard she tried. But she kept trying.

She moved hurriedly throughout the kitchen. She noticed everything. It was the same tour night after night. Ginny followed behind.

"You good girl today?" she asked as she walked.

"Yes, Mother."

Empress stopped at the pans. She rubbed her index finger around the edge and looked at it. Ginny bowed her head.

"Very good."

Pride swam in Ginny. It always felt this way when she got a compliment. It made her want more, like a craving.

Her mother moved on to the grills. They were usually cleaned by the cooks, who didn't want anyone else touching their grill. Her mother made her go over them after they left.

"Don't trust," she said.

She went over each grill and checked them.

"Mmmm. Very good."

Ginny could feel her heart racing. She was going to make it. She could feel it. This was the second compliment. That was rare. Ginny could feel her face turn red. She was happy!

Her mother checked the floors. Ginny knew that they were clean. She scrubbed every inch.

"Very ... very good."

Ginny couldn't hold her smile back. She did it. That meant she would make it home to study. She had so many books to read and a paper to do. She was going to make it.

"I let you go. You do good job tonight. Best I ever see you do." Her mother smiled down at Ginny.

Finished.

Empress walked to the door. She was happy. It had been a good night. Her daughter, though not good, was getting better. Things looked good. She smiled. Soon they would go back to her beloved country, where each person lived in their own place. She walked to the kitchen doors and was about to leave when something caught her eye from behind the door. She stopped and shut the door. In the corner were rags; many of them. She began to see red. Her lazy daughter tried to trick her; again she could not put any trust in her. The anger came from deep within. She turned.

Ginny looked up. She shrank away from her mother. Fear entered her heart.

"Lazy girl. You try and deceive your mother. Too lazy to put dirty rags away. You too busy with dream. Not able to see right in front of you. Make mother look bad."

Ginny backed away in horror. Her mother drew nearer. She could see her mother's hand come up. In the pit of her stomach, she knew there would be no reading until late tonight.

Ginny moved to the windows. They were spotless. She got the rag and sprayed the window, and began to wipe them clean. Nikki-D didn't understand. She wanted the best for her; opportunities that Ginny never had. The window was clean, so she moved on to the next one. She wanted her little girl to go to the best schools. To study and be with friends, not run around with Indians. No! She would not allow it.

Ginny stopped and looked at the vase in the corner of the window. It was part of her heritage. Many connoisseurs, however, feel that the pure white porcelain, called blanc de chine, which first appeared during the Ming dynasty, is the most serenely beautiful of all Chinese ceramics. The over glaze enamel decorations incorporated flowers, foliage, and figure subjects against backgrounds of arabesques and scrollwork. Designs enclosed within dark blue outlines were filled in with brilliant color.

To Ginny, this showed her true worth: Beautiful work and the knowledge of what was put into them to make them beautiful. Feldspar and others produced by fusing silica of quartz or sand by means of a flux. This was Ginny's passion. Her mother could never stop her from learning. Now she had a daughter who made learning easy. She was so proud of her. She loved her, but didn't know how to show her. It was hard and she knew her daughter suffered. If only Nikki-D could see.

I'll show her, Ginny thought, then she went on with her cleaning.

The front door opened and Nikki-D came running in. She stopped suddenly, looking up into the face that was a mirror of hers. Her mother stood in front of her. Fear entered her heart. There had been so much hate and words between them. They both stood for a second, sizing each other up. Her mother opened her arms but she didn't know what to do. She was scared. This is what Nikki-D wanted; for her mother to notice her.

    Nikki-D ran into her mother's arms; into the arms of the woman she loved.

8

LOIS

She watched Jonny sitting on the old, rugged couch. Lois Esque knew something had gone wrong. She could feel the pain coming from her son. It had something to do with the party. Whatever it was, he wasn't saying. He was so silent and solemn sometimes. He moved in still steps, soundless and hushed. She continued sweeping the floor while she watched her son. He seemed so cold and distant to people, but she knew better. She heard the talk from people that didn't know anything: How he was slow and withdrawn in school. They had put him in special classes most of his school years. She let them talk her into it. In her heart, she knew she did the wrong thing.

It was the hushed way he talked; how he said words. He never pronounced them right the first time. Some of them he would never pronounce right; as if his mind just didn't care how the world pronounced words; his way sounded better. Of course, the school couldn't have that. Something wrong with his mind, they said. Needs help. They couldn't see the good things about him. He was such a deep boy. It used to worry her, but now it just made her wonder.

"Do you want some lemonade?"

He didn't even acknowledge her. She hated it when the world hurt her children. It made her feel so helpless. Only on this reservation had she been able to find some form of security. She knew everyone and everyone knew her. They accepted her as she was, never wanting more. They harbored her and watched out for her. Her blond hair and blue eyes were just something they talked about. She was brought into the center with all the information coming from all corners of the reservation. Just like with her son. He really didn't have to say anything. She would know soon enough. Word was being passed from mouth to mouth at this very minute, and soon it would get to her. This was her security. It made her feel warm.

The reservation was her home. She was tired of traveling. Her family had always followed her father around the country. Before that she lived on a farm in Phelps, Wisconsin. She stopped. She could still feel the cold wind of Wisconsin. The coldness covered her thoughts. She remembered it still.

She felt the wind-chill in her bones. The white plains of snow covered everything. Lois was standing at the window looking out over the wasteland. She closed the window and picked up the broom. She began her sweeping. Her mother was in the kitchen making dinner. Her father had left. Where? She didn't know. It had been a while since he left. Her mother brought her girls back home to the farm; Lois and the younger one, Alice. Lois, being the eldest, always had to take care of her sister and her cousins on the farm. There never seemed to be enough time. Her work was never done. The kids always needed something and most of the time she was the only one there for them. It was a hard life for her.

Her mother and family were from Swedish stock. Her father was a Frenchman. He left early after Alice was born. He was a small, funny man who made them laugh. Her mother carried that stoic mannerism that all the Nordic people had; in addition she was in her second marriage, to a man that seemed like her father, always making jokes. There was something odd about him. Dangerous. Sometimes his jokes hurt and he always had the girls sit on his lap. He liked Alice the best. She seemed to take to him right off the bat.

Lois never had any time to worry about those things because of the work she had to do. This morning, she was up at dawn building the fire. Then she got her cousin Bob up and they went out and milked the cows. She woke her mother and the others when the stove was hot and coffee was boiling. They got up and the women began making breakfast. Lois began getting all the kids up and made them go to the bathroom and brush their teeth. Then she got them dressed and down to breakfast before the school bus came.

Her mother relied on her. All she could think of was getting the next job done. She never liked to think too much, anyway. She had troubled thoughts. Things weren't right and she couldn't put her finger on it.

The kids sat down at the table. The food was hot and waiting. They were all still sleepy. They began to jump into the food with relish. Lois waited for them to start. Mornings were always this way. The kids would soon begin to complain, and then they would talk about what was going on, and then they would tell her all the secrets. This was what kept her safe. She would listen and see if anything was out of the ordinary; if not, she knew it was safe.

"I'm going over to Stephen's after school today," said Fred.

"Will you cut my hair tonight, Lois?" It was her sister Alice asking.

"OK, but it has to be right when you get home." Was that look a concern? "What about you, Angie? Do you want me to cut your hair, too?"

Angie kept her eyes down and didn't say anything. She was just playing with her food and not eating.

"Oh no. Not her."

"Did you hear me, Angie?" Lois's heart was beating. She already knew it was too late. Something had happened. When? Last night when she was out working? That was the only time she wasn't around. The other kids were gone, too. Her heart sank. Yes, it was true.

"Is something wrong, Angie?"

The little blond girl just shook her head.

"Daddy was with her last night," Bob, the youngest boy, said as he was shoveling food in his mouth.

All the kids stopped what they were doing and looked at Bobby.

Lois looked at him, too. "Don't talk with your mouth full."

He stopped shoveling and tried to swallow the remaining food in his mouth. Everyone was waiting. Bob couldn't get it all down. Fred, the oldest, got up and stomped out of the kitchen.

Bobby finally stopped chewing. He knew he was on the spot. He squirmed in his chair.

"So what happened?" Lois knew not to press him too much. A little boy only plays to his own tunes. It was important.

"I don't know. I just saw Daddy take Angie with him. That's all." He stubbornly sat there with his arms folded across his chest. He wasn't going to say anything more.

It was worse than she thought. Angie still hadn't said anything. It looked as if her head lowered even more.

She looked out the window. "The bus is here!"

They all got up and ran for their clothes and lunches. Lois helped the little ones get into their coats. When she came to Angie, she bent down and gave her a hug.

"It will be all right."

Angie just waited. Her blue eyes watched her. She could see the hope in them. The little girl wanted to believe what Lois had just said. Everything *would be all right.*

"Listen to me. I want you to stay by me. OK?"

Angie nodded her head in agreement. Lois could feel the tension being released from Angie. It was time to go.

All the kids lined up in front of the door. Some of them you couldn't see because of all the clothes they had on. The chilling cold came right at you when you opened the door. The kids filed out, one by one. She counted heads, as was her custom. One, two, three, four, five, six, and seven. Then Alice and herself. Their books were carried by straps. Puffs of white air from their lungs were visible as they trudged through the snow. The driver waited for them to get to the bus before opening the door. He kept his hand on the swivel. Lois could see small faces against the window watching her and the kids. It was like this every morning: Those blank faces stared at her; rounded red cheeks and round, hollow eyes watching them come to the bus. None of them moved.

Lois was the protector of her group. The kids came to rely on her for everything. In return, she was in control. There was always safety in numbers.

"Bobby, hurry up. The others are getting cold." He was the smallest. He walked in front and the older kids had to wait for him to move. There was only one trail in the snow.

"Come on, Bobby, Lois said to hurry up."

They all walked single-file in the cold.

The door opened and her daughters came in. It was Dani and Claire the middle girls. They looked around, sensing the mood of the room.

"Is Dad home?"

It was the first question out of all of their mouths when they came home. Lois knew he would be home later. He was at the tavern up town. It was going to be a hard night for them tonight.

"No, he's not home. And when he gets home I want you girls to stay in your rooms, out of sight."

They both nodded in agreement. They didn't want to see him anyway. Jonny left the room without saying anything.

"Is he all right?" asked Dani. She was the outspoken one. She was the one well liked by almost everyone. She kept her ears open and listened to what went on.

"Why do you ask?"

Dani looked at her mother, her dark eyes wondering if she should tell and get her mother upset or just let it go. She decided to tell. "I heard that he wasn't allowed into that girl's party last night. They say that all of the kids were making fun of him after her mother wouldn't let him in. Some of them laughed, and said he showed up looking like that little tramp in the movies. They say that he came back and they had to tell him to leave again."

The girls went and sat down on the couch. Claire started talking.

"And you know what else happened? The white boys on the hill went after Jonny and tried to throw him over because they said he wasn't supposed to be up there. But that girl stepped in to help."

"How?"

"I guess she threw a rock at them and told them to leave him alone. Then Caj and some of the cousins showed up and beat up the boys."

Claire and Dani looked at each other and laughed. Lois smiled too.

"Anyway, now its all over the Res. Jonny didn't get to go to the party. The poor kid." Dani always felt this way about her siblings. She thought that they all got the bad luck while she always got the good. She was very popular.

Suddenly, Lois's two little ones came running in.

"Mommy, Mommy," Morgan-Mckenzi yelled as she clung to her mother. She was fighting with her sister again.

"Hush. I'm talking to your sisters." Scout wouldn't let go, so Lois had to put Jonny aside. "I want to talk to you more about Jonny. Later..."

Later was always the way she talked to her son. She knew he wanted to talk most of the time. Time ... that was the problem. She would never have enough time for the older ones. With Jonny, though, she felt like they never needed words; like e.s.p. or something...No, it was an emotional thing. She felt his pain, like it was added to her own. She tried to keep her kids from pain. Most of the time she couldn't. She remembered the pain starts early.

Lois wanted the kids to listen up. It was after school and the grownups were visiting. Her mother went with her stepfather. She had all the kids around her. She kept looking at Angie. The poor thing. So little. I should have been watching. She blamed herself

"Listen up. I want you to listen to me. I don't want you to go with Daddy Henry anymore. I want you to watch out for each other. If he comes for you, I want you to hide. Then come and get me. Do you understand?"

The faces all nodded in agreement. Their feet shuffled.

"Good." They all left. Fred never showed up. His anger was getting the better of him. He would leave soon. Lois felt sad. It was always the good ones that get damaged. He was such a gifted artist; so sensitive. If only home was better. She wished she could do something, but it was probably too late. The helpless feeling came over her.

It was getting late. The night was right around the corner. Lois was deep in thought. Caj came home and demanded that they go up to the rich white man's home and tell them all to go to hell. He and his cousins, Hanford and BJ, wanted to beat up the boy, but Jonny stopped them. As far as he was concerned, he should have.

There was a lot of talking and laughing in the kitchen as the kids ate. It was getting carried away.

"You kids pipe down and hurry up and eat. Your dad will be home and he's going to be drunk. I want you to go up to your rooms. Stay up there."

"You want us to hide?" Caj hadn't settled down yet.

"I don't need any sarcasm from you. Just do as I say."

Nobody said anything. They all went on eating, trying to get as much down as they could before their dad got home. Lois was waiting for him. As long as she kept him downstairs, the kids would be all right. She would fight him as much as she could. If he wanted to, she would let him go to the kids. At least the older ones knew when to leave. They all had their escape routes. The younger kids always hid behind her. It was mostly the middle ones that caught it from their father. She could afford them no protection. She was helpless.

The doorknob turned. The door opened ever so slightly. She waited in fear. She wished it wasn't this way; but it was. Then the door opened wide. He stood there in the doorway. The dark night was behind him. His body swayed back and forth. She knew it was going to be a short night. He was too drunk. It was still early; around six.

"Filthy shits." His voice was creepy and low.

"Be quiet. And get in here before the others see you." She wasn't going to let him start tonight.

Franc staggered in the door, slamming it shut as he came in. Then he stood and stared at her. His black eyes tried to focus.

"Where're are they?" His head fell forward.

"Shhhhhh. Stop yelling." She was holding Shawn in her lap. "Just go to bed."

He stood there staggering. His mind tried to focus; he was listening to the voices from the past. It hurt! It was getting harder and harder for him to make it in the world without drinking. The booze had a hold of him and it wouldn't let him go.

"I want Jonny down here ... now!" He pointed his finger at the floor; barely able to stand. He paused and waited.

Lois didn't move.

Franc hesitated and faltered, his eyes trying to close, his mouth open. Spittle ran down the corner of his lips. He grabbed the chair at the table and sat down. Thump!

His drunken mind was working on the facts of the day at the tavern. People had been talking about his son and the people on the hill. His rage grew as they talked. He sat at the bar and listened to what went on. He kept drinking.

He lifted his head. He must have been out. His mind was reeling. The boys peeked around the corner. When he saw them, the hate flooded through him. He moved with a herky-jerky motion.

"Get in here! I want you in here now!"

Fear showed on the boys' faces. It always did lately. Why? He didn't know. It felt good to see them like this. Franc felt back in control. Control of what? It was hard to think anymore. His head was spinning and his stomach lurched. He had drunk a lot today. Lois got up from the couch.

"Leave them alone. They need their sleep." The little girls were crying and she had to make a choice between her boys and the little ones. The smallest always won out.

Lois left with the little ones and moved the girls upstairs. The boys sat on the couch, their hands in their laps. Neither one said a word. Jonny sat in fear, being the smallest of the two. Caj sat in defiance. He was getting too old to let his dad scare him into submission. His fear was leaving him with each episode with his father. He felt the hate from his father and absorbed it into himself. He used it to fight the drunk man in front of him, and he used it to protect his brother beside him.

Caj looked at his little brother. The tears were at the corner of Jonny's eyes. He was scared, like Caj used to be. His father was getting worse. The drinking was transforming him into some kind of monster to his family. His mother couldn't do anything to stop him. She tried. She talked to him about the war and how it affected his father. Well, what had that to do with them? What had they done that kept their father after them like this. What did he want?

His eyes came closer. The smell of drink was on his breath. His face was inches from Jonny's.

"Say prejudice," he whispered in Jonny's face.

Jonny waited to see if this was what his father really wanted.

"Say it!"

The boys jumped from the rough sound of his voice. Franc knew how to use his voice. He used it effectively at the bar when he was arguing a point. It kept people off balance.

"Mmmm... Prejudice?"

"What? Say it again."

"Prejudice."

"Again!" His voice became louder and immediate.

"Prejudice." Jonny began to cry, scared. He could feel the fear and anger inside him. He saw the confusion; emotions that made him cringe from his father. As he tried to do what his father wanted, their emotions started matching. Jonny's home life was becoming chaotic; the family was in turmoil and it wasn't getting better. His father snarled his terror at his kids. At Jonny. Panic was the emotion of the day, leaving dread for tomorrow.

"Leave him alone. He said the word."

It was Caj who stepped up. He was there for everyone. He tried to keep them from harms way. Jonny could feel the anger emanating from him.

Their father looked at Caj, trying to decide what to do with this boy that was becoming a man. He knew Caj was still too young to take him on, so he dismissed him.

"Get the book." He waited for Caj to get up. Waited to see if his son would make a stand tonight.

Jonny's head was down. He looked sideways at Caj. Jonny was scared. Each time, it came closer and closer to the time these two would fight. He didn't know what to do. He watched his brother get up and leave the room. He was going to get the book. Tonight was going to be long.

His father just sat there looking at Jonny. Jonny didn't say a word. His father started mumbling to himself. He was doing that more, too. It was getting bad.

Caj came back with the book. Big words were written across its cover. "English Dictionary." Caj sat back down with the book. He held it out.

Franc's drunken mind moved inside his head. Thoughts from the past and present ran through it. At the same time, his mind fought to stay awake. It was hard for him. He forgot where he was. The room was spinning. This made his stomach jump. He laughed. Then he opened his eyes. They sat in front of him. The anger flooded his mind again. He knew where he was.

"Look it up. And then I want you to say it."

Caj started looking through the book.

"No, not you. Jonny."

Caj looked at his brother and then handed him the book. Jonny took it and began to leaf through the pages.

He went to the P's. Jonny's fingers were shaking. The words seemed scrambled. He was trying to remember how to spell the word. It wouldn't come to him. The first letter was P. That's all he knew.

Caj leaned over when he saw his father's eyes close.

"P-r-e-j," he whispered.

Jonny's shaky fingers ran down the letters that Caj was spelling for him. His mind was starting to work again. Now he could see the word. He moved through the letters until ... until, "Yes, that must be it," he thought.

prejudice (prehj'uh-dihs)

noun

1. A strong feeling for or against something formed before one knows the facts; bias.
2. Irrational hostility toward members of a particular race, religion, or group.
3. Harm or injury.

Verb: prejudiced, prejudicing, prejudices.

1. To cause (someone) to have a prejudice.
2. To do harm to; injure: "prejudiced his own cause."

Etymology:

<Latin praejudicium.

Derivatives:

prejudicial (-dihsh'uhl) adjective

They sat there waiting for their father to wake. After a while their mother came in. Caj wouldn't say anything to her. She found Jonny sleeping, too. She woke him and told them to go to bed. Caj led Jonny upstairs to their bedroom. Jonny was so tired that all he wanted was to get some sleep. He was glad Caj was there with him. Jonny climbed under the blankets and felt the soothing warmth of them. Caj went over to the window and sat by it.

"Aren't you coming to bed, Caj?"

"Shhhh."

Caj came over and sat on the edge of the bed.

"I hate him. Sooner or later he's going to get his. I swear!" Caj clenched his fist.

"Dad's just drunk." Jonny peeked over the covers.

"Yea, he's always that way."

Jonny couldn't argue with him on this. His father was frightening to him. He could hear his father yelling at his mother. It hurt his ears.

"Thunk."

Jonny jumped. "What was that?"

Shhhh.

Caj grabbed his coat and went to the window. The Henry boys were standing out by the old tree. One of them waved him out.

"You're not leaving, are you?" Jonny's voice squeaked from the lack of air.

"I'll be back. Just don't say anything."

"But what if Dad comes up?"

Caj knew his little brother was scared, but he had to get out. He could no longer stand being the one that held everything together. He needed to do things for him. His life was no longer fun. He wanted to recapture that. He had to go.

"Dad won't be up here tonight. He's already forgotten about you. He's too busy yelling at Mom. So don't worry. OK?"

"Mmm... OK. Maybe they will go to sleep."

"They...

Caj waited for Jonny to form the words on his lips. Jonny tried again.

"Maybe theyyy will go to sleep."

Caj smiled and gave him the thumbs-up sign. Then he was out the window. He ran with the boys into the night.

Jonny watched the window. The shadows ran across it from the old tree. He wanted to shut it. His fear ran deep inside of him. Then he heard the little pup whining. The fear seemed to vanish as he heard the animal's terror. He couldn't leave it out there. Jonny got up from the bed and went to the window. He looked out from side to side. There was nothing there. He quietly shut the window and went to bed.

Lois watched Franc. He ran out of steam early tonight. He was so drunk that he could do nothing else. His mind concentrated on making it to their bedroom. He staggered some more. He didn't even ask for his food; that's how drunk he was. She listened to him yell about Jonny and Caj'. He heard about the party. He was ashamed. He wanted justice. He was going to make his boys stand up to those types of people. There was something wrong with Jonny and people were making fun of him. The boy needed to learn to stand up for himself. There was something wrong with him. And that was it.

Lois watched as he left the room. Soon he would be out. She wouldn't have to protect her kids tonight. They all would get a night's sleep.

The other kids came down stairs. She left them with the older girls. They knew how to keep them all safe from their father if he woke, which was doubtful. She put on her coat and shoes. Grabbing her purse, she went to the door.

"If anything happens you know what to do?"

"Mom. I'm fifteen. Quit treating me like a little girl."

She could see the anger in her oldest daughter's cheeks. Yes, she would be able to handle it. Everyone thought she was so ditsy. That was only part of her character. Her oldest would always step up when she had to. It was hard for her sometimes, because the other kids resented her; especially Claire, the second-oldest. It was the price of being the first-born.

"I'll be back soon." She smiled at them.

Ding-dong! Ding-dong!

The doorbell rang twice; then a third time. Who could that be at this hour? It was dinner time. Don't people have any manners anymore. Ginny got up from the table. Dinner was over anyway. She left the dishes and went to the front door.

Ding-dong!

"Just a minute!" She opened the door and turned on the front porch light. "Yes?"

Ginny looked out in the night. A woman stood in front of her: a heavy-set woman with mousy blond hair and blue eyes. She wore a scarf over her head. She had a worn, old blue coat that covered her heavy frame. There were threads unraveled at the end of the sleeves. The end of the coat was the same way. Ginny could see blue blood vessels running down her legs. She wore sandals that looked too small for her feet. Ginny could see that the woman was uncomfortable, but she saw determination in her eyes.

"Yes? May I help you?"

"I'm Jonny Esque's mother and I would like to talk to you."

The two women stood facing each other in the night.

9

TWO WOMEN

Ginny was sure she didn't know this woman. She looked at her raggedy coat and worn shoes. She wore a scarf on her head and carried a big black purse. Her intense blue eyes watched Ginny, waiting to be invited in.

"Are you sure you're at the right house?"

"Yes. My son came here for your little girl's party and you turned him away."

"Oh, him. I'm sorry, but Nikki-D shouldn't have invited your son. The party was all ready set."

"I don't think it has anything to do with your daughter and I would like to talk to you, but not out here."

Clearly, this woman wasn't about to let Ginny put her off.

"Would you please come in? My name is Ginny Thomas. Why don't you come back to the kitchen and I can make us some coffee."

The two women walked back to the kitchen after Ginny took Lois's coat and hung it up. Lois let her take her purse, too. It was a little heavy from all the things she kept in it.

Ginny put two cups on the kitchen table and brought over sugar and cream. It was too late to be formal. The coffee was already cooked and hot. Ginny was a coffee-drinker so she kept it ready at all times. She poured some in each cup and sat down opposite the woman.

"Well?"

Lois took a drink of her coffee. It was good.

"My name is Lois Esque. I came to talk to you about what it meant to my son to come to your daughter's party. It devastated him when he was turned away. I just wanted you to know that."

"I'm sorry, but as I said, my daughter had no right to invite him because the party was already planned. I can assure you that I had a talk with her."

"I'm sure you did." Lois was getting a feel for this small Chinese woman. She was so reserved and proper. A wanabe.

"I'm sorry about your boy's feelings being hurt."

"I know when you see us, all you see is poor people. Its all right. Because if you can't see beyond the poorness and look at what really is important, then you are really the poor one." Lois blurted this out because she thought this woman would appreciate her directness.

Ginny didn't know how to take this woman.

"I'm not sure what you mean."

"It must be hard to live up to someone else's expectations. Rich people are like that; always worried about how their neighbors will take them. Worried if they are with the right people or if the right people notice them at all. Its a no-win situation."

"What does that have to do with me?"

"Maybe nothing. Maybe everything. Your daughter defended my son; did you know that?"

"No I didn't. What do you mean?"

"She saved him from two of the boys that live on the hill. They said they were going to throw him over the bluff. They were just kidding; probably, but I know how stubborn my son can get when he is challenged. I know he fought for himself, but they were too big for him. Jonny don't talk too good, so he don't say much, even at times like that. He's stubborn."

Ginny smiled. "That's something he has in common with Nikki-D."

"Yes, it sounds like it. Anyway my other boy, Caj, says your little girl threw a rock at them and stopped them from picking on Jonny. He said she was really brave and stood her ground against the two boys. I wanted to thank you for teaching your little girl good values."

Ginny felt a rush of pride run through her. Nikki-D did that? Why didn't she say anything to her? Ginny would have thought differently about the boy coming to her party. She may have let him in.

"I know you didn't want my boy in your house because of his poorness. Maybe you didn't want your little Nikki-D to be around somebody like him. Maybe because of the people that were invited to her party. You didn't want them thinking that you let her run around poor and dirty Indian kids. But you see: that is your fear thinking for you. In the process, what you did is hurt a very nice little boy who has it hard enough in this life as it is. I wanted you to know that. You have taken all the good that Nikki-D did that day and thrown it away. Because of your fear. Not hers."

Ginny listened to this dirt-poor woman talk and for some odd reason, she heard what she was saying. She knew Lois was right even as she denied it. Her life was dictated by others and her fear of how they saw her. It was something she wasn't proud of when someone pointed it out. It was one of the major arguments with her husband. He saw it, too.

"Would you like some more coffee? Maybe we can talk some more."

"Yes, I would like that." Lois smiled at this small woman who possessed so much strength. Lois felt it when she opened the door. She had like her immediately and knew she was right about her when they first sat down and Ginny listened to her. A true bonding occurred between the two of them.

Ginny came back with coffee and sat down. "Tell me again about Nikki-D and Jonny."

Jumping Mouse Returned to the World of the Mice. But he found Disappointment. No One would Listen to him. And because he was Wet, and had no Way to explaining it because there had been no Rain, many of the other Mice were Afraid of him. They believed he had been Spat from the Mouth of Another Animal that had Tried to Eat him. And they all Knew that he had not been food for the One who Wanted him, then he must also be Poison for them.

Jumping Mouse Lived again among his People but he could not Forget his Vision of the Sacred Mountains.

The Medicine Chief reached again for his Pipe, and the little boy ran for a new brand from the fire to light it for him.

"Is this Story about the Green of the South?" he asked as he sat down. "I remember you talked before about the Man of the South and his Sister. Is this Man the Frog?"

"Yes," the Chief answered. He blew a long puff in the air. " the south is the place of innocence. Men who walk there must walk with a heart of trust."

"Those marks are Signs of the Mirroring, just as when Jumping Mouse looked into the river and saw his Reflection," said the Chief.

"But, the little boy added quickly, "that Sign you have upon your Shield is the Medicine Wheel. How is it then also the Mirroring?"

"The Medicine Wheel, my children," said the Chief, "is the Mirroring of the Great Spirit, the Universe, among men. We are all the Medicine River. And the Universe is the Medicine River that man is Mirrored upon, my children. And we in our turn see the Medicines of men Mirrored in the Universe."

"Then who is the Frog? I am confused. I do not understand."

"Nor I," chimed the others.

"Do not make this matter complicated for yourselves," the Chief said. " little Mouse heard the roaring in his ears and sought to solve its mystery. He met Raccoon and was taken to see the

Medicine River, which represents Life. He saw himself Mirrored there in Life.

All of us are so Mirrored, my children, but many men have not visited the Great River and have not witnessed it. Some have followed Raccoon to the River, seen their Reflection, but become frightened and retreated among the mice again. But the lesson is always there for those who seek it. It is in the place of the south. The place of trust."

"Will you explain more to us about the Raccoon?"

"No, because it is for you to visit this place yourself. The Raccoon and the Frog will then become clear to you."

The Chief immediately began the Story again.

The Memory Burned in the Mind and Heart of Jumping Mouse, and One Day he Went to the Edge of the River Place...

"Come with me, children," the Peace Chief said, getting to his feet. They walked through the camp, and past it to the river. Even though it was a warm, almost a hot day, many of the People were still busy about the camp.

10

POEM

She sat on her bed. She was watching the small turtle in its glass cage. The sunlight came through the window in beams. It spread all around. Soft pastel hues and tones overlaid the entire room; it was a good room.

Nikki-D was thinking. Her mind ran through words and immediately discarded them. She was writing a poem. Trying to write a poem was more like it.

"Oh, give it up," she thought. "I can't think of anything. I'm so dumb."

She got up from the bed and went over to the cage. Skippy's food was on the corner of the big tank. Skippy was moving across a small rock on the bottom. A quarter inch of water filled the bottom of the tank. She dropped some food into the food tray. Skippy moved to the food. "He must be hungry," she thought.

Two years had passed since that night of her party. She smiled at the thought of it: Her mother's face as she ran and took Skippy from Jonny's hands. It was a spontaneous move on her part. Her mother fought with her about keeping it. She cried.

Her father came home and she went to him. That night, she heard her mother and father arguing over the small turtle. The arguing wasn't something new, but it was one of the few times that her father stood up to her mother and won. It made her feel good to think about that. Yes, he was there for her.

Since then, she fought her mother on almost all subjects. Her mother wanted her to be the best in school; she wasn't, except for being one of the best-liked girls. She was popular with everyone. Her mother told her what clothes to wear, but it was the Sixties now and Nikki-D was getting caught up in the moods of the nation. The kids of today wanted so much more than their parents; especially the girls. She knew that she could be anything she wanted. It was all there for her. The world was changing fast. She wanted to be part of that change. She needed to be her own person.

"I'm going to be a poet."

Nikki-D watched her mother cringe at her words.

Her father looked up from the morning table. "That's nice, dear. What made you come to that conclusion?"

She could see her father's tired eyes. They were a deep blue. She thought they were the bluest eyes she had ever seen. They were the opposite of her own pearl- black, almond eyes. She often wished she could have gotten some of her father's genes. She used to look for signs of her father in her. She had to admit that there were few of them. She was her mother's daughter. That made her angry.

Ginny came over to the table.

"You can't be serious," she said.

Her father immediately went back to his paper. He knew there was going to be another blow-up between the two women he loved. Why couldn't they get along? It made him sad to witness their battles. His strong-willed wife controlled their lives. He had surrendered that position a long time ago. Now it was too late to get it back. He read the business section of the paper. His ears were closed to the argument.

"What's wrong with being a poet?"

"To be a poet is a condition rather than a profession.
Robert Graves (1895-1985)."

Ginny spoke this even as she cleared the table.

It always stunned Nikki-D that her mother would say something like that, using an example of what she said she wanted to be. It was as if her mother was some great reservoir of knowledge just waiting to show her up.

"Poets never have any respect. They live off others and rely on their families to live. They barely survive. Then they write about the conditions of their survival. That is not what my daughter will be. You listen to what I'm saying."

"I don't care. Its what I want to be. There is more to this world than money. Money doesn't make you happy. Look at you and Daddy."

There was deadly silence for a second. "What did you say?"

It was her father talking. His voice was so low, so menacing that it scared her. He put down his paper.

"You apologize to your mother, young lady. I don't ever want to hear you talk to her like that again."

She couldn't believe it. He acted like it was her fault.

Her mother just stood there with her arms folded and a satisfied smile on her face. Nikki-D couldn't do it. She hated her.

"I said apologize," her father almost yelled this time.

She lowered her head. "I'm sorry."

"Now go up to your room and think about what you've done."

Nikki-D still sat there for a second.

"Now."

Those were the last words from her father this morning. She would never give in. Not to her mother.

"I hate her!"

Nikki-D walked through the apple orchard with Jonny. They were heading up to the old barn. The orchard was a short-cut for them. It got them by the white house with the keeper in it. He acted as if you needed his permission to go and play on the basketball courts in the barn. It really wasn't a barn.

All the Indians came up here to play. Most of the non-Indians played ball in Marysville, at the high school gym. Most of the Indians didn't have the transportation to get there every night.

"Mmm ... you shouldnnnn't say you hate your mother."

" 'Shouldn't,' Jonny. As in 'Should not.' Say it". Its only two syllables. Don't carry the n's."

Jonny lowered his head and tried saying it to himself. She could hear the whisper of the words as he broke it down syllable by syllable. It had become a pattern with Nikki-D to correct him and try to help him pronounce the words correctly. She thought if he could just learn that, they would stop sending him into those awful special classes.

"You shouldn't say that about your mother." His voice strong and confident.

"Good."

She knew it hurt him to hear her talk like this. He was so quiet and thoughtful. It was hard for other people to understand him because he didn't talk much. When he did, the words didn't come out right sometimes. She used to make fun of him. Now she tried to help him. Every time he started talking with a Mmmm in the beginning, she knew he wanted to say another word but couldn't get it out right.

"Mmmm ... maybe she wants the best for you?"

Nikki-D stopped, holding the basketball under her arm. She began tapping her foot. "Are you going to take her side? She wouldn't even let you into our house."

Jonny lowered his head and didn't say anything.

She knew she hurt him. It made her feel bad. He was strong inside. Deep. She could feel it. He knew things, or she thought he did, that she wanted to know. He felt things that she needed to feel. He felt comfortable with who he was, while she never understood who she was. She only understood that she didn't want to be what her mother wanted her to be.

"I'm sorry."

"Its OK. Look-there's Caj."

Jonny waved at his brother and the other kids with him. Nikki-D knew that Jonny was probably related to them all. Her eyes were on Caj. He was getting bigger. Her heart leapt when she saw him smile and wave back. She gave a half-wave in return.

"Come on, lets hurry..."

They both began to run to the barn. The games were going to begin. The older ones let the younger ones play during half-time; or when they all got tired. Nikki-D was one of the better players, boy or girl. Jonny wasn't half-bad either. He wasn't as good as Caj, but he was smaller and played good team ball. Nikki-D was the shooter on the team and she always tried to get matched up with Jonny because he would pass her the ball. The other boys had a hard time with her being a girl and wouldn't pass it to her. Not Jonny, though. He didn't care.

Caj was playing with the big boys. He was getting as tall as some of them, wide shoulders and long legs, his wild hair tied in a ponytail. He was running and dribbling down the floor. On the sidelines, everyone was yelling and screaming for him to make it. Caj's hair flowed behind him as he ran. There were three boys in front of him and he managed to dribble around them. Then he stopped and let it go. The ball went high into the air, heading for the basket, completing the arc from his hand and arm. Swish.

Caj turned with his arms up high, his fists clenched in a victory salute. His smile was wide on his face. He had done it again. He won the game.

Nikki-D sat on the sidelines, clapping. Caj was walking toward her. Her heart beat harder. "He's walking over to me," she thought.

Caj kept walking past her. He didn't even notice her. She was crushed. She felt as if all the eyes were on her. As if they all noticed him not noticing her; it humiliated her. Her face turned red from embarrassment.

"Man's loneliness is but his fear of life.
Eugene ONeill."

Yes, it was the fear of the unknown. Of what was inside her. Who she was? What will she become? Not measuring up to her mothers expectations. Love, hate, sex. There she said it. At least she thought it.

She thought about Caj for days after the basketball game. His smile was the best thing about him. Every time he looked her way, she would try to do something on the court. She wanted him to notice her. She shot the ball and it swished through the net. Clapping came from the sidelines. Caj was one of them that was clapping. Nikki-D smiled the biggest smile in her life. She felt good.

Then they came in. The girls of the tribe. Six of them came in at once. Her mouth fell to a frown. The corners of her lips were touching her chin. They were older girls who picked out the best basketball players. One of them stared at Caj. They all watched him because he was one of the best ball players of the tribe. Even at the age of fourteen, he played with the older guys. That was how good he was. She was the prettiest of the girls. Nikki-D eyed her with hate. Then she saw her chest. No wonder the boys liked her ... Dumb boys.

There was something going on between the two. Even she could feel the attraction. It wasn't fair just because this girl had big boobs. Caj left with her. The other boys and girls left too. Nikki-D's heart left with them.

Everything seemed so jumbled to her. It was confusing. Love and Hate: two emotions that she reserved for her mother. Now, apparently, Caj was added to the list.

"I hate him. He's nothing but a stupid Indian."

She caught herself.

"Nikki-D-you here?" He came up from behind her. She was still watching them leave. Her heart pounded. Jonny stood beside her trying to see what was wrong. When he saw who she was looking at, he knew.

"That's Nilah. She's Caj's new girlfriend. She's a very nice girl. I don't know what family she comes from, but she it's a tribe up north. Canada, I think. She's staying down here with her cousins."

"Oh ... she looks nice. I've got to go home." She didn't really have to go home, but she wanted to see what they were doing.

She walked toward the door with Jonny beside her. He didn't say anything, but he never did at times like this; unless she asked him. She didn't want to talk right now. Her stomach hurt and she was hot.

Outside, the group of kids were sitting around the stone steps. Some were smoking and some were just hanging out. The girl, Nilah, was all over Caj. Nikki-D and Jonny walked on by them without saying anything.

"Hey, where you kids going?"

Jonny stopped for a second.

"Mm ... mm. Nikki-D has to go home."

"OK. I'll see you when you get back. Mom wants you home early."

Jonny just nodded his head and moved off to catch up with Nikki-D.

"Why did Caj pick her? She's just hanging on him like she owns him."

Jonny was walking beside her still. They were back at the orchard. She slowed down, thinking to herself, and waiting for Jonny to say something.

"Caj has a lot of girlfriends. He always did. They seem to like him right off. Not just Indian girls either. All of them."

"I know that. I see him at school. Its probably because he's a jock and they want to be by him. I think its disgusting the way they throw themselves at him." Her anger was rising again.

Jonny looked at her. "Mmm ... you like him don't you?" It wasn't quite a question. She could tell he was fishing, trying to find out her true feelings. She wasn't one to hold them back, much to her mother's chagrin.

"No," is what she said. A lie? Maybe. She didn't know what she liked anymore. She just wanted to get home.

"Mmm ... Caj is a real good guy. He always takes care of me. I wish I could be like him sometimes. Specially I wish I could play ball like him."

"Especially. With an E, Jonny."

Jonny looked taken aback. He walked along with Nikki-D, who was now deep in thought.

"That's all he can think of. Shooting the ball. Why are boys so stupid? Why can't Caj be like Jonny?" But then, she supposed, she would be looking for someone like Caj again. He was so exciting. She was a nerd. The people at school that she ran around with were nerds. Intelligent, but dull. And flat. And ugly.

"I think you have a good shot, Jonny. You're the best point guard we've got. And you pass the ball to everyone to make sure we all get a chance to play."

Jonny smiled. He was obviously happy with the way she pointed out his strengths.

He knew she was the best of their group. She could do things ten times better than most of the boys. They were awkward and falling all over themselves. She was smooth and poised. It was hard for them to accept her. She made the team because of her skills.

Besides, they needed another person to complete the teams. It was something he knew she had to live with. It must be hard to be a girl.

Tammy came running into the room, her blond hair swinging from side to side. She was a bundle of energy, not like Nikki-D, who was focused; at least until this year. Tammy was unfocused energy, spilling out. Her laugh was infectious, her intellect limited. She was a happy girl.

"Hi! Did you hear about the Russians? Its all over the radio and TV. My dad says the communist's, and that damn Catholic will blow us all to hell. Jeez, I hope not. What are you doing? Still thinking about Caj? He's so cute and his smile..." She stared up dreamily.

"No. I'm thinking about a poem I'm going to write."

"Oh, Oh ... your mother again."

"She says she doesn't want me to be a poet," Nikki-D said, thinking, "She wants me to be good. I don't feel good. I've got cramps in my stomach. Its hot all the time."

Tammy went over to the tank. "How is Jonny, anyway. He's so nice. I wish I had an Indian friend, but my mom and dad say they should be left alone. They wouldn't let me go around them. Like I would want to, anyway"

Nikki-D gave her a dirty look.

"Unless its Jonny. He's all right. Don't they have water?" Tammy was getting herself into trouble and she didn't know how to get out of it. She talked faster.

"I mean if they took a bath and looked like they kept themselves clean. Do you see the houses they live in? I couldn't live in something like that. Why don't they build better houses? Dad says they're lazy, that's why. But I don't know..."

Nikki-D didn't even respond. She knew Tammy would talk herself out. She wanted to think about the other day. The walk home. The girls. And Caj.

"Its so hard being a girl. I can't find any clothes that fit me. I'm growing so fast. I'm going to be a giant. I know I am. What do you think?" Tammy surveyed herself in the mirror. Her short blond hair and blue eyes were her main features. She was tall.

Nikki-D didn't say anything. She hated her feet. They were so big. Her mother would have a fit if she knew Nikki-D wanted smaller feet. Nikki-D read about the Chinese women having their feet bound to maintain their beauty. That was going too far. She went to the mirror. Her long black hair ran down her back. It was finally growing back. She loved her hair: Straight and soft, and shiny and hers. She never let her mother touch her hair anymore. Nikki-D ran her hands down her silky-smooth black hair.

"My mother likes Jonny now. I don't know what his mother said when she came that night, but everything changed. She doesn't mind me running around with him. He's my best friend."

Tammy looked at her with horror.

"I mean after you. He's a boy, so its different. We talk about other things."

"How can you understand him? All the girls laugh and make fun of the way he speaks. I mean ... when he does speak." She giggled.

"He speaks good. All you have to do is listen and anyone can understand him. And he knows more than most all of the girls put together. And I don't want you making fun of him again."

"Jeez, Nikki-D I didn't mean anything by it."

Nikki-D lay back down on the bed.

"I'm writing a poem about my mom."

Tammy rolled her eyes again. "Why don't you just leave your mother alone? I swear that's all you think about now. Mothers are mothers and kids can't do anything about it."

Nikki-D thought about this. What was her mother? Think...

MOTHER

Two faces made of the same.
Both looking out. Not seeing.
Hate is love and love, hate.
Which is the one I talk to?
It depends on the face.

Nikki-D thought about the words. Yes, that's it. It was the way she saw her mother. One day, she was very supportive of Nikki, the next, against. Nikki-D wanted her to notice that she was growing up and could think for herself. Well, she wanted Mom to notice her, anyway. Nikki-D was cautious when approaching her mother. She learned that it was easier to wait than to rush it. Even this didn't stop them from fighting. Nikki-D's stomach rumbled.

The cramps were getting worse. She began to cry. Hot flashes came and went and then came back again. The blood began to flow inside her, a flow that would continue approximately every month until middle age came to stop it. The flow of blood found its exit through her uterus.

Bent over in pain, she couldn't move. Nor did she want to. She let out a moan that became louder with each burst of pain. Something was wrong. Frightened, she put her hand between her legs, then removed it and showed it to Tammy. Tammy screamed and ran for help.

Nikki-D lay on her bed. The pain was becoming unbearable. All she wanted and all she could think of was her mother.

11

DUMP

Into the night they ran: Caj and Hanford were in front about twenty yards ahead. Little Buck Jones and BJ ran behind them, and then Jonny. Jonny was slowing down as the other boys ran ahead. He was waiting. He looked back over his shoulder.

Nikki-D was running as hard as she could but was losing ground to the boys in front of her. She almost felt like crying from her frustration. It was hard being "one of the boys." Now that they had finally allowed her to come with them, she was too slow. She stopped for a second and tried to catch her breath. The cold night surrounded her and her body began to sweat. It felt as if her lungs were ready to explode. She watched the older boys running down the road. She moved her legs and tried to get up speed, but she was too tired. A sudden grip of fear went through her as the boys disappeared in the night. They were going to leave her. Then she saw Jonny stop and turn around.

"Mm ... mm. Are you all right Nikki-D?"

"Yes."

Jonny could barely hear her. "We have to get going."

Nikki-D nodded her head in agreement. He was right. She would have to keep up. She tried to move again but it hurt too much. "Can I take another second? I can't breathe."

Jonny looked down the road to see the where the others were. The night reflected down on Marine View Drive. The road seemed to go on forever. Tall trees and bushes ran on both sides of the road. There were no shoulders and a deep ditch abutted the road. Big Flats dump was five miles farther down the road. It sat on the southeastern corner of the reservation. Two rivers forked around the big flats; Ebby Slough and the Snohomish River. Seattle barged its garbage to this site. Northern Railroad's tracks ran in front of the dump and, from there, other contaminates were unloaded. That was where they were headed tonight.

Caj and the others were already out of sight. This scared Jonny. "OK. But we have to go pretty soon."

Nikki-D could only hear her own breathing. It was settling down now. It was so unfair being a girl. Trying to keep up with the boys, finding what they do so easily was always going to be hard for her. They had so much fun, while she had to work. She hated her short legs. She hated being a girl.

"Mmm. You about ready, Nikki?" Jonny wanted to get going. They were falling too far behind the others. The wind was kicking up and the trees began to sing. He felt the hairs on his neck rise.

Nikki-D felt Jonny tense up. This made her tense, too. She had never snuck out of her house like this and now she wasn't so sure it was a good idea. She felt cold even though she had a warm coat on. It must be some Indian thing. Jonny wanted to go and she knew she had to find the energy to keep up. "I'm ready, Jonny."

"Mmmm. We can walk fast until you get your second wind."

Nikki-D stood up and began to walk. Jonny was beside her, slowing his pace so she could keep up. Her legs began to warm up and they lost their tiredness. Jonny moved a little faster. She took hold of the sleeve of his ragged jacket. Together, they walked down the dark, moonlit road that ran through the heart of the reservation. Together, they walked in the night.

The fire was like an inferno rising high into the night. The kids stood around the pile of boxes as they burned. Nikki-D had never seen anything like this. The heat rushed at her, and the yellow flames caught her eyes. She couldn't stop staring at them. The boys all surrounded the boxes and stared, too. She checked Jonny and could see the flames flicker and reflect off his face. It was as if they were all in a trance that only the fire could break. She felt the pressure building around the flames. Excitement was on all of their faces, arousing their basic instincts as the thrill of the flames rushed through them. Nikki-D couldn't believe the feeling in her. She thought they were going to chant in a second. The flames rose higher. The energy rose, too. She didn't know what was going to happen, but she felt it had to happen soon or they all would burst.

She looked around the flames and then up to the sky. The stars blinked in contrast to the fire, as though they knew the flames wouldn't be able to touch them. It was eerie.

Then it happened!

"Heyyyyy! " All the boys yelled at once. Nikki-D jumped out of her skin. They raised their sticks above their heads and lowered their eyes to the ground. She looked down. "Ahhhhh!"

They came one at a time at first; then two, and three, and, finally, too many to count. Their beady red eyes searched for an escape. Nikki-D watched as Caj rushed in for the kill.

"Hiiii-ya! " he shouted, as he slammed down his stick on the head of the dark black rat. "Hiii-ya! " He hit it again. Then he went back to where he stood before and waited, his eyes darting in their excitement for the next victim.

Hanford went in next, then BJ, then Buck. Each slammed their sticks down on the heads of the rats as they tried to escape. The flames were still around the perimeter of the boxes, driving the rats closer and closer until there wouldn't be any room for them at all.

Nikki-D watched the rats as they lay crippled or dying. She heard their cries in the night: Eeeee! Eeeee! Some of them still tried to crawl to safety. She saw their beady red eyes close as they died. This frightened her, but she didn't know why. They were the biggest and ugliest rats she had ever seen in her life. The boys were still clubbing the rats as they ran out. Death was piling up.

The fire burned brightly in the night. Flames shot high in the sky and sparks flew in all directions. Some aerosol cans exploded. The pile of boxes stood about thirteen feet high at its center. Flames began to hit the main pile. Nikki-D stood and watched and couldn't believe her eyes. The pile seemed to move. There it was again. She was sure that it moved. The boys stopped. Again they stared as the flames flickered across their faces. Nikki-D saw something in their faces.

She saw expectation...

The pile moved again and she felt fear come across her. She waited along with the boys. It was all in the passage of rites tonight. There was nothing Nikki-D could do to avoid it. She was one of them now.

A build-up of expectation came until again she thought she was going to burst. Then it happened.

The whole pile lurched. It seemed to lurch in all directions. Nikki-D tried to see what was going on. Her eyes caught the mud under the pile; at least, she thought it was mud. She looked closer. She saw them, their red eyes staring back at her. They were all over, on top of each other. It looked like millions of them to her. Her mind tried to count them but stopped because there were too many of them. At the same time she let out her scream, they streamed out from the pile.

" Aaaaaaaaaagh! "

The rats rushed in all directions. The largest rodents were the last to leave the safety of the pile. Most of them were a foot long or more. They ran with only one thing in mind: to find safety. The dump had many exits for the rats. Most of them had their own escape routes in place but there were too many of them trying to fill the small places. For those exposed to the night, there was no escape; not from clubs.

Nikki-D screamed and screamed. The rats ran up and down her feet and legs. She swung down at them but she couldn't swing fast enough. The terrorized rats fought as hard as her to get away. They bit into her pink-and-white boots that were already filthy with mud. The rats carried the slime and filth of the dump as they ran over her feet. There were too many of them. Fear startled her. She backed up. They kept coming. She couldn't swing her club anymore. Her arms were tired. She wanted help but the boys were all swinging their own clubs and trying to stay out of the way of the on rushing rats.

She began to cry. More and more rats ran around her at high speeds, jumping, flipping and biting, in their attempt to get away. Nikki-D cried harder. She was overwhelmed by the rats. She wanted to get away, yet she was too scared to turn her back on them. She cried even harder as they kept coming at her. Her feet kept moving back, but one of them got caught on something and she almost fell. Scared, she stood there in the middle of the dump, crying. Not moving. In fear.

"Nikki-D! Nikki-D! Over here! Don't stop moving. Come over here on the high ground. Hurry!" Jonny stood on one of the large mounds of dirt. There were several mounds above the slime and mud of the dump. Jonny watched Nikki-D until he knew she wasn't going to move, then he took off from the high ground and ran through the rats.

Jonny got in her face. "Nikki-D, stop crying and come with me. We have to get to the high ground. There're too many rats. Come on!" He grabbed her hand and yanked her with him. She was still crying and watching the rats. They were all she could see. The pile raged with flames; there was nowhere for the rats to hide. They would fight anything in their way. They kept coming.

Jonny and Nikki-D ran for the mound. She felt the rats underfoot as she moved her legs to keep up with Jonny. In the corner of her eye she saw a lone figure in the middle of the killing field, raising and lowering his club. Up and down he swung, hitting and killing any rat that was unlucky enough to be within reach. Nikki-D saw the lone figure standing in front of the inferno killing rats. It was unbelievable to Nikki-D, but he seemed to be in a happy state.

Jonny pulled Nikki-D to the mound and they both stood there as the rats ran around them. They moved so fast! Hordes of them moved in unison across the muddy ground.

Nikki-D did stop crying. She could see that the rats were just as scared as she was – or more so. This gave her some comfort. Jonny was beside her, too. She clung to him to make sure that she didn't fall off the mound. "There're so many of them, Jonny."

"Mmmm! Yea, but we should be all right on this mound and they will be gone in a minute. How're you doing?"

She was still shaking, but not as bad. "Better."

"Mm ... mm. They're slowing down now. See ... no more of them coming out of the pile."

Nikki-D saw it was true. This made her feel better. She had thought they would never end. The other boys were attacking again. She could hear the yells and their clubs and the rats as they died that night.

The killing fields were full of dead rats. Nikki-D could see Caj and Hanford coming over. The light from the fire was at their backs. It was a scary picture of the night.

"Hey yah! Did you guys see that? There must have been a million of them. Man, we got tired of clubbing them. Huh Hanford?"

Hanford nodded his head in agreement.

Nikki-D could see their excitement in their eyes and knew their faces were flushed. Hers was, too. She wiped away the tears. The two boys noticed this.

"Hey! Were you crying, Nikki-D? Scared of some little rats? Ha-Ha, come on. They weren't going to hurt you."

Nikki-D felt the embarrassment creep into her cheeks. She wanted to be one of the boys and she acted like a scared little girl. Anger came. She knew they would be making fun of her now and there wasn't anything she could do. She hated this.

Hanford, with a dark look on his face, said something to Caj. "I told you we shouldn't have brought a girl with us."

"Mm ... mm. Come on, you guys, leave her alone. She almost tripped over there."

Nikki-D loved Jonny. He was always there to protect her when she was in trouble. He knew she must be embarrassed. He knew how it felt.

"Mmmm. Look, the pile is almost done. The rats will be coming out again. We better get ready."

The boys turned and looked at the pile as it glowed in the dark. The heat was almost gone, too. The cold night air blew by them.

"You're right, Jonny. The biggest ones should be coming out now."

They watched the pile some more, none of them saying anything. If a rat came running out across the muddy field any one of the boys would go and club it or chase it until it got away. They all watched for the biggest one and wanted to be the one to get it. While they were standing vigil, Nikki-D watched the last of the pile burning on one end. Her eyes were still hypnotized by the fire when she saw a movement. She caught it with the corner of her eye ... there it was again! Another movement: a rat, but there was something different about this one. She moved her head to see better. The boys still watched the main opening of the pile where most of the rats exited.

It stood there, staring at her, pink eyes, pink mouth, and whiskers, sniffing the air. Nikki-D saw the panic in those eyes as it looked for a way out. There was none, except through the boys and Nikki-D. She saw its white fur and pink tail. The white rat stood out among the filth and debris of the dump. It was beautiful.

"Jonny! Look!" She wanted him to see it, too. Jonny turned around and looked where Nikki-D was pointing her finger. Then he saw it. Jonny smiled.

"Caj! Over there! See?"

Caj turned and looked. Hanford, BJ, and Dale looked. They all saw what Nikki-D was pointing at. The white rat stood by itself in the corner as it looked for a way out.

"Get iiiiit! " Hanford yelled and they all raised their clubs.

"Yeaaaaa! Get the white rat." They all yelled in unison. Each ran hard to be the first one to reach it. Nikki-D felt their rush and was swept up with them. She and Jonny were the last ones chasing the rat, so they looked for the angle it would have to run from to get away.

"Jonny, let's go over there." Nikki-D pointed to a pile on the edge of the dump.

Jonny looked at it. "OK. Lets go."

Caj was the first to get to the rat. He slammed down his club, barely missing its head. The white rat jumped a couple of feet in the air, scaring Caj.

"Jesus Christ!" He jumped back.

"Did you see that?" He wasn't asking anyone in particular. "Shit, it jumped ten feet in the air."

Nobody was listening because they were too busy chasing the white rat. It ran behind burned out cans and sacks of garbage; it ran under anything that would hide it from the predators chasing it. They had their eyes on it now. Its white coat was what gave it away. There was a killing frenzy going on inside each of the kids and it wasn't going to be satisfied until they killed the object of their hate. Pent-up emotions soon emerged and needed to be expressed.

"Heyyy! There it goes." Little Dale moved in for the kill. "Ha! Ha!" He yelled this with each swing of his club. "'Ha! Ha!" Again and again, he swung down on the rat with its sickening pink eyes and pink lips. The rat was too fast for him, though, and he soon tired of running and swinging at it. He stopped and sat down on an old tire.

Hanford and BJ picked up the chase. They both went after it, one behind the other, each cutting off escape routes the rat would take. It was trying to get to the edge of the dump. There, it could burrow down into the holes of garbage. All rats tried to take their own escape routes, but when those were closed, it was always the edge that they rushed for.

"BJ, he's heading for the edge. Go down there." Hanford spotted flashes of white as it ran from one hiding place to the next. "Hurry; this sucker is moving!"

BJ went down about twenty feet and stopped. He adjusted his eyes to see any unusual movement on the ground. Hanford ran up and stuck some cans and mud making them fly all over the place, trying to make it run. BJ saw a patch of white moving. Hanford was right: this one could move. He raised his club. His heart was pounding because he wanted to be the one to kill the white rat. Then the others would look up to him and tell stories about tonight. BJ liked the thought of this and raised his club even higher.

The rat ran right up to him and through his legs. BJ jumped with fear. " Shit!" He didn't even get a chance to swing, it was so fast.

"Christ, BJ, he ran right through your legs! Why didn't you get him?" Hanford ran past BJ as he said this. The rat was getting closer to the edge. Hanford wanted this one bad. He wanted to be the one to get it. He hated white rats and he wasn't going to let this one get away. Not tonight. "Caj, its over here. I think its hiding behind those cans. If we get everyone around it then we got it. Yea, this one is as good as dead."

Everyone circled the pile where the rat was. Each of the boys stood waiting for the command to flush it out. Nikki-D and Jonny waited on the edge. Again, she saw the blood-lust in their eyes. She felt it in her, too. This was it. She could become one of the boys by playing this out. She was scared, not knowing if she could kill. She wanted so much to be accepted by these guys; especially Hanford, who seemed to dislike her. That's all she wanted: to be accepted by these ragged and poor Indian boys from the Res. She needed to feel that she was part of them. This was her home, too. It didn't matter that she came from a rich family. That wasn't important. Besides, she saw how their mothers treated them. It was great. She wished her mother would treat her like that. Nikki-D stopped thinking about it and waited for the command.

"Little Dale, go in and get it." Caj was having a good night. A white rat. That must have been a sign or something. He knew that Jonny would think it was. Bringing Nikki-D along was a good idea, no matter what Hanford thought. Caj had been edgy the past week. Their father was getting real drunk again and getting very weird. Caj tried to protect everyone, but there were too many. The girls and his mother came first. That left Jonny as the one his father went after. Caj looked at his brother. If Jonny could stop that sound he made before he spoke, it would help. He always tried but could never get a handle on it. Scout was another one that his father went after. Poor Scout. She was the one girl in the family that everyone picked on. Caj knew that it was partly her fault. She just acted wrong and said the wrong things and then ran to their mother for protection. This drove his father nuts. It had been a hard week for everyone. Now they'd found the white rat. Caj felt that good things were coming.

Dale ran up and hit the pile as hard as he could.

The white rat moved under the pounding. Fear raced through it, making it bolt from its cover. Once the rat got in the open it was too late. The kids at the dump all saw it at once and the chase was on.

"There it is!" Hanford lurched for the rat but missed it by a mile. It moved to the right, saw the edge and ran for it. BJ was in its way. The white rat zigged and zagged its way through the boys until it was almost free. Then it made its fatal error.

Nikki-D stood with Jonny, waiting for the boys to get the rat. She was praying that it wouldn't make it to her. But the stupid boys were all missing it.

"Mmmm ... Nikki-D, get ready!" Jonny had his stick above his head ready to strike. Nikki-D raised her stick.

"Why don't they kill it?" She saw what was becoming a comical scene of boys running and clubbing at the rat but missing. The rat would jump high in the air when they got too close, and then the boys jumped high in the air to get away from the rat. Nikki-D almost started laughing.

The only problem was that they were heading for her. She didn't want to do this. Even though she was high from the adrenaline, she didn't want to kill anything. She should have stayed home. Why did she always do these things? Her mother told her not to go out at night like this. This was exactly the reason she should have listened to her. Still - how many girls got to go out with the boys and join in their fun? Nikki-D knew that this wasn't something she would think of doing in her life. It seemed natural to the boys to do this. Why, she wasn't sure. It...

"Jonny, its coming to us! Can you see it? Its not turning at all. Jonny...

"Mmmm ... its coming to you, Nikki-D. There it is! There it is! Swing! Swing!"

She did. Nikki-D struck down as hard as she could. She couldn't see because her eyes were closed shut. She felt it, though: a soft splash as her club hit the middle part of the white rat. She didn't think that she had swung that hard but when she opened her eyes she saw the white rat at her feet. It was still breathing but it was dying. All the boys gathered around her and the rat in a sort of ritual. Nobody talked as the last gasps of air left the rat's body. It trembled a little, and then it died.

"Shit! She got it." Hanford looked at Nikki-D.

"All right, Nikki-D! " Caj saw it as a very good sign indeed, even though he didn't believe in that old stuff.

The others nodded in agreement. She was one of them now. She would always be a part of them. The ritual was one they would all remember.

"Mmmm ... way to go, Nikki-D." Jonny stood beside her, smiling. Nikki-D felt the exhilaration of the moment and smiled back.

"You're good luck, Nikki-D. I'm glad you came with us." Caj smiled, too. It was a good night.

After a moment, they heard the sound of a vehicle coming up the main road to the dump.

"Hey, its here!" Caj dropped his club and began running to the road. The others did the same, leaving Nikki-D and Jonny standing alone.

"Mmmm ... are you all right, Nikki-D?" Jonny watched her face; it was full of color. Her cheeks were red and her eyes glowed.

"Where are they going?" She still stared at the dead rat.

"The ice cream truck is here. Come on."

The two friends walked together to the main road. The night was dark and the stars were out. The fire was almost dead and the chill surrounded them. It was a good night.

Nikki-D carried the big, square box with the boys. They were on each corner and she and Jonny were in the middle holding up the center of the box. They caught a ride most of the way with the ice cream man. He let them off at Totem Beach Road and went on from there, waving as he went. She was tired from all the things that happened that night. She could smell the dump on her. It was a smell that wouldn't go away over night. She knew that she would have to wash her clothes as soon as possible before her mom got to them. She smiled at the thought of her mom finding out about her night excursion. She thought about leaving her clothes out for just that reason. She knew she couldn't do that even thought she wanted to. Nikki-D just wanted to enjoy the night.

The boys stopped. They were in front of Jonny's house. The lights were on and the wind was quiet on the bay. Nikki-D could never get enough of the sights of Tulalip Bay. Everything felt right when she was here. This was her home.

"Let's go in. Jonny and Nikki-D, go and tell Mom we got something for the kids. Hanford, you guys can take your share and we'll see you tomorrow. OK?" Caj was happy about the night. Now, if his father wasn't there it would be perfect. He didn't want to hassle with his dad if he was drunk. The car wasn't there. That was a good sign. Jonny and Nikki-D came out of the house and the front porch light was turned on. Caj saw his mother there. He began to pull the box to the house. Jonny and Nikki-D helped him haul the box to the porch.

"What have you got there, Caj?"

"Oooh. Just some stuff for the kids." Right when he said this, the three little ones came out on the porch. Katie, like her mother, stood with her arms crossed. She watched over her little sisters, Alexcia and Shawn, as they waited to see what was in the box.

"Get back." Katie also had her mother's tone when giving orders.

Jonny, Caj, and Nikki-D got the box on the porch. The girls ran up to it and looked inside. Three squeals of delight escaped from their mouths. Lois had a big smile on her face, too. This was just right. Caj felt good. Jonny was smiling. It was Nikki-D who had the biggest smile on her face, watching as the little girls and their mother went into the kitchen and got pots and pans to fill with the contents. They took out the different colored boxes. More and more squeals of delight rang out in the night.

"Ice cream! Ice cream!"

12

SCHOOL

Nikki-D ran down the first-floor hall. She was going to be late for class. It was all right. Her mother had just approved her request to continue her studies in Civics. She was thinking of her future and what she could contribute to the nation. Kennedy was right when he said; "My fellow Americans, ask not what your country can do for you — ask what you can do for your country."

She had decided while in Civics to become a scientist. She would find cures for diseases that would help the people of the world. The year was exciting and fast. Her mother was on her side. Nikki-D could tell her mother was happy with her selection. Nikki-D was happy. Her grades remained at a straight-A level. All her teachers understood that she was way beyond that. She was a thirteen-year-old girl with an extremely bright future ahead of her. She could be what she wanted. What they didn't understand was why she wasn't in a special school for the gifted. It had something to do with her father wanting her to remain normal; there was time enough for her to be special.

Nikki-D didn't care. She liked the classes she took. The teachers would always let her stay and work problems. They would let her go ahead in her subjects. They could see her discipline. It must come from her mother. When Ginny Thomas came to the school, it was for a reason. And the school would answer to her. It had something to do with all the money they had. They were one of the richest families in the region and they were getting richer. Nikki-D's father was turning a small, struggling bank into one of the hottest banks in the region.

Nikki-D worried about her father. He was working more and more. She could tell that her mother was concerned, too. Ginny Thomas had to admit that the move was good for them financially. Keeping her family together was the hard part. She was critical of him no matter what he did. She was concerned about his drinking. She knew the neighbors talked. Ginny wanted him to settle down.

Nikki-D's world was expanding. Her ideology was growing. President Kennedy was her role model. She aspired to meet his request to challenge herself. She wanted to work for the common good of all nations. Even her mother came to like him. He was a good Catholic man. It was important to her that he had faith. Even better that it was the same faith as theirs, although her mother thought Pope John XXIII had ruined it by liberalizing the Roman Catholic Church.

This morning Nikki-D started the day by helping her mother pack sacks of food. Ginny Thomas had helped start a new food bank for the poor on the reservation. Nikki-D knew it was because of that night with Jonny's mother. They would always pack a different sack of food for his family. Only Ginny knew that the family needed it. Of course, Nikki-D never said anything to Jonny about this, even though they both knew it was happening. That was what President Kennedy was talking about: neighbors helping neighbors. He was a phenomenon.

"Huuphh!"

The air was knocked out of her when she ran into someone. It was Caj.

"Hey, are you all right?"

He had her by the arm. Some papers fell to the floor from the collision. Oh god, I'm so clumsy, she thought.

"Here, let me get those for you," he said, smiling. He bent down to get her papers.

She could smell a trace of liquor on his breath. At first she frowned, but when he smiled she forgot all about it. She loved that smile. It wasn't like earlier, when she had a little-girl crush on him. She had matured. She felt right.

Some more books slipped from her hand and hit the floor next to his head. He picked one up and read the title: "The Feminine Mystique." He looked at Nikki-D as he stood up.

"I'm sorry," she said, her face red.

"Come on, Nikki-D, its all right. Don't be so nervous." His dark, candid eyes surveyed her. She could see how exposed he left himself to people. Those eyes were so frank and honest; he took people in the same manner.

It was like him to put people at ease. It was another thing she liked about him.

"Where you going so late? Classes have already started."

"I know. I'm late for my Civics class."

"Civics class. I was never any good at that. Just sports."

"Yea." It was all she could think to say. It was so unlike her. In class she could talk about any subject with no problem. But when she had to talk to a boy like Caj, there were no words. She knew she must look like a dip.

"Where are you going?"

Caj flicked his thumb at the principal's room.

"Heh-heh, forgot that I'm good at that, too."

Nikki-D gave a hesitant smile.

"Well, Nikki-D, nice running into you. I got to go." Then he was off to the principal's office. It was another good-natured run-in.

Yes, Nikki-D thought, the day is going well. Caj! I ran into Caj. Couldn't ask for anything better than that. I know this is going to be my luckiest day. She walked down the hall to her class.

Martin Luther King, Jr., stood on the White House steps, knee-deep in people. His voice carried across the nation. "I still have a dream. It is a dream deeply rooted in the American dream. I have a dream that one day this nation will rise up and live out the true meaning of its creed: 'We hold these truths to be self-evident: that all men are created equal', I have a dream that one day on the red hills of Georgia the sons of former slaves and the sons of former slave owners will be able to sit down together at the table of brotherhood. I have a dream that my four little children will one day live in a nation where they will not be judged by the color of their skin but by the content of their character."

Briiinnng. Briiiiing. The bell rang, signaling the end of class. Mr. Newman got up and turned on the lights. Then he turned off the projector. Students had their hands shielding their eyes, trying to adjust to the harsh light.

"OK, students. I want you to write a paper on what Dr. King was conveying in his speech today. I want it to be at least three pages and not more than five. By tomorrow. Dismissed."

Nikki-D got up. She was almost in tears from what she heard. Emotionally, it moved her. It made her determined to become part of the generation that makes a difference. It was this generation that was distinct: chosen to change the status-quo, to make the world better. He excitement grew with each thought. She practically ran up to Mr. Newman.

"Mr. Newman."

He looked up at her. A frown crossed his face.

"Nikki-D, you were late this morning. Is there something wrong? I waited for our talk."

He was letting her know that he was not going to allow this lazy attitude if she wanted to work with him.

"I know. My mother needed me to help her with the food bank. She usually has our neighbor come over but she couldn't make it this morning."

"OK. Well, you wanted to talk on the changing world and what our roles will be in it. Actually, I have given it a lot of thought. We can talk in our next class. I have a surprise that I think you will enjoy."

Nikki-D agreed and ran off to her next class.

Mr. Newman watched his favorite student as she left. She had so many ideals, so much emotion and energy to be put to good use. He was not an old man ... unless you asked his students. He was young enough to catch some of the joy of idealism that was running through a few of his students. Not enough of them, though. What had to be done for them to catch fire? He went back to the projector.

The hall was full of kids running and talking as they went to their next class. Nikki-D saw Caj standing at the other end with his people. The Indians and the hoods hung around the exit door that ran into the alley way. Most would run out and have a cigarette during recess and lunch. The hoods were loud and obnoxious. The Indians were quiet and watchful.

Nikki-D saw Jonny standing with the others, yet standing alone. She was worried about him. He was solemn and withdrawn. She watched out for him as much as she could. It seemed as if he was drifting away from her. They had study hall together then she went to Math, and they would be together again in Biology. She would have her chance to see him then.

Jonny gave a little smile when she came up to him.

"Hey, Jonny, here comes your girlfriend." It was that smart-ass Madison boy. He ran around with Caj and Hanford and BJ, his cousins. Jonny didn't pay him any attention. He was glad to see Nikki-D.

"Hi," he said.

"Hi Jonny." Her eyes were on Caj.

Jonny noticed when she watched Caj. He felt sorry for her, because he knew that they would never get together. They weren't the same type. He tried telling her once, but it didn't sink in. She had acted like he was jealous or something, so he let it drop.

"You were late today."

"Mom and I had to bring food to the bank. That Nora Livingston canceled at the last minute. Hi, Caj," Nikki called, her attention diverted again.

Jonny looked at his older brother, who barely noticed her.

"He had to go to the principal's office again."

"I know. I met him in the hall when he went. What happened to him?"

"Nothing. He has to stay after practice and work for the principal."

"What did he do?"

"Guess he got caught passing notes to some girls."

Jonny saw Nikki-D turn cold again. It happened every time he said anything about girls and Caj. Poor Nikki.

"Are you going to go to class or hang out here all day?"

Jonny knew it was time to go.

"Mmm ... I'm ready to go if you are."

"Good. Let's go."

Jonny waved at Caj and the others as he walked to study hall with Nikki-D.

"Did you know I'm doing an experiment with Mr. Newman in biology?" She wanted to tell Jonny how good everything was going.

"Mmm..."

Jonny was watching two big boys coming into study hall. They were Indian boys who must be seniors. Nikki-D knew only one of them. She thought his name was 'Chucky'. The other one looked familiar but she knew she had never seen him before. The new kid saw Jonny and gave a little wave. He smiled.

Once she saw that smile, Nikki-D knew. He must be part of Jonny's family. Why hadn't Jonny told her about him?

"Is that your older brother?"

Jonny fidgeted with his pencil, still watching the boys as they went up to the study hall teacher and gave her their slips. They seemed so out of place here – so much older than the other kids in school.

"Well?" She was never really patient even though she knew Jonny would answer her in his own good time.

"Mmm ... the big one's Chucky Jones."

"I know that." Why did he always answer her in a roundabout way?

"Mmmm ... the other one's my big brother."

Nikki-D was knocked over. His big brother. Where has he been? The questions hurled through her head.

"Whaaat?" She said this in a whispered voice so the teacher wouldn't hear her.

Jonny wasn't looking up anymore. He began doodling on his notebook. She could tell it was hard for him to talk about this; at least not here in study hall.

"Your real brother?"

"Mmm ... yes."

The teacher pointed to two desks in the side row by the windows. They walked over to them and sat down. They were so big. Nikki-D knew that there were a lot of big Indians. She saw that after watching them in basketball. In fact, that's where she saw Chucky. He played every once in a while. He was quiet, but what Indian wasn't quiet? At first, anyway. When they trusted you, they would talk your ear off. They always laughed and made jokes. Most people didn't get to see them the way she did. She often wondered how they could keep their sense of humor with the conditions they lived under. Chucky was no different, except he was bigger. Way bigger!

All the other kids tried not to look, but their curiosity got the better of them. She could see heads turning to watch these two big Indians.

"So? What's your brother's name?" Jonny was so exasperating at times.

"Mmm ... mm. That's Gray. Grayam is his real name. But we call him Gray."

"How come you never told me about him before? And where has he been?" A vague memory nudged her. She remembered her mother saying something about it. She knew! It made her mad that her mother knew more than Nikki-D about Jonny's family.

"They sent him away. Been gone for three years. I forget what he did." In fact, Jonny never knew what happened to his oldest brother. The kids all talked about it but no one really knew, except maybe Dani and Clair. His brother had his own life. Jonny was too young to know what it was. Gray ran around with people that didn't know Jonny was alive.

"What do you mean, they sent him away? Sent him where? Why?" She wanted Jonny to back up and start from the beginning.

"Mmm ... they always send people away."

Nikki-D didn't know what to say to that. He acted like it was a nothing; nothing unusual ... life goes on.

"Send them where?"

Jonny was through talking on that subject and Nikki-D knew it was better to move on. "How long has he been back?"

"He just got back and he's staying with Chucky and his family. Mmmmm ... he and my dad don't get along to well. They want him to come back to school because they say he's real smart."

Nikki-D saw that Jonny wasn't going to say too much more. She didn't want to press him. It would be soon enough to find out about this mystery brother. She'd let it go for now.

"Jonny, do you want to come to Biology with me and watch me do the experiment? I get to do it all by myself . Mr. Newman hasn't told me yet. But he said he has a surprise for me." She could feel the excitement running through her. Nothing could stop her today. She felt so good. That's why she wanted Jonny with her when she was doing the experiment. She felt confident with him. This was the first time she felt confident in a long while. Plus, she wanted to talk to Jonny about Caj.

"OK."

"OK. I'll see you there."

Before they could go on talking, two burly policemen came into the room. It was officer Pete and his partner. They looked around the room and spotted Gray and Chucky, pointed their finger in their direction. They called the teacher over and said something, then pulled out a paper and showed it to her. She nodded.

The officers walked over to the boys.

"Gray, we have a warrant for you. I want you to stand up and turn around and put your hands behind your back. The same with you, Chuck."

Both boys did what the officers told them. Everyone in the classroom was hushed. No one could keep their eyes off what was happening. It would be the talk of the school for weeks to come.

Nikki-D watched as Jonny lowered his eyes. She could see his face turn red. Why didn't he fight for his brother and friend? The anger rushed over Nikki-D.

The police officers snapped the handcuffs around Gray's wrists. Chucky was already handcuffed. The boys looked at each other and laughed. Then Gray saw Jonny.

"Jonny, I'll see you later. OK?"

Jonny lifted his eyes to his brother. They both knew that Gray wouldn't be back. His life was forfeited in the war of survival. He grew out of poverty, condemned to the repetitious wasteland of the system, a system that he could neither control nor appeal to. His fate was always in the hands of others.

Jonny felt a kindred spirit in his brother. In his own way, he would always be apart from those around him. They would always hear his words with a question on their faces. Nikki-D tried to help but she couldn't. People would always view him as odd. They would look on his brother with fear.

Gray tried to wave with his hands in cuffs. Jonny put up his arm and waved at his brother and then the police took him from the room.

He could feel their eyes on him. They had questions. They had already made a judgment.

To all the kids in the room, it was just another Indian thing.

The day was strange for Nikki-D. She still felt exhilarated. Life was hers for the grabbing. She had a reason for being on this earth. She had a hero.

Kennedy was the youngest person in American history to be elected president. His administration was dazzling, partly because of his elegant wife, Jacqueline (Jackie) Kennedy, and partly because Kennedy himself was young, handsome, and eloquent.

It was people like him that made America great. Oh, he made his mistakes, like that stupid Bay of Pigs. She blamed his advisors for that one. He stood up like a man and admitted his mistakes. Her mother liked that. She said he had the guts to do that when the whole nation thought of him as their hero. It took a man to do that.

Everything was in front of her. Dr. King was only the beginning. Nikki-D took the words of these men as the gospel.

She watched as Jonny walked back to the hallway where his people stood together. They all knew. How they always knew things was beyond Nikki-D. She just knew that her friend was hurting and this made her angry.

One of these days... They wouldn't be able to walk into the classroom and take someone just because they were Indian. She became more determined as she went to her next class.

Half the class was watching her. The lab experiment that she recommended to Mr. Newman was about to happen. She had sent into motion a sequence of cause and effect. The rats with their long whiskers frisking the cage, were in perpetual motion. Nikki-D would be injecting them with vitamin-C supplements to see what effect it would have on them. But she had added a twist to the experiment. She wanted to see what, if any, effect it would have on the brain.

Nikki-D thought that life was just a matter of cause and effect. Reaction to Action. There was always a duality to nature ... And man. The great Linus Pauling was leaning toward this. She would follow.

The serum was ready. The kids were excited as she prepared to inject the liquid. Everyone was quiet. Her thumb pressed the plunger.

Slam! The door flew open. A senior girl stood in front of the class, tears running down her face.

"President Kennedy was shot. He's dead!"

The pain tore through her body. The ache was immediate and direct. It touched every part of her body. She couldn't breathe. Her fingers twitched. Her eyes clouded. Suddenly, the anguish came. Her mind tried to cope. She focused only on the event. She didn't allow herself to think beyond that. The tears came from so deep that they were like a tidal wave by the time they reached her eyes.

She didn't remember how long she cried. All the kids were crying. It was a national tragedy that no one would forget. Nikki-D recovered slowly. By the time she came to her senses, minutes had passed. She looked down, and her thumb was pressed hard against the plunger. She looked at the cages.

"Oh no...

The rats lay with their heads down ... dead.

LOST INNOCENCE

    Nikki-D sat in front of the television, in mourning. The news of the President's death was broadcast on all the stations for the past few days. The world watched.
    The crushing effects of the shooting left her innocence shattered. The world would never be the same. Americans no longer had the luxury of isolation. Other countries with their wars and deaths a common occurrence, watched their American brothers as they went into shock. Newspapers around the world, said "the Americans have grown up." The world was sadder for it. Nikki-D felt like the rest. Her ideal world died with her leader. Her President was dead. Her face turned shock-white every time they showed the shooting. Then they showed Oswald being killed by another man. Right on TV. People were bewildered and afraid, and wondered how this could happen in America.
    Their America was falling apart bit by bit. The world was in front of her. A young man who was the greatest President since Lincoln had died. He gave his life for his country. Anger ran through Nikki-D.
    The announcer talked as the flag-draped casket was drawn slowly down the street by horses. Uniformed men in dress blues marched beside it. The images! These would stay for life. Nikki-D began to cry again. She hadn't been able to stop crying since the killing. It felt as if her soul was being torn apart. The funeral went on. The old man stood up to speak to the people sitting in the big room. He was an elder. Small and shaking, he rose to speak. People sat in chairs lined up in a row. The building was a gym and it held many people. Jonny stood at the doorway. People were filing in and out. Jonny was one of the kids that had to work to set up the tables and chairs for the funeral and the dinner after. All the kids his age were helping. It was done that way. The kitchen was full of women and kids cooking; outside, men were cooking fish and elk to feed the gathering. There were a lot of people.

Jonny saw Caj and Hanford up on the mezzanine. They were watching in silence. Guy and BJ were with them. Jonny saw his father walk up and take Caj away. They talked to each other, making hand-signs as they walked. Jonny wondered what it was about. The Chairman of the tribe was dead. He had died in his sleep. That's why there were so many people here. He was the dead leader of their tribe.

The tribe was in bad economic times. Sub Williams had resigned as business manager and Wayne Williams was ready to take over. It was hard to get food, and getting worse. Jonny watched his mother as she went about trying to get food and clothing for her kids. She had changed. She always had a smile on her face, as if she knew something that nobody else did. When she came back from the hospital, the kids stood in front of her, not knowing what she would be like. To their delight, the old woman that left in stress and pain had been replaced by a young woman full of life and energy.

Life was still hard. Families had to band together and help each other to find enough of anything to get by. America was in shock and didn't have time for the Indians. The blacks were fighting in the streets for their rights. Indians were not included in this struggle. The President was shot. The Indian community felt the pain of the Americans and sympathized with them. After all, hadn't their own leader died? To them, it was the same.

To Jonny, it meant more worry about his friend and his family. He knew that even though his mother were a happy face, the stress of living was always there. Jonny listened to Caj and Hanford talk. They needed to get away. Have some fun. They were going out tonight. The loud-mouth and BJ would go with them. Jonny was old enough now to run with them. He was trying to make up his mind.

"My people," the old man spoke, "it is a sad time for us. A great man has died. A man who believed in his people. He worked hard to make the world better. To keep his tribe together during troubled times. He fought against the relocation of men off the reservation, he fought those who would take the children from their mothers and families to be put in non-Indian homes, and he fought for tribal rights."

People's hushed voices could be heard all over the gym. The old man looked out over them.

"My people. I offer my sympathy to the family. My heart aches. I know how his family sitting here in front of me feels. They need our support in their time of need."

Now he was warming up to the speech. His arm rose high and he spoke in his sing-song way.

"My people. You must help the family bear their pain. Stand behind them and assist them until they can walk by themselves. Listen to their words of hurt because this will aid them and their spirit. Watch after their children to keep them from harm. Go and hold their hand, this family that is hurting so bad. Help them and in helping this family, you are also helping your people. That is the Indian way."

There were more people who stood up and spoke. Jonny listened to each of them. The way they talked and the words they said were gentle and soft. It was the best time to listen.

Still, only part of him was listening. He thought of Nikki-D. She seemed so down because of the death of the President; like she had never seen death before. That was all the Indian community was about: Deaths. There were a lot of them every year, but this year was one of the bad ones. Nine people died this year and it made people talk. Death came in cycles. Like everything else, this was a down year and the deaths piled up. Jonny rubbed his cheeks. The strain was bad.

Caj came up behind him. "Jonny, we're going out tonight after the burning. Want to go?"

Jonny looked at the four in front of him. He had to go and see Nikki-D: his mother wanted him to go with her to see the family at the burning; and he was still avoiding his father in case he had something for him to do. It seemed as if there were all these duties that he must carry out. There was no time for himself. He was tired. Going with Caj and the rest seemed like it would be fun for a change. He needed some fun.

"OK. I'll meet you at the burning. Are you guys going up to the cemetery now?"

"Yea, we heard this talk too many times before." Caj was sounding more cynical lately. He sounded more like his father.

Jonny watched them go. His father was moving around the room talking to people. He was making his move, becoming a politician. His deep, black eyes seemed to move among the people without ever staying on the person he was talking with. He always looked for the next vote. Franc Esque was a radical. He had found his calling.

Ginny stepped in between Nikki-D and the television. Nikki-D looked up at her. She had been crying again. Ginny didn't understand why she watched the morbid shooting of the President. She would be glad when they buried the man. The drums of the tribe were starting up again and things felt bad.

"Nikki-D, are you going to watch this TV all day?"

Nikki-D just looked at her, not saying anything. She moved her head to get a better view of the television and that was all. Ginny marched out of the room.

Nikki-D moved and swayed as the casket was being drawn by the horses. The nation wobbled and teetered with the procession. At the same time, the drums of the tribe began to beat louder and louder. She knew that the Indians were grieving about their lost leader. It was hard on all of them. The drums had the same rhythm as the television. They were all in this together.

They were walking on the road to the cemetery: drummers beating the drums; Boom ... boom ... boom ... Boom ... boom ... boom ... each in their red headband, singing and drumming. The casket, with its beautiful Pendleton blanket draped around it, was carried behind them by pallbearers on each side. The family and heads of other tribes followed.

Jonny was in the group at the end. It was a large group, even though most of the people got rides up to the cemetery. The group swayed with the drumming, and all were in rhythm with the funeral. All cried and mourned in their silent walk, each trying to determine what this man's death would mean for them. Each lived with the fear of the unknown.

There were those who believed it was a new beginning for their tribe, people who wanted to break the strangle-hold of dependency on the federal government that ran their lives. The next generation's fight would begin today. The old world was crumbling around them, releasing the hate and anger of the younger men and women who wanted more. They were energetic and idealistic and knew that they were chosen to make a change. Their lives depended on the future and not on the past. The past was dying in front of them, inch by inch. They wanted more for their people and were committed to make that change.

Jonny watched his father stand with the new crowd. The same anger that used to be aimed at Jonny was now used to make people listen to him. It started out with the young men of the tribe and had grown and added many women. Children stood outside the circle and listened to the new, angry words. Their learning had taken a new twist.

The crowd stood around the grave. Behind stood Jonny and all the other boys. Caj and Hanford left the group of people that their dad was addressing. All grew silent for the prayer and Wayne Williams thanked everyone and asked them to come and eat at the gym. The burning would be at three p.m. at his home. Others at the grave said their words to the family and the tribe, then moved on, each putting a rose on the casket covered with the Pendleton blanket.

Caj and Hanford moved up to Jonny. "We're heading back to eat."

That was all it was to them. Someone died and they went, watched, then ate. They were so different from Jonny; and from Nikki-D, for that matter. Jonny remembered when she had broken down crying in front of him, not knowing why such a great man had to die. Jonny felt her soul and spirit as it came to terms with its place in the world. He never asked why, but asked how the spirit world worked. It was difference that moved him away from ordinary people and aligned him with the teachings of the elders. Nikki-D would have to find her own answers and all he could do was try to support her. His support was unquestioned and automatic.

Most of the people were gone now. The grave-diggers, who received three dollars for their work, waited for the people to go. The family stayed until last and now they were gone. Jonny watched as the diggers threw dirt in the grave. It was getting time for Jonny to see Nikki-D. He had seen the forces of change today, and he knew that the Sixties would be different for all.

Nikki-D cried hard. The tears kept coming. They flowed from the rustic sun-belt to the rural countryside, north and south. The images of the little boy still haunted her. Standing at his father's grave, confused and fidgeting, he had finally raised his hand in a salute to the greatest man in the world: His father. The President.

She couldn't watch anymore. Anger burned in her. Her model of moderation and progress was struck down by those who opposed change. They struck down her future, her transformation. Like the aftermath of Lincoln's death, the cause would be left with the extreme idealists that had no tolerance for those who opposed them.

Without the vision of their leader to guide them, the metamorphosis could not be complete. All this flowed through Nikki-D – some she understood intuitively, and others would come with time. Like the lost child trying to find its mother, she would keep searching for that which only the President knew.

Shaken, Nikki-D walked to her bedroom. She put on her pants and sweater. She was going out to see Jonny. She needed to talk to him.

It always calmed her, even though Jonny barely managed to get out a umm or huh. She smiled at this thought, one of the few times she had smiled in a long time.

She turned on the radio. New music was coming over it. The Beatles were singing, "I want to hold your hand." What a name for a band. Their music grabbed her immediately. The times were changing and the old music was for those in the past. Nikki-D listened to the future with uncertainty.

Jonny and Nikki-D stood on the small site of Mission Hill. The burning took a little longer than he thought. He was a little late but he made it. Nikki-D called it Indian time. Almost everyone that came in contact with Indians used the term. It just meant that his people didn't follow the clock as much as the whites. He never understood her anger at his being late, but there it was again. She was cooling down looking at the dusk.

Her anger went away and something much worse replaced it. Jonny had so much of it in his life that he didn't want to see it in hers. The sadness. He watched the tears roll down her cheeks. The deep sadness. It was always in his people, so he became somewhat immune to it. He always thought that the rich people like Nikki-D never felt it. Now he knew better. Their President died and it hurt them. Kennedy's funeral was almost like an Indian burial, not the usual burial where nobody showed up. It had dignity. It was the first time he saw the nation cry. He saw some hope for them.

Nikki-D felt the pain again. She hated crying like this. She hurt down to the depths of her soul. She wanted to shake this feeling but didn't know how. Her mother talked to her, and her father talked to her, explaining things to her as if she was some sort of child. Neither one understood her enough to listen. She began to cry again. Her life was so miserable.

"They don't understand me, Jonny. I try and I try but all they tell me is the man is dead and I've got to move on. Like he was nothing or I'm building him up way out of proportion. After this, they want me to just go back to the way it was." She looked at Jonny, a lingering look that didn't swerve from his eyes. "I can't go back." Then she stared out over the water again. The moon was high and the crystal water flowed over the beach below.

She felt his arm go around her shoulders. At first she thought she was imagining it; his touch was so light. His fingers massaged her, bringing her closer, and she began to let go. Her anger ebbed with the tide flowing into the small, silent boy beside her. He understood. That's all she wanted: Understanding. "You understand, don't you, Jonny?"

"Mmmmm ... mm."

Jonny reached out to the sadness. What he received was the anger that was in everybody: His father, his brother, his tribe, and now Nikki-D. The anger grew and grew and it was swallowing him, too. The decade had started out so right; dreams embodied in one man. The man was dead, and the dream was becoming distorted and twisted. The hate and the anger engulfed those who stood in its way. Jonny knew that the coming years would be hard. What else was new? That thought depressed him. He was questioning himself. He could find no answers.

"I have to go, Jonny."

She said those words like they had more meaning than intended. Jonny didn't know if she meant go now or just go. Either way, she was leaving him. He did understand.

He took his arm from her shoulder and stepped back.

"See you tomorrow, Jonny OK?"

"OK," he said in his low voice.

They ran in the night. Caj, Hanford, Guy, and BJ ran together, with Jonny bringing up the rear. He was short and his legs couldn't run fast enough to keep up with them. They were heading to the tracks on Hewitt Avenue in Everett. Hewitt had all the taverns on it. Everett was a city of about fifty thousand people. It was too small to have a red-light district but it sure had its taverns.

They were running in the night, just kids who tried to leave the bad things behind. The decline of the reservation was taking a toll on the people. The lines for food were longer and the food was more scarce. The President was dead and nobody cared.

Jonny was trying to keep up with his brother. Caj and Hanford were running with a case of beer between them. Behind them were BJ and Guy. All were cousins to each other. It was the first time that they let Jonny run with them. The night was theirs.

Caj and Hanford stopped at the tracks that ran through Everett. The huge tunnel mouth was in front of them. It was one of their favorite places. It was just a green patch of grass away from the tunnel. Looking down the tracks, Jonny could see the Hewitt overpass. Small sterno flames shot up under the pass. Bums. They used the underpass to wait for the trains to come, jumping on before the train disappeared into the dark tunnel mouth. Most of them waited until daylight to jump a train. It was too dangerous at night.

"Hey, who has the opener?" Hanford waited. " Shit. Nobody brought the opener!"

The others hung their heads down, not wanting to be the one fingered for not bringing the opener. Hanford went over to the case of beer and tore it open. He grabbed two beers, bent his knees a little and turned one of the bottles upside down, hooking the two tops together and with one twist of his wrist, opened the bottle of beer.

Beer sprayed everywhere; mostly over Hanford. He looked down at his pants. They were soaking wet. He always dressed the best of the group. He was like Caj: Two boys who spent hours on their grooming habits; both with creased pants and shirts.

"God damn it! Look at my pants. I can't go to the dance like this." They planned to go to Normana Hall later on. The YMCA dance was happening tonight. You had to be sixteen to get in. They were going to try to get Jonny in anyway, show him how to have some fun.

To tell the truth, Jonny wasn't sure he wanted to do it. Life at home was so desperate that he had to do something. Even his laid-back attitude couldn't shield him from the poverty and despair on the reservation. There was very little of anything. All the families were falling into drinking. Even the mothers were going out with the men. They drank at the Indian bar until all hours of the morning. Their kids were left to fend for themselves. Every family was affected. Jonny thought about his father and mother. They both had turned very odd.

He thought that his father would be the first one to drink until he dropped. Instead, he had stopped drinking. He still went out to the bars, but only to listen and talk. Then he would come home and sit in his favorite chair in front of the fire and think. He would get up with Caj and head out every morning.

Jonny asked Caj where they went. Caj just told him that they went to the homes of other tribal members and talked.

It sounded like what Jonny and his mother had been doing for most of his life. He didn't see anything out of the ordinary and he let it go.

Hanford opened the beers for the others. Finally, he handed one to Jonny.

Jonny hesitated. It was exciting being with the older boys. But to drink beer? He didn't know about that.

"Go ahead – take it." Hanford wasn't going to let him off the hook.

Jonny looked at Caj. His brother gave a nod: It was all right with him if Jonny tried a beer. Jonny took the beer in his hand. Then Hanford handed one to Caj. They all had one.

Hanford raised his beer to the others, holding it there. "Here's to us."

They all raised their beers. "To us!"

Jonny stood outside the Normana Hall building. The light drizzle of November made the night air chilly. The others all made it in, but the girl at the door said Jonny was too young. He could hear the old dance music coming from the hall. The stroll was being danced. Jonny knew that everyone would line up and couples would dance between them. Nikki-D made him dance with her sometimes and they would dance the stroll. He wasn't very good at it and her friends would laugh at him. Girls were better at that kind of stuff.

Jonny would just leave it alone but the girls wanted boys that could dance. He was beginning to look at girls.

It was almost the end of the evening when Jonny saw Caj coming out with Hanford draped all over him. Hanford made sure that the other guys wore heavy coats so he could sneak beer into the dance. Jonny really didn't like the taste of beer. Personally, he could do without it. Caj and Hanford drank and seemed to have a lot of fun getting drunk. They ended up laughing and talking, making fun of the others and talking about the girls. Then they would stop and look at each other. Deep, troubling thoughts showed on their faces. Jonny and the others would wait.

"Hey, what about that Lena? I wouldn't mind jumping on that."

It was Guy. He always talked big and loud. Jonny and the others mostly ignored him. If that was possible. He sure had a big mouth for such a little guy.

Caj and Hanford made it to the door. Jonny opened it for them. Hanford was drunk; really drunk.

"Yyouull know Caj, I'm going to get a job. Take cacaa-re of my family. Show mmyy father. Yyou..know."

Hanford loved his father. Jonny knew how he felt. His own father never liked him; he thought that Jonny was broken or imperfect or something. It was the way that Jonny talked. His father grew tired of trying to fix Jonny. He kept saying it was all in Jonny's head and he could fix it if he wanted to. Jonny wanted to talk right, and tried everything he could to stop making his dad angry at him. He couldn't do enough.

Hanford was the only one that argued with his father. They would go at it, neither one giving ground. Hanford was almost eighteen and was looking to move out. Caj said that Hanford didn't really want to go but his father was pushing to get him out. His mother was always too drunk to care. His life was built on misery and now he fell into the bottle to battle the misery.

Caj, Hanford, and Jonny walked down the street, singing in high octave, "The lion sleeps tonight."

They gave Hanford some more coffee to drink. Caj wanted to get him sober so he could go home. It was a long night and they were all tired. Jonny was sitting on the green patch of grass where they had started the evening. It was just the three of them. Caj had stopped at a store and bought the coffee. He was a little drunk himself and wanted to get sober.

The night was dark and gray. It always was. No matter what they did, the gray sky hung over them. Small flames of Sterno shot up at the underpass. The gaping mouth of the dark tunnel invited them in to get out of the drizzle. Jonny moved over to the opening, half-in and half-out.

"We got to go home, Hanford. You think you can make it?" As always, Caj was looking out for his favorite cousin. They were very close. All their hopes and dreams and fears – everything – passed between them. They were like brothers. They said they were blood-brothers. Like in the movies.

Jonny saw the light before hearing the train. It was coming. He saw the bums under the pass getting up and moving away from the tracks. They knew better. The flames went out one by one, until there were none.

"I'm not going home." Hanford pushed Caj from him.

Caj got up and grabbed Hanford by the arm. "Come with us. You got to go home. We'll make sure you get there."

"Noo ... I'm not going home. He can kiss my ass. I can do what I want."

His words were clearer. Jonny knew he wasn't as drunk as he used to be. Hanford was feeling good about the job he got just today. The pulp mill in Everett hired him for the green chain. He pulled wood and stacked it. He was right; it was a good job. How he got it, Jonny didn't know. Indians were turned down flat. Hanford looked like an Indian, not like a mixed blood. It was strange.

Caj said the reservation was all a buzz about Hanford, because his father always complained, saying he wouldn't amount to a hill of beans, and now Hanford was the only one that got a job.

"Hey, Cous. I got to go man. You going to be OK?" Caj wanted Hanford to come with them. He kept trying but Hanford wasn't going for it. He said that he was going out with some other guys. It was his life.

Caj let him go. "Who you going out with?" But he knew. Hanford was beginning to run around with rougher types.

"Watch yourself, OK?"

Hanford nodded his head.

Caj looked at Jonny. "Let's go."

They began the long walk home. Their house was about fifteen miles away. Jonny was already tired. Caj walked fast. Jonny walked behind him. Neither one said anything. One of the last sounds Jonny heard was the whistle of the train heading for the underpass.

14

HANFORD

Jonny woke. There was a commotion going throughout the house. Women were crying and talking. He looked around for Caj. He wasn't there. Jonny jumped from the bed, putting on his clothes as fast as he could. Fear started to take hold of his heart. Something was wrong. He had heard these sounds before.

He looked out the window to see who was there. It was the Henrys. Patsy and Mary were crying as they walked into the house. Duane leaned against the old car with a stem look on his face. Other families were watching the scene in front. They knew already.

Lois came into the room. She looked at him, "You better come downstairs."

Jonny heard the concern in his mother's voice. Someone had died.

Jonny walked down the dilapidated stairs to the living room. Roy Henry and the rest of the family were there. All of the women were crying. Jonny looked around the room. Caj sat with his father, not saying a word. He looked down to the floor. Jonny's mother came in with some coffee. She served them all. Then she sat down next to Mary and put her arm around her, giving comfort.

Roy's gruff voice rolled over the room. "Jonny, we want to talk to you."

Jonny sat on the sofa in front of them all. A lot of them were standing because there weren't enough chairs for them. Jonny's heart beat hard. It was bad.

"Hanford died last night." Roy could barely get the words out. The women cried. Then the room grew silent again.

"They found him this morning. On the tracks." With each sentence the women's wails went up again.

"Oooohhhhh."

Jonny's head began to hurt. It was like the world was coming down on him. His heart wouldn't stop, speeding up until he thought it would explode. He began to cry. Hanford was dead. How? His mind raced back to the night before.

A group of young men were riding into the camp laughing and teasing with one another. When they rode past, they turned their teasing to the boy and girl. As they rode by, one of the young men slipped from his horse and walked up to the Medicine Chief.

"Good father," he said, not looking at the Chief, "You are invited to the lodge of my parents for the evening meal. Medicine Crow, my grandfather, has been made well from sickness. The Medicine Power has healed him. My father told me to tell you these things, and also that he will sponsor a dance and Give-Away to the People in the thanksgiving tonight."

"A dance!" Squeaked the Children almost together. "We must prepare," the girls explained to the Chief, and then they were off, running hand in hand to prepare.

"Well, it appears that now only we three are left," said the Chief.

As they began to walk again.

"This," explained the Chief after he and the little boy had reached the brush and trees along the river, "is where Jumping Mouse began. Do you see the lodges of our People? Those, my son, we will pretend are the Sacred Mountains. Lie down here upon your stomach and see how a Mouse would perceive the Prairie."

He laid on his stomach and looked. The expanse of Prairie appeared to him as a measureless sea of grass. The chief helped him back to his feet and found them a cool place to sit. There he began to Story again.

Jumping Mouse went to the Edge of the Place of Mice and Looked out onto the Prairie. He Looked up for Eagles. The Sky was Full of many Spots, each One an Eagle. But he was Determined to go to the Sacred Mountains. He Gathered All of his Courage and Ran just as Fast as he Could onto the Prairie. His little Heart Pounded with Excitement and Fear.

He Ran until he Came to a Stand of Sage. He was Resting and trying to Catch his Breath when he Saw an Old Mouse. The Patch of Sage Old Mouse Lived in was a Haven for Mice. Seeds were Plenti-

ful and there was Nesting Material and many things to be Busy with.

"Hello," said Old Mouse. "Welcome."

Jumping Mouse was Amazed. Such a Place and such a Mouse. "You are Truly a great Mouse," Jumping Mouse said with all the Respect he could Find. "This is Truly a Wonderful Place. And the Eagles cannot See you here, either," Jumping Mouse said.

"Yes," said Old Mouse, "and One can See All the Beings of the Prairie here: the Buffalo, Antelope, Rabbit, and Coyote. One can See them All from here and Know their Names."

"That is Marvelous," Jumping Mouse said. "Can you also See the River and the Great Mountains?"

15

CHRISTIAN

Ginny watched her daughter. It was hard to see her go through this grieving so hard for the man she worshipped, her ideals destroyed by Oswald's hate. Destroyed by a single bullet. Maybe I sheltered her too much? Ginny had thoughts that all mothers had when their child was in pain. It was so hard to see them grow up.

"You better get your coat. Its time to go."

The sky was dreary with drizzle coming down. Jonny's people were all in mourning. Their leader was dead. What was it like for them? Ginny looked out the window to the waters of the sound. The water was dark and waves climbed the beaches. The drizzle blended its gray coldness with the dark water. Everyone was hurting so bad. She felt the tears at the corners of her eyes.

Ginny and Nikki-D stepped out of their house. Nora, the neighbor, was coming out of her house, too. She was heading for the church in town.

"Hi, Ginny. Can you believe those people and their drums? Allll ... night long.

Every night. Nobody can sleep with all that racket. I called the police and complained but they told me to call the Indian tribe. Can you believe that? I told them we were tax-paying citizens and I wanted something done about the noise. You can hear the noise clear across the reservation. And you know what? The drumming stopped. Just like that. I guess I told them. Heeh-Heeh-Heeh."

Ginny just ignored Nora. The Indians probably stopped on their own.

"Hi, Nora. On your way to church?" Ginny could feel Nikki-D pulling on her sleeve. Nikki-D didn't like them and wanted nothing to do with the Livingstons. Probably something to do with Jonny; those two were inseparable.

Nora no longer bothered her. She felt sorry for the women and others like her on the reservation. Ginny met with them all, for school and roads and funding for the heart foundation and other events. She knew their fear. Her mother the Empress lived that way and to some extent so did Ginny. Not anymore. She ignored Nikki-D.

"Yes. Can you believe the world today?" Nora moved off. "Some communist shooting the President. What's happening to us?"

"Yes its sad times for everyone. The Indians lost their leader too. That's why the drums are going all night long."

"Oh-that's what happened. Its no reason for them to wake everybody. I would think they could find some other way to bury him. After all, its not like he's a president or something."

Nikki-D was pulling harder now. They were on the road outside their fence. They both stopped and looked. The old cars and campers were everywhere, parked in every spot that was open. Now they were parking on both sides of the road coming up to their house. Ginny knew it would mean trouble. Nora was in for a surprise.

Ginny and Nikki-D got in their new car. Nick was rushing out of the house to catch up. Nikki-D sat in the back. They watched as Nick fixed his tie and smoothed out his suit. His hair was thinning. He was putting on some weight and was beginning to look older. He worked so hard.

She leaned over and moved the rear-view mirror. Ginny looked at herself and beyond. The mirror showed Ginny's future. She stared at the image that was her daughter. She was a girl so different from her; as different as Ginny was from her mother. Yet as she thought this, she looked deeper at her own face.

It was an uncompromising face, even as Ginny looked at herself. Unbending, she maintained her composure. Life was work. She was not inflexible, but kept to her unalterable position of inner strength. She was persistent in her belief that she would not break, exacting in her demands that her family follow her example, keep to her ironclad rules. Ginny was stern and demanding with Nikki-D. She wanted her to work for perfection. Her love was conditioned. It had to be. Or...

Ginny watched Nikki-D, who was looking out the car window. She was so obstinate for her age. She was a real beauty, but her beauty was wasted, because her daughter never thought of it. She was so headstrong in her resistance to Ginny that it made Ginny laugh. Nikki-D looked at her with an expression that asked how Ginny could laugh on such a sad day. Her daughter brought to Ginny the gift of symmetry. More important, she brought to Ginny a friend in Lois. Changes were coming fast. The world was growing up. The safety net was being cut. Ginny watched her daughter's ideals crumble as her own grew. It was so strange.

Nick finally had the car going. They drove down the little road from their home. The cars were there and they could barely get by. It was slow-going. Ginny watched the people in the cemetery. It was another funeral. Their leader just died and now Hanford was gone. They gathered halfway up the cemetery at a grave. Women wailed so loud she could hear them from here. Dark faces watched them as they went by. They were faces of the poor and impoverished. A memory flickered in Ginny. It was of the first time they came to this place. A funeral was going on. She remembered the loud wailing then, too. She heard a moan from Nikki-D. Sensitive to their tears, it brought up hers, too. There were so many of them. Most of the time you could never see an Indian. Ginny had to wonder: where do they all come from?

They went by the Indians of Mission Hill, to the Church at Totem Beach. They drove up to the corner and Nick parked the car on the grass to the side of the church. A long dock headed out from the beach with small docks snaking from it like fingers. Small boats with white adults were heading out from Stouts Marina. On the hill right in front of the church were the restaurant and store. It was used by the whites on the reservation. Ginny looked down the beach at Coy's, where young Indian kids swam in the summer. There were none there now; only a couple of boats tied to the docks. The Indians mourned their leaders for a long time. While they did, their kids stayed home. The docks looked empty as she walked into the church.

Ginny Thomas bent down and crossed herself. She had always been deeply religious. The Church of St. Marie's was one of the better ones she had worshipped in. The Father was a young man with roots in this country. Father Bucharest was the great nephew of the missionary priest sent out from the East in the late nineteenth century. The government gave each church a reservation. The Catholic church was awarded Tulalip.

The first two buildings built on the reservation were the church at Totem Beach and the mission school at Hermosa Point. Both were a success for the church. Each one taught the natives the Catholic dictates that went into life. Seventy-five percent of the native population went to the church. All of the natives were the sons and daughters of the children of the old mission school.

Ginny Thomas heard about the history from the good Bishop, as did all the parishioners. It was good story, even though he never mentioned that the natives still worshipped their own religion. It was something that the church tried to stamp out, but the natives steadfastly refused to give up their belief. No Father was going to change that.

Today Ginny Thomas prayed for the world. After the assassination of President Kennedy, she saw the country sit in stunned silence. The greatest country in the world, having all of its leaders killed – something was wrong.

She could see how it effected Nikki-D. The girl seemed destroyed after that day. Her mood immediately changed. Most people couldn't see this, but Ginny was her mother. It was life: Events that make you grow up in a hurry. It was hard for everyone. This assassination would go down as one of the defining moments of the Sixties. Ginny was sure of that.

Ginny prayed again. She watched the people file in and out, waiting for them to find their seats and sit down. Her daughter came in and kneeled down, crossing herself. The weight of the world seemed to be carried on her shoulders. Nikki-D's ideals were crushed under the rifle of some small man in Dallas. It would take a while for her to trust again.

"For we are born in other's pain, And perish in our own."

Ginny knew the country was paralyzed by what happened. The President was dead. Birmingham was the site of extreme racial violence. American families watched helplessly on the sidelines. Each family stood blunted in the face of history. This is where faith stepped in to soothe the total indignation that all people felt. Ginny made her daughter come today. In the silent church she watched her child trying to piece together her broken world. Ginny crossed herself and prayed.

The good father came in. The service was about to begin. Father Bucharest moved up to the podium. His young face belied the hidden age from working in this parish. To him, it was one of the most satisfying. It was a gift from God to give him the same people that his granduncle taught. He saw more people coming in, all seeking answers from the world – a world that was becoming more violent.

He looked down upon his parishioners. "Let us pray."

Lois sat in the back of the church with Jonny and her smallest children. Jonny had come with her because he had some sins to confess. She knew that he went out with his older brother. It made her sad that he had to find that type of release. Times were hard, but if there was anyone that she hadn't had to worry about it was Jonny. She watched all the people around her. Their sad faces showed strain and stress. She knew though, that the people that died would be all right. They moved in this world, then they had to go. The tribe was right. The spirit rested in all of us. Good spirits, bad spirits – who knew? Being prepared and accepting was the way to battle them. She went to all the churches now. She listened to all the old women of the reservation. It was different now; after the pain came... enlightenment. She smiled at the thought.

In the back were the Indians. They always sat in the back. Why they did, Ginny never understood. From her side pew she could see Lois and some of her kids. The woman had made such a turnaround. As the world had gotten worse, she had became calmer.

Lois saw Ginny and smiled. She smiled back.

Ginny saw Nikki-D sitting by Jonny. It was good that she had a friend to turn to. Sadness washed over Ginny as she realized that she wished that she could be her daughter's friend. It was a feeling that left her alone. She looked up as Nick sat down beside her.

Nick was the one that sat with Nikki-D as she cried and cried through those days. He could be so right sometimes. Her husband stayed by his family no matter what. As she grew older, Ginny made fewer demands on him. It was enough that Nick was there for her. He helped her drown her fears. It took so much energy. There was so much misery on this reservation. She wondered what would happen next.

Jonny sat and sang with Nikki-D. She had moved to the back to sit with him. He could see her parents in front singing the songs of the church. The last few days had been hard. He drank his first drink and then ran with the boys at night. He hadn't seen Nikki-D for a while. She looked the same. Not as sad as she was at the funeral. Things were settling down on the reservation. It was so different.

Nikki-D was holding his hand as she sang. His mother and little sisters sang next to them. They always loved singing in church and he wouldn't be surprised if they didn't form a singing group. He never sang. To him this place never meant much except that it helped his mother and family. It preached beliefs that seemed to contradict the old people of the tribe, and everyone here acted as if they had no spirit at all. He knew that his thinking was becoming skewed for some reason. He was thirteen now and didn't really feel right all the time. Nikki-D said she experienced this, too. Hormones. Time for the kids to become adults. He was beginning to feel urges.

He immediately turned to look away, embarrassed. He was hot and her hand seemed like it was melting him. The urges kept coming and grew in his pants. He was mortified. He knew his hand was sweating. He squirmed a bit. Nikki-D stopped singing and looked at him. He could see in her eyes that she knew. She just looked at him and squeezed his hand and went back to singing. Jonny gave a sigh and went back to listening to the songs ringing in the church.

Jonny and Nikki-D looked up as soon as they heard his weeping. It was Caj. The tears were running hard down his face as he looked at Hanford's casket. It was a closed casket and a picture of him stood on top, surrounded by flowers. The moaning and crying coming from Caj unnerved Jonny. He had never seen his brother like this. Tears came to his own eyes. Nikki-D put her arm around him for support; she was crying, too. Caj was being comforted by Hanford's family but it did not stop the tears. Nikki-D put her head on Jonny's shoulder. "It will be all right, Jonny. Caj needs to cry. It will be all right."

"Mmmm ... mm. Mmmm ... mm. Caj."

The sounds of death once again ran through the halls of the church.

"I don't know about those two." Lois watched their two kids walk to the car. "They're going to have such hard lives."

Ginny didn't want to hear that because it was exactly what she thought. Or feared.

"Wandering stars, to whom is reserved the blackness of darkness forever," Lois looked at her. She smiled at Ginny. "From darkness comes enlightenment, from chaos comes order."

Now it was Ginny's turn to be surprised. "Why, Lois, that was so profound. Where did that statement come from?"

"Oh, I don't know" Lois smiled.

"Well, when I see bad things you always manage to bring out the good. From the moment you came to my house you've been like that; now more so. How have you been, anyway? I see your man talking around the reservation." Ginny stood primly next to her friend. She enjoyed the conversation.

Both women stood under Ginny's umbrella. The drizzle came down from the gray clouds. She saw the same dark clouds in the future where Lois saw the sunshine. How was that possible? She prepared for the worst while Lois waited for the best. Ginny never understood how she could be this way. She believed that the Indians had some influence in that. They had so little that anything was better than what they had. Maybe that's why they laughed all the time. They had to make light of their position. Or maybe it was something more.

"My Jonny is beginning to run around with the older boys. I worry when he gets in late. Or that he's drinking. But I don't worry about him."

It was odd how Lois put things. How could she not worry about him when she is worried about him? Ginny stopped. She wasn't making sense herself. All she knew was that Nikki-D was pulling away. She wasn't the same. How that affects the rest of her life, she didn't know. She wanted to protect her and keep her safe.

It was sad to hear that Jonny was running with those boys. Such a shy boy. With his speech impediment, Ginny knew why he hardly talked. His future was bleak as it was, but having something like that, too? Well...

"The one I worry about is Caj. He's like his father, seeing only what's in front of him. He drinks now. He doesn't learn anything in school. He has already hit his peak in school, with his sports. Now the real world is closing in on him. His sports can't protect him from the poverty we live in, and his classmates are leaving him. I wish he wouldn't drink and run around. But he needs something, or someone. And if its his cousins, then that's fine with me."

Ginny knew what she meant. The real world had closed in on all of them. She was glad that she had money and a good position in the community. Nobody would think of walking away from Nikki-D. She was still one of the most popular girls in school and had many friends. She wore the best clothes, even though Ginny had to go out and buy them for her because Nikki-D wanted to wear blue jeans and sweaters. Ginny thought after Nikki-D had her period, she would turn more into a woman. It was wishful thinking on her part. Nikki-D was blessed with beauty and brains, as many women were. Nikki-D just ignored the beauty.

"Its so sad about your little girl. Jonny has been talking to me about her. He's been telling me that she's hurt from the death in the country. She's such a little beauty. The boys will be after her soon. Then you'll be pulling out your hair in bundles." Lois laughed as she said this

"I wish. Nikki-D doesn't seem to worry about those things."

Lois looked at Ginny. Didn't she see the way Nikki-D looked at Caj? He was too old for her. She had those puppy-dog-love eyes every time she looked at him. Caj thought it was funny. Lois knew that in a few years he wouldn't be thinking like that. Ginny wasn't going to be ready for it. Lois remembered her own two daughters, Claire and Dani. Those two would make any mother go crazy. She stopped ... and laughed. They made her crazy. It was all right to think this, but she had to remember not to say things like that. Her kids took her words so seriously.

"I know. Jonny is slow like that, too. He's a deep thinker, so sex and things like that are going to be hard for him. Sometimes I wish I could put some of Caj in Jonny."

"Is it his speaking disorder?"

"I think so. They say so at the school. Always putting him in special classes. I don't know if it ever helps. Its hard to see him trying to talk like normal people. His father is ashamed of him. That makes it harder. He wants to speak right so his father will accept him. But that's not going to happen. He can't see that his father has his own problems. It hurts me to see him keep trying though."

"I guess its the opposite for Nikki-D and me. She has so much potential that she could do most anything. Her stubbornness keeps her from reaching that potential. Her father loves her so much that he lets her do almost anything she wants. I have to fight him on every issue when it comes to her. I'm always the bad guy. Lately though, he has been listening to me. He's not so quick to be on her side. He sees that she's special." Ginny watched her daughter as she spoke. All the love that she never received came rushing to the surface. Nikki-D is special.

"That's nice. She's so pretty."

"Yes. Beauty and brains: maybe I prayed too hard to have a perfect baby." They both laughed.

"Jonny is special in a different way. His thoughts are so deep. He seems to know what people are about right when he meets them. He's very spiritual. They say he saw his spirit power at a young age and it makes him see things that others can't see. He's such a little Indian. Acts just like them. And yet his father can't see it. A shame."

Ginny looked at this Swedish woman beside her. Lois had all the characteristics of the Swedish people. A tall woman, compared to Ginny; strong and stoic, with a determined mind. They must look like a sight, standing together and talking and laughing about their kids. They were from opposite backgrounds. It didn't mean anything to them because now they were friends who had the same fears about their kids as anyone else. Ginny looked at this gentle woman and was happy that she was her friend.

Ginny frowned. "How bad are things?"

Lois looked at her for a second. Then she looked at the ground. "Everyone is having a hard time. These people lost everything and barely make ends meet ... you know that. They always were able to make fun and laugh at their hardships. Now they don't laugh. I can see the deep hopelessness in their eyes. Its going to be hard. I don't see anyone helping them very soon. Most of the white people on the reservation would rather they just slip away and sink under the sea. Its lucky they're so communal, or I think it would be a lot worse."

"The church does all it can." It was all Ginny could say. In her meetings with other women, she could hear their fear of the Indians. Then they stared at her because of the way she looked, with her Asiatic features that most of the Indians had. She could see these women putting her in the same category as the Indians and that made her mad.

"Oh I know. I wasn't saying anything or accusing. Its just reality. We have to search hard for the things we need. The drinking is getting worse. It has to get worse before it can get better. Franc drank then stopped. He says its because his people need him..."

"Nick still drinks with the men at the club. But he's not an alcoholic."

Lois frowned at Ginny.

"I mean ... I'm sorry, Lois. He drinks like the others. The fighting and screaming has stopped, but that's all. He's a good man who takes good care of us. Nikki-D adores him. That's what makes it so frustrating sometimes. She's just like him. And I don't know if that's good."

"I guess we just try the best we can and go on from there." Lois listened to her friend. She remembered being like that once. Then she saw the light and the weight came off her shoulders. She smiled at this. The memory made her feel good. "I have so many kids that I barely have time for one when the next demands my attention. Franc is gone most of the time. We had no money. It was getting hard. But Jonny ... You could see the disappointment on Franc's face. Jonny must have represented all the disappointments in Franc's life, because he would not let the boy alone, demanding Jonny talk right. It just wasn't going to happen. Franc took it hard and now he hardly talks to Jonny. It hurt

Jonny bad, but its probably best for him because he can just be who he is now. A very special little boy."

Ginny could see the love in her friend. They both had their special kids with their special problems for them. Thinking about it, she knew that, given the choice, neither one of them would give them up. It was the one thing going for Nikki-D and Jonny.

The wind kicked up from the beach. Clouds moved in from the Northeast. Winter cold swept past them. The clouds grew darker and heavier and lower. Ginny watched Nikki-D and Jonny. Storm clouds hung over them as they talked. The rain started coming down hard. It was time to go.

"I guess we should go before everyone gets wet. I'll come and see you later. OK?"

Lois just nodded her head. She was watching them too. The two women moved down to the cars to get out of the storm.

16

SPIRITS

He stood on the little dirt road in front of Tulalip Bay. Rows of eight houses sat facing the bay. They stood in between Totem Beach and Hermosa Point. The houses were nothing more then little shacks. Gray and decrepit, they barely stood against the east wind that came from the mouth of the bay. The two points acted as a buffer against the wind so not much blew through. Except during thunder storms. Then cold winds came flying in from the North, kicking up the waves and surf, sending its frozen fingers to make life miserable for those in its path. It was like that tonight.

Jonny was cold from the wind. He looked at the gray shack he called home. Its colorless exterior blended with the gray clouds and wind. Its old wood, worn and aged, tried its best to stay together. He stood there, not moving; uncertain whether he should go in or not, or even if it would be warmer on the inside. The house looked hostile and unfeeling.

The wind picked up some. He was getting cold. He watched trees behind the houses blow back and forth, indicating how much the wind was blowing. There weren't many trees: twenty or thirty in an orchard, mostly apple trees. Up above them, between two silos was the old barn. It was the basketball court. Most of the people went there to play. Jonny used to go there but he stopped. He had no interest anymore.

The wind gusted up again. He looked down to the docks. He watched the boats bobbing up and down against the wooden planks. Coy's dock went out to the channel. A big, red building covered the high dock that ran from the road. Sitting high on its pilings, it provided cover for those who wanted to unload their nets into their boats. There would be no loading tonight.

Jonny decided to go in. He had no other choice. Walking to the house, he looked back one last time. The clouds in the sky were moving faster. The waves beat against the rocks and cliffs. He shook his head. It was going to be a miserable night.

The darkness hit him when he went in. The house was completely dark and he stood waiting for his eyes to adjust. There was no electricity, so he searched around for a candle. The living room table was to his right and a candle was standing in the middle of it. Jonny moved toward it.

He tripped over something and froze. Something on the floor was moving. Hair rose on his arms. He moved back a step. His eyes adjusted and he could see. There were blankets everywhere. He knew there were people sleeping under them. He didn't know who. His mother must have let another family stay there for the night. She always did that: Let people stay and eat with them. Most would stay for a week, never any longer than that. When the thrift store opened at the beginning of each week, they would be in line waiting to get their commodities and then they would go home. He never understood how she had enough food for them. It amazed him that she could feed her family let alone others, but she did. Jonny stepped over the body on the floor and grabbed the candle. There was a box of matches next to it and he picked that up, too. He took one out and closed the lid, striking the match against the rough grain, once, twice, three times, until it flared. Putting it against the wick of the candle; he waited until it caught fire. Another flame shot up; now he could see the dank living room: the old, ripped-up couch sat against the big wall, a couple of chairs, and that was all there was to it. A feeling of despondency came over him. He desperately wanted to change all of this. He didn't know how. He put the candle out once he had gotten his bearings. His eyes worked at readjusting to the dark. It took a little longer, and he waited.

A sound floated toward him, caressing his face then floating on by. A murmer ... he never moved. He waited for something to happen, but nothing did. The sound came in her soft voice. Her voice was a hushed secret in the shade of the night. She was in the dark somewhere but he couldn't see her. Shhhhh ... her undertone voice came to him like a light in the night, warning him. He tried to see her but it was too dark. He could imagine her blond features, her blue eyes on him. Her voice was a voice of love floating to him in the dark. He followed it to the kitchen. The dark was broken by the crackling of the fire. The peat in the wood popped and burned in the night. Still he couldn't see his mother. She was in her bedroom with his father. There were no lights.

Even if there were, she wouldn't turn them on for fear of waking the man beside her. Jonny could feel her watching him. He checked the wood in the stove, but she had already put some in and the flames would burn most of the night. It amazed Jonny that she could keep the stove going all night. It was as if she never slept, always watching over the big brood that was her family.

"You're home early." Her soft voice still floated to him.

He tensed his throat muscles to whisper. "Mm ... mm. I know." He never said much. He wanted to, but if he stayed too long, he might wake his father. She would never move until she was absolutely sure his father was out for the rest of the night.

"There's some food in the pan on the table." She knew he would be hungry. His mother knew everything about her kids.

Jonny went to the table and lifted the pan, finding some cornbread and beans in a bowl. He sat at the small table facing the dark doorway to his parent's bedroom. Jonny was alert. Eating his food fast in case his father woke. He got up and put the bowl in the sink, gray and cracked. The grayness of everything depressed him. He needed to talk. It was late as he looked out the cracked window at the night-sky. It won't get any better, he thought. Jonny walked to the stairs in the hallway. The world was coming down on him and he had no one to turn to.

Then he heard the sound float to him. Her voice was no more than a whisper in the night, "We'll talk in the morning."

Jonny began to feel better. Jonny couldn't wait any longer. He had to get out; find some freedom from the depression. He stopped listening to the words of the old ones. They lived in the past. Jonny saw the world today. It was getting bad. His spirit was dead. Nikki-D was the only one that he talked to. They both knew it was bad and tried to find a way out. Nikki-D wanted to go away. She said she needed to find herself. She said her mother wanted to send her away to a private school. Nikki-D was thinking about it.

Jonny never thought of leaving the Rez. It was his home. His people always lived there. His father left to go to war a long time ago. He came back; as far as Jonny could tell, everyone always came back when they left. It would be no different for him. He wished Nikki-D wouldn't talk about leaving. He wanted her to stay. He was smart enough to know that it would be a mistake for him to say that. She had to go. Her people were like that.

"Jonny. Let's go." It was Caj, in front of the house. It was time to go out. There was a dance tonight, one he could attend. His heart started beating faster. He wanted to go. There were a lot of girls at these dances. Jonny never danced, but it felt good to watch them. He liked girls.

"Jonny, if you don't hurry we're going to leave you." Caj had already started drinking. He had been cut from the team. He was tired of it anyway. The coach kept him on the bench even though he was better than some of the other kids. Everyone on the Res. knew why the coach did this. They talked among themselves but never talked to the coach about the prejudice. The coach never saw himself as he was.

Jonny ran to catch up with Caj. Time was running out. They had to hurry. Jonny was running as fast as he could. He had been running for most of his life. Sweat ran down his light-brown hair, down his forehead, into intense, brown eyes and down his face. His body was hot despite the cold outside. He sweated. His body came from his father's people: people who worked in the waters and woods all their lives. The weather made his clothes stick to him and he felt muggy. He saw a small, white fence behind the 76 station and rushed over. The lights of the night caught his silhouette as he disappeared.

Jonny looked at his hands. They were turning blue and he could see his veins sticking out of the skin. He must have passed out. Lying in the ditch, he rubbed them together again. The drizzle fell from the sky. A cold, gray, cloudy sky loomed over him. Fourth Street had lights on every corner. Dimmed by the overcast nights, they gave little light. Jonny looked at the neon signs of the gas stations. 76, Chevron, and Shell were the highest and the best lit. He turned his eyes away. The light hurt. He looked at his hands again. They were cold; real cold. His whole body felt wet because of the drizzle. His head was spinning. Jonny closed his eyes for a second. The spinning settled down and he opened them again.

"I'm not here." Hopelessness came to him in the dark gray clouds above. His life was over. He was fourteen. He hung his head low in the mud, runoff water flowing around him. He lay in the small town of Marysville, Washington. Jonny thought about his death. His life was meaningless and empty. No happiness came to him; even if it did, he wouldn't know what it looked like. The coldness of the coming morning seeped through his pores. Jonny began to cry, his head lying in the mud and water of the ditch. He was too tired to raise it above the wet earth. He no longer wanted to.

The gray clouds in the sky parted and a big thunder clash burst through the dark night. The rain poured down in torrents. Jonny's heart jumped. He was afraid. He closed his eyes again, squeezing them together as hard as he could. Another clash came from the sky. He shivered and sank back against the fence. The black-and-gray clouds swirled above him, showing their force to him. He wanted some place to hide, but all he could do was lie there in the mud, his mouth open, head spinning. The world was swallowing him up into a huge vortex, spinning faster and faster until he couldn't stand it anymore. The thunderstorm kept up, clashing and splitting, the rain pouring down from the sky like tears that wouldn't stop. Jonny's tears joined the rain. His small body shivered in the cold night. Suddenly the clashing stopped; silence followed. Jonny waited for the spinning to stop. The rain no longer came down. The spinning slowed. His eyes opened.

"Ah-chee-dah." The words came out of his mouth before he could stop them. His whole body clenched up. Fists balled, ready to defend himself. He couldn't believe his eyes. "What the hell."

A ghostly wolf-pup stood in the distance. Shadowy, it stood with its head down in front of its huge paws. It stayed there, not moving closer. Gray eyes watched his every move. The pup's head swayed back and forth. Then it jumped up, leaping in the air, its spirit alive and wanting to play. It bounced back up, bringing its head down to its paws, kicking out and then down. Then it stopped. Looking at Jonny, it began to walk to him, sniffing. As it came closer it began to change.

He must be dreaming. He would close his eyes and then it would be gone. Jonny did that. He closed his eyes, then opened them.

"Holy shit."

The wolf-pup's face was only inches from his nose, his soulful gray eyes penetrating and absorbing. Jonny couldn't move. A tranquil peace came over him as he stared into those eyes. The wolf-pup's serene presence luminesced in the lights of the town. It moved over and surveyed the street, where cars waited for the traffic light to change. When it came back, it continued to watch Jonny. Then it looked out, across the town and its streets. It looked beyond the lights of the town into the dark underpass. He kept staring beyond the underpass to the reservation.

The reservation. Officer Pete didn't understand the people on the other side of the underpass. It was as if they lived in perpetual darkness, the evergreen trees hiding all those that relied on the light. The starlight couldn't even penetrate the trees. It was the same with the people of the reservation: small, dark people who kept to themselves. Savages, really. The thought didn't surprise him. He always had these thoughts about them. Where the thoughts came from, he didn't know or care. It was just him. He compared that darkness to his side of the town. He loved his town, even though he lived on the Rez. He grew up here, as did his father, and his grandfather before him. It was his town and being the law of the town kept anyone from saying different. As officer Pete tried to see beyond the darkness, he sat in the comfort of his town.

Jonny understood what this was. The fear in his heart grew. His heart felt like it was going to explode, and still the fear grew. The wolf-pup stood there. Like an extension of Jonny, it had ashen skin, brown veins, limp and pallid, with large gray eyes. It was spooky.

"I must be dead," Jonny said.

The fear still grew inside him. His breathing was labored and uneven. The wolf-pup just stood and watched. Jonny began to stiffen, his body like a corpse. The air escaped from his lungs and he couldn't get it back in. No! He didn't want to die. It wouldn't stop: his heart beat faster, his body became stiffer, the fear grew. Then he looked toward the apparition that brought the fear: the wolf-pup.

In that second, Jonny could see. He watched the spirit-pup, and a peacefulness started to form. It was way in the back of his mind. It was there, and it was growing. He knew the wolf-pup was there to help him. Jonny had faith in this. The peaceful feeling expanded, catching the fear that wanted to overwhelm him. The battle was between the two. Jonny became a spectator as fear and faith raced against each other. The wolf-pup watched.

Suddenly the wolf-pup started moving, stepping over the small, white fence that surrounded the 76 station. It's legs moving faster and faster as the cars waited for the light to turn green. Jonny wanted to call out to him; warn him about the cops. He kept his mouth shut. He didn't want to get busted himself. "Hey, every man for himself." The alcohol justified his reasoning. He looked up again to see the wolf-pup at the underpass. Its dark shadow concealed him for a second, then there he was, waving at Jonny to come. It stood underneath the pass getting dry, watching him, making Jonny want to go. Fear kept him looking for the unseen men in brown. Then he decided. He was off, over the fence, and running for the darkness. Well, more like staggering toward the darkness. He was moving, and he was picking up speed.

The wolf-pup walked into the shadows and disappeared. Jonny had to reach the underpass and the reservation beyond. Only then would he be safe. Officer Pete jumped as he saw the boy running across the station.

"There's the little shit! Let's get him." He and his partner were sitting in the alley, waiting, since the taverns shut down. It was two in the morning and the parties were over, too. Now it was just waiting. There was only one way out of town that lead to the reservation and he knew they would have to come past them.

"How did he get past us?" His partner's brow furrowed as he asked. "Probably crawled on his belly." He didn't care as long as they could get him now. The chase was on. Their lights blazed around and around as they moved out from their hiding place. Tires screeched on the cold, wet cement. It would only take them a few seconds to get to the underpass; a few seconds to stop him from returning home.

Jonny could hear the sirens coming around the corner. He knew he only had a split-second to react. The light at the intersection turned green. The cars began to go and then hit their brakes as Jonny ran in front of them. Angry drivers yelled obscenities at him.

"Get off the road, you drunken Indian."

He heard their voices, yet didn't hear, as he chased his spirit. It was raining now.

Hard droplets hit his face; his wet hair stuck to him. He kept running as the police car roared closer and closer. Finally, he made it across the road to the other side. The underpass was in front of him. Dark trees stood high on the other side. The darkness comforted him and he knew it was home.

"Faster, or he'll make it to the underpass." Pete hated the Indians: the way they looked, their total drunkenness. As if they were in some other world and didn't give a shit about what went on around them. Pissing anywhere they wanted, fighting and passing out on the sides of the buildings. He hated their indifference to going to jail when he busted them. He hated them being in his town. What he hated most....

"Look—he's slowing down. He doesn't know we can go beyond the underpass now. He thinks we have to stop. We got him." Officer Pete's partner sped up. The chase was almost over.

Jonny was at the underpass. His adrenaline ebbed, and he slowed to a walk. He was safe. He made it. Walking, he looked at the trees. The wolf-pup was standing at the edge. The pup jumped up and down frantically. Something was wrong.

They say spirits always talked like that. Sort of off to themselves, using their own language, and it was up to you to figure them out. Suddenly, Jonny's antennae went up. His ears could hear the tires coming. The police car was racing to catch him. His blood rushed to his head and body and he began to run again. Something's wrong. They aren't supposed to come past the underpass. He looked back and the red-and-blue lights were almost upon him. Panic hit him as he knew that he made a mistake. His legs moved faster, digging into the ground, pushing him towards the trees. It was darker on this side of the freeway and if he made to the trees they could never find him. Only twenty more yards.

"Shit! He's heading for the trees." Officer Pete's tense body was sitting high in the seat. His face was against the front window, trying to see in the rain. Dark clouds, low and ominous, hung next to the ground. He could barely see the boy running because there were no lights on the other side. The dark frightened him. He could see the boy go into the woods. They were too late.

Jonny stood in the shadows of the trees, breathing deeply. Wet foliage grew knee-high, the shrubbery keeping the forest floor alive and vigorous. Pristine and primal, a low cloud of mist hung next to the ground. Wildflowers stood high above the mist, attracting insect and animal life. This was nature's way. It felt like his lungs were going to explode. The tree he was standing by hid him from the road. He looked down and saw a large, black beetle crawl across his shoe. Slugs slowly moved, leaving a light trail of slime behind them. Jonny looked up. The police car came to a screeching halt and he saw the one man he hated get out of the passenger side.

He knew they would never come into the woods. It disturbed him that they were coming out further and further. They held their long, black flashlights above their heads. Two beams of light flashed through the woods. They could only see the light and nothing else. Jonny smiled. The wolf-pup turned and headed into the reservation.

Looping down the trail, the pup's head moved back and forth, sniffing the night and the dark-green leaves and bushes. The pup blended in with the white mist that covered the ground. The woods began to look ominous and threatening. Jonny saw the pup jump from something on the trail. It whined and moved on down the trail. Jonny looked back at the road, but he knew he couldn't go that way. He hated walking through the woods at night. He knew it would be only a short trip until he came out on the main road. He moved off, following the shadow in the night.

Finally! The cold, black road lay in front of Jonny. The road cut through the reservation, giving light and a clear path for those who walked it. It was eight miles to where Jonny had to go. It would take him some time when he had to walk. He never liked to walk.

He had been walking for miles and the weather was letting up. The cold wetness chilled his body.

Standing on the hill just above Priest Point, he looked around. In the darkness, eerie shadows danced. The wolf-pup was twenty yards ahead of him. Its loping stride carried it down the road. Then it stopped.

The wolf-pup began to whine. Nose high in the air, it sniffed, trying to determine who was there. It moved to the side of the road, poking his head into the tall grass that grew just before the forest. Jonny watched. He stopped walking, not knowing what was happening. Suddenly the pup jumped back and let out a yelp. It ran back to Jonny. Jonny's heart raced.

The tall grass began to move and a rabbit ran across the road. The wolf-pup moved forward and back. It walked ahead of Jonny, keeping its head down, and sniffed side to side were the rabbit crossed. Jonny could see the fear in the pup. Its whine became louder and louder; then it took off running.

"That's all I need." Jonny watched with disgust on his face, "A cowardly spirit."

The green fir and alder trees on each side of the road hid things ... bad things. The Stee-tots and Stick Indians moved just beyond the tree line. Fear rushed through Jonny as he thought he heard something. They were moving closer. People say they get close to you so they can use their powers: powers of the mind. They talk to you in silent voices.

"Shit." Jonny looked from side to side as he walked. Fear kept him alert and he clenched his fist, ready for them if they came. The wind blew through the trees, tense and continuous, singing its songs, talking to those who would listen. Jonny listened with fear. Something was there. He couldn't tell. His ears picked up only the sounds humans can hear. He couldn't hear the voices that he knew spoke between the trees. He slowly lowered his head and moved on down the road, eyes watching the sides of the road, fear keeping him on edge. He was determined not to let them take over his mind.

The wolf-pup moved down the road. His four-legged gait kept a good pace for Jonny. Jonny watched its shoulders rise, then hunch down low. Suddenly, it stopped. The wolf-pups ears perked up, pointing toward the distant trees.

Jonny's ears perked up, too. From the distance came a familiar sound; a sound that comforted him, and told him he was almost home. It was the percussion sound of the drums. Thump-thump-thump, thump-thump-thump, thump-thump-thump..thump thump. It carried over the winds and rested in his soul. His heart raced and he picked up his steps. He was close. Heading due west, he turned on the Old Tulalip road. He walked until he came to the white totem poles that split the road in two directions. Each road went to one side of the bay. Voices followed the drum beats: human voices, singing. Jonny went to his right, where the drums and the voices were the loudest.

In the dark he could see the plank-cedar building that hid the fires. The lone dirt road with its big potholes led to the long house, to his people. Jonny was at the beginning of this road. From the distance, he could see shadows dancing on the side of the Cedar building. It was the long house. Jonny smiled and began to walk down the lone dirt path.

Outside the long house, one big fire burned. His people were playing another tribe in the Slahal (bone) games. Eee-oh-oh, Eee-oh-oh; their voices sang in unison. They were singing the Tulalip song. The other tribe was listening. All were swaying-Eee-oh-oh, Eee oh-oh - the music came from the Tulalips. They were singing their song and swaying back and forth with the rhythm of the drums. Both sides faced each other next to the fire.

Raymond Moses sat in the middle of the line and swayed more than the others. His hands moved in front of him, then behind him as his people drummed their songs. He held the bones in his hand and the man directly across from him closely watched his hands. It was up to him to pick the right hand with the right bone in it. Kneeling, the two groups of players had people standing in back of them, drinking and betting on the outcome of the bones.

Everyone was having a good time. Their voices and the drums told all those within the reservation of their fun. Jonny came up to them and watched for a second. The flames crackled and the heat warmed his cold body. The rain had quit and the cold morning clouds were all that was left. He looked out onto the cold, black water of Tulalip Bay. The cool water rippled inside the bay. Jonny could see the point beyond the spit, the mouth almost closed by the two points of Mission Hill and

Hermosa. He moved closer to the fire, putting his hands out to warm them. It felt good. It all felt good to him. He was home.

He had been sitting on a log next to the fire for some time. Jonny was sad. He couldn't make sense of his world. It all became meaningless and destructive. He gave a big sigh. No longer wet, he looked for the wolf-pup. It was standing by the door. The long house doors were open. The people inside were waiting. Jonny got up and walked to the door. It was time to go in. He took one look back at the fires rising high into the sky, the people singing, and the drums beating. Then he walked in. He walked into his death,

17

DROWNING

"Noooooo"

"Crash!" the bowl with the water fell and hit the floor. Jonny's fingers shook from his mother's scream. He was never so frightened in his life. Something was extremely wrong.

"Its too hot in here. I got to get out." She rolled over and over on her bed. Dani and Clair were trying to keep her quiet, but she was too far gone.

"Jonny is bringing some water to cool you down, Mom. He'll be here in just a minute." Dani looked at her sister, who was crying as she held her mother's arm.

"Yes Mom, Jonny will be here in a second with the water." Clair watched her mother in agony. She was the sensitive girl who always wanted things to be right. She always helped her mother; not like Dani, who never seemed to be here until something bad happened. She was glad Dani was here now. She always knew what to do. She took control. Something like this was too much for her. Clair felt like everyone was drowning and there was nothing that they could do.

"Jonny ... We need that water." Dani was of the same opinion. She couldn't show how frightened she was. The other kids needed her now. Why was it always her? She was supposed to go with her friends tomorrow but now she wouldn't be able to. Dani wiped her mother's face and forehead with a wash cloth. Her mother was sweating tons of water. Dani didn't know why. The night was cold.

Jonny ran to the old sink, put the bowl under the spigot and turned on the water. The water rushed out, filling the bowl. He didn't turn it off. Taking the bowl, he walked as fast as he could with his eyes on the water, trying to balance it so none would spill.

The lamp by the table was on and the girls were sitting beside their mother on the bed. His mother lay there as if nothing was wrong. She turned to him as he came into the room with the water.

"Jonny. My little boy. Come here and give your mother a hug." She smiled.

Jonny looked at his older sister. Dani had a frown on her face. He didn't know what to do. His mother scared him.

"Don't worry, Jonny. I'm all right." She smiled again.

"Bring that water over here, Jonny. I need to get this cloth wet."

Jonny brought the water over to Dani. He could tell that her hands were nervous, too. She went on like nothing was wrong and everything was in control. Jonny admired his sisters for that. They were always the ones Mom would turn to when she needed help. It was a comforting thought for him.

"Where's Caj?" Dani didn't have time to think - she just wanted all of this to end so she could get on with her life.

Jonny shrugged his shoulders. Caj left when his mother started getting worse. He didn't stay around much anymore.

"Where's Dad?"

Jonny pointed out to the living room. His father was passed out on the floor. He had one of his fits again. Epilepsy. He was a grand-mall epileptic. He was having more and more fits when he came home. The drinking wasn't helping him much. Now he was yelling about the politics of the tribe, about the people who were running the tribe and how stupid they were. Jonny didn't know who he was talking about. He would hear the names, but he was too young to know them.

Tonight his father started out the same way. He wanted the tribe to fight the white people – something about Public law 280, a law that put the tribe under state jurisdiction. His voice would rise each time he brought it up. The little ones were crying because of being sick all week. His mother was trying to take care of them and listen to their father at the same time.

"Arr ... you listening to me! Those bastards. They're selling us down the river. I want to write a letter." He was sitting in his chair with his legs crossed. His head would go down and up. Most of the time you didn't know if he was acting; trying to catch you off-guard.

"Just be quiet, Franc. Can't you see the girls are sick?"

"I don't give a shit! I want to write a letter now!" He pointed his finger down. Then he started coughing. He put his hand over his mouth. The spit still flew out.

"Get the damn paper out."

The girls cried louder. His mother didn't go to them like she used to. She didn't do anything but stand there. The week had been rough for her. The kids were sick. Franc was drinking more and more. He became more erratic. She wasn't getting any sleep. She was going out every day standing in line to get food. She had to go to the food bank and get commodities.

Sometimes Nikki-D's mother had been bringing food for them. She would sit and have coffee and they would talk. Most of the time the kids were in school so they could talk freely. She had become a good friend to Lois Esque.

Jonny's mother had been deteriorating until she finally collapsed into her own world. He could feel the pain of her life. The failure.

The kids could see it coming for a long time. At first it was the little things that didn't add up, like the time when Jonny was watching his mom make a bottle of milk for the baby. Everything seemed to be going OK, except Jonny noticed the milk smelled bad.

"Mom I think the milk is sour."

His mother put her little finger into the milk and tasted it. Yes, it was sour. Then she went right on filling up the bottle.

"Isn't it sour? It sure smells." He was sure it was sour because the fridge broke down last week and the milk didn't last long.

Shawn was ready to eat.

"Mom..."

Then Caj came in and took the bottle from her.

"Its all right, Mom." He looked at Jonny to tell him not to say anything. Jonny was silent.

"Why don't you take a nap, Mom." Caj wasn't going to let her do any feeding that day.

It was other things like that. Sometimes she was there and sometimes she wasn't. The house was messy and nothing was getting done. She still went to get food, but you never knew what she would bring back to eat. It was scary.

They could see the crippling effects of depression attacking her. She was no longer the mother they knew, nor would she be ever again. The house rested in its own gloom. The core had been attacked to a point that left it helpless and floundering. That was their mother.

Then she had begun to cry. First it was lone tears at any time. They would run down her face as she was talking, or whenever. It was eerie to Jonny to watch his mother cry without acknowledging she was crying.

It was beyond her control. The silence of her tears hurt. What could you do? She acted as if it wasn't happening.

It was her dreams, and all the hopes that were her life, leaving one by one until she came to the end. Could they all have been illusions? Her mind grappled with this. The rainbow was heavy with rain. Drowning bubbles floating from her body. At the same time, the crushing weight of reality forced her down grinding her inspirations into the fictional creations of her fantasy. Her mind unable to cope, she destroyed both reality and fantasy and was abandoned to the shadows.

More and more, she would stay in bed. The girls would have to get food as best they could. Their father was no good. He just went to the tavern to avoid his life. At least they didn't have to listen to him night after night.

He would come home with his drunk family and friends. Lois tried to maintain her house through the shouting and fighting, but was it breaking down.

"Dirty fucking pigs!" Frank argued about the tribe.

"Yea, Franc, they're ripping off the money that belongs to us. How do they all get food when we go hungry? I don't see them standing in line." Georgie, his younger brother, was talking drunk again. It was always the same old line.

"I think we should get a petition going to find out where the money goes." Franc always said this when he talked about money and the tribe.

"Hey, did you drink my beer?" Georgie looked around but couldn't see anythingbecause he was too drunk.

"No."

"Yes you did."

"Fuck you! I did not." Franc stood up while he said this, his anger rising. "You calling me a thief?"

Georgie swung at his brother and everyone got out of the way.

Its funny how the kids all began to talk lower. In whispers. There was less and less talking for fear of disturbing their mother. Jonny's father wanted her to be the woman that he married. He wanted control back in his life.

"You're weak, woman!" he yelled at her. "You're just doing this! Using your weakness to get out of what you're supposed to do. I want some food! I want it now."

The kids didn't hide that night. They weren't going to let him hurt her anymore. They stood together, all yelling at him to leave her alone.

It was too late. Their mother heard the words of her husband. She was weak, powerless to do what she was supposed to do, incapable of being a wife to her husband. The more he said, the more wooden she became. She was paralyzed.

Caj always moved when there was trouble. It was better than just standing around doing nothing. He knew there was something very wrong with his mother. His emotions were immediate and strong, and he had to do something to help her. The others looked like ghosts hovering over her trying to make her life easier. He knew that it wouldn't help. He had to find someone who would bring back his mother. He had to do it fast.

Most of the people of the tribe were in the same kind of trouble and couldn't help even if they wanted to. There wasn't much hope for any of them. Caj was going to change that. He would break away. Somehow. First, he had to take care of his family. His mother needed him. He wouldn't let her down.

When he ran out of the house, he really didn't know where he was going. It was a spontaneous thing. He saw the look on the other kids' faces when he left but he didn't have time to worry about that. When he passed his father stretched out on the floor he wanted to stop and kick him for what he did to their mother. It wouldn't do any good. What he needed was someone to help. There was only one person that he knew of that might be able to.

He stood in front of the big house, like Jonny must have, years ago. He didn't go in and didn't leave. Caj had known about Nikki-D's mother coming down to the house. At first, he was skeptical. Then he started putting two and two together. Each time Ginny Thomas would come to the house they would have food to eat. It was good food, too; not commodities and food-bank food. The kids would try not to attack the food as their mother put it on the table. The older ones held back so the younger kids could get their share first. When their mother heard them eating and laughing, they could see a smile cross her face. It was the only time they saw it in the past year. Caj knew of one person that may be able to help his mother. He walked up to the front door and knocked.

Rap-rap-rap. It was the door. Someone was knocking. They all remained silent. Rap-rap-rap.

"Answer the door, Jonny." Dani soaked the cloth again. Their mother was asleep; At least for now.

Jonny went to the front door and opened it.

She stood there all prim and proper. Jonny couldn't believe his eyes. Not knowing what to do or say, he waited.

"Well, aren't you going to invite me in, young man?" Ginny Thomas didn't have much patience at this hour of the night.

Jonny looked back at his sisters for help.

"Well......" Her steely eyes narrowed.

Jonny opened the door wider for her. She stepped in.

The room and the house were in chaos. The mess was overwhelming. Ginny crinkled her nose. The smell and the stink overpowered her. She looked down at the floor at an inert body: Lois's husband lay prone in a drunken stupor. Face to the side, his eyes were closed and the way he was snoring, he wouldn't wake for some time.

"Where's your mother?"

The young man trembled in front of her, so different from the boy who defied her at her daughter's party. She could see deep strength in him, the same strength she saw in Lois. She began to make her way through the clutter on the floor, tip-toeing around things she could not identify. Jonny led the way.

The room was dark, lit by one old lamp without a shade. Lois lay in the bed, heavy blankets over her. Two young women held each of her hands as she tried to get up. They were talking to her. They talked at the same time.

"Mom you can't get up. You're sick."

"Please, Mom, don't do this. We'll take care of things."

They both shut up when they saw Ginny standing there. She went right over to the bed. Looking down at Lois, she could see that the woman was in bad shape.

"You, I want you to go and get a big bowl of water." Her finger was pointed at Dani. Dani frowned, but did as she was told.

"You, what's your name?"

"Clair." She liked this woman who ordered her older sister around.

"Clair, I want you to go to my home and tell my husband to call Dr. Johnson. Tell him that I want him to come here at once. Do you understand what I want so far?"

Clair nodded her head yes.

"Good, then I want you to wait until the doctor gets there and bring him down here. You understand?"

Clair nodded again.

Ginny waited. "Well, what are you waiting for?"

Clair got up to go.

"Oh, and tell my husband to feed you something while you wait"

Then Clair was out the door. Ginny looked at the face of her friend. Lois's skin was pale. There wasn't enough blood flowing. Not only was her skin pallid and anemic but so was Lois, her movements slow and disjointed. Ginny's heart sank. This woman was so strong when they first met... to see her reduced to this!

Lois's eyes opened. They had deep, dark circles under them. She tried to focus, but it took too much energy.

Ginny could tell that the woman was split. On one hand she was trying to fight for her life and on the other, not caring to live. It was something Ginny went through many times in her life. Now her friend was fighting the battle. All Ginny could do was remain by her side and help.

And one other thing.

Ginny knelt beside her friend and held her hand in hers. She brought both hands up to her forehead. She lifted her sister back into her arm with her knee. She was slipping down. Morgan-Mckenzi nodded yes. She was tired. Now that there was a grown-up here to take charge, they could go to sleep. Right now that was all she wanted to do.

"OK. Go to bed now."

Morgan-Mckenzi went up with the little ones.

Ginny could see that there was much work to be done. She took off her coat and hat.

Dani came in with the water. She and Jonny were talking as she got the water. She wanted to know who this woman was, coming into their home like this. As usual, Jonny just shrugged his shoulders.

"Here's the water."

"Good. Uh...Dani."

"Dani ... we have a lot of work to do. I want to know who and what everyone should be doing. Tonight, in the morning and so on. Do you understand?"

"You don't have to keep asking if we understand. We do..."

Ginny could tell she was making a mistake with this young woman; such a pretty girl. She must be a heartbreaker, used to having things her own way.

"I'm sorry. But we need to work together to get your mother through this. I'm her friend. I want to help. I'm here to help. But I will need to know things. I need you to work with me on this. OK?"

Dani knew she was right. She had such a strong presence, everything so proper. Her dark eyes watched Dani as she thought. She began to think about who and what the kids should be doing. She began to recite them to Ginny.

At the end, Dani talked about Caj going out to check the nets. He probably wouldn't be home and someone would have to go out to the nets. Jonny went out with Caj, but Caj was the fisherman. Jonny would have to go himself.

Ginny watched the boy as his sister was talking about him. There were so many of them. All tried to do their part for the family.

"Are you able to go out on your own?"

Jonny shrugged his shoulders. "Mmm-mm ... yes."

She could tell he was nervous with her there. He still remembered her crass treatment of him. She detected no animosity nor hate from him. Such a strange boy. Lois's arms moved out. "Jonny. I'm all right. You do as they say. You go out tomorrow."

She was sweating gallons of water. Ginny didn't like this.

"Go to bed, Jonny, and get some rest before you go out." Ginny gave him a small smile of encouragement.

"Jonnyyy ... come here and give me a hug. Jonny. I can't see you. The fog." He didn't move, Looking at Ginny to see if it was all right.

"Give your mother a hug."

Jonny went over to the bed. He looked down into the sad eyes of his mother. She was leaving him. This he knew.

She was fading fast. She no longer made sense. Lapsing into times before and after. Today's life ebbed into the gulf. The relentless pounding of her life gave way to tranquillity. At the same time, she surrendered her mortal existence. She passed into the next phase of her life. She looked at Jonny one more time. He was the only one that understood.

Jonny could feel the pain as grief overwhelmed him. He didn't cry. So many years of suffering made his grief that much more. He grabbed her hand. He didn't want her to leave him. It was selfish. He was just a little boy who wanted his mother. The same one he always knew. He was afraid of change.

He felt the pressure in his hand as she let go and the fog clouded everything. Ginny felt worn and tired. The doctor had come and he put Lois in the hospital. He said she was having a nervous breakdown and would have to be watched for some time. They came and put her on a gurney, tying the straps around her so she wouldn't hurt herself if she woke. There wasn't much chance of that since the doctor had given her a heavy sedative. Ginny held her hand over to the ambulance, never letting go. She was brought to the Providence hospital.

Dani was with her all the way. Ginny was so hyper from all the commotion that she told her husband that she needed to stay and clean up. He came down with the doctor to make sure she was all right. Then he left and said he would stay home tomorrow and wait for her.

Since then, Dani and Ginny worked hard to clean up the house. It was such a mess. How could people live like this? Clair went to bed after admitting she was very tired from the last week.

Ginny looked at part of the reason for the pain in this house. Franc Esque was snoring in the bed that Lois just left. It took all their might and persuasion to get him off the floor and onto the bed. Together, she and Dani managed to put him to bed.

Then they went to work on cleaning up the house. She would have to come daily and make sure the kids kept things clean. They had no food. She checked the cabinets to see. There was just powdered milk. Her anger was building. Now she knew why it was important for Jonny to go out and check the nets. They needed food. It was that simple.

This wasn't the America Ginny knew. It was so hard to see people still so poor that they couldn't even put food on the table. She knew that Lois's house wasn't the only one in this condition. She passed the church with its line of Indians waiting for their food.

She would always be embarrassed because she saw this blond woman standing among the short, dark women, talking and laughing with them. Ginny couldn't see how they could laugh with all their suffering. They were all alike. Lois was a part of them. She remembered Lois telling her once that everyone suffers sometimes. Some people just don't want what to admit it. Then she looked at Ginny.

Now Ginny had her sleeves rolled up, cleaning. It took her away from the suffering.

Jonny sat in the murky fog, his mind dulled by the recent events. The boat rocked in the still water. He felt in a trance. He gazed out but could see nothing. He was trying to stay awake. At least he didn't have to go to school today. It was Saturday. When he woke, it was still dark. His befuddled mind rebelled against being forced to wake. He had to get up and check the nets.

He was sitting on his net, the boat tied to one end. His eyes refused to stay open. The daylight would tell him to pull the net and pick the fish. Caj never came back. Jonny didn't know what was going on with his brother, except Jonny knew Caj was tired of what was going on at home. Caj's moods and attitudes were changing. Jonny knew he was sensitive when he was unable to help his family. Most of the time he was still the same old Caj. Everyone was different now.

Jonny closed his eyes. The sleep caught him.

He was dreaming. There was a white mist with a sound behind it. He couldn't make out the sound – like an engine running. He saw his mother walking through the mist.

She walked away from him. He didn't want her to go. He ran after her. But he could never catch up to her. Then she disappeared and Jonny stopped running. He was surrounded by the white mist. Fear rushed him because he couldn't see where to go. He was trapped in the white mist. Waiting.

"Hey Jonny. You awake?"

Jonny lifted his head, blinking his eyes. The fog was still there. It was morning. He could see the murky light in the sky. The fog should be lifting soon. Jonny looked over to who was yelling. It was the Jones boys, Richard and Marvin. It was Marvin yelling in the fog.

That's no way to fish, with your eyes closed. You better start picking or the crabs will be eating your catch. Its lucky we came by or you would still be sleeping."

Jonny waved at them as they motored their small skiff to the docks. He watched them disappear in the fog. Then he stood and stretched.

His mind wasn't on fishing. Even if it was, he was too tired, and he couldn't stop thinking of his mother. She really scared him.

He took the rope and untied it from the boat and pulled it in, hand over hand, until he reached the net. The water was cold: winter water. At least he was in the bay. It was choppy, that's all. The five-inch web dripped cold water as he pulled. Still the cold didn't bother him because of his thoughts. He was pulling the net and piling it in the front of the boat. He would push down to tighten the bunch. There were no fish yet. He knew that he would have three piles of net by the time he was done. The first one was done, so he climbed over to start another. Because of his worries and pain, his mind wasn't sharp. He felt his foot get caught on some web. He tried to twist and when he did, he lost his balance.

There was a big splash as he fell into the cold morning water.

His mind was immediately alert. He held his breath. He began to swim to the top. The net was wrapped around his boots and was floating away from the boat. It was pulling him down further and further under the water. He panicked and tried to swim harder. Bubbles were escaping from his mouth. His eyes, wide open, looked at the top of the water above.

He was tired from flapping his arms and kicking his legs. It dawned on him that he was going to drown. He took off his coat and shirt, freeing up his arms. Then he bent over and tried to take off his hip-boots. He could see the net wrapped around his ankle. He would never be able to get the boot off. The cold wasn't so cold anymore. More bubbles came from his mouth.

There was nothing he could do to save himself. Truthfully, he didn't know if he wanted to. Life was so hard anyway. Pain seemed to be the bigger part of his life. Nothing seemed to go right. Maybe it was time to give up. Jonny closed his eyes.

When he opened them, a pale, gray wolf-pup was dog-paddling in front of him. Back and forth the wolf-pup swam in front of Jonny. Jonny didn't know what to make of this. The wolf-pup wanted him to swim with it. Dog-paddle. His air was gone. Slowly Jonny began to dog-paddle.

He broke clear of the water with such force that his head came right out. He sucked as much air as he could before the net dragged him back down to the depths. The water was not deep, but deep enough if you had a net attached to you. Jonny could see his boat floating away. It was about twenty yards from him. He would never be able to get to it. Then his head went back under.

The water was full of bubbles. He floated back to the net. Bent over, he tried to free himself. It was hopeless. He never felt so helpless.

The pale, gray wolf-pup was back: there he went again, dog-paddling to the top; and back down again. He was becoming frantic and tried to get Jonny to follow him. All the energy was gone from Jonny's body. OK, Jonny thought, "You try doing the dog-paddle with a net tied around your foot."

Jonny tried one more time, paddling and pulling and kicking as much as he could. The wolf-pup was right in front of him. Jonny was right next to the top. One or two more paddles and he would be there. His lungs were demanding air. The wolf-pup waited for him. Jonny stretched his arm out.

A hand plunged into the water and wrapped around Jonny's, pulling him to the surface. He breathed and air flooded his lungs. Another hand grabbed his arm.

"Jonny! Jonny, grab the end of the boat. I can't hold you." It was Nikki-D.

She brought his arm to the boat and Jonny grabbed the edge. Nikki-D pulled with all her might. Jonny got halfway in the boat and Nikki-D unwrapped the net from his ankle. Then he fell into the boat; plunk!

He was coughing and spitting water. Nikki-D had never been so scared. Luckily she knew where he fished. When he hadn't come in with the other boats she decided to go looking for him. She thought he would have heard her engine. Her heart was pumping a thousand times a minute.

Jonny sat up. She could see emotions working behind his pale face. He was a mask of emotions. He tried not to show them as his lips pouted and he averted his eyes from her. Then he could hold them back no longer. The deep sadness covered the face of her friend. She reached out to him. He fell forward into her arms, burying his face in her lap. He grasped her legs with clenched fists. And ... then she heard the deep moan of the helpless young man who was her friend. Nikki-D and Jonny sat together in the boat. They floated together in the white mist of the quiet morning.

18

GOOD-BYE

Nikki-D bolted up in her bed. The pain rushed through her head. She wasn't feeling good at all. Her heart was being squeezed to death. It hurt bad. Her blood stopped at the heart, building up like a dam, then rushing to her head. The pain was deep and penetrating. "Mommm..."

Deep in her stomach was a vacant emptiness, devoid of anything but fear. Sweat was on her upper lip and rolling down her forehead. The pain in her heart grew. Nikki-D bent over with her hands on her chest. Everything seemed so wrong.

Ginny came running into her bedroom with concern on her face. "Nikki-D, what's wrong?"

All Nikki-D could do was cry. She wanted a release from this pain. "I don't know what's wrong. My heart hurts so bad."

Ginny wrapped her arms around her little girl. Nikki-D leaned her head into her mother's shoulder, still crying.

"Shhh... its all right." Ginny began to cry, too. Nick looked in at the doorway. He stood watching mother and daughter as they cried. It was hard on him. He remembered the conversation with his daughter when he had to tell her that he agreed with her mother and she would be sent to a school for special children. It was a boarding school for girls.

"No, I'm not going. I told you I don't want to go to some dumb special school. I'm happy here. My friends are here." Nikki-D was mad. She had looked at her mom. Her mom just sat there, staring at her. She was always in control. It was her fault.

"We know you have your friends here, honey. But your teachers say that this school is holding you back." Nick was doing the talking. He and Ginny decided it would be best if he was the one to tell Nikki-D.

"You, you want me to go Daddy?"

He could see the tears in the corner of her eyes. The truth was, he didn't want her to go. His little girl was the one bright spot in his life. He always looked forward to coming home to see what new and exciting thing she discovered that day. It was even hard for him to keep up with her sometimes. She learned at such a fast rate. She passed everyone. He looked at Ginny. Except one.

"No honey, we just want what is best for you. You need to go. Can't you see that? Its not what we want but its what we need to do. Your mother and I love you and we want what is best for you." Nick's heart ached as he saw the tears in his little girl's eyes. They started falling now. He wanted to reach out to her but Ginny told him that he needed to be strong. They were a united front against this girl with so much energy.

"She's the one who wants me go." Nikki-D kept crying but she was also seething with resentment at her mother, the one person that she always had to compromise with. It made her furious. "I won't go."

The night was long. Nick had to get up early and get to work. Nikki-D would be all right. She was with her mother. As Nick walked, he found it funny how Nikki-D always ended up with her mother when she needed help.

Shadows ran across the walls of the night. Nikki-D was still in her mother's arms. The tears stopped. "Hic! " Her body jumped. "Hic! Hic-hic-hic."

"I'll get you some water."

All Nikki-D could do was nod, her eyes down. "Hic." She lay back down on her bed. She stared out of her window into the raining night. Soft pebbles of rain lay against the pain. Nikki-D told her friends she was leaving ... most of them. It was harder than she thought. They were sorry to see her go. So was she. She didn't want to leave. She was scared. What would happen to her life? All the comforts she knew wouldn't be there for her. Not her family. Not her mother. Not Jonny.

Ginny came into the room with the water. She looked at Nikki-D, asleep and lightly snoring on her pillow. She had cried so hard it must have taken all the energy out of her. Ginny went over and sat next to her daughter. The night would be long. Putting her hand on Nikki-D's shoulder, she began to hum like she had when Nikki-D was a little tiny thing. She hummed songs from her childhood. She hummed Chinese songs, passed down from her mother.

Nikki-D and Jonny sat under the tarp on the hill. The tarp kept the rain off them. She wanted to see him again. All of her fighting and words and threats hadn't changed her parents' minds. She was leaving. It would be soon.

"I hate her. She's the one who wants me to go."

Jonny nodded his head. He didn't agree with her but sometimes it was better to go along with Nikki-D. She could make your life hell if she wanted to. He didn't want that. There were other things on his mind.

"I mean, what is so wrong in staying here? I've lived here all of my life."

"Mmmm ... mm, no you didn't. You came here from back east."

Nikki-D looked at him with disdain. Jonny bent his head down and didn't look back. Oh-oh ... a mistake.

"I knooow ... where ... I came from!"

Jonny could feel the ice in those words. Yep, it was close. He kept staring down.

"I think she hated me because of my father. Now she turned him against me."

Jonny hated the thought of Nikki-D leaving. He was as angry as she was. If he had his way, they both would stay and grow up right here where they belonged. But the world wasn't made like that. She would go and nothing was going to change that.

"When are you going?"

"In a month. I'll start next quarter there. Its so mean to send me in the middle of the year. They planned it this way." Nikki-D was venting her anger. It was all that she could do.

Jonny listened for a second, then he had to say something. "My family has to go to court on Monday." There! It was out.

"What?"

"They're bringing us to court on Monday. To find out what to do with us. They say that my mother can't handle us and that we are getting into too much trouble."

"On Monday? This Monday?" Nikki-D didn't know what to say.

"My mom and dad met with the BIA the other day. And me and Caj and Dani and Morgan-Mckenzi had to fill out some papers."

"Papers for what?" Nikki-D didn't like the direction this was taking.

"Papers to get into Indian schools in Oklahoma. They only had enough openings for the older kids."

"You mean you're moving to Oklahoma?"

"Not all of us. Just some of the kids. So I guess we both will be in a boarding school." He looked at her. Her black hair was tied in a tail in the back with the front short and in a puff. Her eye's were red and tired.

"Just you four?"

"Mm ... mm. Yea, if the judge says its OK. Then we leave next week."

"What?"

Jonny moved on fast so he could get it out before she took over. He wanted to tell her everything. Wanted to tell her how he felt, tell her about the awful feeling of despair that crept into his thoughts all the time. How he would miss her and would write every day. He would call her, too. He wanted to tell her that she was his best friend and that there would never be another like her. He wanted to tell her how angry he was ... and how afraid.

"We leave next Wednesday if everything goes right."

"But how can they just send you away like that? Its not right." Nikki-D was desperate. Her life was crumbling in front of her. They're taking Jonny away. He would be gone when she came home for holidays. She won't be able to tell him about her new school, or run through the woods or sit on the bluff and talk with him. The stark reality was hitting her all at once. It will never be the same anymore. She began crying.

Jonny looked away. He didn't want to cry. Men shouldn't cry, although, he saw many of the older men of the tribe cry. His lips trembled as he tried to talk.

"Mmmm ... mm, Mmm-mm ... mm, its better than them taking all the family away. And the government will give my mother some money for food and clothes. They say we will get three meals a day at the school. Sort of like Christmas."

Nikki-D was crying so hard that she couldn't listen to him. She turned and hit him in the arm. Hard. "You're so stupid for drinking. Now look what you've done." She got up and ran home.

Her accusation hurt Jonny. She was right. He was part of the problem. She didn't understand that he stopped. Ever since that night with the wolf-pup, he knew what direction he had to take. He watched her as she ran. He watched his best friend run from him. He began to cry.

Lois Esque sat in the chair in the hallway. The court hearing had been going on for some time. Her kids sat next to her. Franc refused to come. The dull, pea-green hallway had paint peeling from it. She didn't know how things were going to go. She knew it would be all right. There was no problem she couldn't overcome. She was resigned to the fact that they were going to take half of her kids from her. She knew that she had to let them go. It would be better for all of them. They were teens now and their world demanded more from them. She couldn't control what they could do. Caj and Dani, the two most popular of the group, would be all right in this new school in Oklahoma. She was concerned about the others. Jonny and Morgan-Mckenzi. They were her youngest ones. They were different, those two. She prayed that they would be all right.

Jonny watched his mother with the little ones in her lap. Silence pervaded the hallway. They all waited to hear their fate.

Judge McVee sat as they all marched into his office. He had spent the better part of two hours talking with the agencies who controlled this family. All these many years hearing cases from those whose job it was to tell him what is right for this Indian family or that Indian family, secure in their knowledge that what they recommended was right. As he watched this family walk into his office, he wasn't so sure.

They all stood there, heads down. Kids. All he knew was Indians had a lot of kids. Over time, he understood that's what Indians were: family. It was his job to take this family, listen to the agencies, and then tear them apart.

"Lois Esque, I have heard all of the evidence and the recommendations of the BIA and the Welfare. Do you have anything to say before I sign the order?"

Lois stood with a little girl standing beside her. "I know you have to sign the order sending my children away. But I was wondering ...."

She had to stop because of the tears in her throat. Then she went on.

"I was wondering if they will take good care of my children?"

He heard this all the time. The mothers just wanted to make sure the government takes good care of them. He wished it was so. He had one of his staff look into the treatment of the children in the Indian schools. The report wasn't good. He looked at this woman, a white woman who acted just like the Indian women. Asking the same questions. Questions he couldn't answer.

"I'm sure they will, Mrs. Esque. Now, at this time, do any of you kids have anything to say?" They never did. Meek and docile in their demeanor, they always looked at the floor. They never looked him in the eye. How could these kids always be in trouble?

"Since no one has anything to say, then I pass judgment and sign this order that; One, Morgan-Mckenzi Esque is hereby remanded to the BIA boarding school in Oklahoma. To attend Chilocco Indian boarding school. Two, Dani Esque is hereby remanded to the BIA boarding school in Oklahoma. To attend Fort Sill Indian boarding school. Three, Caj Esque is hereby remanded to the BIA boarding school in Oklahoma. To attend Concho Demonstration school. Finally, Jonny Esque is hereby remanded to the BIA boarding school in Oklahoma. To attend Fort Sill boarding school."

Silence followed.

"I think you should look at this as a new opportunity. Dani and Morgan-Mckenzi, I hope you will stop your fighting and truancy in school and take to the books. Its your only way out. And you boys: Caj, you're one of the best athletes in school. Its such a waste to have to see you like this. Drinking and fighting. Your peers look up to you." When he saw Caj look at him he knew he hit a nerve. They probably took his sports from him. It always went that way for these Indians. Good until the middle-school years and then reality hits. The coaches have enough good kids so he doesn't have to play the Indian. After all, the Indians never complained, while the white parents called him and complained every day. Better to sit the Indian down, no matter how talented.

"Well anyway, I hope things go better for you at this school. Its up to you. If that's all you have to say, then this court is adjourned."

Nikki-D woke in the night. Guilt ran through her. She hadn't talked to Jonny since that day she whined about her life. She was so mad at the world. She wanted it to stay the same. No matter how hard she cried and fought against the change, it was coming anyway. Now Jonny and his family were being torn apart. They didn't even have any say in it. It wasn't fair. She could feel the same juices of injustice surge through her. She felt as if she had no control over any part of her life. Jonny must have even less. She was determined to do something about it. What, she didn't know. She pledged her life to help those people that needed help the most.

This helped her with the pain in her chest. Now she had to say good-bye. Tammy cried. Nikki-D was wrong to close her out of her life because of what she said about the Indians. Now she knew that she should have brought Tammy in, so she could learn that the Indians were people like her. Pain shot through her as Nikki-D thought of this. The one person she never said good-bye to was Jonny. Now he was leaving her. The pain raged again. She did so many things wrong. Now it was too late to do anything about them.

Tomorrow was the day. They were sending them away early in the morning. Nikki-D had her alarm clock on. He mother said she would get her up. Nikki-D saw that this affected her mother, too. She never saw this side of her mother until something bad happened. Then her mother would sit and say nothing. Passive and contemplative, she tried to understand the world around her. Then she would pray.

Nikki-D tried to sleep.

"Hurry up or we'll be late," Nikki-D was yelling at her mother and father. Time was running out and she couldn't miss seeing Jonny and Caj off. "Will you hurry, Mom?"

"Quiet down, Nikki-D, we're on time. Nick, bring the car around front. Nikki-D, grab that food in the kitchen and we'll go." Ginny Thomas was nervous, too. She wanted to be there for Lois. Ginny knew it would be hard on her watching half of her family being sent half way across the nation. She knew that she would be facing the same fears when Nikki-D left in two weeks. She hoped she was doing the right thing. A mother never knew.

The car was in front and Nick was helping them load the food into the back seat. Ginny looked at the sky. The rain was falling some grape-size drops. She knew there would be a downpour coming. "Nikki-D, go inside and get the umbrellas. Don't forget yours. Its going to rain hard today. I don't want you catching a cold."

"Mom ... we have to get going."

"Do as I say." She wasn't in any mood to put up with her daughter.

Nikki-D ran back into the house. She took the stairs in twos. She ran to her bedroom and grabbed her umbrella, then to her mom's room, grabbing that one, too. She flew downstairs and out to the car, slamming the front door behind her. Her parents were waiting in the car. She climbed into the back seat and they drove off.

The buses were lined up for the kids. Greyhound was transporting the kids. Lois stood by the front entrance of the bus station in Everett. She was making sure that the kids all had their tickets and money for food while they rode the bus. It would take them three to four days to make it to their schools and she didn't want any of them to run out of money before getting there.

"OK, do all of you have your money?"
They nodded.
"How about your tickets?"
They nodded.
"Your luggage?"

They pointed to the cardboard boxes wrapped with tape two or three times around them. Only Dani had luggage. It was used.

Lois looked at the people milling around the station. There were more kids from other reservations there, too: some Lummis and some Nooksacks. Kids stood without parents around. They must have ridden down here on the buses. They came from the North, near the Canadian border.

It was so sad looking at these kids, children of all ages being sent to all parts of the country. Lois cried again. Dani saw her sobbing and began to cry, too. She walked over to her mother and put her arms around her. "It will be all right, Mom."

Lois wiped her tears. Dani always stood up when needed. She went over to her little sisters. Shawn, Katie, Alexcia and Scout. Clair was with them. She would stay home and help her mother. Scout moved off. She was added to the list of kids going. She was next in line after Jonny. They were sending her to Concho, too. At least her older brother would be there for her. Scout was hanging onto Clair, crying as loud as she could. Each of the children went up and touched her to let her know it was all right. Then she settled down.

The rains were falling hard. The clouds were almost black and swirling. Lois worried about the road conditions and asked the drivers about it. They assured her that they would be able to drive with ease through the rain. The buses were the best thing to travel in on days like this. The chartered buses would only have the Indian kids on them. There would be no stops to pick up any passengers after leaving Everett.

Lois checked the routes again. They would all ride together to California and cut across from there. They would continue together until they reached Amarillo, Texas. Then they would split up and go their separate ways, each one sent to a different school. She prayed her kids would be all right. In her heart she knew that, for some of them, there would no returning home. She held her handbag in the crook of her arm as she tried to pull her worn gray coat around her. She was a mother caught with no way out. She wept because that was all she could do.

Ginny watched the road through the hard-driven rain. They were eight miles inside the reservation. The road was narrow, winding through the hills. She could barely see through the rain. "Nick, are you sure you can drive in this?"

"I can drive. Just let me do it, OK?"

Ginny and Nikki-D could tell he was nervous. It was harder to drive than he let on. They both sat up, tense and watching. The black concrete of the road blended in with the sky and rain. Nick steered, keeping his front wheel on the yellow line in the middle off the road. He was only going twenty miles an hour. Ginny thought that was too fast. Nikki-D thought it was too slow. Both were wrong.

Suddenly, Nick put on the brakes as other red brake lights flashed in front of him. A car was slowing down.

"What's wrong?" Ginny didn't like it. The rain sounded as if baseballs were being dropped on the hood of the car. The windshield wipers were on high and it was still hard to see.

"Nothing, honey. Just a car slowing down."

Nikki-D wished he would just speed up. She knew that time was running out. It couldn't end this way. She never said good-bye. She never got to tell Jonny how much she would miss him. She never got to say good-bye.

"Dad, will you hurry up?"

"Be quiet, Nikki-D. Yelling at your father isn't going to help his driving." Ginny gave Nikki-D a stern look, then looked at Nick.

"You can go a little faster, dear."

The luggage was loaded. The kids were standing beside each other, some already making friends. Faces, some light-brown and some dark-brown, watched the people around them. Their eyes showed concern. It was time to load up, a time everyone dreaded.

Jonny was standing by the doorway. He had been watching Colby Street ever since he got here. If Nikki-D was coming, she would be coming down that road. He shuffled his feet. Time was running out.

Finally they made it off the reservation. Nikki-D breathed a sigh of relief. They would make it on time. Already picking up speed on highway 99, they should be there in a few minutes. The car slowed. Nikki-D looked. "Oh, no..."

There was a wreck in front of them. The right lane was blocked and cars had to go around the wreck, in the left lane. Nikki-D was desperate. The line was moving slowly. Each car waited for a car in the right lane to move over. They made it up to the wreck, but it took some time.

It was a bad wreck. People's lives were at stake. Nikki-D watched as they passed.

Jonny hugged his mother. The others were in the bus. He was the last. He waited as long as he could. She never showed. His face burned with rejection. He wanted so bad to talk to her. Now it was too late.

"Don't worry, Jonny, I'll tell her you waited." Lois said these words as she hugged him.

Jonny just nodded his head. He climbed aboard the Greyhound bus. The dark interior was lit by small lights at the top of the bus. The driver sat in the lower portion of the front while the passengers sat in the higher section in the back. Jonny walked by the kids sitting in the blue seats. Most of the movement stopped. The kids put their things in the overhead rack, so there was nothing to do except wait.

Jonny sat with Dani. They were both going to Fort Sill, so they sat together on the left side of the bus. He sat next to the window. The roar of the engines silenced everyone. They heard the air hissing as the door shut. Nobody said a word. The bus backed up. Lois and her family stood with the other Indians, watching the bus leave.

Nikki-D pointed. "There's Mrs. Esque! Pull over there."

She saw the bus back up. She was too late. They didn't make it on time. "Stop!" She screamed the words at her father. He put on the brakes and she was out of the car. She ran to catch the bus.

She passed Mrs. Esque. She ran through the gateway and out to the bus. It slowly started pulling forward. Nikki-D was on the right side of the bus. She tried to find Jonny, but he wasn't on that side. She ran around to the left side. The bus was passing her. She strained her eyes, looking for Jonny. Then the bus stopped before pulling out to the street. She searched.

There he was ... sitting next to the last window. She waved. "Jonny!" Tears ran hard in the rain. She was too late. Still she waved. "Please let him see me," she prayed.

As the window went by, she could see his sad eyes staring at her. She saw his face in the window. She saw his hand give a small wave as his lips moved. "Good-bye, Nikki-D."

She sat in the train station. It was Nikki-D's time to go. The tears ran out long ago. She hugged her parents one last time, then she boarded the train. She gave the steward her first-class ticket that gave her a private room. She went to her room and sat next to the window.

The train pulled away from the station. She waved to her mother, who was crying. The train was taking her away from her home. The world was moving fast. Everyone she cared about was gone. Nikki-D didn't mind leaving.

She opened her diary. She entered the date, "Oct. 28th, 1964: a new beginning."

"Yes and No," Old Mouse Said with Conviction. "I Know there is the Great River. But I am Afraid that the Great Mountains are only a myth. Forget your Passion to See Them and Stay here with me. There is Everything you Want here, and it is a Good Place to Be."

"How can he Say such a thing?" Thought Jumping Mouse. " The Medicine of the Sacred Mountains is Nothing One can Forget."

"Thank you very much for the Meal you have Shared with me, Old Mouse, and also for sharing your Great Home," Jumping Mouse said. "But I must Seek the Mountains."

"You are a Foolish Mouse to Leave here. There is Danger on the Prairie! Just Look up there!" Old Mouse said, with even more Conviction. "See all those Spots! They are Eagles, and they will Catch you!"

It was hard for Jumping Mouse to Leave, but he Gathered his Determination and Ran hard Again. The Ground was Rough. But he Arched his Tail and Ran with All his Might. He could Feel the Shadows of the Spots upon his Back as he Ran.

All those Spots! Finally he Ran into a Stand of Chokecherries. Jumping Mouse could hardly Believe his Eyes. It was Cool there and very Spacious. There was Water, Cherries and Seeds to Eat, Grasses to Gather for Nests, Holes to be Explored and many, many Other Busy Things to do. And there were a great many things to Gather.

He was Investigating his New Domain when he heard very Heavy Breathing. He Quickly Investigated the Sound and discovered its Source. It was a Great Mound of Hair with Black horns. It was a Great Buffalo. Jumping Mouse could hardly Believe the Greatness of the Being he Saw Lying there before him. He was so large that Jumping Mouse could have crawled into One of his Great Horns. "Such a magnificent Being," Thought Jumping Mouse, and he Crept Closer.

"Hello, my Brother," said the Buffalo. "Thank you for Visiting me."

"Hello, Great Being," said Jumping Mouse. "Why are you Lying here?"

"I am Sick and I am Dying," the Buffalo said, "And my Medicine has Told me that only the Eye of a Mouse can Heal me. But little Brother, there is no such Thing as a Mouse."

Jumping Mouse was Shocked. "One of my Eyes!" he Thought, "One of my Tiny Eyes." He Scurried back into the Stand of Chokecherries. But the Breathing came Harder and Slower.

"He will Die," Thought Jumping Mouse, "If I do not Give him my Eye. He is too Great a Being to Let Die."

He Went Back to where the Buffalo lay and Spoke. "I am a Mouse," he said with a Shaky Voice. "And you, my Brother, are a Great Being. I cannot Let you Die. I have Two Eyes, so you may have One of them."

The minute he had Said it, Jumping Mouse's Eye Flew Out of his head and the Buffalo was made Whole. The Buffalo Jumped to his Feet, Shaking Jumping Mouse's Whole World.

19

CAMPUS

Jonny stood poised to attack, his fists clenched. Navajos were surrounding him and some of the other Washington kids. Bear from the Herrera tribe, was in the lead. He was short and squat with wide shoulders. All of these people looked like that: strong and dangerous. He took the point in the battle. PeeWee, of the Umitilla tribe, stood to one side with John, from the Spokane tribe. The fight was between Washington tribes, with some Oklahoma tribes, against the Jo's and their allies. There were a lot more of them.

Jonny said nothing. He never said much. The fight was because of his cousin Guy's loud mouth. It didn't matter, because the Washington tribes were the fighters of the school. Their small, husky bodies could do some damage to the long and lanky Jo's and southwestern tribes. Jonny fought because he had to, not because he wanted to. Most of the kids were that way; just trying to get by.

"Yea, you queers better back off."

Jonny raised his eyes. There was his cousin Guy, mouthing off again. It was his way of being accepted, which is what they all wanted. They wanted to be part of something. Jonny watched his cousin from the beginning. He always talked and bragged with the others. Jonny didn't like it, but that's the way his cousin was. Everyone knew he was his cousin. Now it came down to this.

"Yaht-tah-hey, you bastards. Come and get us if you want."

A big, dark boy stepped up: Roger Jim, who ran with the gang of Jo's from one of the other halls.

"You have a big mouth, hey? Maybe we won't fight today. Maybe we will. But you will still have a big mouth."

Bear looked at Guy. Then he began to laugh.

"You're right about that."

Jonny knew there wouldn't be a fight today. The kids began to break up and go back to their halls. Jonny watched them all. The knot in his stomach loosened. He walked back to Quanta Hall. His home.

Its flat red face matched the grounds around Ft. Sill. Rows of windows lined the face. A big doorway gave way to a wooden door that opened to the inside of the building. Jonny walked through the door. He passed the matron's office on the right. A small white woman was the matron for the weekend. June was her name. She was OK. Jonny liked her because she read a lot of books. She would talk to him about the things that he read. There was no concern about her. She was in total charge of the kids of the hall and they knew it. Jonny walked up to the second floor. The floors were shiny from all the buffing the kids had to do on Saturday. In the middle of his bay there were long rows of bunk-beds, painted dark green, lined up back-to-back. They must have come from the Army base next to the Indian school. They were so ugly.

Jonny's bed was at the very end of the bay. He was one of the last kids to arrive at the school so he didn't get to pick where he slept. He got the last bunk because the kid who was supposed to come didn't make it and Jonny was his replacement. The place was empty today. Jonny went to the window and looked out. Some kids were still milling around, but most were leaving to go to town: Lawton, Oklahoma. Jonny heard it was nothing but a truck stop. He hadn't seen it yet. He kept to himself. You weren't supposed to lie on your bunk until after three in the afternoon. Nobody ever stayed around on the weekends so Jonny was able to lie and read or think on his bed. Today, like most days, he thought about home.

Guy came walking in behind him.

"Man Cous, heh-heh, that was close." He was sweating.

"Why you sweating, Guy?"

"Oh nothing, you know some of them wanted to talk."

Jonny knew that they must have chased him down. His cousin was a strange duck. He always talked and caused trouble and worked to get out of it. Most of the kids just tuned him out. Jonny couldn't because they came from the same place. They must have chased him until they ran out of gas. For a little kid, he could sure run. Nobody that Jonny knew at school had caught him yet.

"Going to the dance tonight, Jonny?"

Jonny shook his head no. He had no money. The BIA was supposed to send him money every month. All the other kids got their money, but Jonny got nothing. He was getting desperate because he needed the money to buy toothpaste and things like that. Jonny borrowed money to call home. He talked to his mother every week. He started writing letters, too. He could say so much more if he didn't have to talk.

"I'm going. I want to dance with Jenny. Man, she's a fox. You know what? I saw her panties when we were in Math today. I think she wanted me to. She opened her legs a little and I had my head laying on my arms on the desk. And I was looking. White panties. You know how I sit in the front of the room by the teacher's desk?"

Jonny knew that Mr. Ansion seated Guy next to his desk to keep him from making any trouble and keep him quiet in class. He was a real motor-mouth.

"Anyway, I know she saw me looking and then I saw her legs open a little wider. Man, it was great. I couldn't stop looking. Now I know why the teacher has his table that way. I bet he can see all of the girls."

Jonny was uncomfortable with the kind of talk that he heard from his cousin. He looked at the clothes he was wearing. His pants were worn and you could see the threads. His shoes were worn, too. No girls would want someone who can't even afford to buy any pants. The Jo's got new clothes every month.

Guy watched him for a second. "Hey, I got some clothes if you ... you know, need some."

"No. I'm not going to the dance anyway."

"They're treating you wrong, man. Why don't you call them and tell them to send you down your money? I would."

"I have called. They told Mom that they sent it already."

"Yea, right. You want me to call my dad or something?"

"No."

Jonny wished he could tell his cousin to go away but he and Dani were the only ones from home. And Jonny was lonely.

"Well, I got to go. The bus is going into town and I have to buy some clothes. See you around."

Jonny moved from the bunk beds in the middle of the bay to the window. He watched as the kids lined up to go into Lawton. Guy ran up to the end of the line. Jonny watched as two Jo's came up from behind. They stood on either side of Guy. Jonny knew that it was going to be rough, but he knew that Guy would get out of it somehow.

Jonny went back to the bed. There were so many books for him to read. He loved reading. It was the one thing they couldn't take from him. Jonny was homesick. He felt cut off from his world. He had never been alone before. He was always around his family. It was nothing like this, isolated and alone. It hurt. He knew he was having severe reactions from being separated from home but there was nothing he could do to stop it. He called his mother whenever he could but it wasn't enough. He was detached from everything.

Funny – even as his world grew, he felt so imprisoned. So many new things, yet he wanted the old. He was shrinking inside himself. What he needed had to come from within. From his people. To Jonny, this small world of the campus paled in comparison to the unlimited world of his people. The stories told him all. His spirit watched the earth from a distance and it was a very small place, compared to the real world within him.

Caj was at home in his new environment. The school was made for him. Concho Demonstration School in Oklahoma. BJ was here with him. That made it easier to deal with the kids from the other tribes. They both watched out for each other. Nobody messed with them. That was good.

"Hey, Caj, come here."

It was Coach Donnell. Caj picked up his helmet and ran over to the coach.

"Caj, I want you to run through the slot. You understand? Through the slot."

Caj nodded. He wore the yellow-and-black uniform of the Concho Eagles.

The quarterback lined up behind the center. "Ready, set. Nine-fifty-four-nine-fifty-four, hut, hut."

The ball was snapped and the quarterback faded back with the ball. Then he rolled to Caj and slammed the ball into his stomach. Caj was waiting for it. He took off running. The defense was coming in. Caj dodged one guy and made a move on another, then the slot opened up and he headed for daylight. But there was Benie, the big bastard, standing right in front of him. Caj set his feet. He could out-run Benie if he wanted to. Caj needed to make a point. He lowered his head and hit Benie under the shoulder pads, ramming his helmet into the midsection. Benie went down in a heap. Caj looked up. The end zone was twenty yards in front of him. Nobody touched him. Touchdown!

"Yea right that's the way to do it, Caj. Did any of you others see that? He's our boy. Yea..."

Caj smiled. It felt like he was home.

Ever since he got here he knew it was the place. Caj walked down the hall. The books felt good in his arms. He was the man again. BJ, was waiting for him at the chow hall and he was hungry. The food here was great and he couldn't get enough of it. He was growing and filling out. Soon he would look like BJ, who was eighteen now. He checked his watch. He was late.

"Caj"

He heard the sweet, soft voice of Mariann. She was a tall, slender Sioux girl. She was a cheerleader and the prettiest girl in the school. Mariann wore a light-blue sweater and pants. The sweater had a big C with an Eagle on it. It looked great on her. She carried some books in her arms. She had the long, black hair of her tribe. She had an oval face with brown eyes. She was part white.

"Caj, I was wondering – could we talk?"

"OK." He flashed his smile at her.

"I'm going to the dance Saturday. I wondered if you wanted to go."

"I thought you were with Benie."

"No, I'm alone." She started crying. She moaned and slumped down.

Caj was unsure why she was crying.

"Are you OK? Come on, lets go over and sit down."

He led her to a bench and they both sat. She was really crying. It made Caj uncomfortable. It hurt him for some reason.

She hid her face from him.

"What's wrong, Mariann? Why are you crying?"

She squirmed in her seat. She rubbed her eyes with a napkin and looked at him.

She moaned, "I'm leaving in a couple of weeks. They're sending me to Ft. Sill. Benie doesn't want to be with me because we're too far apart. I don't know what to do. I feel so alone. I don't want to go." She began to wail in her napkin.

Concho was a small school for those students who were waiting to get into the larger Indian Schools. Most of them would leave in the first three months. If they didn't get into another school by then, they stayed for the full year. Caj had his name in for the Art School in New Mexico. Like the rest of the kids, he was just waiting for his number to be called.

"Hey, it will be all right. Man, its rough; leaving like that. I'm just getting ready for the football game and my number may be called at any time. Its tough. Benie doesn't know anything. It will be all right. My little brother is there. I'll tell him to look out for you. OK?"

She didn't move. She was bawling even harder. Caj didn't know if he helped any at all.

"OK?" Caj almost shouted this to her. She was one of the first girls he met when he came here. Word was out about her. He had wanted to get some of it, except he really liked her now that he'd met her. She wasn't like they were saying. He became friends with her. Besides, she was Benie's girl. That was enough for Caj to take her to the dance.

She smiled at him. "OK, Caj."

"Then I'll go to the dance with you."

Nikki-D moved along the corridor. She didn't want to miss the lecture in the dance hall. Everything in the school was bright and airy. She liked it. She realized now that she was holding herself back. Her mother was right; as usual. It was so exciting. People here talked about the world like they made a difference. They were people like her. She began running. Time was short.

Nikki-D looked around the seats. The auditorium was full. There were only a few seats left. She spotted one in the corner on the left. The room was well-lit, no shadows or anything like that. The windows had snow on them. The chill remained outside.

"Excuse me. Excuse me." She moved in front of the girls who were already sitting. "Excuse me."

She finally made it to her seat. A light-brown-haired girl sat next to her. Nikki-D put down her books and took out her notepad. She always took notes. The girl next to her watched.

"Came prepared, huh?"

Nikki-D nodded, a pencil in her mouth. She removed her coat. She wore a white sweater and a skirt. She filled the sweater enough that boys noticed her. It wasn't something she thought about. She felt older than the other girls. Why, she didn't know.

"Uhmm ... uhm! My name's Annie. What's yours?" Annie was a Jewish girl with a pretty face and a thin body, wearing glasses. Her hair was in a ponytail. It was how she always wore it. She was a very bright girl who believed passionately in her ideals, which had nothing to do with her parents.

"Nikki-D..."

"That's a nice name. I wish my parents had the foresight to give me a decent name. Makes you wonder what they were thinking or if they were thinking."

Nikki-D giggled at that. She knew how the girl felt.

"You're Chinese aren't you?"

"Half." The question disturbed Nikki-D. No one really asked like that.

"And the other half'?"

"Welsh."

"Nice touch. I can see it in your eyes. I wish I had your looks. But then, I guess I wouldn't be me. Lucky me."

Nikki-D tried to listen to the girl but the lecture was about to begin. The Professor stood in front of the podium on the stage. She was a small woman. The seats were all tiered down toward the stage so that the students in back would have a view. Nikki-D took out her camera. She checked the flash bulb and made sure the film was ready.

"Ladies... I'm here to talk about the world today and how it applies to you as women. Today, the US government passed a new law, called the Civil Rights Act. This law says you can't discriminate against a person because of his race, creed, or color ... etc. etc. Except they left out women. Now, we have a number of women who have come to the forefront and are fighting for the rights of women. They include Gloria Steinem and Betty Friedan. I want to talk about the beginning of the future." The young women in the auditorium sat enraptured by the speaker. Nikki-D couldn't stop listening. It was as though she was talking directly to her. Nobody said a word.

They came rushing out of the auditorium. Nikki-D got her pictures and wanted to get them processed. Annie was with her as they came through the doors. Annie seemed nice enough. She was a bit plain. She didn't take a single note. Nikki-D wasn't sure how to take that. Most of the girls here had some real brains.

"Annie ... Annie! Over here." A dark-haired girl was waving in the crowd. Annie waved back.

"Martina. Hi! Come on with us. We're going over to get Nikki-D's film processed."

"OK." The dark-haired girl worked her way through until she reached them.

"Didn't you love the lecture? So much knowledge in one person."

"Come on, Martina ... you're not going to bring up the ERA again."

Annie pulled Nikki-D aside. "Watch her or she will get you going to her meetings. Women's suffrage, you know."

"Martina, this is Nikki-D. Shake hands and come out fighting."

Martina and Nikki-D looked at each other and shook hands. They were both beauties. Martina wore a brightly patterned, flowing dress. She was a looker. She filled out in all the right places and it caused much anxiety in the other girls around her. Boys could never take their eyes off her. It was one of her strengths and it was her weakness.

"Come on, let's go."

They were all sifting in Nikki-D's room. She had found the friends that would last for the rest of her life; girls who thought and acted in the same manner, wanting the same things, fighting for the same goals. They all wanted the same things.

"Nikki-D, do you think I look good in this makeup?"

"Annie, leave Nikki-D alone. She should be thinking about going to the meeting tomorrow. Its important. Besides, you look great. You always do but you never believe it."

"Right, Martina. I have the natural beauty of my parents flowing through me like you and Nikki-D. An Italian princess and a Chinese empress..."

"Stop it, Annie. Nikki-D isn't even aware of her beauty. And I'm enslaved by mine. You should be happy."

Nikki-D was considering going to the ERA meeting tomorrow. She, like the rest of the girls, was taking college classes. Her brain had to work overtime for the first time in her life. The activities and the classes brought out the best in Nikki-D and she glowed. She had decided she would go to the meeting.

Martina and Annie were getting ready for the dance at the boys' school. Nikki-D thought it was stupid of them to get all dolled up just so some boys could look at them. Nikki-D knew her two friends wanted to look older, something she never wanted because she already felt older. She was excited to go to the dance with her two new friends. Everything seemed exciting to her now. Things were great.

A feeling of guilt hit her. She thought of Jonny and Caj and Tammy, back home. She felt disloyal. She was no longer homesick. She was home.

Most of them were gone now. The cool night air flowed through the windows. Jonny sat in front of the window, watching the stars. He remembered home and his friend Raymond Moses who told the stories of the tribe.

"Ouuuu ... Raymond would say. I tell you a story about how the beaver got his tail." Raymond would dance around and point his finger at you. Make you listen to him.

Jonny would always listen to Raymond and his stories. The evening was so quiet. It always was. He could see for miles in all directions from his window. He hated it. He wasn't used to seeing so far and seeing the sky without having to look up. The giant cedar trees back home were so high that you had to look straight up to see the stars. Now, he could see the sky forever and it scared him. All he saw was darkness.

The pain of separation left him feeling singular and alone. He no longer felt connected to anything. Jonny was detached from the others in school. It didn't matter.

Leaving home…cut him off from his people. His learning was cut short. He would never need the teachings of this school. His spirit was low and Jonny knew that he had to get back home.

"Wahahahaha!!"

Jonny looked down by the flagpole in the middle of the campus. He saw Guy running from some bigger boys. They were trying to chase him down. Jonny watched as Guy dipped and ducked away from the grasp of the boys. Then he turned and ran into the darkness.

"Wahaahahah!"

Jonny smiled and then he laughed to himself. Maybe the place wasn't all bad.

20

AWAKENING

The dance floor was slick. Nikki-D sat in the corner with her friends. She was nervous. It was her first dance without her mother being there. She was excited. Martina and Annie, two of the most unlikely friends, accepted her as one of them. They began to go everywhere together.

Nikki-D looked around. It was dark in the auditorium and she had to squint to see. Straight across from her was the entrance. Party papers hung from it. Two chaperone's stood on either side of it. The stage stood to the left of the entrance. Tonight they were playing records. One of the school chaperones played them on request.

Most of the girls sat on the same side of the dance floor as Nikki-D. The older ones moved about, talking with each other. The boys moved all the time. They wanted the girls to see them and they flashed shy smiles as they walked by. All of them were dressed in their best dresses and suits. Nobody was allowed in unless they dressed properly. Nikki-D didn't care much one way or the other. She wanted to see what it was like. She wore her white dress, like the others. Actually, it brought out her eyes and hair, which she liked. She noticed the boys noticing, but she was feeling different about their stares. Something moved inside her; a feeling, but more. An awakening.

Nikki-D watched her friends look at the boys. Martina smiled with her head held high and cocked to the side. She smiled right back at them. Flirting, inviting, she controlled them with her eyes and demeanor. Martina was happy and bubbled over.

Annie sat, nervous and hopeful, ready to verbally rebuff any intruder, but wishing for one to come to her. She kept up her defiant stares until boys came too close; then she would lower her eyes. She used makeup to compensate, but she used too much and it left her looking too old and out of place for the boys. The teenage years weren't being kind to any of them.

Nikki-D still wasn't sure why this dance seemed different to her. She refused to wear makeup that made her look older. She thought she was old as it was, and didn't need any cosmetic aid to add to her age. That's why she never understood Caj, always calling her a little girl. She still felt the rejection from that statement. Jonny understood her; why couldn't Caj? She didn't care what boys wanted or what they thought of her. She was always too busy.

The boys knew she was a real beauty. They would walk in front of her staring, not taking their eyes off her. Annie leaned over.

"Nikki-D, did you see how those boys were looking at us?"

"I think they're looking at Martina."

"I can see why. The way she flaunts herself."

Nikki-D decided not to say anything. It didn't matter to her, anyway. She never understood why Annie put herself down and at the same time condemned Martina for being ... well, Martina. The way she said it right in front of Martina, made Nikki-D uncomfortable.

Martina shrugged it off. She got all the boys anyway. She was a girl that wanted it all. She never understood why the girls and women she listened to thought you had to give up boys to bring up women. She found boys fun and funny. They played by their own rules, outside women, whether women liked it or not. Martina was glad they did, because it made life more challenging.

Annie and Martina were sixteen, going on seventeen. Life was facing them. They made their move in the courses and the activities they participated in. They brought Nikki-D with them because they wanted her in their corner. They both were making their contacts that would last a lifetime.

All three looked up as a boy walked over to them. He nodded at Annie and

Nikki-D.

"Would you like to dance?"

Martina smiled at him and got up. She took his hand and moved out to the dance floor. As they walk out to the floor, Martina looked back and smiled.

Annie stuck out her tongue. Annie always wanted what Martina had. She never understood fun for fun's sake. She was rooted in the deep liberalism and dogma of the times. She was pushed to find success through self-discovery. She really just wanted to have fun. Maybe that's why she chose Martina as her best friend. Now Nikki-D, a cross between both of them, had come and made the threesome. She felt they would watch and take care of each other for the rest of their lives.

"Isn't Martina a bitch?"

Nikki-D giggled. She watched them as they said these things to each other. She never could be outspoken like they were. When she spoke out, it was for a cause. She treated friends like she wanted to be treated, so it was all right for her to laugh at comments from Annie, but nothing beyond that.

"Shit, I wish I was her."

"The boys sure like her." Nikki-D was amazed how much.

"Yea."

Annie saw a boy staring at her. She smiled. The boy came over.

"Would you like to dance?"

"Sure." She was relieved that he didn't come over to ask Nikki-D, although she could tell by the way this boy dressed and acted that he would more than likely ask her.

"My name's Tom. What's yours?"

"Annie. Plain and simple."

"That's all right. I like the simple things in life."

Annie smiled at this. She liked it. She liked Tom.

Nikki-D sat there alone. She thought about the classes and her studies. One thing that her friends got her hooked on was the new age of thinking. She was fast becoming a feminist. In addition, she felt part of the Great Society that was America today. Going to these meetings only reinforced what was already there.

Nikki-D felt thirsty. She decided to go and get a cup of punch. The floor was full now. These were kids who were confident and in charge of themselves and she was one of them. There was no childish separation here, although, she noted, they still went to separate schools and chaperones had to be on hand. Nikki-D got up, smoothing out the creases in her dress. She wore white gloves to go with her dress, which was the latest style, thanks to Martina and Annie. She moved off to get some punch.

She walked between a couple dancing. The boy looked awkward but determined to get the dance right. The girl patiently waited for him to move in unison with her. Nikki-D thought that all the couples looked good. She often wondered what it would be like to dance with Caj as they moved to the beat of the music. She used to dream about that a lot when she was at home. Now it seemed so long ago. She thought about the reservation as her home. Here, she was so busy that often she didn't have enough time to think about home. Then out of the blue, homesickness would hit her. Like now. Nikki-D moved faster. It wouldn't do any good to be sad.

She happened to look over to the other side of the dance floor and saw a blond head bobbing up and down. The head was moving as she moved. She stopped. The blond head stopped. Because of her height, she couldn't see who it was. There were too many bodies between them.

She began walking again. The table was in front of her, white table cloth covered with food and a big punch bowl in the middle. Small glasses hung from its edges. Nikki-D was hot and needed a drink. She passed over the plates of food. She decided against eating anything. She liked to eat, but she didn't want to spill anything on herself. It was her first dance and she didn't want to make a fool of herself. She passed on the food.

Her hand reached out for a glass. Clink. The sound seemed to roar over the sound of music. Nikki-D looked around. Nobody heard it. She felt some perspiration. Some boys stood in the corner watching her with envy in their eyes. She was too beautiful for them. They couldn't even talk to her, let alone dance. She was having that effect on them.

The red punch splashed into the bottom of the cup. She stepped back so none would spill on her. She kept up her appearance, her hair braided the way she liked. She still didn't wear makeup, although Annie kept after her, telling her how much more beautiful she would look. Nikki-D didn't go for it. She felt they were acting like kids.

"Can I help you with that?"

Nikki-D jumped. The punch swayed back and forth in her cup. She almost dropped the cup. A hand grabbed her hand and steadied it. Nikki-D turned around and looked at the boy with the deep voice.

He was tall and good-looking. He had blue eyes and blond hair; like her father's. His smile was wide and deep, with pearly white teeth. His eyes twinkled.

"My name is Beau Culvier."

She felt his hand leave hers. Her heart was beating fast. His smile was like Caj's. Instead of dark eyes, he had the deepest blue eyes she had ever seen. The way he stared at her made her uncomfortable. He was older, and obviously in control. All Nikki-D wanted to do was slow down her heart.

He was the blond head that followed her across the floor. He was about six feet tall and it made her feel self conscious about her small stature. But she liked it.

"My names Nikki-D Thomas."

Her cheeks were red. She could kick herself. Nikki-D sounded like a little girl's name.

"Nikki-D. I like it. I noticed you sitting by yourself and I wanted to go over and talk to you. You got up and left before I could get there. I tried to catch you but the dancers got in my way."

Nikki-D giggled. "I know. I saw your head bobbing up and down. It was strange because I couldn't see who you were."

"Well now you know." He smiled again.

Nikki-D smiled back. She glanced over to the table to see if her friends were back yet. The music had stopped and she was sure that they would be there. She didn't know what else to say to this boy.

Then the music started playing again with another slow song. "You've Lost That Loving Feeling." Nikki-D loved the music that was coming out. It was nothing like her parents' music. Not even like Elvis. She had tried to get Jonny interested in the bands, but he didn't listen. It was so hard to get Jonny to do something if he didn't want to do it. She would use all the persuasion she could muster and still not get him interested. Listening to the music tonight seemed to have a special meaning.

"You want to dance?"

She looked at him. Her tongue was tied to the back of her mouth. She could barely get the words out.

"OK."

Beau took her hand and walked her out to the floor. The Righteous Brothers were singing on the record. Beau turned and took her into his arms. She felt light-headed. She melted into his arms. Awkward, she began to move with him. Nikki-D felt as if she was floating. Her mind closed everything out except the beating of her heart. She couldn't hear the sounds anymore; the music was coming from her. She leaned her head against his shoulder. Something was awakening inside her; something good. She never felt this good. She could dance forever like this. With Beau.

Beau moved away from her.

Nikki-D looked up. She looked at him. He was smiling again. She felt her cheeks become red from embarrassment. She felt lost, with no control. She wished she was still dancing. She liked the feeling of a never-ending dance; but the music had stopped.

"Thanks for the dance."

"OK."

"You don't say much, do you?"

This irked her. Now her cheeks were red from anger. "I say enough."

"I didn't mean anything by it."

Martina walked by. "All right," she said, and winked.

Nikki-D lowered her head. She got embarrassed by anything now.

"Hey, its all right. I think I'm the lucky one here. I've been here for some time and this is the first time I've seen you. I wanted to meet you." Beau was a person who was comfortable in the presence of people; especially girls. He was the quarterback of the football team. He came from a well-connected family. This never went to his head. All of his friends swore by him. Almost everyone liked him.

Every time Nikki-D looked at him, she went blank. He was one of the best looking boys she ever saw. The only one that could compare would be Caj. He was an older boy. If her mother knew, she would immediately stop her from seeing him. Nikki-D was glad she was here and she was certain she wanted to see him again.

Beau took her arm and led her back to her seat. Annie and Martina watched them walk back. Nikki-D never noticed. She was trying to listen to what he was saying. She tried to walk without tripping. All types of fears entered her mind as they walked. His voice was strong and confident. She loved his voice. It was the only thing her ears could pick up. They made it back to the table.

"Well, thanks, Nikki-D."

"You know my name."

"I know. You told me."

Nikki-D blushed in front of her friends.

"Are you going to introduce us?" It was Annie. She and Martina were smiling at her.

"This is Annie and Martina." Nikki-D didn't say more. "Oh thanks, Nikki-D. That was some introduction."

"That's all right. My names Beau Culvier. Nice to meet you." He looked at Nikki-D.

"I think we will be seeing a lot of each other."

Nikki-D smiled and blushed. She wished she would stop doing that.

Beau Culvier smiled down at her and then turned and left.

The girls watched as he walked out of the dance. Martina and Annie didn't say anything to their friend. They could tell by the look on her face that she wouldn't hear a thing that they said anyway. She was too far gone.

Jonny had been watching early-morning television. There were protests going on at some colleges. The Marines had landed in some country that he couldn't remember and the students didn't like it. It interested him because of the tactics they used to protest: a peaceful sit-in. They just sat waiting for the establishment to do something to them. Jonny felt something stir. It was as if the people on TV were showing him what to do in his life - how to fight and stand up for what is wrong without worrying about the consequences. They sat there in defiance ... never blinking an eye.

Jonny knew he had to do something about his condition at school. He looked at his clothes; the rags he had to wear. Every day. the same pair of pants, the other kids making fun of him. Girls didn't look at him. They were nice to him because of his poverty. He felt it and knew it was true. He was in no better condition here then he was at home. He was the poor kid on the block. He had nothing to offer, nothing to give. It should not have been this way – the BIA was supposed to send him his check. The defiance he saw on TV was now in him. He wasn't going to take it anymore.

Jonny walked out of the main TV room and went to the janitor's closet. He knew what he was looking for. It was hanging on the wall; a rope with a half-inch thickness.

Jonny walked out of Quanta Hall. He had the rope with him. Standing in the entrance, he looked around the morning campus. Everything was quiet. Clouds moved fast across the sky. The wind blew. Even so, it wasn't cold. He wore his blue wind-breaker. The cafeteria would be opening for breakfast soon. He needed to get set up before all the kids rushed out of their dorms to eat. Jonny saw the flag as it went up the flagpole in the middle of the campus. The wind whipped it to and fro.

Jonny had seen it on TV: people throwing the flag down and stomping on it. There was nobody around this early in the morning. Most of the kids had to do their chores. Usually it was a fight just to get them done before breakfast and school. Jonny didn't do his chore this morning. He was through with that until he got what he wanted. He wanted some fair treatment. He wasn't going to live like this anymore.

Standing in front of the white flag pole, Jonny looked up to see the flag waving in the wind. The dark-red sand blew past him. The wind was still blowing. A gust of wind kicked the flag and it went into a flurry of motion. A burst of energy went through Jonny. Excitement erupted and he had to smile. He was in control.

Kids came out of the dorms. Boys and girls ran through the wind. They hid their faces from its biting force. Not Jonny. He would go with the wind. No more hiding.

Boys stood in front of their buildings waiting for their girlfriends to come out. The girls always took longer. The older boys would smoke a cigarette while they waited. Most of the kids, both boys and girls, smoked. Jonny didn't. He never understood why anyone would want to. It smelled bad.

Bear and PeeWee walked by.

"Hey, Jonny, what you doing?"

"Mmm ... mm, nothing."

"Why you got that rope?"

Jonny shrugged.

PeeWee hit Bear on the shoulder. He pointed to a girl walking out of her dorm. The wind kicked her hair. She was holding her books and trying to keep her skirt down at the same time.

"Bear, there's Arleen."

"I see her."

They waited until she got to them. Arleen was Bear's girlfriend. She was a small Colville girl. She wasn't that good-looking, and not particularly friendly. Only Bear could love someone like her. At the same time, she ran rough-shod over him.

She stopped in front of him.

"Well, aren't you going to help me with my books?"

Bear moved over and grabbed her books.

"You're looking good this morning, Arleen," oozed PeeWee.

PeeWee was always kissing her ass. He was the biggest kiss-ass on campus. That's why he ran around with Bear.

Bear and Arleen stared at each other. It was obvious that they wanted to kiss or something. It was against the rules for a boy and girl to touch or kiss. They could hold hands on campus; that was all. Most got around it. Jonny looked at the woods in the distance. Most of the kids found places they could go, away from prying eyes.

"I'm hungry, Bear."

"Let's go, then."

"What's Jonny doing with that rope?"

"I don't know. You know Jonny; he's crazy."

"Oh."

"I think Arleen wants to eat, Bear."

Bear gave PeeWee a dirty look.

"I know. Let's go."

They moved off to the cafeteria. Jonny watched them. There was something sad about them. He sat down in front of the pole. It was time to tie himself up. Time to make his statement. He was almost done. He tied so many knots that nobody would be able to untie the rope. Kids were walking fast in the wind. Most of them walked by without noticing him. Jonny just sat there tied to the pole, his hair blowing in the wind. He had his wind-breaker zipped up to his throat to keep warm. He faced the administration building. It was there that he aimed his protest.

Kids were now noticing him sitting tied to the flag pole. Some pointed. Some laughed. The kids thought Jonny was strange anyway. He kept to himself, mostly. Even in the Indian culture, you opened up after a while and talked. Not Jonny. More kids came out and looked. Girls would go by and giggle. Most of the kids talked to themselves and murmured their thoughts about Jonny.

Jonny didn't care. He was going home. He made up his mind. He had enough of this school with all its different kids. None of them looked alike. It was different to see all these tribes represented. Those people who say all Indians are alike should be sent to this boarding school. Then they would know.

Jonny saw Miles, the matron of Quanta hall, come out. Miles walked fast. He wore the white outfit that matrons had to wear: white shirt with white pants, contrasting with his dark Indian skin. Miles had the classic features of an Arapaho Indian: high cheek bones and long nose; black hair that wasn't long, but cut short, Fifties' style.

"Hey, Jonny."

Jonny didn't look up. He kept his eyes on the ground.

"Jonny, what are you doing, tying yourself to the pole like that? Trying to become a protester? Listen, I want you to cut yourself loose and come inside where we can talk. OK?"

Jonny stared at the ground, not saying anything.

"I know you got problems. This ain't the way to settle them. Its only going to get you in trouble with the authorities. You don't want that, do you?"

Jonny still didn't look up.

"OK. If that's the way you want it. Its too late now, anyway."

Now Jonny looked up to see what he was talking about. He saw them coming; three men in suits. They came from the Administration building: Mr. Robertson, the principal, Mr. Demouns, the administrator; and Mr. Addams, the exec of the school. They were the three white men who ran everything. Nothing went on without their knowledge.

"What in the hell is going on here, Miles?" asked Mr. Demouns.

"I'm not sure, sir. Seems like Jonny has a problem."

"Jonny? Jonny who?"

"Jonny Esque, sir."

Mr. Demouns looked at Mr. Robertson. The principal didn't say anything. Mr. Addams stepped up. "He's the young man that hasn't gotten his money yet. His mother has called numerous times, asking us to help him. We can't seem to find out were his money is."

"How long has it been?"

"Ever since he got here."

"Shit."

Mr. Demouns waved Miles over to him. He leaned close to him.

"Miles, is this student in your dorm?"

"Yes, sir."

"I want him off this campus and in school before noon. We have the BIA coming today and we can't afford to let them see this. Now, these are your people. They talk to you. I want this settled. You understand?"

"Yes, I do."

Then Mr. Demouns looked at Jonny.

"I want the rope off you in five minutes. You understand me?"

Jonny kept his eyes down. He didn't look at any of them. He closed them out of his hearing. The world around him faded as he thought of the sights and sounds of home. He smelled the beaches of Tulalip. Jonny ran among the evergreens. Their aroma surrounded him. He was in his world. He was home.

The three men left. Miles shook his head. He bent down to try to untie the rope. He couldn't. The yellow rope was tied tightly around Jonny's body. His blue wind-breaker contrasted with the red-and-green ground and the white flag pole. The wind still kicked. Miles was stumped, but then he began to laugh.

"You know Jonny, as far as Mr. Demouns is concerned, I should know you like one of my tribe. You're fighting some ignorant people."

Jonny kept his head down. He was home.

"Jonny, I know you will sit here until doomsday. You've reached your limit and can't take anymore. I know this. But they don't know it. You have to understand that they have all the power and they know how to use it. Eventually this will come back at you. They have long memories."

Jonny kept his head down.

"OK. I have to go and get wire cutters to get you out of this. Maybe it will do you some good to get your anger out. Sit here and think. I'll be back."

Jonny sat in the middle of the campus as the school life went on around him. The other kids stayed away from him because word got out that Mr. Demouns was mad. They knew what that meant. Kids learned fast what they could do and what they couldn't do, and who they can talk to and who to avoid. Jonny was on the shit-list.

Jonny's stubborn streak rose up. He didn't care what they thought. He was sticking to his guns.

The morning went by. Jonny was tired from sitting. His head was hanging down from exhaustion. He was tired. His eyes closed. Sleep overcame him. He twitched and then fell to sleep. After some time, he began to dream. His eyes darted side to side under their lids. Like spirits, dreams moved in their own time and place. Jonny was sometimes a spectator and sometimes a participant. In his dreams, Jonny talked to himself.

His mother and Nikki-D's mother were walking in front of him. They were walking to the trees. Jonny could see them, high in the sky. They were so far away. Jonny was thirsty and hungry. He had been following them for some time. He couldn't catch up with them. A weight was tied to his back and it made walking hard. Jonny wanted to let go of the weight, but the rope was tied with the knot where he couldn't reach it. His mother and Ginny Thomas stood at the edge of the trees, waving for him to come. He was too tired. Jonny looked around ... no trees anywhere. He hated it. The heat was taxing his strength. He sat down to get some rest. The weight was too much. Something moved in front of him. It was the wolf-pup, panting, waiting for him. Jonny couldn't move. He wanted to but the weight prevented it. He needed help.

"Jonny! Jonny! Talk to me." He could hear her voice. Nikki-D was calling to him. She came up and grabbed his arms, trying to lift him up from the ground. She wanted to help him. "Jonny, I'm here to help you."

Jonny's eyes flickered; his head was down against the wind. Jonny could still hear the voice. She would help him. He went toward the voice. He opened his eyes and lifted his head.

"Jonny."

Jonny could see her in front of him. She knelt there, her long, black hair falling forward. Her eyes watched his every move. Blood rushed to his head as the excitement built in him. Nikki-D was there.

"Nikki-D."

Jonny focused his eyes. She was in front of him.

"Jonny Esque? I'm Mariann. Are you OK?"

Jonny could see now that this girl in front of him wasn't Nikki-D. Suddenly he felt alone again.

"Why are you sitting here tied up to the flag pole?"

"Mmmmm ... mm, who are you?"

"I came up from Concho. Caj said to look you up when I got here." Mariann wondered about the boy in front of her. Caj said he was a little quiet, but he never said anything about this. Mariann knew something was going on here. She wasn't sure she was going to get an answer from this boy. She was scared being here. It was always hard going into a new school. She looked down. She missed Concho.

Jonny perked up when he heard his brother's name. It was like Caj to be there when he needed him. Jonny looked at this girl. She was thin and lanky like the Plains tribes. He would guess that she came from one of the tribes around here. Maybe a Sioux or a Pawnee.

"Mmm ... mm, you know Caj?"

"Yes. I met him at Concho."

"Mmm ... when did you get here?"

"Today. I'm on my way over to the Administration Building. I saw you. I knew it was you, because you look so much like Caj."

"Oh."

"Yes. At first I thought there was something wrong, but the closer I got, I couldn't believe you were tied to the pole. I didn't know what to think. I almost called for help but I saw other kids just look at you and go on. Are you in trouble?"

226

"Mmm .... mm, mm ... mm, a little."

"Can I sit here? I think its lunch time. I don't think I want to go into the cafeteria just yet. I ate this morning. Why are you in trouble?"

"M ... I want to go home. They haven't sent me my money. I want them to help me but they don't listen. So I thought I would try this."

"I think I saw them doing this on TV. They called it a sit-in."

"Yea. That's where I saw it, too."

"How long are you going to sit here?"

Jonny narrowed his eyes. "Until they help me."

Mariann liked Jonny. He seemed the opposite of Caj. He was so serious. He looked like a ragamuffin. His clothes were worn and torn. Why didn't he just order some new ones, like at Concho? Mariann looked over to the Administration Building.

"I think they're coming to help you now."

Jonny watched the four men as they stomped their way across the school campus. He knew it was now or never. They had determined looks on their face. He knew it was time for the showdown. He was just as determined not to back down.

Mariann moved back. "Should I stay?"

"Maybe not."

"OK. I'll talk to you later." She headed off to the Administration Building.

He watched her go. She had a nice walk to her. Jonny couldn't take his eyes off her. Then she passed the men coming for him. He couldn't see her anymore.

Mr. Demouns was coming right at him. "God damn it! I want you up and out of here now."

Jonny could see the veins in his neck, and his face was red. He was that angry. Jonny didn't move. He lowered his head, so as not to look at him.

"I mean it! I want you back in school and off this campus now."

Jonny still didn't move.

"OK. You had your chance. Cut him loose and get him out of here. I'll deal with him later."

Miles took out the big wire-clippers. They had green handles on them. He moved over to the rope. The Exec had another pair and began cutting the rope, too. Jonny didn't fight them. They worked as fast as they could. The rope loosened.

Jonny turned around and grabbed the flag pole. He wrapped his arm around it and locked it to his other arm. He was going to make it as hard as he could for them.

"Come on, Jonny. Give it up." Miles and the Exec grabbed his legs and tried to pull him from the pole. Jonny held on. The kids were watching. If it wasn't so serious, it would be funny.

Mr. Demouns came rushing in, his anger at a peak. He reached in and took Jonny's thumb and bent it back as hard as he could.

"Let go of the god damn pole you little shit!"

The pain shot through Jonny's arm. Tears immediately came to his eyes. He kept his head down and didn't let them see. He let out a little moan. That was it. Mr. Demouns took his other thumb and bent that one back, too. The shock of the pain ran straight to his head. He thought he was going to pass out from the pain. Jonny couldn't hold on anymore. He had to let go.

The tears came from his eyes; not only from the pain, but partly from the failure he felt. He could barely see because of the tears and the pain. They were dragging him away.

" Stop it! Stop it! You're hurting him! Can't you see that? You're breaking his thumbs." Mariann was crying and screaming at the men. They stopped.

Kids were standing around in a semi-circle watching them. Miles and the Exec dropped his legs. Mr. Demouns still had Jonny's fingers but wasn't bending them anymore.

"You kids get back to school. This has nothing to do with you."

None of the kids moved. They knew something bad was happening. They were kids brought up on the reservation. They were taught never to question the authorities; always do what they told you to do, or else. Even with that they didn't move. Something stirred in them. In that moment, Jonny came to represent a will to fight. They felt inside that if they let the authorities treat Jonny like this, then they would be next. Most of them watched their parents treated like second class citizens. They saw how that affected their parents. They instinctively rebelled against it. They were not their parents.

"I said go back to school. And I mean now!" Mr. Demouns couldn't keep his anger in.

"Mr. Demouns. I think you better let this one go." Miles moved away from Jonny. He saw something that the white people couldn't see. They were too used to being in charge, used to having their demands met. They had become blind. Miles was staring at the new world. Miles knew the old order was going to fall.

"Jonny, are you all right?" Mariann ran up and grabbed his hands. She began to rub his thumbs. It was soothing to Jonny. She didn't even think about it. She wanted to help this young man who was so stubborn.

Jonny was crying. He didn't want to, but when Mariann started rubbing his thumbs, the pain began to subside. All his fear left. She helped him beat the authorities. As Mariann rubbed his thumbs, Jonny looked at her. The girl stared back at him and smiled. As they sat there, the men moved off to the Administration Building and the kids moved off to school. Suddenly, they were two kids that weren't alone anymore.

Caj watched as they showed President Johnson's message that he had sent Marines into Vietnam. Wherever that was? He watched as the Marines came off boats carrying their duffel bags and rifles. Caj was excited. It was going to be a big war. The thought pushed his adrenaline up. He couldn't take his eyes off the TV.

Caj stood on the sidelines with BJ. He was nervous all day. Practice was bad for him. The coach gave him the hook. BJ didn't play ball but he came out with him to watch. They did most things together.

"Hey man, you hear about the war?"

"What war?"

"I saw it on TV. Johnson sent in the Marines. I was thinking about us. We're going to be out of school soon. Unless we go to college what do we have back home? There's no jobs. I think we ought to check it out. You know, the service."

"Man, are you crazy? Why would you want to do that? Where are they fighting, anyway?

"Vietnam."

"Where's that?"

"Shit, I don't know. All I'm saying is we should check it out. What you going to do, go back to the Rez and drink yourself to death? Let's check it out."

"OK. OK. I think we can do it here. They say the army recruiters come here for the seniors; you know, give them a lecture. We'll see them when they come."

"Ahh man, I'm not going in any Army. Let's check out the Marines. I saw them on TV. They looked pretty good."

"Are you nuts? I ain't going into any Marines."

"Come on, lets check it out."

BJ knew better than to talk to Caj now. His mind was made up. All BJ could do was try to talk him out of it. Besides, what would it hurt? They ain't going to join anyway. Why would anyone want to go to war? Doesn't he know that you can die that way??

The practice was over. Caj came out of the locker room. BJ stood against the door, smoking a cigarette. He forgot the talk they had. He wanted to go and get something to eat. After that, he wanted to go to the Rec. room. The girls would be there and he had his eye on the one named Sally. BJ knew she was watching him, too. BJ couldn't wait to see her.

Caj came up to him, his wild hair wet from the shower.

"Well, you ready to go find them recruiters?"

21

ROTC

She felt his hand as it moved up her leg. Her body tingled from the pressure of his fingers. She couldn't move. She didn't know if she wanted to. Nikki-D was hot. Her body was running over with heat. She tried to catch her breath, but his mouth was over hers, his lips strong and forceful. So much so that it scared her.

Nikki-D turned her head from him, tearing her lips from his. Breathless, she spoke. "No. Let's stop, Beau."

She peeked over at him. His face was red and sweaty, his blond hair disheveled and out of place. His blue eyes were excited and unfocused. His brain must be gone. She giggled.

Then she saw the anger cover his face. She knew she had made a mistake.

"What's so funny?" He jumped up and straightened out his clothes.

"Nothing." She looked down. She didn't want to anger him any more. It was an ongoing battle to keep him off her. At the same time, she was fighting herself, because she wanted him so bad. Her body was on fire from his touches. She looked at the spots where his hands had been. She thought she could see the red prints of his fingers. Then her body began to tingle again, and she felt the sharp stab of lust hit her loins. It was hard on them both.

"I have to go."

Clearly, Beau was upset with her again. Nikki-D thought it funny – a boy of his age acting like a child at times like this. It made her feel in control. She liked this feeling. It made her love for him stronger, because she knew he would do anything for her. She looked at him.

His strong lean body was molding into a man's body. He was seventeen, going on eighteen and it was important for her to remember that. He wanted to be a man so bad. He worked out all the time. She found out his heroes were men with power. He read books on McArthur,

Patten and Montgomery. She was a little disturbed that he thought of men of war as heroes. He talked of joining the Marine Corps after high school. That was at the end of the year. Nikki-D didn't like to hear it. The war in Vietnam was escalating. The world was a scary place. All you had to do was read the paper in the mornings.

"I'm going to work out. I need to take a shower."

"No, I don't want you to go."

"Listen Nikki-D, you may be able to handle being turned on and off like a lamp, but I can't. I need to work off all of this tension."

"Why are you tense?"

"Don't act like a little girl. I know you're one of the brightest girls at school. So don't play games with me."

"OK." She pouted her lip. "I just don't want you to leave me. Can't we just sit here and talk? Please."

She watched him as he thought about this. He sighed and sat back down next to her.

"Just for a little while. I have to finish my homework and then go to practice."

She smiled. "OK. Just for a little while." She snuggled up to him. She wrapped her arm around his stomach ... his fine stomach.

"So what's going on in the world today? I know you and your girl-friends must read every paper put out." He rolled his head into hers, his blue eyes only inches from her deep, dark eyes.

Nikki-D knew he didn't approve of her friends and their wanting to change the world. She went to all the meetings with them, read the latest books on the changes in America. She read about the black movement and its leaders, Malcolm X and Martin Luther. Whites attacked the blacks for fighting for their rights as Americans. She could only watch and listen to the world in its turmoil. But not for long. They were planning on going to a protest march next week. She got excited thinking about it. Nikki-D kept their secret from Beau. He didn't agree with their politics. He was America, love it or leave it. He wasn't comfortable with blacks fighting for freedom when he thought all Americans had the same ability to succeed. All you had to do was work hard. He was conservative like his family. She would change him, though. Nikki-D was confident of that.

"Don't tell me. It will only lead to a fight. I got something to tell you. I've picked my college and I've joined the ROTC."

"What do you mean you joined the ROTC?"

"Its the way I want to pay back my country."

"But don't you know that they're sending more and more troops over to Vietnam?"

"Yea. I'll still be in college when that's over. We'll go in there and kick some butt and get out." He got a dreamy look in his eyes. "I wish I was part of it."

Nikki-D was steaming. "You can have your damn war! That's all you think about. Doesn't it bother you, killing people?" She felt her chest constrict. How could he do this?

He knew how she felt about it. People were in the streets fighting against oppression, here at home. Why didn't he see this?

"No, I don't think about it. I want to serve my country, not tear it down. You keep bringing up your hero, John F. Kennedy. Well, isn't he the one that said, "Ask not what your country can do for you, but ask what you can do for your country?""

She felt his sarcasm as he said the words to her. Nikki-D was fighting mad. It was part of their love. Argue, and make up, argue, and make up. She fell into it every time. It was different now. She was planning to go to her protest and he was joining the ROTC. They were two kids that the world was causing to grow up fast.

"Do what you want. I thought you had to go!" Her icy eyes never left his. The challenge was there, neither one giving in on this one. Suddenly he broke contact. He got up and put on his coat.

"You're right. I should get back to school and so should you." They were at his friend's apartment. It was one of the bennies of coming from a well-to-do family. Nikki-D could have brought him to one of her cousin's homes. She knew it would get back to her mother. She couldn't have that. She told her mother about Beau. Her mother would have a fit if she found out how much Nikki-D was seeing him. Her mother could never understand something like love. She still thought Nikki-D was too young to date. Nikki-D watched as Beau stomped around the apartment getting her coat and checking to make sure everything was in place. Yes, it was better not to tell her.

Ginny Thomas was on the bottom. Nick covered her with his body. He was beginning to heat up and made faster pelvic thrusts. Without thinking, she matched his thrusts with her own. Her eyes closed as she felt him move against her. She could feel the orgasm build in her. She opened her legs wider and stuck her head in the nape of his neck. The thrusting became more immediate and final. Ginny grabbed his buttocks and moved faster. The orgasm rushed through her body, flooding her brain.

"Oh ... oh ... oh ... oh!" Her body tightened up for the release that she sought. Her eyes rolled under their lids. Her mouth let out air and sweat trickled down her forehead. Nick was still pounding against her but her mind was somewhere else. She heard his grunts as he climaxed in her. Finally there was no movement at all as Nick laid on top of her. Nick was a dead weight, but she didn't mind. She was happy.

"Are you all right?"

"Mmm ... mm."

Ginny discovered that she loved this man, her husband who had put up with her all of these years. She was so scared after Nikki-D was sent off. Everything was so hard for her. Nick showed her how much he really cared for her. Just thinking of Nikki-D still sent a stab of pain through her heart. Now she knew that she had Nick here. She squeezed him.

"Ohhhhh..." Then he let out a sigh. "What was that for?"

"I don't know. I wanted to hug you. Show you how much I love you."

Nick looked down at her. Ginny watched his eyes as he averted them. She used to think he averted his eyes because he was weak. Now she knew that it was just his way. He was a man of strong character and backbone. That's why she married him.

"I'm going to the bank early tomorrow morning."

Ginny's ears perked up. It was time for her to ask Nick.

"Its Saturday tomorrow."

"I know."

"We had things planned for tomorrow."

"I know."

Ginny's anger flared. "Do as you please."

"Listen, Ginny, you're always asking about the bank. Why don't you come in with me?"

"You want me to come in with you?"

"Sure, why not..."

"There is a man I want you to meet. His name is Bob Bryce. To tell you the truth, he's the reason I am doing so well; without him the bank would be in trouble."

Ginny thought about going in. It wasn't exactly how she thought a person should spend a Saturday afternoon. Her interest picked up. She did need to know some things about the bank. What better way for her to achieve her goals then by going in with Nick? She had really been missing Nikki-D lately and maybe this would help her. Pain came over her when she thought of her little girl. She needed to do something.

"OK. I'll go in with you."

Nick saw the pain and determination in her eyes. He moved off her and looked at her.

"Nikki-D didn't call today. Maybe we should call her to see what's up."

"No, I don't think so. She's trying to show us that she's grown up. If we start acting like parents to her she will just turn stubborn and not call us at all."

'But what if something has happened to her?"

Ginny could see the concern in his eyes. It almost made her want to call right then. She held the impulse down. "Nothing has happened to her. The school will call if that happens. We just have to wait. After all, she's fifteen-almost-sixteen and is growing fast."

"That's what concerns me. Kids today are growing up so fast. The streets are all on fire. Blacks are protesting and I don't want Nikki-D harmed. With the way she looks."

"What did you say ... just how does she look?" Ginny turned to instant anger with her husband. She hated him saying things like that.

"I'm sorry. But Nikki-D has all of your looks. And that's Chinese. I don't understand why you get mad at that. You have a beautiful people, and..."

"I'm American. My people are American. That's all I'm saying."

"I know that. We're all American. You're Chinese-American and Nikki-D is half Chinese and you both have the looks. You never let her see that side of you. Now she has to come face to face with it. The world today is changing."

Ginny knew he was right. She couldn't bring herself to talk to Nikki-D about her ancestry. It was too painful. She wanted Nikki-D brought up in a wholesome environment, brought up American. She succeeded at it. Nick was right. The world was changing so fast. She could no longer hide from it. Even in Tulalip. Here they fit in so well.

She thought about the streets and the blacks and the protesters. Fear entered her heart. Nick was right. Her little girl could be in danger just because of her looks. The fear kept growing.

"Maybe we should give her a five-minute call."

Nick smiled. He leaned over her, picked up the phone and dialed the number to Nikki-D's school.

Jonny felt the big hands take him by the throat. They were on the elevator to the jail. The doors had just opened and Jonny, frightened and unsure after seeing all of the orange bars, refused to walk out. The two men beside him had his arms and one of them twisted hard. Jonny let out his breathe.

The principal began to squeeze Jonny's throat. He fought for air but his windpipe was being crushed. Jonny thought he was going to pass out.

"Hey you bringing a little boy for us? He can share my cell." The prisoners laughed and made crude jokes as the guards took Jonny from the principal and his staff. Jonny fought them all the way, digging his heels into the floor as they dragged him. The guards led him through the jail, walking by the prisoners. Jonny kept his head down. He thought better than to fight the guards. The look in their eyes told him that they didn't take any shit from anyone.

The cell door opened and Jonny faced the orange room. It was so bright with orange bars that it almost hurt the eyes. The cell was sparse, with only a commode sitting in the middle and steel bunk beds on one side of the cell. The guard pushed him in and Jonny heard the cold, hard steel bars shut behind him. He was alone.

The other prisoners walked by his cell. Jonny had been there for a couple of days. The guards never gave him any bedding, so Jonny had to sleep on the hard steel. The first night he cried like a little baby. He kept his tears low because he was scared of the other prisoners. After the second day of sleeping like this, Jonny began to get used to it. A prisoner came up to his cell.

"Hey boy. Why they bring you here? This is adult jail. What you do – kill someone?"

The man was big and built hard. He had a shaved head and Jonny knew that nobody messed with him. He had mean eyes.

"Mm ... mm. I tied myself to the flagpole and refused to go to school." Jonny was embarrassed by this because of what the other prisoners were in for. He heard them talking about what they did that brought them here. It was bad.

"Is that all? Shit, why don't they give you some bunk?"

"Mm ... mm. I don't know."

"What's wrong with your speech? You one of them stutterers?"

"Mmm ... mm. Mm ... mm."

"Hey, that's all right. We'll get you some bunk. Shit, putting a kid like you in here just for that. You one of those boys from that Indian school, aren't you? They usually send them to the juv. Seen those fences over there. Must be hard to be locked up all of the time. Ain't like the school I went to."

Jonny watched the man. He was big but he sounded like he was going to help him. He said nothing.

"Guard. Guard. Why haven't you got this boy some bedding?"

Some time later a guard came and unlocked Jonny's cell. "Come with me."

Jonny got up and followed the guard to a room were bedding was stored. "Hold out your arms." Then the guard loaded Jonny up with bedding and they went back to his cell. The other prisoners, who played cards outside Jonny's cell, had already put a mattress under the cell door. Jonny got back and saw this and began to make his bunk. At least he wouldn't freeze tonight. He looked over at the big man.

"Hey, boy. You be all right. That shit is something every man has a right to. Even in here." Then the big man went back to his cards. Jonny would be all right until he got out. The school wouldn't break him. Jonny smiled.

Jonny stood with the pitchfork in his hands, throwing horse manure into the wheelbarrow. Soon it would be time for lunch. His stomach growled. More hungry than he thought. He leaned down and picked up some more manure. He was cleaning out Lightning's stall. He was Jonny's favorite horse. Mr. Demouns sent him to the barn as punishment for not obeying the school authorities, but it didn't bother Jonny. He liked the horses and the hard work. It took his mind off home.

He couldn't stop thinking of home today, though. He really missed them on weekends. Most of the kids went to town and he was always left here to work. At least they paid him a little money for cleaning the barn. Sometimes, even hard work couldn't stop him from feeling lonely. Today, the thoughts of home almost made him cry.

He needed to be strong; like his father said. He had grown up some since coming to school here. The work had hardened his muscles and his light-tan body grew another couple of inches. He was five-foot-eight and his dark-brown hair was shaggy now. He let it grow because he knew the school authorities couldn't have made him cut it. Part of his heritage. Jonny smiled at this. While he was growing up, most of his people had short hair and didn't let their kids have long hair, either. Caj was one of the exceptions to this. Caj did what he wanted anyway. Now it was Jonny with hair to his shoulders. He was shedding his baby fat and his body was sculpting itself into the man he would become. His deep brown eyes grew more intense and serious as the world forced him to participate in it. He was lean and scrappy; and he was angry. Or was it sad?

Creak!

Jonny stopped and bent up. Someone was here. The gray stalls were too high for him to see over. He put the fork in the ground by his boot and leaned on it.

"Who's there?"

Creak!

There it was again. Jonny felt fear. He took the fork and grabbed it by the neck. He moved out of the stall and looked at the barn door. Daylight came in. It shone on one spot in the center of the barn. The barn was big enough to hold twenty horses and the stalls ran on both sides of it. In addition, it had a ceiling floor where straw grass and horses feed was kept. Jonny labored long and hard to load the rafters with the sacks of food.

Jonny's eyes searched out the intruding noise. He was sure he heard it. He stood at the very end stall. The front barn doors seemed a long way away. He looked down the rows of stalls and didn't see anything.

Creak!

Jonny heard it again. Now he knew someone was in the barn. He moved toward the sounds. It came from the bales of hay next to the door. Jonny moved slowly, his heart racing. There was still a couple of the horses left; they moved against their stalls. They knew someone was there, too. Jonny called out again.

"Who's there?"

The sound caught his ears. Weeping. A girl crying. He moved faster to the hay. Then he saw her sitting on one of the bales. Mariann. She had her head down and she was crying. Jonny stood in front of her.

"Mmm ... mm. Are you all right, Mariann?" He felt stupid after asking. He didn't know what else to say.

Mariann looked up. Her eyes were red with tears. Her face looked so sad. She wore blue jeans and a plaid shirt. It looked new. She wiped her eyes with a towel.

"I didn't know you were here." She tried to smile. "I'm all right. I just feel bad today. I get like this sometimes. It seems like sometimes I have no one in the world and I'm all alone. Sometimes I can't take it and I break down and cry. Stupid isn't it?"

Jonny didn't know what to say. No, it wasn't stupid. She was talking about the things that he felt. Mariann was lonely. So was he. It hurt.

"Mmm ... mm. I don't think its stupid."

Jonny felt small next to Mariann. She was older than him: a sophomore. This made her one of the worldly type people that Jonny always tried to emulate.

Jonny looked at her. She had long, coarse black hair that hung down her side. Her eyes reminded Jonny of Nikki-D: slanted and very wise. She spoke in a small voice. Jonny sat next to her. He felt stupid and unsophisticated. He knew he should do something. He put his arm around her shoulders. She slumped against him. He could hear her heart breaking inside. She had a special smell to her. Jonny loved the way the girls smelled, except when they used too much perfume. Not Mariann.

She was crying against his neck. Jonny couldn't help feeling her against him. He could feel himself become excited and immediately felt he was some kind of pervert. He was ashamed of thinking about sex when Mariann needed someone to help her. Jonny pulled away a little to see if that would help. Mariann stopped crying and looked at him.

She quickly moved toward him. Her lips sought his. She wore a light lipstick that tasted funny to Jonny. They kissed hard and long. Heat rushed through every pore of his body. Jonny felt himself grow. She smelled so good. He kissed back. She moved her body against his, both of them fighting the loneliness they felt, both wanting to be somewhere else but stuck here together. Jonny moved his hand over her, and Mariann put hers on the back of his head, forcing his head down. The heat overcame them and they began removing clothes. Jonny froze for a second. Everything was going too fast. He wanted to catch his breath but she wouldn't let him. She needed someone.

Jonny brought her behind the bales of hay. There they laid out their clothes to lie on. He felt her breasts with his tingling hands. They were both naked and kissing. He was so hot. He lay beside her. Mariann looked down his body. She softly grabbed him in her hand. Blood rushed from Jonny's brain down to his groin, and he thought he was going to pass out. His eyes rolled back. It felt so good.

Her soft hand started moving up and down, caressing him. Jonny couldn't stand it any more. He tried to get on top of her. She moved under him; her soft breasts touched his chest. Her nipples caressed him. They both were holding their breath at the same time they kissed. Their movements were of two forlorn kids trying to end their desolation and loneliness. It was a loneliness caused by years of neglect and abuse in their home-life. A young girl who had to grow up through a school system because her parents were too drunk to want her. A home where sex was the only way to get attention. Staying in the system so long that now she was lost. A boy who knew his only chance in life came from his inner-self that only his people could bring out.

Jonny and Mariann were fighting their loneliness the only way they could and in the only way they knew how. It was Jonny's first time with a girl. He hated this world that he was sent to. Maybe that's why Mariann was attracted to him. It was the only world she knew and Jonny hated it.

He fought it and never gave in. His loneliness was condensed into this one school year. They wouldn't let him go out but they would never get him back again. Controlled by people that knew nothing of what was needed for true growth, they set up a system of suppression. Jonny would fight them until the day he was home.

Jonny moved his groin against her, hard. His anger at these thoughts made him excited.

She moved back. They both were too hot to know if they were doing it right or not. Jonny wasn't even sure if he was in her or not. It didn't matter. It had nothing to do with sex. It was his passage into life. Like his political education, he was now finding the physical realm of life. It left him, for better or worse, a man.

Mariann didn't care about the man or the politics. She just wanted someone to hold her. To love her. If her sex brought love to her, then she would use it. She needed Jonny. There was no one else. This was her home now. The kids of this school would be her family. Jonny would be her lover. She wouldn't let him go. She wrapped her legs around his as he moved on top of her. She matched his every move. Jonny thrust faster. His head felt as if it was going to explode. He thought of nothing else. The world faded in and out. Finally a great release came over him and he came inside her. Breathing through his nose, he made only a small sound. It was enough for Mariann. She began pumping her pelvis against his before he went soft. Soon she too felt the release from the pain and tension that was her life. For a second, she felt love as only it can be; in its physical form. Jonny filled the emptiness that was inside her.

They lay there for some time afterward, then they got up and put their clothes back on.

"I'm sorry for crying on you. I just needed someone."

Jonny was embarrassed by what he did.

"Mmm ... mm. Its all right."

"You don't talk too much. Caj talked all the time."

Jonny nodded at this.

"Why do you fight the school?"

"Mm ... mm. I don't like the way they treat us."

"I know. But this is the only place I know. I've been in Indian schools since I was a little girl."

"Mm ... mm. Don't you miss home?"

"This is my home. Its all I know."

"That's sad."

"Yea. I guess it gets a little tiring. I feel alone all the time."

"Mmm ... mm. I know what you mean. I felt like that when I first got here."

"I'm glad you're here." Mariann looked at him, waiting.

"Mmm ... mm. I'm glad you're here, too." Jonny was embarrassed. He thought about what they just did. It was like he took advantage of her, forgetting that she was the one that made the first move and came on to him. He felt ashamed.

"Maybe we should go."

Mariann saw the fear in him. She knew he was embarrassed and wanted to go away.

"OK. Let's go horseback riding."

This caught Jonny by surprise. He thought she would want to go back to the halls.

"Mmm ... mm. Are you sure?"

"Yes. Aren't you?"

"Mmm ... mm. Yes, I want to go." Still, it was clear he wasn't too sure about this. Jonny wasn't equipped to handle this girl.

"OK, let's go down by the creek. Its a good spot to be alone. Can you get me a soft, quiet horse to ride? I don't want to fall off or something."

"OK."

Jonny jumped up, Mariann put her arm out and he pulled her up with him. She moved close, only inches away. Jonny stepped back and went to get the horses. He was thinking of what horse would be right for her. He knew that he would be riding Lightning. He knew it would impress her.

    Lois lay in the dark. The little ones were in bed with her. They kept each other warm on these cold nights. The clock ticked on the old night-stand that Franc brought home from the thrift store. He slept out on the couch. Lois heard his snoring. He drank hard tonight. She tried to quiet the kids when he got home, but she was becoming tired of the fights. His drinking was worse now.

    Now she had to put all of her energy into the little ones growing up. Lois knew she let the older kids down. All of her life she had felt if she could look back at the end of her life and say she did her best, then it would be all right. She wasn't so sure anymore. Trying to protect her kids was a full-time job. She wanted Franc to be the head of the house and take care of the hard decisions. She knew that wasn't the way it was. He was like a kid to her. She made all the decisions for everyone. She now knew that Franc would take things only so far and didn't have the fortitude to go to the end.

    His patience was short. He felt he should have been put in charge of the committee to build the new building. They passed him over for one of their own. Franc had to take a back seat because he demanded they build it his way. Finally they got rid of him all together. After that, the committee was able to form a consensus and the new building was being built. Money came from the government. It was going forward.

    Shawn kicked out under the blankets. The girls moved all night long. It was okay because Lois sat up at night thinking. She never felt trapped in her life. She felt she was born to have a family. She felt trapped in the poverty. It was so binding on the people here. Her mother couldn't understand how she stayed. Lois knew. The people of Tulalip had something more than the material things that her family used to gauge their lives. She remembered all the fighting over who owned what, and how much each of them had in life. Even in this poor state, Lois knew that she saw more happiness here then she would on the outside. Inside of her she knew there was a barren spot. It was Franc. They no longer touched each other or talked. He talked at her, not with her. It was so different from when she met him. He was so happy and carefree that he swept her from her family and friends, who warned her that he would turn out like all the rest of the Indians. Drunk!

They were right. They didn't understand how much more she got out of her marriage. Franc was just the beginning. In between, she fell in love with the Indians and their way. It was her way now.

Shawn stirred. She rubbed her eyes with the back of her hands, half-asleep.

"Mommy, I got to go the bathroom."

"Shhhh. You'll wake the others. Hurry up and go. Put on my housecoat. And keep yourself covered."

Shawn nodded her little head and yawned. She put her mother's housecoat on. Lois watched her little girl at the end of the bed. She almost laughed. The housecoat was too large for her tiny frame. It was an old, brown, worn housecoat, but it was warm. Lois didn't have to worry about Shawn getting a cold. Even now, she could see the white puffs of Shawn's breath. Her little girl got up and ran to the bathroom next to the bedroom. At least she didn't have to run all the way upstairs. Lois kept the fire going downstairs but that didn't help up there. She was glad her kids were sleeping in a warm room at the Indian Schools. At least she could afford to keep the three girls down here with her now. Soon they would be big enough to where they could sleep upstairs and keep warm under the big blankets she had. Now they slept with her, and it was enough.

Lois watched as Shawn came back and took off the housecoat and folded it in the chair next to the bed. She jumped under the covers and snuggled up to Lois. Soon she began to warm up again and Lois felt her heavy breathing against her. They slept like that most nights. They kept each other warm from the cold world. Lois heard the snoring coming from the front room. Franc, drunk most of the time, slept alone. Lois listened for a minute and then leaned over and turned out the lights.

The house was cold and dark.

22

GIFT

Caj ran for the bus as it started to pull away. It was one of those old yellow buses that carried the kids from the schools. He almost missed it because he was talking to his recruiter. It was a final deal. He was in the Marine Corp. BJ backed out from going in but Caj never had a doubt. The Marine Corps. was calling and he wasn't going to hang up.

Caj caught the bus and, while running along the side of it, he began pounding on the door.

"Hey! Wait for me. Stop the bus." He pounded some more. He heard BJ calling to the driver from a seat in the back.

"Driver. Stop. We got one more coming. You're going to run over him."

That got the driver's attention. He put on the brakes and the bus skidded to a halt. The red dust from under the wheel kicked up in Caj's face. He turned his face away and covered it until the dust subsided.

The bus was for the students who weren't on the football team. Caj always rode the student bus anyway, so he could ride with BJ. This was a special trip. They were going to play Ft. Sill tonight. He was going to see Jonny. Caj knew from his mother that Jonny was having a hard time at the Indian Schools. Caj wanted to find out for himself. Caj never had to worry about money or the Administration. He was one of the stars of the team this year. They all helped him if he needed it. It was just a great school. The door popped out from the bus and the driver yelled.

"Come on. We got a deadline to meet. Get aboard."

"OK. I'm coming."

He ran and hopped aboard the bus, jumping up the black rubber steps and running down the isle. He saw BJ, who saved a seat for him. Abigail, Benita and Cari sat in the seats opposite them. The girls looked at him as he walked down the aisle. He could see the want in their eyes.

He smiled at them. Caj wanted them, too. Most of them he went out with. Some of them he went to bed with. He wasn't sticking with just one girl. He never felt the need.

BJ, with his big smile and white teeth was laughing as Caj sat down next to him.

"I never thought you would make it."

"It was close."

"Well. Did you do it?"

Caj shrugged and nodded his head. "Yep."

"All right. My man. Joining the Marine Corps. I can't believe it. Hey, you dorks, Caj is going to be a Marine."

Kids turned and looked back. Caj, sitting on the aisle seat, looked at them. He could see questions in their eyes. Some of the girls looked at him with new respect. He would have to call Sunday and tell his mother. He knew she would have some problems. His father? Caj wasn't too sure. Maybe he would get some respect from him; maybe not. It didn't matter to Caj at this point. He knew he would not be going back home. The world belonged to him. It was what he wanted.

Jonny waited by the front gate of the compound. Fresh white puffs of air came out of his mouth. He watched the road for the buses, then his eyes shifted to the road to town. There were two reasons he was waiting. His brother Caj was coming for the football game and dance, and his cousin Guy was coming with a special gift from town. Jonny kept his hands in his pockets for warmth. He was still on probation and they wouldn't allow him to go to town himself. They couldn't stop him from seeing his brother Caj and this would be the first dance he was allowed to go to.

The matrons and Miles stepped in for him. They told Mr. Demouns it was policy to give students special time for themselves and he couldn't keep Jonny from going. It must have angered the hell out of him. The thought made Jonny smile.

The yellow bus rose in the horizon. Jonny stepped up to the fence, a cold, light-gray metal fence that kept everyone in. Most of the boys and some of the girls climbed it and headed to town most anytime they wanted. The students had elaborate systems against being caught. The bus was bigger now. It was the school bus from town. It was full of students. It got back at three every time it went to town. It was the last bus from town, so it was the fullest coming back. Jonny moved from the front gate on the northeast side of the school and began following it down to the north gate where the kids would be let off. By the time he got there, the bus had already pulled up and kids were getting off. Jonny watched them until he saw Guy. His cousin was talking to some girl from another hall. She was trying to get away from him. Jonny could imagine what Guy was saying to her. It was usually something sexual. The girl finally got away from him and Guy unloaded from the bus. Seeing Jonny, he waved and came running over.

"Say, Jonny ... didn't see you there. See that girl over there? I think she likes me. I had a hard time getting her off me. Ha-ha."

Jonny gave a weak smile.

"You bring back the gift?"

"Are you kidding? I worked a great deal for you. Got it right here in my pocket."

Before Guy could bring it out, he saw two kids who looked like Sioux or Cheyenne. They looked as if they meant business. Guy started walking faster.

"Listen, Jonny, I got to go."

He was moving faster now; trying to pull the gift from his coat pocket at the same time. Guy gave one big pull and it popped out. It was wrapped and tied, a square box wrapped in red. Guy threw it at Jonny. Jonny barely caught it.

"Listen, Jonny, you can pay me later."

With that, Guy was off. Running for where, Jonny didn't know. The two boys ran past him, giving chase.

Jonny looked at the present. He smiled. Jonny liked the feel of it. It was what he waited all day for; such a small thing that meant so much. He knew when he gave it to Mariann that it would say all the words that he could not get out. He felt the excitement in his stomach. Jonny was never in love with anyone before; not until Mariann. He couldn't think of anyone else. Every time she walked by, he watched her. Sometimes he would walk through the halls of the school waiting for her class to get out just so he could see her. He never thought that he was making a fool of himself. When you're in love, it doesn't enter your mind; not Jonny's anyway. Now he had her gift for Christmas. It was going to be the best Christmas of his life. He spent all of his borrowed money for this gift. It didn't matter to him. He wanted to make her happy. He wanted to be with her for the rest of his life. Jonny knew they were made for each other and she felt the same way.

Jonny looked at the gift wrapped in the bright red paper one last time. He put it in his coat pocket, keeping his fingers around it. He walked home, thinking of tonight. Yes, this was going to be one of the best days of his life. Jonny had to smile at that.

Mariann was looking in the mirror, holding a green dress up in front of her. She had another one in her other hand. The mirror reflected her bed in the background. There were dresses and clothes covering the entire bed. She was impatient. She wanted to look right. She wanted everything to be right. Mariann tossed the dress onto the bed with the others. Nothing worked. She had to get to the game.

She wore clothes to keep out the cold: a team coat with a skirt in the red-and-gray colors of Ft. Sill. Mariann covered her legs with an Indian blanket, wrapping it under her to keep warm. She looked at the clock. The game was going to start soon. Mariann sat in the bleachers watching as the football players ran out on the field. She couldn't keep her excitement down. Then she saw him run out. Caj was a little smaller than the linemen of the team. He was their leading runner. She knew them all. She blushed at the memory of the boys she went to bed with. That was in the past. Now she was there to see Caj.

She jumped up and yelled. "Caj, yea, go team!"

Some of the kids around her looked her way. Mariann didn't care. This was her first team. Her school. Caj was her friend. She couldn't wait to see him afterwards. She would have to wait until the game was over. Then the dance. Her eyes took on a dreamy look at the thought of dancing with Caj. A shot shook her out of it and the game started.

Caj took a shot from the linebacker, dropping him two yards behind the line of scrimmage. A jolt shot through his body, rattling his teeth, like a dentist drilling without Novocain. He staggered back to the line.

"Hey you guys, a little help!" Caj smiled that big smile of his. The linemen knew he was kidding them. That's why they liked him so much. They knew he must be hurting. The whole game was like that. They played their hearts out. Ft Sill was the bigger school and they weren't supposed to have a chance. Most people already wrote them off. But they believed, like Caj. They were down by three points. All they needed was a field goal to tie the game. That was a win for them. The only problem was they had to go sixty-five yards, or there about, to get it. It looked bleak.

Mike the Mountain grabbed Caj's hand in the huddle. "Sorry man." It was his block that let the linebacker get to Caj.

"Hey no problem, that big sucker moves fast."

Jay, the quarterback, came back into the huddle. "Shut up in the huddle. I want to talk. Coach called a draw play. Caj, be ready. Mountain, let your man come in and then go to the middle and block the one backer. You got to hit him good. Caj, run as far as you can but when you go down, call a time out. Remember, everyone, call time out. OK. On two. Go."

They clapped their hands and ran to the line. Caj eyed the backer who just hit him. The backer was on the line again. The backs behind him spread the field with the wide receivers. That left the middle wide-open. They were expecting a pass. They just wanted to cover in zone, play it safe, let the game end.

Caj liked the call. It was his time. He lined up behind the quarterback. He was the only back. He bent over and put his right hand on the ground, using his knuckles as leverage.

"Ready set. Fifty-two ... fifty-two, hut ... hut."

The ball was snapped. Caj watched as the line fought off the defense. He kept his eyes on Mountain. Mountain was backing up, letting the linebacker come in. Jay was running backward with the ball up, as if he was looking to pass. The linebacker bit on the fake and rushed harder. Mountain let him run by him. and then he headed downfield. Jay was right in front of Caj with the linebacker, about to make the tackle. Jay turned at the last second and put the ball in Caj's stomach.

"Oomph." The linebacker hit Jay and they went by Caj.

Caj could see the field was wide open and he began to run. Then Mountain came in to view. Caj headed for him. He passed the line of scrimmage. Still no defenders. They were too far down field. The receivers took them out. Now Caj saw his receivers turning and trying to block some of the defenders. He was at the forty and moving.

Mountain saw the two defenders come for Caj. He moved to the right and took them both out with one block. Now it was up to Caj. It was all slow motion. He already passed the point where Coach thought he had to get to make a field goal. Caj was thinking touchdown all the way. This was what he lived for: the excitement, the thrill, the adrenaline rush. He could hear the fans in the stadium calling his name. He loved it.

"Go, Caj, go!" Mariann screamed at the top of her lungs. She was standing now. She and all the other kids. All screaming. Most in her section were yelling for the defense to stop Caj. But not her. She wanted Caj to make it. She screamed louder, "Go, Caj..."

Caj was at the twenty with two defenders coming in on him. They came from the sides of the field and had the angle on him. He didn't think. Reacting instead, he juked the one on the left and the defender fell. Caj could hear his breathing. It was labored now. He didn't have enough energy to fake out the other guy. This was where his heart came in. He sucked in the last breath of air before he was hit. He used his last bit of energy.

"OOOmphhh!"

"Oomph!" Jonny tripped over his shoes. He was getting ready for the dance. First he had to see Mariann. Caj came today and brought some new jeans with him. Jonny could wear them and they actually fit him now. He'd grown over the past few months. He felt good in new clothes. A new Jonny: he liked that.

Jonny glanced over on his bed. The little red box lay there waiting for him to snatch it up. He took an extra-long shower to get as clean as he could. It was his first dance and he really overdid the preparation, but he didn't care. Jonny remembered Caj when he and BJ went out. They would take hours just getting ready. Now Jonny understood why. They wanted the girls to notice them. Jonny wanted only one girl to notice him. Mariann. She went to the game to root for Caj. She said she would root on Jonny's behalf too. Jonny hadn't seen Caj yet, but the package he got from him told Jonny that he was here. He wanted to talk to his brother but there wasn't enough time. Caj had to get ready for the game. Caj was always on the run anyway. Jonny wanted to talk to him about Mariann and how to approach her with his gift. Now Jonny would have to talk for himself.

Jonny began combing his wet hair again. He was nervous. The game was over. All the kids were getting ready for the dance. It would start in a few hours and Jonny wanted to find Mariann before it started. He wanted to give her his gift and see if she accepted it. Jonny felt a wave of panic.

The box was so small. Jonny kept turning it over and over. Why do they put a ring in a square box? It didn't seem right. Guy said that he could get him the best ring his money could buy. But could he trust Guy? Jonny raised his eyebrows. No!

Jonny knew he had to tear the wrapping off to open the box. There wouldn't be any time to re-wrap the gift. He desperately wanted to peek inside to make sure, but had to trust Guy this time. Jonny vowed that if Guy didn't do right, he would get him. He wasn't kidding on this. It was too important.

Time to go. A good feeling of anticipation washed over Jonny. It was going to work out right. He smiled, flipping the box in his hand. He couldn't wait to find Mariann and go to the dance and see Caj. They were the two people he loved most in his life.

"OOOmphhh..." They both fell to the ground in the old hay loft. Mariann was on top of him. She kissed his face all over and then found his lips. She kissed him long and deep. Seconds went by. Then they broke apart.

She smiled and nudged him with her nose. Happiness flooded through her. She was excited. She was ready. "Mmmm-mm..."

Caj laughed. "Mariann, I missed you." He didn't think he had it in him after the big game. The adrenaline was still rushing through him from the big win at the football game. He was happy. She was there. It was time to take her.

They never saw the shadow come in and stand in the corner, watching.

They moved to their clothes, pulling and unbuttoning and dropping. Soon they were naked with Caj on top of her. She felt him inside her. He was so excited that he ejaculated his semen in her only a few seconds after entering. A seed would grow from this. Neither of them could see it now. They were too young. The seed of love and passion would grow with time. Mariann needed it. It would sustain her in the coming years.

Caj lay at her side, naked; he watched Mariann as she dressed. The sweat on his body began to dry, giving him a sticky feeling. The cold air outside never penetrated the barn. Heaters kept it warm and dry, and the horses were harbored from the weather. Caj looked up at the loft. A small door was open and he could see some snow falling from the sky. He smiled.

Mariann saw that smile. It was the main feature that everyone liked about Caj. He accepted life as his own personal challenge and it showed in his smile. She felt she could hold him for the rest of her life. She smiled, too. "What are you grinning about?"

"Snow."

Mariann went over and looked up. The snow was coming down hard now.

"Let's go up and look out."

Caj looked at his watch. This sent a chill down Mariann's spine. He would be leaving soon. The bus was going to leave right after the dance. The dance stopped at eleven that night. It was seven now. Four hours. That's all.

"OK. I want to see what it looks like from up there anyway."

Caj moved to the stairs. She followed. Looking down at the barn, they could see the horses shuffling from foot to foot. The large lights kept the barn well-lit. At the top of the loft they sat down under the small door to the outside. From the barn they could see the school and the field. Some kids moved around the field. Most of the kids were in their halls getting ready for the dance. Out to the left Caj saw the lights of the small town of Lawton. Over the administration building were the Army clinic and hospital. From there was flat land as far as the eye could see. It was so different from home.

"I never get used to the flatness."

Mariann heard this all the time from the western tribes. Kids from there felt naked in the great expanse of the plains. She herself couldn't understand a place with trees everywhere. When she rode the horses through the trees by the creek, it always made her claustrophobic. Mariann looked at her arms; they had goose bumps rising on them. No, she didn't think she could live in a place like that.

"It just shows how big the world is, or how small we are."

"I know. I felt my reservation was too small for me. I want to see more of the world. I like the idea of seeing for miles. Back home on the water, you could see for miles. After a while you couldn't judge distance because it went on so far."

"Your people fish all the time, don't they?"

"Yea. They fish all the time. And they carve, and paint. Like most of the other tribes."

"Jonny told me about your people. He misses them. All he wants is to go back home. He hates it here. I don't blame him. He hasn't been off probation since I got here."

"That's what I hear. It sure don't sound like the little brother I know. He was the one always doing what he was told. He would sit and listen to anyone that wanted to talk. Not me. I left as soon as I could. I needed action."

"He said your father drinks all the time. My parents drink, too. He talks about things that I don't know about. He seems so old some times. He fights the administration here all the time. He sticks up for other kids, too. Doesn't matter to him."

"Boy, he really must have changed. I guess I better go and see him. I got something important to tell him."

Mariann watched him hopefully. Then she had to ask, "Are you going to tell me?"

Caj thought about it. Then decided, "I'll tell you at the dance."

Mariann seemed satisfied with this. "Then give me a kiss and then I have go and get ready."

Caj leaned over and lightly touched her lips with his. Both kept their eyes open. There was nothing to hide between them. Then he pressed down harder and she responded. Their eyes closed. The kiss went on seemingly forever.

In the corner of the loft, Jonny stood watching them. They never heard him come in. He turned and ran from the barn. To the two lovers locked in their embrace, it was as though Jonny was never there. Jonny ran from the barn. Emotions were churning through him. He was hurt. The pain was caught in his throat. From his throat to his heart, the pain tore at him. Tears wanted to come to his eyes but Jonny gulped down some fresh, cold air. He stopped running and slowed to a fast walk.

It felt as if he was going through his own death, his fate determined by two people he loved. Dark and black thoughts entered his mind - sullen and mournful thoughts. Jonny kept thinking about what he had seen. He tried not to think about it. He shook his head to push away his thoughts. It did no good.

The cold snow fell to the ground in front of him. Jonny kept his eyes down. The flakes of snow were getting bigger and wind made them swirl around in the air. Jonny was in front of the dining hall and was heading back to Quanta Hall. After the panic came and left, it was replaced by anger. The anger flooded his brain and he wanted to lash out. A figure stood in front of him and he came to a halt.

"Well, Jonny Esque..." It was Mr. Demouns. Before he could say another word Jonny pushed him aside and went on by him. As he went by, Mr. Demouns grabbed at his arm, tearing Jonny's hand from his pocket. The red box flew out and landed on the snowy ground. Jonny jerked his arm back and kept moving, not looking or turning back.

"You struck me! Young man you get back here. Did you see that? I want him written up and I want to file charges against him. He's suspended, you hear? I don't want to see that boy at any functions of this school. That includes tonight's dance."

Miles bent down and picked up the red box, listening to the tirade of Mr. Demouns and watching Jonny headed for his hall. He knew something was wrong with Jonny. Miles thought about the girl. Mariann. It must have something to do with her. He would have to find out later. Right now, Mr. Demouns wanted him to go and sign as a witness to the written complaint he would file. Miles shook his head as he watched the boy disappear into the snowy night.

Miles and Mr. Demouns stood in the great hall. Kids wandered around the dance floor. Wilson Picket was playing on the record player: "Wait for the Midnight Hour." Miles liked the new music. Rock and Roll. His eyes caught the couple on the floor. The boy looked like a bigger version of Jonny. Caj was his name.

Miles had watched this boy with the big smile destroy Ft. Sill in the football game. The standings may not have indicated it, but Ft. Sill didn't have a chance. It was their first loss to such a small school.

Now Miles watched this boy move around at ease with the kids in the hall. A clear leader. He must have been a leader back on his reservation. Miles thought about all the different cultures in this hall. The kids may not have known it, but they represented Indians from one extreme to the next.

Caj was the opposite of Jonny. Miles could see that right off. This boy was open and fun and willing to converse with anyone. The young ladies watched him as he danced around the floor, waiting their turn to dance with him. Miles knew this boy could get any one of the girls this night if he wanted, yet he stayed with Mariann; a girl from Concho. That's probably where they met. Still, she did have a reputation as a loose girl; a girl that didn't think twice about going to bed with the boys. She wasn't really a troublemaker but she did stand up to those who wanted to put her down.

The song ended. The final dance was coming on. Then the kids would all go back to the halls. The Concho kids would load the bus to go home. It was a long night for Miles, who had to chaperone all of them. He found some boys in back of the building sniffing glue. They were out of their heads and he sent them to the infirmary. The last dance was a slow dance and Miles watched Caj and Mariann as they came together for the last time.

Miles knew what Jonny was going through: his older brother taking away the girl he thinks he loves. So many of these kids needed love. When they thought they found it, they took rejection hard. Jonny was a kid that really needed someone. His life was in the worse condition of all the kids: a boy who talked funny, making the other kids look at him differently. He had no money at all. Miles knew that Jonny's brother and sisters got their money. Jonny was the only one that had to fight every month for his money.

Miles would see him waiting in line at the student bank with the other kids; always in the back. He was the very last kid, waiting in line and not saying anything while the others would laugh and have a good time. The girls would talk about shopping trips they would take. Jonny couldn't even leave the campus. Miles would watch as Jonny went up to the bank window to give his ID and name. He would wait while they searched their records to see if money had come in for him. They would shake their heads, "no". Jonny would fill out the forms to request a search for his money and the bank would have him fill out a special form for a loan until his money came in. They could give him enough money to get by on, but nothing for an extravagance or any mad money. Miles could see the hurt on Jonny's face every month. Even the other kids felt sorry for Jonny. It was hard.

Now Miles watched as the kids filed out of the dance hall. Caj was kissing Mariann good-bye. Miles walked by them and whispered.

"You know you're not supposed to kiss in public. Once more and you're out of here."

Caj and Mariann smiled at Miles. They moved off for a final kiss. She began to cry. Caj was talking to her, telling her he would come back to see her. Then they had to go.

"Will the Concho students move off to the bus at the north gate? Make sure you have everything. We will be leaving in one half-hour." This message was blared over the loudspeaker and the kids headed for home.

Miles saw Caj run for Quanta Hall. He must want to say good-bye to Jonny. Miles thought he better hang around to see what happened.

"Jonny! Jonny!" Caj ran through the huge bay floors. He knew Jonny lived in one of the bays on the second floor. Most of the kids hadn't made it back yet. Caj wanted to say good-bye to Jonny. He didn't have much time left.

One bay didn't have any lights on and Caj went by it to the other bay across the hall. He walked through the bay looking at the beds and searching for Jonny. The rows of bunks never seemed to stop. Caj knew he couldn't live like that. Two to a room was enough for him, and only if BJ was his roommate.

Caj heard snoring coming from a bed and went over to look. It wasn't Jonny; it was two boys sleeping together.

"Must be Navajos."

Caj moved on but Jonny wasn't in this bay. He walked out and went to the other bay. Like most schools, this one was almost empty until 12:00 p.m. on Saturdays. The kids just stayed out most of the time on weekends. Like any teenagers, they liked to have fun and not go to bed too soon. With the football game, he knew some of the kids were partying somewhere around here. They always did.

Caj walked across the hall to the next bay. The darkness caught him. It was like the one next door. He could see most of the kids in this bay. They were nerds and academic types. Most of the beds had someone sleeping in them. Kids that liked to party probably asked to be moved and the ones in here probably wanted to be here. Except one.

Caj saw him sitting in front of the window looking out into the night sky. He hadn't seen his brother in months, so it shocked him to see that he'd grown so fast. He was almost Caj's height. Still slender. His hair was long and curly flowing to his shoulders.

"Jonny?"

Jonny looked away from the window. He sat there staring at Caj. Feelings of hurt ran through him. Angered flared for a second, but then it was replaced with sadness and grief.

Caj saw the pain in his brother's eyes.

"Jonny, you all right?" Caj could see that Jonny was having a hard time here.

Mariann told him that Jonny fought with all the administrators, always trying to change the conditions of the school. Caj couldn't believe she was talking about his little brother: the kid who never said anything unless he had to.

"Mmmm ... mm Caj."

Caj smiled. "Yea its me."

"Caj"

"What's going on with you? I heard you got into some trouble before the dance."

"Mmm ... mm." Jonny was caught between his emotions on seeing Caj again and remembering what his brother did.

"I have to go and I wanted to talk to you. I have something to say."

Jonny arched his brows in curiosity.

Caj laughed. "Heh-heh, I've joined the Marine Corps." Caj swept his arms out, waiting for Jonny's reaction.

"Mmmm ... mm. What?" It was just like Caj to do something like that. Jonny knew that his brother had no idea that he had hurt Jonny. He didn't care like Jonny. "Live today, gone tomorrow" was his motto. To him, love was living, doing the things you want and letting others do their thing. Now he popped up with this.

"Yea. I went and signed the papers before I came here. I go in after the end of the school year. Said I didn't have to wait. How about that?"

Jonny was suddenly very scared for his brother and hurtful thoughts were swept away. "Mm ... mm. You didn't!"

"Yea I did. I'm going to be a Marine."

Jonny could feel the pride coming from Caj.

"Mm ... mm. Why'd you do that? Don't you know there's a war on?" The war was on TV all the time now, mostly scenes showing soldiers walking through some jungle in Vietnam.

"Yea. That's why I joined. Its the only war we're going to have and I want to be part of it."

"Have you told Mom?"

"Of course, stupid. She knows its what I want to do. She wasn't too happy at first but then she knew all I had to do was sign my name and there was nothing she could do about it. So she told me to write and all that stuff."

"Mm ... mm. Don't you want to go home?"

"Why would I want to go home? The best thing to happen to me was getting away from the reservation. I need to find out what I'm about. What would I do back there? Listen to Dad cry about the tribe and what its doing to our people. That's not for me. I've heard enough. I like it here at school. I want to go in. There's nothing back home for me. Its like I'm free."

Jonny couldn't fathom this. Home was all he thought about. He listened to some of the seniors talk about the war. It didn't sound right to him. He should write Nikki-D and find out more about it. She would know. It didn't sound right to him. If anything, Jonny couldn't wait to go home and be free of this place.

"Hey, Jonny. I hear they're after you all the time. I hear that you start fights with them and won't back down. Why? You've changed so much. Oh, yea! Mariann sends her best. She's some girl, huh? I met her at Concho. She always cries, but she's the best. Listen, I got to go. The bus is waiting. I'll see you the next time we get together. Tell everyone I said "hi" when you call home. I hear Morgan-McKenzie is coming down with her boyfriend; sounds serious to me. BJ says hi. I see Guy hasn't changed. He almost got into a couple of fights with some pretty big boys at the dance. He'll never change." Jonny and Caj laughed over this.

"Mmm ... mm. I'm going to miss you, Caj."

Caj was taken aback by the emotion coming from his little brother. He went up and put his arms around him and gave him a hug.

"Don't worry, little brother. Nothing's going to happen to me. Hey, I'll be home before you. You still got a couple of years to go before you graduate."

"MM ... mm. I know." Jonny gave him a weak smile. He knew that Caj had taken that next step in life. He would join the world of adults while Jonny had to fight them as a kid. Jonny knew that Caj had already left him behind – him and all the other kids who thought about growing up and being on their own.

"Listen, man, I got to go."

They shook and hugged again. Then Caj was out the door and gone.

Jonny sat down next to the window. The snow was falling hard now. The school buses would be home before the snow did any damage to the roads. Jonny could see the snowflakes falling, each one of them on its own, seemingly unconnected. If Jonny looked out farther he could see that they were all part of the snowstorm that blanketed the area. All Jonny had to do was look out farther. Then he would see.

"Thank you, my little Brother," said the Buffalo. "I know of your Quest for the Sacred Mountains and of your Visit to the river. You have given me Life so that I may Give-Away to the People. I will be your Brother Forever. Run under my Belly and I will Take you right to the Foot of the Sacred Mountains, and you need not Fear the Spots. The Eagles cannot See you while you Run under Me. All they will See will be the Back of a Buffalo. I am of the Prairie and I will Fall on you if I Try to Go up the Mountains."

Little Mouse Ran under the Buffalo, Secure and Hidden from the Spots, but with only One Eye it was Frightening. The Buffalo's Great Hooves Shook the Whole World each time he took a Step. Finally they Came to a Place and Buffalo Stopped.

"This is Where I must Leave you, little Brother," said the Buffalo.

"Thank you very much," said Jumping Mouse. "But you Know, it was very Frightening Running under you with only One Eye. I was Constantly in Fear of your Great Earth-Shaking Hooves."

"Your Fear was for Nothing," said Buffalo. "For my Way of Walking is the Sun Dance Way, and I Always Know where my Hooves will Fall. I can Always Find me there."

"Come with me," the Chief said. "Let us walk to the pines on the hill."

"Tell me, what is the meaning within this Teaching?"

The chief walked in silence until he was almost to the top of the hill. A coyote jumped from behind a small rock and ran over the top of the hill, but not before stopping once and looking back at them.

The smell of the campfires and cooking food drifted up from the camp below. The voices of children laughing at their play blended with the sounds of the wind in the pines and the songbirds of the prairie.

"When you experience this seeking," the Chief began, "You will meet the Old Mice of the world. They can name for you the beings of the Prairie, but they have neither touched nor known them. These People have received a great Gift, but they spend their lives hidden within the sage. They have not yet run out on the Prairie, the everyday world. Like Jumping Mouse, they fear the spots the most.

"But remember, my son, the Mice see clearly only that which is very near to them. To those people who perceive in this way, the sky will always be full of spots because of their near-sightedness. And of course in their fear they will always perceive them as Eagles," the Chief chuckled.

"But Jumping Mouse does not stay, he runs. As you already know, the Buffalo is the great Spirit's greatest Gift to the People. He is the Spirit of Giving. Jumping Mouse Gives-Away one of his own eyes, one of his Mouse's ways of perceiving, and heals the Buffalo."

"Why must he Give-Away an eye to heal the Buffalo?"

"Because this kind of person, this Mouse, must give up one of his Mouse ways of seeing things in order that he may grow. People never are forced to do these things. The Buffalo did not even know Jumping Mouse was a Mouse. He could have just stayed hidden like the Old Mouse."

DREAMS

But I, being poor, have only my dreams.
I have spread my dreams under your feet;
Tread softly, because you tread on my dreams.

William Butler Yeats

Nikki-D ran down the hall of her building. The girls' doors were always closed. She was heading for Annie's room. The rally was on. The protest march in New York brought it out. She was excited.

She came to the door with a psychedelic painting on it: a picture of Jimmy Hendrix in all of his beads, with smoke floating around him. Nikki-D could hear the loud throbbing music coming from Annie's room. "Are you experienced," the singer asked and the guitar blared out the answer. Nikki-D knocked on the door. There wasn't much time left for them to get started. She told Martina first and now she wanted to get Annie ready. She knocked on the door again. The music's beat increased and Nikki-D heard the new song: "Purple haze is in my brain/ Lately things don't seem the same."

"Annie, are you in there?" She knew it was a dumb question. The way Annie had been behaving lately made her cautious.

Nikki-D opened the door an inch. Smoke came rushing out. The acrid smell of marijuana hit her and she wrinkled her nostrils. "Ugh!"

She pushed the door open some more. The room was dark and a light was blinking on and off. A strobe light. The smoke danced in the air. A psychedelic array of colors and dance and sound rocked the room. Nikki-D adjusted her eyes. She tried not to breathe. How anyone could do this to themselves was beyond her. She moved slowly into the room.

The room was a mess. Only a pig would stay in something like this; or someone who was abusing dope. Nikki-D and Martina tried to talk to Annie about the dope. She wouldn't listen. She said that it was a new world. She wasn't going to hold herself back. If anyone embraced the turbulent sixties, it was Annie.

They were lying in the bed. Both of them were naked. Nikki-D turned her head away, not wanting to embarrass them. Neither of them moved. Nikki-D looked again and saw that the boy was out of it. He smiled and turned his head from side to side. He must be on something strong; acid, probably. He was a pale, skinny boy with long, blond, curly hair, lying flat on his chest. The hair was the only thing covering him.

Nikki-D looked down further. She quickly passed the groin area where a bush of pubic hair surrounded a flaccid penis. Sheets covered the boy's legs. The sheets were dirty and gray instead of white like they were supposed to be. Nikki-D moved over to the side of the bed where Annie lay. She was half-awake. There were a bunch of butts in an ashtray sitting on the lampshade. Annie smiled up at her, not trying to cover her pale, white body. She was naked, too. Her small breasts pointed to the ceiling. Nikki-D always thought Annie had the perfect body. Now, though, she thought Annie looked horrible. She had dark patches under her eyes that contrasted with her white skin. Her veins were blue and running up and down her body. She was wasted.

"Nikki-D." She smiled. Her speech was slow and methodical. "The music."

The sound was blaring in the room. Nikki-D was glad Hendrix was over. You had to be on pot to listen to him. She went over to the record-player, picked up the needle arm and put it on the rest. The record she let run around and around. She wasn't about to put another screeching sound on. She didn't want to touch anything. The room was filthy. She made a note to talk to Martina again. She would help her with Annie. Strangely, Martina was so stable in working with Annie. She was really the only one who could have any control over her. Nikki-D tried to stop her, but Annie never listened to her. Nikki-D could only get so close, then Annie would shut the door.

Nikki-D turned off the strobe light and the room became dark except for the light coming in from the door. It was eerie as her eyes adjusted to the dark and she went looking for the wall switch to turn on the lights. When she found it, she flicked it up and the light flooded the room. The pale boy put his arm over his eyes to keep the painful white light away. With his other hand, he pulled up the sheets and rolled over into a fetal position. There he lay, staring at a spot on the wall, not moving again.

Annie picked herself up on her elbows and stared out, too. She was coming down. She cleared her voice.

"Why'd you do that?" Her slightly husky voice was accusing.

"So you will get up? Man, Annie, you have to stop this." Nikki-D knew she started off saying the wrong thing.

Annie fell back down on bed. "Come on, Nikki-D, you're not going to play mother, are you?"

"No. I'm not going to mother you. Are you going to get up today?" Nikki-D was angry.

Annie looked over at the boy next to her. "Groovy."

"Groovy, yourself Get up and let's go." She went over and pulled Annie by her arm.

The naked girl got up and walked to the bathroom; staggered, actually. Nikki-D could hear the shower come on and decided Annie would be down after jumping in. Annie always took cold showers. Nikki-D and Martina never could understand why. Annie was strange.

She went over and looked at the record collection. Hundreds of records stood in their sheaths. Everything else in the room was a disaster but when it came to Annie's music she made sure every record was kept clean and in its proper place or she would have a fit.

Nikki-D felt creepy in this room. It wasn't how she wanted Annie to be. The past year was the worst. Annie still went to the protests, but she moved in a different direction. She bought into the drop-out culture and started taking drugs and espousing free love. Which meant she went out with lots of boys; and men.

It made Nikki-D embarrassed because she knew Annie was sleeping with all those guys. She could never do it, although she had considered doing it with Beau. In fact, she had decided that she wasn't going to put it off anymore. She was seventeen now. She loved him and knew that they would be together for the rest of their lives. Loving him was the most natural feeling for her. Putting off sex with him didn't make sense anymore. He was taking her to dinner tonight. He said it was a special occasion. Nikki-D could only surmise that he was going to ask her to marry him. Her heart leaped at this thought.

She would be going out to California to go to college. Cal-Berkeley. Her friends were going out there, too. They decided they wanted to go to college together and they all applied together. Of course there was no problem with them getting in. Nikki-D was sent so many offers from so many colleges that she couldn't even make it through them all. So had her friends. They would stay together.

Beau would be out there, too. He had transferred there to complete his ROTC program. He was ready to graduate. They all were leaving in the coming weeks. Go home, then head to college. She thought it would be hard not being with Beau, but she knew that after tonight she would be with him for the rest of her life. This made Nikki-D giddy and faint-hearted. She knew she was acting like the girls she always hated, but couldn't help herself. She was in love.

"Well?" Annie was standing in the doorway. Apparently she had been waiting while Nikki-D daydreamed. She wore bell-bottom jeans with a psychedelic, flowered blouse that hung down to her waist. "Are we going or not?"

It sounded like the old Annie. Nikki-D knew she was down from her high. She was glad because she hated to see her with her brain floating out there somewhere. Annie flipped off the light and the room was dark. Nikki-D felt creepy again. The smoke still floated around parts of the room. It came from the incense on the table in the center of the room. Nikki-D didn't see it before but could smell it now as it rose and wafted over. She didn't mind that smell. It was the pot that bothered her. It was there every time she came into the room. Annie wouldn't quit, though; she made new friends and the boys always had some for her. What she had to give back, Nikki-D didn't what to think about. They both moved off to the door and left.

Martina was running toward them. Nikki-D and Annie stood watching as she came closer. The field was filling up with people who were getting ready to march. Nikki-D was excited. She observed the people. They wore various outfits in bright colors and patterns. Head-bands and bell-bottoms were worn by both men and women. The crowd was charged with an electricity that Nikki-D could feel. It was exciting.

Martina had her hair in braids, like an Indian. She wore a flowery red skirt and light-blue blouse. A man was running beside her and they were smiling at each other. She waved.

"Hi, you guys. I thought you wouldn't be coming. I was worried about you."

The sun was coming out. Nikki-D could feel the soft warmth on her body. She loved the sunshine. The day was going to be good and she felt this was going to be the best march ever. Her dream was to stop the war and she worked hard at it. For the first time in her life, Nikki-D felt part of a bigger picture. Her life had meaning. She felt alive. Nikki-D looked at Martina. Martina always had this effect on her. She was so carefree and full of life.

"It doesn't look like you were too worried."

Nikki-D jabbed Annie in the ribs.

Martina just smiled, as if she didn't even notice the sarcasm.

"Its going to be great today. We'll stop those warmongers." She was so perky and fun.

They both looked at the boy next to Martina.

"Oh. This is Brian. He's going to march with us today. He's against the war, too."

"No shit."

Nikki-D jabbed Annie again.

"Yea. He says he used to work for some chemical company that is making some sort of spray that they drop on the people over there."

Their ears picked up on this. Nikki-D read about the chemicals they used over in Vietnam. Everything was getting out of control. She felt out of control.

"Well, are we ready?" Martina and Brian led the way as the four of them merged into the huge crowd of people joined for one purpose: to stop the war.

The crowd sat in front of the draft building. Nikki-D and Martina were locked arm in arm. It was their sit-in. The police were standing; rows of them with their batons in their hands. They had on their white helmets and black uniforms. Right out of the Gestapo. Nikki-D talked with Martina while they waited for something to happen.

"Martina, what would you say about Beau taking me out to a nice dinner tonight?"

Martina looked at her friend. "I guess I would say he takes you out all the time."

Nikki-D put more meaning to her words.

"I mean he's asking me out. Polite. You know what I mean."

It was clear Martina was wondering what her friend was getting at. But she played along. Nikki-D was so bad at this. Now, if it was Annie, she would know right off what she was talking about.

"Oh."

Nikki-D wanted to slap her friend. How come she always understood Annie?

"I mean, I think he's going to ask me something tonight."

"Oh.!" Now Martina understood. Beau was going to ask her to marry him. At least that's what Nikki-D thought. Jesus, she should have seen that coming. Nikki-D was so serious all the time. Shit, she's going to get hurt.

"So what are you going to do?"

"I don't know. I love him." This was true. Nikki-D had loved him from the moment she saw him. They were inseparable since that day. Everyone knew they would end up getting married someday. Nikki-D knew, too. The thought never scared her when it came to Beau. He reminded her of her father.

Martina saw the frown come over Nikki-D's face. Then she saw something from the corner of her eye. The police were moving in. She felt Nikki-D tense up but she didn't know why.

The clubs came swinging down on some of the demonstrators. Nikki-D and Martina tried to hold their ground but the line broke and students began to run everywhere. They hung on as long as they could but there was too much confusion. They looked at each other and got up and began to run. The police shot tear gas into the main crowd but Nikki-D and Martina were already out of the line of fire. They began to walk home.

"So...are you going to say yes?"

Nikki-D didn't answer.

The evening was calm and silent. The lights were low and romantic. It was a five-star restaurant that they came to. Nikki-D sat in the table booth with her hands folded. Beau sat across from her, acting bored, as if it was just another evening. Nikki-D's heart was pounding. Part of it was from the protest march today but most it was from anticipation of the question she knew Beau was going to ask her. She had practiced her answer in her head all day. Even when she was with her friends she thought about this moment. She was going to remember everything about this night. She would write it down so she could show her kids when they grew up. Shit! she wished he would hurry up and get to it.

Beau sat there with this big, dumb smile on his face. She was the most beautiful girl he had ever seen in his life. He was in love. He loved her eyes, those black pearls of wisdom that showed him her soul. He knew they would live their life together. It was in the stars. A shadow crossed over his mind; he would have to wait for that lifetime together. Right now he had to talk about something else. He reached over and took her hand. Their softness always surprised him. Slender fingers brought back memories of Nikki-D massaging his back after a game. She was magic.

"Is there something on your mind, Beau?"

Beau looked up. The spell was broken. He came here to tell her of their future. It wouldn't be fair to deny her that.

"Yes. I have something to say to you. I need you to listen to me for a second before you say anything. OK?" Beau looked at her until she nodded yes.

"I know we had plans for our future, but something has come up." Beau rushed to get it all out. "They've let me graduate and join the Marine Corps and they're sending me overseas." Beau stopped here and watched for Nikki-D's reaction.

Beau was in the Marine Corps and he was a happy man. He stood for everything she fought against. He wore the uniform that she hated. He dropped the bomb on her as if it was nothing.

"I've volunteered to go overseas."

Nikki-D's happy mood was gone.

"What do you mean, you volunteered to go overseas?" She knew what overseas meant. Vietnam. He didn't even have the balls to say it. "Where overseas?" Nikki-D wasn't going to let him off the hook. He could say it, damn it!

"Well, I thought..."

"What? What did you think? That's your problem: you're not thinking. Why would you want to go over there? You can't even say the name. What is this some macho-man thing? What about me? Did you think about me? I'm going to college. I picked the college in California to be next to you. Now you're telling me this. What about me?"

"Stop it."

"No! You stop it." She was crying now. "We had plans. What about them? What am I supposed to do? My friends protest against that war. I protested against that war today. How could you do this to me?"

"You! That's all I hear. What am I doing to you? I've always been up front with you and your communist, pinko friends. I told you when I first met you that this is what I wanted. I believe in my country just as much as you and your damn friends believe in your cause. Should I throw that away because I love you? You're wrong. This isn't about you. Its about me. I graduated. I can't wait two years. I'm a commissioned officer and I will be going eventually, anyway. Don't you understand? At least I will be going on my terms. This is what I want. This is who I am."

JONNY

Jonny stood in the cold, dark long house. The cold gray planks ran around the building, providing seating to all the people that came. His dream brought strange sights to his mind. The music played slowly, repeatedly. His senses stretched and touched his soul. The end of the long house began to fade, it was so far away. The end of the house was moving away from him, growing in the distance. The darkness came from there. He ran toward the darkness but couldn't catch it. The end of the long house kept moving away from him.

An illusion or reality? Jonny couldn't tell anymore. Fire rushed up and cackled at him. People walked by and he didn't notice them. He heard voices; voices from the distant past that called to him. Jonny wanted to go to them. He wanted to see who spoke. He moved toward them.

Jonny wanted to go back because he was scared. He had no confidence in himself. His dream was a nightmare, his nightmare a dream. He wished Caj were there with him. Or Nikki-D, who always protected him. The fires were hot and lay in a circle around him. He thought he was going to burn up. There was something in front of his eyes and he had to see through slits, making the fires seem more sinister. It was too hot and he wished his mother was there. She would pull him from the fire. His mother wouldn't let any harm come to him. He needed her.

His mother was one of the faces in the crowd. She watched as his power surrounded him. He felt her soft energy touch him. He never saw his mother like this. She was larger than life. She had her face on. That can't be right! She was white but Jonny saw her face painted all red. Her blue eyes stared out from the paint. Then he saw her smile. This made Jonny feel good. He wasn't as scared anymore.

Jonny's head-dress fell over his face. He wore the regalia of the red face dancers. His family was an off-shoot of the Jimicums of Monroe; river people and red face healers. He clung to his staff to keep his balance. He was tired, and he went right into his trance, and his dream. The song began to play in his head again. The shadows moved around the fire. His power took him with them. He could feel the earth beneath his leggings and his feet. It felt solid to Jonny, but soft at the same time. Jonny moved with the shadows around him. He began his dance.

Jonny's fear grew as he moved toward the end of the long house. Shadows stood around the two huge fires. They poked at the fire with their long sticks, making the fire rise higher. More faces came and went as he moved. Some of them he knew. Mary Stewart in the corner and Juanita Morales, his cousin, sat with her; they were from the Jones family. They both had their regalia on. Raymond Moses stood at their feet. Marvin and Richard Jones just came in. They weren't dancers, but they followed the smokehouse people's ways. Their eyes watched him. He stood alone in the shadowy world.

A thing moved into his world. His power. Jonny could feel it in him. It controlled him. Like a hurricane, his power rushed in, throwing him aside. He became all-powerful. He became one with nature. It picked him up and carried him around the long house; his long house. The voices cried out with pain and joy at the same time. More and more voices surrounded him. They all sang. Deep-throated songs and drums pounded next to him. The words made no sense. Jonny didn't understand those who were talking to him. He began to sweat in his dream. Then one voice came through. It was loud and clear, singing the same thing over and over again. Jonny understood it. Other voices joined in and they all sang. Jonny moved again. He could feel its power. It rushed through him and brought those around him into his song. He sang the song of his power. Jonny smiled; he grew in front of them, he grew above them, he grew within them until he filled the whole room around the fire. Jonny watched the fire from above and below. It felt good. Then he looked down the long house as it continued to grow. There were so many more fires to go through. It would take Jonny forever, but he didn't care if it did; he had the time.

The spirits of all his people, past and present, entered the long house. Their knowledge combined to form the world in which Jonny lived. He danced his dance that was their dance. He believed.

The faces came to him in his trance. He saw the old man with his silvery mane, Jonny's mother, and others. One face kept coming back to him.

There was something wrong. Someone was not with him. He saw a shadow in the distance. A face that he couldn't see. A face that didn't know how to sing. Jonny needed to show it how to sing. He moved toward it.

He wanted to help the face come into his power. The face stood alone watching him. Jonny thought he could recognize the face if he got closer. He just knew that he wanted to help whoever it was. He knew the face needed him. He could feel the pain coming from it: a pain that could only come from the heart. Its pain confused Jonny's power. He needed to get closer.

25

SHADOW

She watched him for a second. He was a shadow on the dreary road. Her heart leaped. She tried to see with hope; hope that Beau had come for her.

Nikki-D was home. She needed time away to think. She was miserable. She hadn't told her parents yet. Nikki-D needed her mother. Sometimes she made her so angry, but she had no one else to turn to. Beau had left last week. Nikki-D said good-bye to him along with his family. His family couldn't understand why he would volunteer to go to war, either. Nikki-D hated him and wanted him at the same time. The commercial planes flew in and out of the terminal. Beau would be sent down to North Carolina first for staging, he said, and then he would fly over to Vietnam.

She hated him for making her go through this when he didn't have to go. He was rich and his parents could pull strings to keep him out of the war. His father had said he would when Beau took Nikki-D to tell them he had volunteered.

Nikki-D thought someone would finally talk some sense into him but as he said the die had been cast and he was leaving.

She cried. They cried. Beau was in her arms and then he was gone. The ache in her heart never left. She missed him from that point on and never stopped missing him. The shadow moved on the road. It was coming to her.

"What are you doing up so early?"

Nikki-D felt her mother come in. She didn't answer. They were like that now. Still stubborn with each other, still fighting for their rights. Nikki-D put her face against the cool window. The snow fell outside. The weeping in her heart couldn't be stopped. The tears fell. She felt her dream fade and she didn't know how to save it. She wished Beau would walk up right now. That's how much she missed him. Then she saw the shadow of a person standing in the snow. Her heart leaped. Nikki-D wiped her eyes, squinting to see who it was. The figure stood watching. It was Beau.

"What are you doing? Is something wrong?" Ginny knew that something happened between Nikki-D and Beau and had been waiting since she got home for her to say what it was. Nikki-D wasn't making it any easier.

"He left for Vietnam. Beau left me." Nikki-D couldn't stop the tears now. She stared out into the snow flakes. She stared at the figure on the road. He was coming to her now.

Ginny went over and put her arms around her. She watched all the fine boys being sent over there and didn't know what to do about it. Caj was gone and now Beau, and who knew when, or if, they would come back. Ginny figured this would happen because Beau joined that ROTC program. Young men, don't they know what they do to their young women?

"I'm sorry, honey. Why didn't you tell us?"

"It was so fast. I thought he was going to ask me to marry him and then he volunteered to go. We had a big fight and then he was gone." Nikki-D was in her arms, crying now. They were tears of love and loss for a boy who left her to fulfill his dreams, leaving her to come to terms with the loss of her own dream.

Ginny knew her little girl was in pain and she wanted to make it stop. Then she noticed Nikki-D staring out the window.

"Is someone out there?" She leaned over and looked out of the window. She saw a shadow, a man standing on the street. She looked harder. It was Jonny.

"Look, its Jonny. He must have come up to see you." Ginny thought this would pick up her daughter's spirits. She wondered how Jomy managed to show up every time her daughter was in distress. It gave her an eerie feeling.

"I know."

"You don't seemed pleased."

"I thought it was Beau at first."

"Well, we have to bring him in out of the cold."

Ginny leaned to see again. She saw Lois coming around the front hedges.

"Lois is with him. I'll go and get some coffee made. You bring them in. We'll talk about this later; OK honey?"

Nikki-D nodded her head and wiped her eyes but didn't stop staring out the window.

26

COFFEE

Ginny moved to the window with her daughter. She could see Nikki-D wipe her tears away. It always made Ginny feel like a failure when she saw her daughter like this. "Are you all right?"

Nikki-D felt her heart drop. For that one moment she had imagined the man standing in the falling snow was Beau. But it was Jonny. She felt angry, and anger found its release in the young man walking up her driveway with his mother. Jonny always showed up at these times to screw up her misery. Well, fuck him! She wasn't going to let him stop her this time. She felt embarrassed by that word, but found herself using it more and more. Annie must be rubbing off on her. The anger continued to flow through her as the tension of school came back to her.

Ginny felt her daughter tense up. She had her arm around Nikki-D's shoulder, trying to comfort her. Ginny knew it was going to be a hard Christmas now that she knew about Beau going into the service early. She saw her daughter's plans go down in flames. Ginny knew how hard it was when that happened. She knew the best thing was to get over it and go on. The world was a big place and there was enough room for new plans. It was always that way. Ginny looked at her daughter's face, swollen from all her crying. She sighed. It was just so hard to go through the pain.

Ginny went to the front door to open it for her good friend Lois. She stood there in her scarf and ragged coat, hanging on to her son's elbow. Her boy Jonny had turned into a fine young man. Ginny was surprised at how much he had grown since he went away to school. When Ginny talked to him she knew that he had changed. There was a seriousness to him that she never saw before. He moved with confidence and direction. He still didn't say much, but she knew that he didn't have to in order to get his message across. He would be a force to be reckoned with in the future.

"Lois, what are you doing out in this weather? Come in and let me get you a hot cup of coffee. Jonny, take your mother's coat and put it up; Nikki-D is in the other room, You can join us in the kitchen if you want. God, it must be twenty degrees outside and you walk up here. Come in and get some coffee."

"Oh, thanks," Lois said. "It isn't so bad. We wanted to come up and see how Nikki-D was doing. Jonny was coming anyway and I thought I would join him and visit for a while."

Lois moved her plump body across the room, following Ginny into the kitchen. Jonny watched them go and then went into the other room where Nikki-D was sitting at the window. He saw her in the window as they came around the bushes. He knew she saw him, too, because her face lit up for a second. She must have thought he was someone else, because her face had dropped when she recognized him.

Ginny was glad that they came over. If anyone had an effect on Nikki-D, it was Jonny. Ginny was amazed at how he could cut right through the stubbornness of her daughter and get her to listen. She knew he took some heavy verbal attacks from Nikki-D but he seemed to not notice, or he just let them go by. Ginny smiled at the thought of her daughter coming home in a rage because of Jonny. Sometimes she was so mad she could only stutter, and finally give up, and just say "Jonny". The funny part about it to Ginny was that she could see the love coming through at the same time.

Jonny wasn't the problem here. When Ginny found out about Beau signing up for early entry in the service, it was all she could do to calm her daughter down. When he signed up to go overseas, Ginny felt the cold fear of pain that Nikki-D was going through. The war was on everyone's mind. It was getting worse. Ginny still believed that they must fight communism in the world. It was a word that she heard most of her life. It was a scary word, a word used for hate. It was part of Ginny's upbringing with her mother – part of her nightmares. Now it was affecting her family again.

Ginny was glad Lois was here. Caj was over in that God-awful country. He had left before Beau. Ginny remembered Nikki-D crying about him too. Her little girl wasn't getting any breaks in this one. Caj was her first puppy-love. At first it scared Ginny, then as she got to know him she knew that it was okay. Caj was a boy with a heart. He wasn't mysterious like Jonny, but open and full of life. His laugh said everything about him. It was no wonder Nikki-D fell in love with him;

he was a heart-breaker.

Now he was over in a country full of killing and destruction. Nikki-D marched against the war; it was too bad her side didn't win. Ginny refused to watch television anymore at night. All there was on the news were the body counts; more and more bodies, either theirs or ours, all dying for freedom. Such a noble cause, but it left no one on the sidelines. Either you were for, or against the war; there were no in-betweens. It made her sad.

Still, she thought we couldn't let the communists win. If they do, then they will be at our door next. She remembered her mother's word of warning against them and if anyone knew about the communists, it was her mother. Ginny shook her head; she didn't want to think about that time of her life. It was too painful.

"Sit down. Let me get the coffee."

She wore her house robe this morning. It was Saturday, so she hadn't fixed herself up this morning. She had put a lot of work in at the bank. Her eyes were barely open this morning and she let her hair down. She was becoming comfortable enough with herself to let this happen once a week. Lois always told her that her eyes were her best feature. She said Ginny had soft eyes and a hard exterior. Lois would always laugh when she said this. It made Ginny feel good that her friend thought of her this way. Only Lois and Nick had ever said anything like that to her. Her reserved nature probably kept most people from seeing that. Ginny knew she didn't have the warm personality of Lois; maybe that's why they got along so well. They were opposites.

Lois moved to the kitchen table. She wore a plain dress she had made herself with patterns she got from the thrift shop. Lois always wore a dress because it was a ladylike thing to do. Her hair hung to her shoulders. The gray was more pronounced now as she moved into the mid-years of life. Ginny felt bad for her friend. She knew Lois would always be poor, but did the years always have to be hard?

Ginny set out two cups, and then brought out two more. She had forgotten that their two youngsters were now coffee drinkers. She didn't like Nikki-D drinking it, but knew that it was a small concession on her part. Better coffee than all the drugs and alcohol they drank nowadays. She put two teaspoons of sugar in Lois's cup, stirred it and then brought the cups over and sat it down in front of her.

"Nikki-D, Jonny-bring your cups over and sit down. Nikki, they walked all this way in the snow to visit and talk."

Nikki-D looked horrendous. Her eyes had black circles under them from crying and lack of sleep. They could tell she was having a hard time just concentrating. When she didn't move, Jonny got up to get the coffee.

"Mm ... mm. I'll get them."

His voice shocked Ginny and Nikki-D at the same time. It was so deep. His was a man's voice; more confident, almost commanding in its rich tone. Ginny saw Nikki-D look at Jonny to see if that was really his voice she heard.

Lois sat with a smile on her face. "Jonny's voice has changed hasn't it?"

Jonny looked over at his mother. He never liked being the center of conversation. It was hard on his mother since Caj went to war. Now she used him as a substitute. It was something he had to get used to. Jonny thought she was using him to calm her tensions about Caj being over there, like some sort of transference.

He had changed, though; even he could tell that he was more of a man than a boy. The last year was the kicker for him. He was close to five-foot-ten now and knew that it was the tallest he was going to get. He let his curly dark hair flow down his shoulders. He thought it made him look more Indian. He had broad shoulders, though not as broad as Caj, and a long, lean body with golden, dark-brown skin. He became attractive to girls now. They boldly came up to him and began conversations with him like they used to do with Caj; just not as many of them. Jonny knew it was because he didn't smile and laugh like Caj. That was all right, too. He was himself and there were more important things in life.

He brought Nikki-D her coffee. She looked bad. Jonny hated seeing his best friend in pain. Ever since she fell in love with this Beau guy, she had been up and down emotionally. Now they were all sitting in the kitchen because the lives of two people they loved, Caj and Beau, were affecting their lives and they had to work it out. Caj had stopped writing to them. He had been over there for four months now. He used to write every week; almost every day. Now they were lucky to get a letter once a month. You couldn't help thinking something bad may have happened. A flash of anger went through Jonny. Caj should have the common courtesy to write and let them know he's all right. He should at least do that.

Ginny sat next to Lois and the two kids sat opposite them. She could sense the tension in the room. It was time to move on.

"Lois, I hear the tribe is having trouble finishing their Multi-Purpose building. It seems a shame that they can't get it done."

Lois knew this was an opening for her friend to help. She knew her long enough now to see when Ginny had something on her mind.

"I don't see how they can finish it. Franc says all their money has run out. Politics got in the way. Every family wanted something to do with the building. I guess Franc found out that its easier to vote for a new building than it is to build one."

Ginny was going to say something but Jonny stepped in.

"Mm ... mm. I know how we can get it done."

Ginny smiled at him, a maternalistic smile that told him she appreciated his comments, but this belongs in the realm of adults. He was still a boy. Anyway, she had an idea she thought she could pass through the bank board that would get the Indians their needed money. She wanted them to put up some land for collateral and then they could get enough money to finish the building. It would be a start for their tribe. She wanted to run it past Lois, who would get the message to the right people. Franc wasn't the man for the job. He was a drunk, crying about how the tribal board was ruining his chance. How Lois ended up with that man, she'd never know. Lois was her friend, but this was business and she would demand that someone else manage putting the building together. Ginny saw Jonny was still talking.

"Mm ... mm. If your bank would take our land for collateral then we could finish the building and we could do a lot more."

Jonny was saying the very thing she had been thinking. Ginny felt a rush of blood, knowing now she'd obviously better stop thinking of Jonny as a boy and listen to what he was saying.

"Excuse me, Jonny. I'm sorry. I wandered off for a second. Could you go over what you said one more time?"

Before Jonny could say anything else Nikki-D stood up.

"No, he can't. Come on, Jonny, let's go up to my room." Nikki-D took his hand and led him out of the room.

Ginny watched the kitchen door swing back and forth. A slow anger toward her daughter began to build. She would have to talk to her about her rudeness. Ginny wasn't going to take that in her own house.

"Ginny, you look like you're doing a slow burn." Lois laughed as she said this.

"You have to excuse Nikki-D. She's got her problems. She's concerned about Beau. She's leaving to go back to school after the holidays. I hope it works out for her, because when she comes home she drives me nuts."

They both laughed. Lois was thinking about Caj.

"I'm sorry Lois, have you heard anything from Caj yet?"

"No. He just stopped writing. I think he might be sick or ... something."

Ginny wanted to comfort her friend but there really wasn't anything she could do. She felt so helpless like this. She knew she would have to find ways to be there for her daughter as the year went on. Was that how long they stayed over there? A year didn't seem like a long time. Ginny looked over at Lois, whose face was falling from the impact of what could happen. Ginny would have to watch herself and what she said around Lois and Nikki-D. That damn war turned everything upside-down.

"I'm sure he's all right."

"I've asked the Marine chaplain to check. He said he would get back to me. He said this is the way it usually is; that boys go over there and find it exciting at first, but then the boredom sets in and letters begin to fall off. The chaplain said it probably was nothing more than that. What do you think?"

"I think he's absolutely right. Everything's going to be fine. OK?"

Lois nodded.

"Good. Now, let's talk about that building. Did I hear Jonny right that the people of the tribe want to put their land up to get a loan?"

"Yes, they all voted on it. Franc wasn't there. He's back in the tavern. He wasn't getting anywhere with the families of the tribe so they appointed someone else to try to get the money; Williams and some other people. But they don't know how to get the it. Jonny says we have to take a risk. I agree."

"Good, because I've talked to Nick about it and he agrees it can be done. It will cost you some, but in the end it will begin to give the tribe credibility with the banks."

"Why are you doing this, Ginny? The tribe hasn't done anything for you."

"Its about dreams to me. I've always wanted to do things in my life. I remember when I was a young woman," Ginny said wistfully. "I had dreams back then of going off to school and becoming a doctor or something ... you know, to help people. I wanted to write. I wanted to explore the soul of people. I let go of all my dreams for profit. My mother always warned me that my dreaming would hurt me someday, so I let them go. Then I realized that I had become my mother. She could only see her value through a dollar. The more money she made, the more she grew in her own eyes. She taught me that money is the only thing that people listen to."

Lois looked thoughtful. "I guess most people with money say that. I had my dreams, too. I think you let go of dreams the older you get. The little girl becomes a woman. I know how your world is. I found peace here among the Indians. They believe that dreams and visions move alongside the real world. There is no difference. You are what's inside of you. And that never changes."

"Maybe so. The Indians live in isolation from the outside, but the outside is coming and they will have to face it. They have to change or leave. Right now, there are more whites than Indians living here. What will they do when more come?"

Ginny stopped talking and thought for a second. She waved for Lois to follow her into the living room. They both picked up their cups and walked out of the kitchen. She led Lois to the big bay windows. The gray clouds sprinkled small snowflakes from the sky and the water was black and moody. Ginny stood in front of the window as Lois sat on the sofa. It was a majestic view of the sound. Hat Island loomed in the forefront, and on the left was Everett with its jetty. In the distance Lois could see small tugs moving with the tides, pulling their piles of logs behind them. It was the great Northwest in its most picturesque form. It was the reason most people moved here. It was why more would come.

Ginny turned around and sat next to Lois. "You know, when I first came here, I hated it. I couldn't believe Nick would do this to us. I had friends and family where we lived. I thought life was good. Then when we moved here, so far from everything and on a Indian reservation, I thought he'd completely lost his mind. We had some terrible fights over it. I made him suffer for it. The drums frightened me. On the first night here, they kept going and going, on and on, and I didn't know what to think. Then I saw my precious daughter hanging onto the window and staring out with her little hands against the window pane, like she was trying to join those people who were drumming. I panicked and went after her and yanked her from the window. Then Nick came at me. It was so hard for me. Nikki-D jumped in between us and asked us not to fight anymore. It was like cold water being thrown in my face. I began to see that it was my fear that was the problem."

Lois moved and took another drink of her coffee. She felt Ginny made the best coffee she ever tasted. Ginny always gave her recipes for cooking and they had become best friends over the years. Lois was learning more about her now. She was opening up and letting the real Ginny come out. It must have been hard for her under the Empress. Now she was letting go of some of those fears.

"Ginny, you have never told me anything of your people? You're Chinese but you stay away from them. Why is that?"

"That's another story. This place is my home now. I love everything about living here. I'm happy and at the same time I'm sad. The world is blowing up in our faces. The children are fighting for a better world. I want a better world, too. I have money and power. I want to do some good in this world. I know you are the same way. You want these people to have a better life. You want a better life. We can do it together. The tribe has to get stronger before the whites take over the whole reservation. It will happen, unless we help. I think the new building has to be built. I can get them a loan to finish it."

"Then what?" Lois was listening to her friend with some wonder. She was going to make this happen. Lois could feel it. Jonny could do it, but it would take him longer to get the building built. This way might work.

"Then the tribe and its people will be forced to make payments, and find other sources of revenue. The government has them. They give them money and then they take it away. The Indians don't have a chance under those kind of conditions. They have to learn to become independent. They have to break away from the easy money with no responsibility. They have to earn their way."

Lois's face was red from the way Ginny talked. She could pepper her speech with hard words like any man. Lois found this fascinating in Ginny. She felt Ginny was right about breaking the dependency. She wanted her children to have a better life than what was being offered. They deserved so much more. The government was something evil in Lois's eyes. It broke the spirit of the men of the reservation. They had no jobs. They drank. The women had to buck up and fight for what little there was for their families. Lois no longer had any fears. She was beginning to fight back. Her way.

Ginny watched her friend calculate what she had said. When she saw the small smile come over Lois's face she knew she had her. They would form a coalition for the future of the reservation. Their reservation ... their people ... their lives.

Nikki-D and Jonny sat on her bed in the bedroom. She had just put a record on. She turned it up. She and Jonny liked loud music, although Jonny didn't like it as loud as she did. The song came blaring over her small speakers.
"This is ... dedicated to the one I ... love./hooo,hooo,hooo."
The Shirelles, an all-girl group, were singing the song. They were one of Nikki-D's favorite groups nowadays. They sang "Soldier Boy," and "Foolish Little Girl." She felt the words as they were sung. She thought of Beau. Her heart was breaking, like so many other young girls and women with their men sent off to war. She didn't think any one could feel the anguish of women. They were left alone to wait. Wait in pain. With a leaden heart that would stop beating at every thought of death. She was alone.
"I don't know what is happening to my life, Jonny. I was looking forward to my future just a few months ago and now I can only think about my past and Beau. I'm in limbo. All I can do is wait. I feel like I'm all alone. I have nobody."
As she said this, Nikki-D leaned her head into the only shoulder that she could always rely on. Jonny had his arm around her and began to rub her arm. She rested with the dark thoughts of fear as they came and went. His strength held her as she rested in his love. Jonny never said anything as he held her. There was nothing to say. They were together.

27

VIETNAM

The truck hit a bump in the road, making it rise high in the air and it came down with a thump. Caj woke with a jolt, his eyes immediately scanning the fields. It was nothing. He rubbed the sleep out of his eyes. He always slept on the long trips from the main base. Caj felt the heat on his body. The smell of the country would stay with him for the rest of his life. He was soaked from his own sweat, and his head hurt.

The driver was smoking a reefer from a five-pack he bought from one of the boys at the check-point. The kids would stand there waiting for the convoy to come through to sell what ever wares they had. Most of the drivers bought five-packs to smoke as they drove down the main roads. Drivers weren't very secure people. They hated being exposed on the main roads. Any sign of danger and they slammed on the gas and moved out.

Caj looked out the window to see down the road. It was a long convoy today. They were heading to Chu Li, an Army camp south of Danang. Way up at the front of the convoy, Caj could see an old man with a boy, pulling an old, brown wooden wagon with their belongings stacked high. Dust, kicked up from the trucks and the refugees on the side of the road, blurred Caj's vision.

"Crack-crack-crack!"

"Bruuup! Bruuup!"

"Holy shit! what was that?" The driver was up now his hands on the controls in case he had to kick the truck into high gear.

All the people on the side of the road fell to the side of the ditch. Women and children stared out from under their round white hats. Caj tried to see what had happened and where the shots had came from. He had his rifle at the ready. His heart was pumping.

Trucks moved down the road in a hurry. The driver changed gears and their truck moved up. Caj was watching out in the fields, but something caught his eyes on the side of the rode. They drove by as Caj felt numbness crawl through his body. He kept watching the side of the rode.

The old man lay there with blood flowing out of the wounds in his body. The little boy stood over him, crying. Caj watched a patrol heading out in the tall grass. They would be after the sniper. Their truck rode by and the boy was right next to it. Caj could see that the old man was dead. He was hit by return fire from one of the gun-trucks or the 60's on the jeeps. Caj watched the little boy as he cried over his grandfather. The numbness crawled up his neck and surrounded his brain. The numbness kept down the panic and the pain of the scene.

Caj watched the little boy as they drove down Highway One in Vietnam. The little boy's hand was in his mouth as he screamed over his grandfather. Nobody went to him. The trucks were moving faster, putting distance between them and death. The distance took Caj from the scene that was etched in his mind forever. Distance from the pain was all he could ask for.

Caj woke with a start. The dreams were getting bad. The February sun was up already, burning through the mosquito net around his hooch. His eyes were wide awake and attentive to what was going on around him. The other guys were still sleeping. They didn't have to get up for a couple more hours. Caj sat up on the side of his bunk, pushing the netting aside. He watched men coming off perimeter-watch slowly walking back to their hooch's. Everyone seemed to drag around with no energy at all. Caj felt that way the more he went out on the road. He was halfway through a forty-five-day detail to truck convoy. At first he was excited to get out. Something strange was changing him. He lost his exuberance. He lost his sleep.

Caj climbed into his clothes. They were smelling pretty good after so many days of use. He sent his other fatigues to get cleaned and the Momma-san hadn't brought them back yet. It didn't matter anyway. Every one smelled out there. He hated the smell of the water after it overflowed. It came out in the wash. Caj put on his flak jacket and helmet, then picked up his rifle. It was as clean as a whistle. He spent most of the night cleaning it after he tried to fire it one time on the road and nothing happened. The driver went nuts on him and told him he should have the rifle clean and ready to go the next time he went out. Since then, it was a ritual with him to clean his rifle at night before he hit the sack. He checked everything out and then headed out to the staging area to catch his next assignment.

The sun was up now and the dust was rising. Caj watched and heard the sounds of people stirring to the new day. A deuce-and-a-half rolled up to the men standing in line to load. Most of them had coffee cups in their hands, trying to shake the night away. The clubs were always full at night and the booze flowed freely. Caj started going to the club with the other men because he couldn't sleep anyway. The drinks helped him and it was fun. They could talk about all the things going on in the war. They flirted with the baby-sans who worked the clubs. Caj thought back to meeting one last night.

"Hi."

She laid down the drinks on the table full of Marines. She had the whitest smile that Caj ever saw. Long, black hair ran down her back. She had a thin body and lively eyes. It sort of reminded him of Nikki-D. His heart gave a tug when he thought of home. Even he got homesick.

"Hi. My name is Caj. What is your name?" He said it slowly so she could understand him. She wasn't wearing western clothes like the other girls. She wore the traditional white cloth split up to the waist and underneath she wore black pants. She looked good to Caj, who was feeling horny anyway.

She smiled and Caj smiled back. They were talking without talking. She used her eyes to glance at him. She couldn't understand this American but she knew that he noticed her. At the same time, Caj was watching for any signal that she was interested, too. He noticed her sideways glance at him. She bent over, and with the softest voice Caj heard, she whispered to him.

"Need money."

Suddenly anger exploded from Caj. It rose so fast that it scared him. She was a hooker, just after money from him. That's all these people were after. He desperately wanted her to be different, but she wasn't. He needed something to make sense to him again.

"Why don't you go fuck yourself'?"

She was taken aback by his angry outburst. She didn't understand his words, but she knew this big American wasn't saying anything nice to her. It was hard to understand them. They say things different, always laughing, then angry. She stepped back.

"Need money ... for drink."

Caj was embarrassed. She only wanted the money for his drinks.

He hurried and got money from his wallet. He tipped her and she moved back to the bar. Caj watched her for a second. He had already ordered another drink. He downed his beer. He needed another. Even though he knew he had misunderstood her, every time he saw her the anger came back to him. The anger wouldn't go away.

Caj hopped on the truck sitting in the convoy. They were heading to Baldy today. It was about thirty miles south of Danang. About ten trucks were riding with a larger Army convoy until they reached Baldy. They would stay there while the main convoy headed down to Chu Li. Caj checked out the driver, who was already lighting up a joint. It didn't bother him anymore that most of the drivers smoked dope. Shit – he was still buzzing from last night. The beauty of riding shotgun was he could sleep during most of the trip down. Caj put his food on his side of the cab and then went with the driver as he checked out his truck for the last time.

The truck checked out okay. The driver got back in the cab and Caj climbed on top of the load. The trucks carried anything and everything, from C-Rats to Ammo. Whatever was needed by the troops in the outlying areas. Caj settled down on top, in the middle of the load. He must have been about twenty feet from the sound; a good viewpoint. His truck was carrying some dehydrated foods. Caj ate some of them and thought they were better then the C's that everyone else ate. They weren't in tins, either. He liked that. The truck lurched and they were off. Caj looked back. Most of the shotguns were standing on their loads as they left staging. Caj was heading for Baldy today.

"Ka-boom!" The earth shook from the explosion. Caj watched as the black cloud went up. Everyone ran to get their weapons and then rushed to the edge of the perimeter. Guys watched as the gun truck came racing back to Baldy. He could see the gunner on the Fifty-Cal, swaying all over the place as they came into the compound. Everybody ran to their trucks. Most of the trucks were unloaded or being unloaded so the men were either sleeping or at the underground hole that was the bar. Caj was sleeping in his truck when he heard the explosion. He jumped up and was ready for anything. He checked his rifle again. The gun truck came to a screeching halt and the lieutenant ran up to it.

Caj could see the fear in the eyes of the driver and the gunner. The truck that was with them never came back. The black cloud was a sure indicator of that. The gunner's arms were waving as he gave his report to the lieutenant. Then both of their arms pointed out toward the area were the truck was hit. The lieutenant pointed over to Caj's truck. It was due to be unloaded here at Baldy. It was an ammo truck. Caj watched the black cloud in the horizon with trepidation. He knew that he was the next to go down that road.

It was a cloudy, windy day that brought the heat straight to your body. Caj was sweating, but it wasn't from the heat. He was on top of his truck again. This time the fear was growing in him. The word all day was about LZ Ross being over run by NVA regulars. The whole place was hopping. Caj could smell the fear in everybody. He could feel it in himself

They moved slowly down the road. Each minute felt like an hour. Caj sat rigidly in his seat, watching the hills around them. The tank was slow and they moved at a snail's pace. He turned and saw the tank behind them, too. Two Cobra's flew by the hills, each ready to attack any position that the rocket came from. It didn't make Caj feel any easier. He could feel the blood pulsating in his brain. His head hurt. No wonder the drivers smoked pot all the time. He would, too, if he was on the road all the time. He popped a couple of pills to help his headache. He needed some relief

The truck moved up to the hill. It was a small LZ. LZ Ross looked as if it was hit good. Most of the hootches and bunkers looked like they took a direct hit from rockets. Caj watched the men moving around. A man came up to the truck.

"I'm supposed to show you where you go on the perimeter."

Caj saw a real distance in the man's eyes. He saw an old face in a young man's body. Dark lines hung under the man's eyes. Caj got out of his truck and followed him. The man didn't say anything until they reached a hole at the base of the small hill. He saw the wires were blown away. Men were threading concertina wire together. Caj saw the razor blades sticking out and the men wore heavy gloves to thread the wire. The clouds were still in the sky but it didn't stop the heat. He was sweating.

A chopper flew toward them. Under it hung a long rope with a net at the bottom. The net was full. Caj watched it with fascination. Then a cold numbness hit him as he saw what was in the net. It was like a sledge hammer hitting him in the head and stomach at the same time. The numbness never stopped, running over his body and mind repeatedly.

Bodies! The net was full of bodies. Dead! Dead bodies hanging everywhere. Arms and legs and ... Faces! A man's face pushed against the net, frozen in a last, permanent scream. His eyes were open ... seeing nothing.

The chopper flew directly over them. It was as if the chopper was bringing the bodies over so Caj could see. Then it flew off.

Caj lowered his eyes. He tried to listen to what the man was saying to him. His head hurt so much. He had a sinking feeling in his stomach.

The lieutenant came running up to Caj.

"Get back in your truck, Private. We're leaving."

Caj woke with a start! The day was beginning again. The sun was coming up and he could feel the heat running though his hootch. He reached over and took the bottle of pills from the floor. He popped two to get some relief for his head. Caj got up and put on his flak jacket and helmet. Slowly he pulled his sixteen up and hung it from his shoulder. Tired. He wasn't getting much sleep anymore. He was drinking more. Dreams invaded his nights. The days were long and weary as he headed down Highway One. He needed some coffee.

The dust was clogging his mouth as they traveled down the road. The sides of the road withered away; crumbling from the combination of the rains and then the sun baking it to a hard clay. Suddenly Caj's truck veered off to the left, the driver speeding up as they went around a bend. The rice paddies lay flat along the dikes. People were already bent over planting rice in calf-deep water. Caj watched them work. Most of the time, peaceful sounds floated by in a lazy sort of way. Nobody moved very fast once you got off the main road. Two worlds occupied the same place and time. The Americans could never understand these people because you had to live with them over generations to do so. Caj could. He thought of his own people, the ones he tried so hard to get away from, those lazy days he fished on the beach, with a peaceful wind floating off the waters.

The truck rounded another curve in the road and Caj's eyes locked onto men walking the dikes in the paddies. They were walking toward him. It was a Korean patrol. The point was watching the ground as he walked. There were about twenty of them, with the ones behind the point laughing and smoking as they walked. In the middle of the pack two men carried poles between them. Caj looked closer. Jesus. They had something hanging from them. It was the bloody bodies of the enemy. The Koreans tied the hands together and the feet together and let the bodies hang, the heads falling back from their shoulders, almost touching the ground. The bodies bobbed with the movement of the men who carried them. The Koreans' point looked up and saw Caj's truck. A big smile came to his face and he pointed to the dead enemy hanging from the poles.

"Marine! Marine! Number one."

Caj smiled and waved. They were right next to them now. The truck sped by them as the Koreans kept waving. Caj could see blood running down the face of one of the dead. A numbing sensation covered him. He didn't even feel the headache anymore. Just tension. A slow, creeping tension that never went away. They were just dead people. Not even alive. It didn't mean shit.

The truck raced down the dusty dirt road. Caj looked back at the shrinking Koreans. His driver was humming as he drove the big deuce-and-a-half. He was happy to get away from anything that looked like danger. He took another toke and then handed it to Caj. Caj took the joint and lifted it to his lips, inhaling deeply. He could feel the tension lift a little as the smoke swirled around him. Yea, fuck the war.

The fucking sun was rising again. Caj could feel its heat before it rose in the sky. There was no way to escape its rays. The sun burned into Caj's morning, never letting him get any rest. He lay in his hootch waiting for the sun.

He got up slowly and put on his pants and shirt. They were worn and rumpled from no wash. He smelled, but nobody cared. They all smelled. Caj reached for his pills and popped a couple for his headache. His bunk was in the corner of the hootch and right now it looked like a shambles. He put on his jacket and helmet and slung his rifle on his shoulder. He looked out of his hootch, checking out the long line of hootches. They were the hootches of the blacks. Caj didn't want to run into some black who wanted trouble; nor did he want to spend ten minutes shaking hands in some meaningless black-power handshake.

The hate between the blacks and whites was getting nasty. The Chicanos ran with each other, but sided with the blacks most of the time. Caj didn't give a shit about any of them. They were all American as far as he was concerned. Besides, nobody could get more American than he. He was a fucking Indian, for Christ sake.

Caj saw no one out there. He moved out and headed for staging just as the sun rose in the sky. Caj put on his shades. Sunglasses made you look cool no matter how much you sweat. He could feel the draining power of the sun hit him. It sucked the energy out of you. It dried up everything in its path. It was going to be another hot one. Caj wondered where he would be heading today. Sweat ran down his back. He was so tired.

He sat in the tower at ASP-2 watching the rice paddies as the sun went down. It was dusk; a long day ended. Caj was put on shit-duty today. He was sent to clean up somebody else's shit. He lifted up the lid of the latrine and pulled out the round barrels full of shit. He put his T-shirt around his mouth and nostrils to hold the smell down. Then he poured diesel fuel over the contents and lit it. A puff of black smoke rose from the container. Shit burns, like anything else. There was no ocean to dump it into here. The wind shifted and the black smoke was pushed into his face. Caj stopped breathing for a second and moved away from the smoke. It didn't matter; he wasn't even sure he could smell anything anymore.

He was put on wire duty after burning all the shit. He strung wire around the perimeter. It was an easy day. Nothing much happened. In fact, Caj liked the work. He wore a T-shirt around his head at high noon to keep the sun at bay. The sweat poured off him while he strung the wire. His muscles ached. All of them ached. He felt good.

Sitting in the tower, Caj watched the peaceful world of war in front of him. Quiet wind brushed his cheeks. He put his face to the wind. He wasn't sweating. The day was coming to an end. Caj felt good; it was a good day. He closed his eyes and thought of home: the quiet beaches and the boats packed up to go home; smiles on everybody's faces because of the fish they caught that day. He kept his eyes closed and the wind here felt just like the wind back home. Soothing.

Suddenly there was movement. Caj jumped up, his eyes wide open. His heart beat faster and the sweat came back. He searched the surrounding area as he reached for his rifle. He barely saw the boy before the first shot.

Crack!

Caj saw the dirt kick up. He saw who it was. Nooooo! Caj felt the numbing coming over him as the second shot was fired.

Crack!

He just stood there, watching, tension running deep in him. The veins in his forehead were bulging from the blood-rush. He could hear the radio cracking and the officer of the guard asking what was going on. The rifle was right in front of his face. The man behind it was aiming again.

Crack!

Time stood still. Caj stood still. His mind raced. His heart beat hard in his chest. His stomach heaved in fear. The numbing came again. It was almost over. Soon it wouldn't matter. It wouldn't matter that the little boy got too close to the wire. They were all the same to Caj now. He learned to expect the unexpected. He learned that when he let down his guard he would get hit. Nothing was normal here. Nothing made sense. Nothing mattered; least of all, human lives.

Caj woke up to the blinding sun. The heat. He didn't think he could raise his head, it hurt so much. He swung his arm out to the pills and the drink on the floor. Caj popped a couple of them and then took a swallow of warm beer. It was always warm. He needed to get up and take a shower. Not only did his clothes smell but he was beginning to smell bad, too. Foggy, he got up and grabbed his kit.

The shower was a cold slab of concrete with four wooden walls. This one held four spouts where cold running water trickled from the faucets. There was a cracked half of a mirror in his kit and he laid it down and looked in it. Dull, red eyes stared back at him. Caj got naked and stepped under the shower. The cold water hit him like a sledgehammer. His body responded immediately. He felt the tingling of his skin. His mind seemed distant so it was a purely physical reaction. Caj ran some soap through his hair. Luckily his hair was short or it would be matted. He washed the crud off his body and then stood under the cold water, staring at nothing.

Caj's eyes watched the movement of the two women; a young girl and an older woman. They came in to clean up the place. Once they saw Caj, they bowed down and then went on with their business. They saw his eyes and knew he wasn't with them. The older mamma-san knew his eyes would watch every move they made. The younger one could feel the tension coming from the American. She tried not to look at his nakedness.

Caj tensed up around the women. Anything could happen. His mind raced. He never thought of covering up as they worked. They were just gooks. What did it matter if they saw him naked? Besides, his mind was too numb to think about it. He had to get ready to head out. Time was running short. The sun was almost over the horizon.

"Hey, Caj, you're on my truck today. We got another Louie taken over the middle. Guess they sent him back from the bush. Let's see how he likes being exposed on the roads all the time. It never works you know; to send a guy from the bush to ride the roads. They get spooked over everything. Its hard, man."

Caj looked at his driver, a redhead with whom he had ridden before. Caj didn't care about a new lieutenant. They came and went. Most of them served six months before being reassigned. Caj's world was becoming more isolated. Keep to yourself and things would be all right; that's what he thought.

"Hey, man. We got the white truck today. Easy riding today, man. You're going to be cool back there. No heat today man."

The redhead talked like a "head." They all must be dopers to drive down these roads. Caj wondered what the guy was taking. He looked to be around eighteen. Caj knew that eighteen meant a lot of years over here. You seem older when you sink into yourself and become reclusive. What you say and what you think are totally different. It was ironic that all the guys opened up and drank and partied all the time while being lonely boys on the inside. Caj felt like that. He didn't give a shit anymore. Besides, it was going to be a cool day. Get out of the sun. Yea.

He sat among the boxes in the cool, white truck, a refrigerator truck that carried fresh produce to the bases. The going was slow. Caj didn't care. They could take all day if they wanted to, as long as he got to stay in here. He felt safe in there by himself, a secure feeling that came from having four walls block out the outside world. A light was always on in here. He could just lie back and be safe.

Suddenly he detected a movement. It was the door handle. He opened both eyes now. There it was again. It was a small movement at first. Caj stepped back. He had his back against the far wall. He brought his sixteen around. It was locked and loaded. The handle moved again. Caj's mind started racing. Someone was playing a joke or the driver wanted to get something out of the truck. That's impossible. The truck was still moving. His mind locked on to the handle. He knew it was the enemy.

He became claustrophobic, the walls no longer his friends. The door handle jerked again. It was the enemy. Caj's mind raced. He couldn't fire his weapon – he might get hit by the ricochet. More movement. The enemy. Grenade! It would be thrown in and the door shut, blowing Caj to hell. Shit, that ain't right! He was already in hell. The handle came up. Caj took out his K-bar with its long, dark blade. His head was splitting. The door began to swing open. Wait … wait …. wait. Now!

Caj ran up and kicked the door. A small face looked at him in shock as it floated in the air away from the truck. Caj watched as the small body landed. He watched as the small head turned at an odd angle from the body. He watched as the small body lay in the middle of the road while the white truck raced on down the road.

Caj walked down the boardwalk between the hootches. His head was down. The white side was cooling down from the daily sun. It was a long day for Caj. His helmet was off and hanging on his side. He had his sixteen slung over his shoulder; it felt weightless. Almost everything he carried attached to his flak jacket. When he took off the flak jacket everything came off with it. Caj was dragging. He didn't look up when he walked. He couldn't wait to get to the club and down a couple of beers.

A hand reached out and grabbed him. Caj jumped away from the hand.

"Whoa, Caj, its me."

Caj saw Muff standing in front of his bunker. He was a skinny black guy who used to bunk in Caj's hootch until all of his brothers forced him out. They beat him until he joined them. Caj knew he was a good guy and didn't understand why they forced him to take sides. Race was the big issue in the rear. There were more Dixie and Black Power flags hanging from hootches then Caj could remember. It was ugly.

"Caj man. Don't go to the club tonight."

Before Caj could get out the question, Muff was gone. He wondered why Muff would give him this warning. He didn't remember being particularly close to him, nor had they talked much while Muff was in the hootch. Still, Caj felt a tingling going up his spine at the warning. He thought about it and decided he really didn't have to go to the club to drink. He had his own stash of hard whiskey. Maybe he better stay home tonight.

The dream was so vivid. Caj heard the explosion as though it was right next to him, but far away. His brain was foggy. The night carried weird sounds and images. Caj felt the vibrations of the explosion hit his face. Then fear hit him and he was wide awake, his eyes darting around the area. He saw the black cloud rise in the sky.

"Incoming!"

Even as Caj heard the warning, he knew it wasn't incoming. This explosion came from the club. His mind locked on the image of fragging;

the warning to him. His mind raced. It came down to this: Americans killing Vietnamese; enlisted men killing officers; blacks killing whites; whites killing blacks; Americans killing Americans. The hate dug deep into the psyches of all the people involved. It was their hate for the Vietnamese, their hate for the Americans, their hate for each other, and their hate for themselves. Caj watched the black symbol of hate rise in the night sky for a second, then he laid back down.

It didn't matter to Caj. Fuck them. Let them kill each other. He didn't care. Angry only that the explosion woke him from his sleep, he slowly closed his eyes and went back into his troubled sleep. The sun would be up soon.

28

THE ENEMY

Beau lay wide awake with his troops. The trees and brush hid them from any danger as they lay in wait. The night was spooky and he wished the sun would rise. After four months in country he was ready to call it quits. He felt his whole life had changed in a dramatically short time. He knew that nobody could have explained war to him so that he would have understood it. Its something you had to experience firsthand. It changed you.

He was a man's man. That was how all the young guys said it. He came in like John Wayne, ready to take on the enemy. It was bad luck for him that the Cong was willing to show him what that really meant. Lieutenant Beau Culvier knew what war was all about now. He moved a bit, pulling his rifle next to him. They were a couple of clicks out from the LZ Baldy. Their mission was to set up an ambush by one of the main trails heading for the main road. NVA were spotted heading in their direction and HQ wanted to make sure that they were ready for them. As far as Beau cared, they could walk right on by. He prayed for this to happen. The last thing he needed was another fire-fight.

The enemy came at him out of nowhere, his bayonet raised high. Beau could only watch in horror as the blade went into his abdomen, penetrating his skin and finding muscle underneath. Beau went for his rifle, but it wasn't there. He looked around for his men. Why hadn't they heard what was going on? He did the only thing he could; he let out a scream. As hard and as long as he could.

"Aaaaaaaagh!"

Corporal Bodoni jumped ten feet in the air. The hair on his back shot straight up, tingling. Through the bushes he could see the lieutenant screaming. He ran over and jumped on top of him and put his hand over the lieutenant's mouth, pressing down hard.

"Jesus mother fucking Christ! Shut the fuck up!"

Corporal Bodoni was tired from holding the lieutenant down. They were all out there too long, fighting too much, just trying to stay alive. He could cut the fear with a knife, it was so thick. They all generated fear. It was the common denominator, the one constant that kept them alive. It kept them in control. It bottled up their normal emotions somewhere deep. The deeper, the better.

Fear was like an addiction. It numbed you out in the beginning, slamming down any emotions that wanted to come out. Like a drug, the more you used fear to stay alive, the more you needed to stay in that constant state. Emotions don't go away. They fight you at every turn. Each corner you walk around, fear is ahead of you. Every village you come to, fear enters first. It was your brother, friend, and protector. It was also your destroyer.

When the emotions erupt they don't care where you are. That's what was happening with the lieutenant. His emotions used his dreams to break free. That wasn't good on night patrol. It was bound to happen. The guys in the squad knew it was coming, but didn't know when. Most of them avoided the lieutenant as he began to break down. They could see each new break in him. He quit talking about home. He isolated himself from the others. He didn't write home anymore. He was breaking contact with the world because he couldn't afford to let any emotions come out. He couldn't afford to let those back home in their safe world bring thoughts of comfort and calm. He couldn't think about the future or he wouldn't be here in the present.

Beau opened his eyes. Corporal Bodoni let go of him when they focused. He knew the lieutenant was back among the living; back where the fear of death was the only emotion that mattered.

Beau immediately forgot the dream. His eyes checked out the area. Corporal Bodoni was beside him. Fear thrust deep in his heart. Everything seemed normal. The bushes and the trees waved slowly in the breeze. As long as his senses could feel the world around him, he felt safe. His eyes adjusted. He stared at an object next to a tree. Something was out of sync. Something was funny.

The enemy moved fast. The bayonet pointed out from the rifle. The enemy ran with the rifle in front of him. Before Beau could shout, he watched the bayonet go into the abdomen. The blade disappeared as it was pushed in deeper, searching for the deep recess where the emotions hid. Beau watched the blade as it went all the way in. The enemy twisted his rifle as he pulled the blade back out. Beau watched the bloody blade as it was withdrawn. He let out a scream.

Corporal Bodoni went down. Loud machine-gun fire erupted from the right. Beau could see the red tracers following their flight through the trees and bushes. More of his men opened up. Beau fired his weapon at the enemy in front of him. Corporal Bodoni lay with his life-blood flowing out of him. He was already dead. Beau fired some more rounds into the lifeless body of the enemy.

They carried the body of Bodoni out in his poncho. It was like this all the time. One man here, another there, never knowing when or who would get it next. It had been a hell of a month for his people and for Beau. Last night was one of many fire fights, and it wasn't letting up at all. The whole country was under attack by the enemy. Beau learned what everybody knew: that the enemy never cared how many they lost as long as the war was going their way. Beau walked among the bodies of the enemy; there were twenty dead of theirs for every one of ours. A killing field.

Beau woke. He was lying in the bush on the night patrol. He was sweating from his nightmare. His nerves were on edge and his senses tried to reach beyond his body. Again, he adjusted his eyes to see. The trees and bushes carried their shadows. Beau hated the shadows. He learned quickly that they hid the enemy, an enemy that killed.

Beau wasn't getting any sleep. He was left tired and lonely. He thought of Nikki-D. He wished he would have listened to her when he had the chance. He knew now that the war was a mistake that would haunt him for the rest of his life.

Beau felt the chill of the night, although he wasn't sure the chill came from the night. His body responded differently back home in the world. In the world, his body knew there was little chance of danger, so it responded slower to stimuli. Over here, Beau could feel it responding to the slightest twitch. His eyes felt as if they were sinking to the back of his head. Beau already had the stare: a stare that had nothing to do with the real world, except that it came from the real world of war. His war.

Terror is what came from the stare. Nothing but blank thoughts dwelled behind the eyes. The mind needed to protect itself. It needed to allow Beau to rest. He stared. At nothing. For no reason. To rest. There was no rest in Vietnam; just death. Violent! Barbarous! Cruel! Savage! Sudden death. Beau's mind recoiled from these thoughts. Its best not to dwell on those things that can't be controlled. In Vietnam, there was no control. That terrorized the men. That was what they ended up fighting for ... control. If they couldn't keep control, then they were dead; that simple.

The days and nights were dragging on. Nineteen sixty-eight! The year of Tet. That was what they were calling it on US television. Back home. There, Tet was just another word that people never understood. Now they think Tet is a word for war. It is a word for war. For the past thirty days that was all it meant to the men from Baldy and the surrounding bases. Attacks were coming from all parts of the country. People were dying in huge numbers every day. Bodies on bodies, killed for the sake of one ideology or another. Both sides destroyed people and their country. They were simply cannon fodder for some obscure little men who had political power and wanted the world to know it. Beau knew it.

He checked out the men on patrol. Most of them were wide awake, waiting to be hit again. They stayed away from Beau. They thought he was bad news. "Look what happened to Bodoni. He's dead." They didn't want to be like that. Survival was on their minds. That meant staying away from any one who could get you killed. They couldn't understand why the brass sent out somebody like Lt. Culvier, an ass-hole who couldn't handle the pressure of the war. The day-to-day shit was what they all had to put up with: the day-to-day death sentence that nobody wanted. Morale was low. They'd lost too many men. There was no relief in sight. Then the brass sends someone like the lieutenant! They felt the scythe of death hovering around them.

Beau moved among the men that hated him. He knew that he was in the wrong place at the wrong time. Morale was killing them. The men said it was Beau that was killing them. That must help morale. Beau went back to his hole. The night moved in its own time. Every man wished it would end; it never did. They suffered in the darkness, a darkness that seeped into their thoughts and souls. Each left to fight their own inner war, as well as the jungle war they lived in. They lived their lives by the seconds of the time clock; seconds that ticked in eternity.

Beau saw the movement in the trees. A shadow! Then another! They walked in single-file; small men with their little round hats. NVA! He waited, his rifle ready. Then he saw one of their faces. The bile rose in his throat. He looked again. The man saw him and attacked. His rifle was high, the bayonet gleaming in the night. Beau couldn't take his eyes off the face. It was Bodoni. Beau wanted to throw up. Instead he screamed in the night.

"BODONI!"

Beau woke. The night was silent. His thoughts of the men weighed heavily on his mind. He was losing it. Beau saw the men watching him. They hated him. He knew. The past months had worn them all down. The fighting never ended. They were always on patrol. This last one was thirty days, humping the boonies. They made contact almost every day and were hit most of the nights. They were dragging. Beau knew it. He blamed himself. Bile remained permanently lodged in his throat. His men were dying. It tore at his confidence. The brash young man out of college no longer existed. Nikki-D would never recognize the man Beau had become. He spoke very little. He averted his eyes when someone stared at him. He could no longer hold his head up. The men's morale wasn't the problem; his was.

His men came back to him in his dreams. They came every night. Collins and Degas were the first two of his men to die. It was his fault. Beau was too cocky. He didn't listen to the old salts that tried to tell him how to set up his ambush. There was cross-fire. Beau could still feel the rounds hitting around him. It was the most scared he'd ever been in his life. But they won the battle. The enemy withdrew with heavy losses. The prize for the win was Collins. Beau set him up in the cross-fire. Collins was hit by his own men. Collins was dead because of Beau; everyone knew it. Nobody said anything, but everyone knew. They all watched Beau from that day forward. The first casualty of Beau's war was trust. The men would never be able to trust him again. He would never be able to trust himself again.

Beau woke again, not trusting his instincts. There was something out there stalking him. It was a shadow of the enemy. His eyes adjusted. The misty night kept its secrets from him. His senses were on full alert, waiting for any kind of sign that would give the enemy away. Beads of sweat formed on his brow. His eyes sucked in any light that would help him in the dark. Chills crept up his spine. Beau watched the trees.

The enemy attacked. Beau saw the reflection of light off the bayonet. Beau froze, unable to move, watching time come to a standstill. He knew he was going to die and there was nothing he could do about it.

A shadow crossed in front of him. Bodoni stepped in front of Beau and took the bayonet in the belly. The blade went through him until the tip came out of his back. Beau watched it in slow motion. Bodoni went down and at the same time Beau heard the crack-crack-crack of his rifle.

Beau woke. Sweat ran down his face. The war no longer stayed in reality but now entered his subliminal center. The war owned his body and was fighting to take over his soul. The battle raged on different grounds. The dreams never left him alone. In each dream, he was fighting a losing battle. The war was almost over.

The heat of the sun hit his face. His men were getting ready to head back to the base. Beau wanted to get back as soon as possible. He would take the fastest route to get there. He got out his map and checked the coordinates and drew the route of their return. When he was done, he called over Sergeant Stokowski and showed him the route. Stokowski tried to tell him that it would be safer going a different route. Beau wanted to get back, so he dismissed this and told the sergeant that it was the way they were going. Stokowski stormed away from Beau before he said anything that would get him court-martialed. Beau didn't care.

The men watched the exchange between their sergeant and the lieutenant. They knew it was going to be bad going back. Grumbling and bitching was part of the service. These men were beyond that. They only thought of saving their lives and having some dumb second lieutenant come in here and play with their lives, was not to their liking. They could smell the fear coming from the lieutenant. They knew it could get one possibly all of them-killed. They waited for their Stokowski to tell them what was up. He would protect them from this dumb fuck. If he couldn't, they would defend themselves.

The explosion was deafening. Beau and the other men hit the dirt with their eyes scanning the horizon. Screaming came from the point. It was Private Degas. Beau moved up to see what was happening. The screaming became louder the closer he got. Then it stopped. Deathly silence hung over the trail. Beau came to the men standing around in a circle. He looked down at the body of Degas. His guts were hanging from his belly and blood was everywhere. The explosion took both his legs off, too. The men standing around turned and looked at Beau. Their eyes told him everything. He was responsible. He was a piece of shit. He was a dead man.

The dead man woke. He lay in the bushes waiting for any sign of trouble. Fear seized his every thought. His eyes watched the trees, and watched his men. Living in fear was a terrible way to go. Beau's eyes adjusted in the night. The night was against him and he prayed for the light of day. Only then would his fear subside for a bit. He was jumpy and on edge. His men never said anything to him. He was a persona non grata. The funny thing was, they all were acting on their fear. It was persuasive and potent. When fear was corralled and used right, it was a powerful tool in war. If it got out of hand, then it turned on you; exhausting you and making you feeble and weak. Fear worked on you until you became afraid of fear itself. Then there was no turning back.

He watched the trees where the enemy was waiting. Beau knew the attack would come from there. The enemy was predictable, too. The men had all been through this before. They were ready this time. Beau made sure of it.

Beau watched the night sky. Stars blinked at him as though they knew what was happening with the world today. The war was going bad. The world back home was erupting into an inferno. Beau worried about Nikki-D on the college campus. Social unrest started from there and moved out into the streets. She was so headstrong for such a small girl. Beau had to laugh at that. She was so intense about her beliefs. He wished that he could be like that. He was once. It seemed like such a long time ago. It'd been about only six months since he left that world behind him. Beau knew that when you count time by the seconds, six months turned into an eternity. He could barely remember that confident boy who signed up to come here. That boy was lost forever. He was replaced by the shaking man lying on the ground waiting, waiting, waiting.

Beau panicked. He tried to bring up an image of Nikki-D, but couldn't. She was being lost to oblivion along with other things in his past. He wanted desperately to remember her, to remember her face, to remember her smell. Beau squeezed his eyes shut, concentrating, tighter and tighter, until tears flowed through them. Nothing. Sadness rushed through him. Numbness descended over the emotion until he couldn't feel it anymore. It don't mean nothing, anyway. It was a second of contemplation and then Beau went back to checking out the trees. The trees where the enemy would be. The trees where the attack would come from. There was no time to think about anything else.

Time was so precious over here. Time was your enemy and time was your friend. During the day, time went by too fast. Dog-tired, you try to get some rest. Let your mind wonder about nothing; conscious only of time ticking away. You only wish that it would slow down. At night, time slowed to a crawl. In God's wicked way, you get your wish; tick, tick, tick. The bushes move; tick-tick-tick! The enemy; tick-tick-tick!

Adrenaline rush; tick-tick ! Fear; tick-tick.!

Attack; tick!

The attack came from the trees. Beau wasn't even aware that the enemy was there. He was daydreaming when the attack came.

A little man with a round white hat charged at him with his bayonet high. His AK47 was firing rounds as he ran. Beau was shaken out of his daydream. It was too late. He would never be able to get his weapon up in time to fire before the bullets hit him. The first bullet struck him in the leg. The second hit him in the arm. Beau felt shearing pain from his arm as if somebody had broken it. He watched the determined eyes of the enemy as he closed in on Beau. He watched the eyes of the man that was going to kill him. Beau wanted to find some hate in them. He wanted his enemy to hate him for what the Americans had done to him and his country. Beau wanted the enemy to have a reason for killing him; not like the Americans who used platitudes and insipid words as their reason for killing on a mass scale. Beau wanted his enemy to be different. Beau wanted to die for a reason, even if was the enemy's reason. Pain crushed his body. Pain from the soul. Beau was about to pass out when he saw Bodoni rush in front of him. Bodoni fired his weapon into the enemy. Beau went out.

Beau woke. The heat of the sun was coming through his hootch. It was another day in the rear. He looked over the white salt flats of FLC. Force Logistic Command, Camp Butler was his new duty station. He could almost see the heat-waves as they floated by on the hot air. The dream was bad last night. Beau didn't know if he would ever stop dreaming. The war had a way of sticking with you.

After he was evac'd out of the jungle with the body of Bodoni, the men of his unit made it very clear that if he came back he would be dead. After all, they wanted to live and if it took killing a dumb second lieutenant to stay alive ... well, that's the price they would pay. Transfer orders were sent out within the hour by the executive officer following Beau to the hospital. He was awarded the purple heart by an officer who didn't know under what circumstances he had been wounded. Everybody learned not to ask questions over here.

Beau knew he was better off as the supply officer. He got up and went to work daily and went to the club drinking every night, a ritual that helped him cope. That was his new life. Coping. Nothing more.

Beau walked into his office. The place was a mess. Beau felt a cold chill go down his spine. Someone had come in and torn his office apart. A message was written on the wall. "We are all men who want to be treated as men." Beau read the message repeatedly. Panic ran through him as he thought of his men from the bush coming to get him. No, it wasn't them. The men in the rear fought a different war. The race thing tore at every one. Martin Luther King had been assassinated and the blacks were a hot bed of unrest. Beau didn't understand it. As far as he was concerned they were all Americans. Wasn't that the important thing? Doesn't every one have a place in America? What the hell were they fighting for?

Beau felt the same suspicion that he got from his men in the bush. It was no different wherever he ended up in this damn war. Beau was like all the rest. He just wanted to get home. The war was a mistake. His dreams of being a hero had long vanished; now it was just survival. He did his time and he was getting short. He did as little as possible with the men. He didn't trust them anymore. They had become the enemy; the same men who were cleaning his office right now. There was no middle ground over here. You had to stand for something. Beau was an officer. He stood for the men that sent brothers out to get their asses shot off. It didn't matter to any of the men in the rear that Beau was one of the few who came in from the bush. It just meant he was dumber that the rest. Respect wasn't a word the men used anymore. They all lived in a world of chaos.

It was chaotic times for Beau. He had to learn to live with his limitations. He had to learn to live with reality. Reality forced him to cope; drinking helped. He became a drunk over here. When he got off he was going to the club. He had to go there now. He felt the eyes of his men as he walked out of his office. He didn't know who the enemy was anymore. The hate was clear. He was the enemy.

The stars were out winking at him, just like in the bush. Beau was walking to the club. He carried no weapon here. He wanted to get to the bar before all the cold beers were gone. Being an officer, he drank hard drinks too. He always started out with a cold brew. He liked to keep to his patterns. You followed the same pattern over here because if you didn't, something could happen. You learned that if someone walked over a spot then it was safe, so you walked where everyone else walked.

Beau became a man of habit. He walked to the club the same way and at the same time every night. He did the same thing tonight.

The hootches had loud music coming from them. Beau couldn't get used to the loud noise in the rear. He watched as he walked through the black hootches. It was funny how they segregated themselves from each other; whites with the whites and blacks with the blacks. Beau tried to understand but couldn't. It bothered him that men hated each other so much because of their skin. There was too much hate in this world.

The black men watched as the white lieutenant walked by. They gave the signal when he was past them. The meeting went on. Straws were drawn. Four men came up with the short straws. It was time to set their plan into action. It came down to this. They had to make their statement to the world about the condition of the black man. This time it would be their hate that triggered events. They no longer would stay on the sidelines and wait for whitey to shoot them down. For every one of them that was killed, there would be one of the whitey killed. The four men dressed in fatigues made their amends to their brothers. They walked out of both ends of the hootch. It was time to make their statement.

Beau got his beer and sat at a table by the door. The club was air-conditioned so he didn't have to worry about the heat. The floor show was about to go on; some Korean band playing rock and roll. It was always a Korean band playing rock and roll. Beau took a sip of his drink. It was cold. It made him feel good that he got some cold beer. He also had a rum and coke on his table. He drank that right down and felt the soothing warmth of the alcohol. Yes, it was going to be a good night – he felt the fear flow away.

The night went on while Beau drank himself into a stupor. The band would be coming on in twenty minutes and the night would pick up from there. Beau wanted to see the women. They always brought women with them and the officers would try to get to them. Beau had himself a couple of the women before. They represented sex to him. Nothing more. It never bothered him that he was cheating on Nikki-D; it never entered his mind. She was a person in his past at this point; nothing more. His only concern was having fun today. Having sex was part of it.

Beau was getting excited about meeting another woman and having sex. His emotions digressed to a very basic level. He was a man of war. He was enlightened with insight to who he was. He had to live with himself. Nothing more. Nothing else had any meaning to him. His future had been determined for him. If the doors to the club hadn't opened, he would go home in a few months. If the men behind the doors hadn't had so much hate, he would go home. If the men hadn't acted on their hate, he would go through numerous jobs, always leaving for some reason or other. If the men hadn't swung their arms, rolling their grenades into the club, he would end up in failed relationships, one after the other, always wondering why the woman left him. If the grenades hadn't stopped right under him, he would find himself hanging out at the corner of some liquor store trying to get another drink. If Beau hadn't let down his guard and understood who the real enemy was, then all of his future would still be in front of him.

The explosion was deafening. Beau didn't have a chance. He died instantly. The men who did the fragging ran back to their hootches. The people in the club were in a world of chaos. Beau didn't have to worry that it was his fault. He died wondering whose fault it was anyway. He died not knowing who the real enemy was. His death saved him a lifetime of pain and disillusionment.

The black cloud rose in the sky. The explosion woke dead men who would go back to the world and live their lives the same way Beau would have; fearful men who only wanted the world to be as it was before the war. Their eyes darted in the night, seeking out the enemy that wanted to kill them; seeking out the enemy within.

"What would have happened if he had let the Buffalo die?"

"He would have had to live with the stink of the rotting flesh, my son. Or he would have had to retreat to the place of Old Mouse. And if he had decided to live there instead of moving and growing, then he would have experienced thirst. The chokecherries he would have eaten would have made him thirst mightily for water. Believe me, many men have reached these places. Some choose to live with the stink, and others, refusing to leave the Old Mouse's place, thirst constantly. Still others run endlessly under the great Buffalo. These are probably the most powerful of men, but no doubt the worst. They have the power, but they speak always from fear. Fear of the great hooves of the Spirit, and of course the fear of the spots, the high Eagles, the unknown."

"Is there yet more?"

"Yes,, there is," answered the Teacher. "But do you wish to eat first?"

"No. I can eat later. Please finish the Story."

The Old Man smiled and let his eyes rest on the camp below him.

Jumping Mouse Immediately Began to Investigate his New Surroundings. There were even more things here than in the Other Places, Busier things, and an Abundance of Seeds and Other things Mice Like. In his Investigation of these things, Suddenly he Ran upon a Gray Wolf who was Sitting there doing absolutely Nothing.

"Hello, Brother Wolf," Jumping Mouse said.

The Wolf's Ears Came Alert and his Eyes Shone. "Wolf! Wolf! Yes, that is what I am, I am a Wolf!" But then his mind Dimmed again and it was not long before he Sat Quietly again, completely without memory as to who he was. Each time Jumping Mouse Reminded him who he was, he became Excited with the News, but soon would Forget again.

"*Such a Great Being,*" thought Jumping Mouse, "*but he had no Memory.*"

Jumping Mouse Went to the Center of this New Place and was Quiet. He Listened for a very long time to the Beating of his Heart. Then Suddenly he Made up his Mind. He Scurried back to where the Wolf Sat and he Spoke.

"*Brother Wolf,*" Jumping Mouse said...

"*Wolf! Wolf!*" said the Wolf...

"*Please, Brother Wolf,*" said Jumping Mouse, "*Please Listen to me. I Know what will Heal you. It is One of my Eyes. And I Want to Give it to you. You are a Greater Being than I. I am only a Mouse. Please Take it.*"

When Jumping Mouse Stopped Speaking his Eye Flew out of his Head and the Wolf was made Whole.

Tear's Fell down the Cheeks of Wolf, but his little Brother could not See them, for Now he was Blind.

"*You are a Great Brother,*" said the Wolf, "*for Now I have my Memory. But Now you are Blind. I am the Guide into the Sacred Mountains. I will Take you there. There is a Great Medicine Lake there. The most Beautiful Lake in the World. All Lodges of the People, and All the Beings of the Prairies and Skies.*"

"*Please Take me there,*" Jumping Mouse said.

29

HOME

Too hot to go to Church? What about Hell?

Lois waited at the wire-link fence that stood about ten feet high. She watched the lazy afternoon sun shining down on the planes as they came and left. She wore her best dress for this occasion. Jonny was next to her. He never moved or said much but watched the planes, too. The sun was bright today. It was a good sign. The dark clouds had been heavy for the last few days and the sun broke through on this day. July was unpredictable. Lois was just glad the sun was here. Today was special. Caj was coming home.

Jonny went over and sat down with Ginny and his sisters. Lois looked at her dear friend. Ginny's features were sagging. She worked so hard at the bank. That wasn't the reason for this change, though; it was Nikki-D. Lois remembered when they found out about her boyfriend. He died over in that dreadful war. Nobody could understand how the women and mothers and girlfriends and wives felt when their men went off to war. The waiting was so hard. Then every day the news was on television. It brought the war home to them. They all watched it: the bodies and the men out in the fields who died for their country. Each woman had her worst fears presented to them on the six o'clock news, each day of the week. Then their worst fears were confirmed when a strange man in uniform come up to the door, or the parents of the boyfriend call with the bad news. That's what happened with Nikki-D.

Lois felt so sad for Ginny and Nikki-D. Ginny's little girl was trying to escape her mother's life, only to run into the same life. Jonny thought Nikki-D would be searching most of her life for something that was right in front of her. Sort of like Caj. Wanting more. Lois perked up when she thought of her son coming home safely. He wasn't wounded or anything thank God! That's why it was so hard for Ginny and Nikki-D. They had to face loss when Lois didn't. Life worked out that way.

Ginny came over.

"When do you think his plane will be in?"

"I don't know."

"Nikki-D called this morning. She sounds better. I hated her going to that college in Chicago. I wish she would have stayed around here. She sounded so sad."

"I know."

Lois rubbed her friend's arm. It had been about six months since Beau's death and it still was hurting Nikki-D. It would probably take a lifetime to get over. He was her first real love.

"I was wondering if Jonny could give her a call. She always feels so much better when he talks to her. He was with her a lot when Beau died. I think she stills needs him."

"I'll talk to him."

Lois thought about Jonny and Nikki-D: two of the most unlikely friends she ever saw; true friends who would do anything for each other. They fought for each other and loved each other more than Lois could understand. She thought it odd that they never got together. The attraction was there. Kids nowadays made their own rules. Lois liked that. She and Ginny were brought up with harsh restrictions for women of their day. The choices were limited. For Nikki-D and Jonny, the sky was the limit and Lois was rooting them on. The world was so hard. She looked at Ginny.

"He'll call her."

It was a dry day in the July heat. Lois could see the heat-waves rising off the landing strip, an optical illusion that rose over the wings of the waiting planes. It was in the high eighties. It was too hot for her. Lois wore her favorite print dress today. She made it herself from one of the patterns she got from the thrift shop. The chill was out of the morning now and the heat would rise until late afternoon. The kids wanted to get back so they could go down to Coy's dock and swim. Most of the reservation kids hung around down there. All the kids swam like fish, so there was no danger of drowning. It left Lois free to do her chores and visit. She and Ginny visited the site of the new General Building being built. When it was done, they would all go to the grand opening. Lois was making herself a nice dress for that occasion too.

Ginny walked away. She was always so active that it took Lois some time to catch up with her. They worked together well. Lois could hear the pride in Ginny's voice when they talked about the new building. It was mostly Ginny and Jonny who got the loan through the bank. Jonny was becoming a leading spokesman for the project. They asked him to speak at the opening. Lois felt pride well up in her, thinking about her son speaking in front of the whole reservation. It was his destiny.

Now she worried about Caj. He had stopped writing many months ago. Lois remembered talking to the Chaplain at the Red Cross. She was so nervous, and worried. He was a nice man. But what he had said scared her.

"Mrs. Esque, I want to say something to you and I hope you will keep an open mind about it," he had said in his soft, chaplain voice.

She nodded.

"Sometimes when young men are sent to war ... it changes them." He looked at the ceiling trying to find the right words.

"Changes them?"

"Yes. Its a different world. All the things and people back home become just memories. That's where they like to keep them. Some of them..." He looked down at Lois. "Some of them change dramatically. War makes them do strange things. Then they become strange to us. You understand?"

It was obvious that she didn't. The Chaplain decided to try the direct approach.

"Caj said he would write when he is ready."

Lois's heart sank. Ginny was next to her and she grabbed Lois's arm. Her face must have fallen after hearing his words.

"Is ... Is he all right?"

"Yes! Yes! He is with his unit. In the rear. Not much action going on there. He is in one of the best places for safety. I assure you of that."

Lois began to tremble. The Chaplain was lying. Beau died where Caj was, Lois knew this by the way Ginny squeezed her arm. The lies were put forward to save the innocent from being hurt. Lois could only imagine what would make her son decide not to write to her.

"Could you check on him ... and ... let me know?"

The chaplain nodded his head that he would. He scribbled on his note pad. He would forget until the next time this woman came in asking about her son. He saw it on all of their faces: the uncertainty, pain, and anguish of not hearing from their boys as the war turned them into men. He knew that when Mrs. Esque left, there would be another mother coming in to ask him the same questions and he would have to give the same lies to them. The truth was that he didn't know how it was over there. He had never been over to Vietnam. He could only give them the company line and act as if he knew. This would leave an imprint on him for the rest of his life.

"Mom. The little ones want to get out and play. I think its going to take longer than we thought for Caj's plane to get here."

Lois turned to Jonny who stood by her. He stood tall now. Both sides of the family had tall genes so it didn't surprise her that Jonny picked them up. Where he got his gentle demeanor, she didn't know. His father was such an angry man. So was his grandmother. Part of the Jimicums. Esques came from some Frenchman trapper that came into the region in the 1800's. Jonny had Shamans on his side; a very great spirit-power. Lois liked that; a healing power. She knew her son would be a leader in the tribe. She knew he still had many trials to overcome. Nikki-D was one of them.

"OK. Let them out, but keep an eye on them. Jonny, I want you to give Nikki-D a call. Ginny says that she hasn't recovered from Beau yet. You're the one she needs to hear from."

Jonny looked at his mother. She saw the deep, soulful eyes; like a wolf's. He nodded at her that he would give Nikki-D a call.

Jonny remembered as he walked away. The bad news came to him from his mother. She had just come back from Nikki-D's place. Jonny saw her hurrying up their front yard. The April wind was blowing off the bay. Her print dress was blowing all over and she hid her face under her scarf Jonny knew something was wrong. The whole day seemed to rise up in the rough wind. It blustered over the dark water of the bay.

Whitecaps rose inside the bay, telling Jonny a storm was coming. Small boats at Hermosa Resorts bobbed against their mooring. Jonny remembered.

Jonny's heart sank when he saw his mother's face. She was crying. Maybe it had something to do with Caj. He knew instinctively that it wasn't Caj. Nikki-D! He went running for the door, swinging it open for his mother as she climbed the front steps. She stopped and looked up at him. The tears were still falling down her face.

"Jonny. Its ... Its Nikki-D. Her boyfriend..."

Jonny didn't have to hear anymore. He helped his mother into the house.

"Mm ... mm. Where is she?"

Lois went over and sat down in her favorite chair; pulling off her scarf at the same time. The kids ran up to her and she put her arms around them, as she always did when something bad happened. The kids were silent. They knew. Jonny got his coat.

"Mmmmom...?"

"She's home ... Ginny is taking care of her and trying to talk to his parents. Every one is so scattered. I told Ginny I would come down and get you. Nikki-D needs you, Jonny, it..."

Jonny didn't hear the last part because he was already running down the road to Nikki-D's. Lois was left to get the kids ready and find someone to baby-sit them. Franc was gone to Seattle; he had been there for about a month. Looking for work she said, but everyone knew that he was drinking on First Avenue. It was all right though, because when he was out of the house the family was allowed to collect welfare. At least they had food and rent for the month. Jonny worked at odd jobs to help his family but it was barely enough to get by on.

Lois ran over to Elliot Brown's home. Sheila Brown would baby-sit. She knocked on their door. Sheila opened it and gave Lois one of her smiles. She always had a great smile; one of her best features.

"Hi, Mrs. Esque."

So polite.

"Sheila, can you baby-sit for me? There's an emergency up at the Thomas's house and I need to go back up there."

Sheila saw Lois's face and knew it was serious.

"Let me ask if I can." She waved Lois in. The house was hot. Their wood stove sat in the middle of the room. A bed sat in the corner of the house. They liked to keep the wood burning. An old pot of coffee sat on the stove. Steam was coming out of the spout. Sheila went in the other room and then came back with her coat. " I can stay with them."

"Thank you. They shouldn't be any problem, its bedtime."

"Its all right. Is Jonny there?"

This surprised Lois. She was used to girls asking for Caj, but Jonny was different.

"No; he went up to the Thomas's."

Lois watched Sheila's face fall. She would have to watch this one.

"Is Nikki-D all right?"

Lois liked this. The girl obviously liked Jonny and knew that Nikki-D was one of the important people in his life and she still thought of her. Sheila had some values.

"They're all having a hard time up there. Especially Nikki-D."

Lois didn't have to say any more. The reservation knew about Nikki-D's boyfriend going to Vietnam. Now they would know that he was killed in action over there. Sadness washed over Lois. Her friend Ginny would need her. She knew that Nikki-D would have to blame someone for his death. The mother was always the first one to blame. Ginny's relationship with her daughter was so strained, yet sometimes so close. It was something she missed with her own kids. Still, she felt close to them all. The problem was she had too many of them right in a row. It was hard to give to those who needed it when there was someone younger who needed your attention more. So she did the best that she could and moved on. That's all anyone could do.

Ginny opened the door, her face ash-white and her lips trembling. Jonny felt the sorrow coming from the house. He knew that the house had too many bad spirits that still hung around. Soon he would suggest to his mother that they come up and sweep out the house. The spirits would remain until this was done. Jonny felt this.

"Mmm-mm ... Is Nikki-D here?"

"Come in, Jonny. She's upstairs with her dad now. You can wait in the living room. I have to make some calls."

Jonny noticed Mrs. Thomas checking out the stairs going to Nikki-D's bedroom. She was worried about her, but had to wait for the signal from her daughter. It was a game that mothers and daughters played with each other and it baffled Jonny. He saw it in his own sisters. It was a deeper understanding than he or other men could achieve. They had to remain silent while this secret communication went on around them, never understanding what was being said. Whether it was a stormy tale or a humorous adventure, it was between them. Jonny felt that women thought too fast for men. This scared men, so they formed their own groups that kept women away. Maybe that was what Beau was doing when he joined the Marine Corps.

It seemed as if Jonny waited for a long time before Mr. Thomas came in. He was white and pale. Jonny could see his pain. Nikki-D was his only daughter and she needed him. He tried to be there for her but he never knew if he helped or not. Jonny waited for him to say something.

Nick shifted on his feet a couple of times to get his emotions under control. He stood by the fireplace, not saying anything. Finally he was ready.

"Nikki-D's mother is with her right now, Jonny. Can you wait a little longer? I know she would want to talk to you."

Jonny nodded his head. It was going to be a long night.

Jonny walked into her bedroom. The pink room was what he called it. Nikki-D and her pink! She claimed she hated it and she only had the color because her mother wanted it. Jonny didn't believe that for a moment. Now the color brought back the little girl that Jonny met when he was ten. He looked around the room at her life. She wasn't neat like her mother. She wasn't dirty either; just messy. Jonny could see a sense of order in the mess though. Especially her pictures. They were in order on her desks. A big one of her and Beau stood out in front. Then there were pictures of all her friends and family. Nikki-D must have taken a million pictures. Her whole life could be told by them, and the smiles of their faces. Jonny knew most of them.

He heard the little sobs coming from the big bed. He saw her eyes sticking out under the covers. Nikki-D looked like shit. His heart lurched for a second. Jonny never saw Nikki-D this bad. Her eyes were swollen and red from crying so much. There were black rings under each eye. Tears trailed down her face.

"Mm ... mm. Nikki-D?" He called her name softly. "Nikki-D?"

She never moved. Her father said that the doctor gave her a shot of something to calm her down. Jonny went over to the bed and sat in a chair in front of her. She would sleep on and off through the night.

A sound came from her lips. She was talking to him. Her voice was so low, barely audible.

"Jonny ... I hurt so much ... it wouldn't stop hurting..." Little sobs escaped from her. "My life ... my life is gone ... they killed my life, Jonny."

Jonny reached out and took her hand between his, gently rubbing it.

"Shhhh ... Nikki-D. They say you should sleep."

"God ... took him away from me ... I never... never even slept with Beau ... he wanted to ... but I said we should wait until we're married... I loved him ... Jonny."

"Shhhh ... Nikki-D."

"What do I do now ... Jonny?"

Jonny didn't know.

A last small sob came from her lips.

"Shhhh ... Nikki-D."

Jonny got to the car and opened the door for his sisters. It was an old car, so the doors were hard to open. It was better than nothing. They all piled out into the sunshine. Ginny watched him. He was such a good boy and the girls were all getting big. He worked hard to get the tribe to go after a loan for their building. He was only eighteen and already making manly decisions. She felt sorry for him. Those decisions never got any easier. She knew.

Ginny was hurt from the loss of her daughter. Nikki-D would be running from home for some time. She knew the hurt that she went through. Lois helped Ginny through the pain of accusations coming from Nikki-D. Nick was there for her too. He would always step in when the words became too hurtful between her and Nikki-D. She couldn't understand why Nikki-D blamed her for Beau. Ginny liked the boy. Thought he was going to be something in life. He was someone she would be interested in if she was that age. It made no sense to her.

Lois came over.

"The plane is coming in."

"Right on time." Ginny saw the red in her friend's face. She was excited about her boy being home from that awful war. Ginny was, too. She raised her eyes to the sun and caught a glimpse of the plane before she had to look away. It was on its final approach.

Jonny had the kids at the fence, showing them the plane.

"Did he fly straight back from the war?" Ginny couldn't understand the Army's sending these boys back without some sort of rest. It didn't sound right to her.

"Yes. They said he had one stop in California and then he flies back here. I think its a civilian flight from there."

Lois's face fell. Ginny could see the concern on her face.

"What's wrong, Lois?"

"I don't know. I wonder how the war affected Caj. What will he be like? I see them on TV, and they all look so scared. We have some of the men from Korea who are called crazy. Raymond Moses calls himself the last of the wild ones. You know the war affected him. Franc came back from World War II different. He lost all of his charm and humor."

"That's what war does to people. Its like we have a deal with the men ... or boys and take care of them when they get back."

"The only time Franc could talk about the war for a long time was when he came home drunk. I could see his eyes: cold and black, with depths so vast that I could never understand what he saw. An empty soul. That's what they showed me. He's still that way.

"Lois ... Caj is different. Remember his smile and the way he swaggered when the girls were looking? He was always having fun. He always wanted to climb the next hill. I think you raised a very good boy there. He's a good boy."

Lois nodded her head. Caj was the one that could have anything he wanted in his life. Well-liked by every one, Caj walked through schools and life. Yet he was the one that had to leave. He was stifled by the reservation. He couldn't accept life's limitations. Caj ran toward all that life gave. Maybe he ran too far.

"Yes, Caj was the golden boy of the family, I think; Franc was proud as a peacock when he heard Caj joined the Marine Corps."

Ginny noticed Lois tense up every time she spoke of Franc. He must be drinking heavily again.

"The war is destroying so many people. I wish it would just end." Lois looked up to the sky, waiting for the plane.

"As flies to wanton boys, are we to the gods; They kill us for their sport."

"That was a line from King Lear, by William Shakespeare, spoken by the Earl of Gloucester." Ginny moved closer to Lois as she spoke.

"They express a bitter sense of the meaninglessness and brutality of life." Ginny again noticed the tension from Lois.

"Lois, its over for Caj and your family. He's coming home."

Lois just watched the plane as it landed. She and Ginny walked to the fence and stood with Jonny and the little ones. They watched as the men and women departed. Most of them were rushed by their families as they walked to the terminal.

There were no uniforms in the first wave of people. Then two men came out of the plane. They wore the uniform of the Marine Corps: the green dress uniform with red stripes. They put on the hats. Round black rims that reflected the sun circled the green hats. Under the rim, the two men wore the darkest sunglasses that Lois had ever seen. She wondered how they could see.

They were both taller than Caj so Lois knew they weren't him. The first one looked over the entire field, moving his head from right to left. The second one was doing the same thing, except his head was moving left to right. It was as if they were synchronized to catch at a first glance as much of the territory as they could. Then their heads moved over the people at the gate and fence. Lois could feel their eyes surveying each person in the crowd. She felt their eyes on her, checking her bags, checking the kids. It was as if they expected the kids to harm them. Fear went through her. They began to walk down the steps, the tall one first, while the other watched. Then he headed down, too. When they reached the bottom their families rushed to them. They waited and watched.

Lois waited some more. The two men were gone now. The wait was long. Lois knew that they didn't have to wait much longer. He wasn't there. She watched Jonny and Ginny go to ask questions. It wasn't necessary; Caj would not be on the plane. The fear that Ginny noticed came true. People said that the boys coming home were better off than the ones that returned in a body bag. Lois watched the plane as it was unloading a gray casket. Those people were wrong.

She looked up at the empty plane. Caj would not be coming home.

30

TOGETHER

Nikki-D rode down Interstate 5. It had been a long time for her. School was out and she graduated with high honors. That wasn't enough for her. She was a product of the Sixties. Her generation would always grow up with angst. For Nikki-D, that meant she needed to find out who she was. The questions mounted with no answers, leaving her with the feeling that she didn't belong anywhere in the world. School had given her freedom to reach inside and seek her true self. The war taught her life wasn't fair and she had to deal with that. Now she had to know what her life meant. She had the tools, except some pieces were still missing.

This couldn't keep her down. She was home. The Res. She saw all the big evergreens standing tall along the island split by rivers. She could see her home from the freeway. A small dot in a small clearing, but it was her home. It always excited her to come back here. Even more so now.

Nikki-D had come to terms with her past. She had been wild the last couple of years, but in her final year, she quit all the sex and drugs and drinking. Partying was part of college life and she took advantage of it. Now she knew it was because of those unresolved problems in her life. He mother, her father, herself – all came under scrutiny during her classes. She graduated with a BS degree in psychology. She went to so many classes on emotions and hurting that she felt as though she knew herself better than any time before. She smiled at that. It made her feel good to be in control of her life, at least to the point of knowing what she had to do. She was excited to be home.

The taxi driver was watching the signs on the freeway. He didn't want to miss the exit to the Res. They had a long way to go. Nikki-D hired a taxi from Seattle; she wanted to have a nice, leisurely ride home. She wanted to enjoy it. There was so much going on in her mind: things that she needed to do and say. An image of Jonny entered her mind. It was a good image. He stood so tall and handsome; she was by his side. It made sense. They were meant for each other. It wasn't like Beau, who was her young, intense love. It wasn't like that. She and Jonny were together from the moment they met. She was sure there was a spark even at that young age. She just didn't see it.

Nikki-D remembered Caj and Beau as so exciting to her. They represented those things that she couldn't control. That drew her to them. They were so handsome that she remembered melting every time they were around her. Caj was the first one. They were never together. It wasn't meant to be. Her mother and Jonny's mother would always say that. If its not meant to be than it wouldn't be no matter how hard you wanted it. Now she believed them. Her puppy-love of Caj had come and gone. Her heart had to deal with it. Of course, she blamed her mom. Her mom's concerns were valid. She knew that at that age if Caj had wanted sex with her she may have given it to him. It was hard to admit that, since she always wanted to be a good girl. It embarrassed her.

Then came Beau: that was her first true love, so intense in its emotions that she could fall under its spell. It was love on a grand scale that brought them both to new heights of understanding and wanting. Her regrets about sex and consummation were no longer there. Her morals were tested and found wanting after Beau's death; but before that she only belonged to him. Marriage would have brought them together in a life that, she knew would have been long and happy. It was never meant to be.

She had thought it all through. Nikki-D resolved never to be afraid to act on her feelings again. That is why she was home: to settle things. It felt right for her to be home now. She even felt good about seeing her mother again. The truth was, she wanted to see her mother. She had missed her so much during her pouting years. Nikki-D realized she locked out her mother at the time. It was something she had to do although it hurt them both. She was glad that her mother and father didn't see her at the time, anyway. It wasn't something she was proud of doing. Like she said, those days were over. The Sixties were bad years for everyone. She didn't even like to think about them now. It was too painful.

The taxi turned onto the off-ramp. Marysville still looked the same, gas stations on every corner. Fourth Street still had its stacking lanes of cars waiting to get on and off the freeway. Nikki-D had forgotten how much fun she used to have walking down the main street of Marysville with her girlfriends, young girls giggling while they walked with their skirts swaying and sweaters emblazoned with their school logo, the tomahawk. She remembered the boys watching them and how much they liked to be watched then. It was all just fun and games to them; games with serious undertones.

Nikki-D remembered her friends; special friends, like Tammy, whom she hardly even talked to anymore. She made a mental note to contact Tammy and see how she was doing. The shops where Nikki-D and her mother used to shop - they were all changing now. The small shops were closing for bigger shopping complexes. She had heard that there might be a big mall built there soon. That would be something for this little town. The citizens fought to keep it small and comfortable but the times of change were on them all. Nikki-D knew what change could do to you.

The taxi turned left traveling through the underpass that brought them to the Res. Home. Nikki-D was already feeling good. She rolled down the window and smelled the fresh evergreen trees. It was completely different from Marysville. The Res. had only one road that ran around the 76 station in an S-curve, cutting through the trees before disappearing across the Quil Ceda river. Nikki-D smiled and leaned out some more. The sun was shining down on them. It was around eleven in the morning and the sun was getting hot. She loved the summertime in Washington: so much growth, wild-flowers, wild berries, and more. The lazy waters teeming with running fish brought cool relief from the summer sun. All of this brought girlhood thoughts to Nikki-D. Yes, she was glad to be home.

Caj sat on the steps of the Indian tavern on State street. He was one of many Indians sitting in the morning sun, drinking and talking. Mostly drinking. He couldn't remember the last time he was home. The drinks were eating at his brain. This binge was one of his longest and it was having an effect on him.

"Caj! Hey bro! You got another drink?" Mike Dunn was sitting next to him. They both had drank for the last two weeks straight. Their words were slurred and their movements sluggish. "Give me another drink, bro."

Caj must have passed out for a second because he didn't remember having the bottle. He looked down into his hands and saw the can of beer. It was still full, so he must have been out for a second. He felt ragged. Caj hated waking up.

When he woke, the sadness was always the first thing that hit him. Caj always felt like crying and didn't know what to do about it. It was ironic that Caj was considered the life of the party wherever he went, smiling and laughing, and generally having a good time. He liked a dare and anyone foolish enough to bet him on a dare usually ended up paying.

"Caj, you going to give me a drink?" Mike was getting upset. His friend just stared into space now. He noticed Caj staring more and more. He used to be concerned about him when they both sobered up, but Caj came out of it more times than not. Mike just wanted a drink now. His eyes were barely open, the laughter was over and he was getting down to some serious drinking. Mike was already thinking about calling the cab home. They were down to their last dime, and it was getting hot. He took the can of beer from Caj and took a drink. Its cool foam ran down his throat. His brain was swimming and he knew his buddy Caj must be in worst shape. They had different drinking patterns and Caj wasn't a binge drinker, so he must be suffering now. Caj was a daily drinker and stayed in the taverns most of the time, only stopping when he ran out of money or when he had to attend some family get-together. Mike wasn't sure where Caj got his money, but he knew Caj liked to buy for everyone when he did have money. Now this binge was almost over.

Mike looked at his buddy; Caj sat in his own blood, his face broken and beaten from the fight last night. Mike doubted if Caj even remembered.

Caj was sore. He knew he was in a fight but couldn't remember why. He never did. There were so many fights lately. He began to remember the three men as they put the boots to him lying on the floor of the tavern. Everyone watching as they kicked the shit out of him. They watched him laugh after each blow as though he enjoyed it. Maybe he did. He usually put up a good fight until they wore him down. Then the beating would begin. The kicks were so hard this time and they were hitting him in the head. He felt the blackness come to him: It is what I seek.

Caj couldn't even feel his lips. The sun was like a burning ball in his closed eyes. He hated waking up. He hated it all.

"Hey brother, you look like shit. Ha-ha!"

Caj knew he probably looked bad because he hurt like hell.

"I'm all right. Time to go home. You keep the beer." Caj wobbled up to his knees, then tried to lift himself up. His head swam and his stomach lurched from the motion. He wasn't going to make it. He leaned down with his head against the pavement. He was sick.

"Hey, Caj, you going to make it?" Mike was laughing at his buddy. He tried to get up and fell back down himself. "Whoa! Are we on water or something?"

Caj laughed. He licked his lips. His mouth was dry. His stomach was dry, looking for something to throw up. His head wouldn't stop swimming. Caj waited for a second more, until the motion sickness went away. He stayed very still.

Mike was up and heading back into the tavern. " I'm getting a cab. Time to go home, Caj. You wait here. I'll be out in a sec. OK?" Mike staggered in the dark doorway, where there seemed to be cool air.

Caj wished he could move so he could get out of the sun. It was burning into his brain. Just like Nam. There was no way to escape from it. It wasn't only the sun but the heat that got to Caj. The heat made his head hurt. The heat always did.

Mike never did come back out. Caj waited because he couldn't move. He was going to pass out again if something didn't happen soon. He could feel himself slipping away. He could almost feel the dark blackness upon him again. It was what Caj wanted, if something didn't happen soon.

Nikki-D was happy. She knew what she was getting into and didn't care. She thought of Jonny and wished that the cabby would drive faster. This was going to be her special day. The sun was brighter than any time that she could remember. The summer wind was bringing her home. She was a young woman now, experienced and ready for anything the world sent her. Her life made a difference, or it would soon. She had let go of those young-girl worries and moved on. The world today was different than those ten years ago. It wasn't time to drop out or tune in. It was time to enjoy what life afforded you and not ask too many questions. She wasn't a sell-out because she never completely bought into that Sixties' mantra. If this was cynical, then that was fine with her. She wanted her happiness and she didn't want to wait for it.

The excitement was reaching a peak for her. The left turn on Totem

Beach Road was up next. Then another left to Mission Beach Road, where her home was. She knew her mother and father were waiting for her. They never met her at the airport because they never knew the appropriate thing to do. So they waited. Nikki-D realized it was her attitude that they responded to, but she was different now. They would see. The taxi turned left. Nikki-D could smell the ocean from here. Her senses were alive to the sights and smell of the Res. Her home.

She giggled. The taxi driver looked in his rear-view mirror. She could see his eyes on her. She didn't care. The happy feeling was a rush.

The cemetery. Nikki-D was afraid to look up at the cemetery. She didn't want to see any burial today. She looked anyway. The green, fresh-cut grass lay around the headstones of the graves. A single road ran in and around the cemetery and out again. She looked to see if anyone was there. Not today. Nikki-D felt relief and the happy feeling came back to her. No problem. This was her day. She was home.

The taxi stopped at the curb. It was a yellow cab that looked as if it had hit too many roads. He could barely see it through his blood-shot eyes. Mike must have called it. Caj was thankful for Mike. He knew that people had been passing by and seeing him in a bad position. Caj laughed at the thought of a drunken Indian outside a small, run-down tavern, and here he was. The thought never bothered him but he did see the irony in it. He could barely lift his head, so he waited. He didn't have to wait long. With his blood-shot eyes, he watched the pair of legs walk up to him. He could see a set of small cowboy boots come to a halt in front of him. They were too small to be a man's; Caj tried to figure out who wore boots like that from the Res. He couldn't think of any woman he knew.

He tried to lift his head again. The pounding in the back of his skull was getting worse. Caj knew he had to go home and get some sleep soon. Or ... No: there wasn't any or, - he had to get some sleep; it was that simple.

"Well, I never thought I would find you like this."

It was a soft, feminine voice. Caj knew he'd heard that voice before, but he couldn't place it. Now he wanted to look up. When he did, the sun bore down on him, blinding him for a second. The blurred figure had long hair. He saw that for sure. Everything began to wobble again, so he lowered his head between his legs. He let out his breath. "Shuuuuu!"

"That's all you have to say to an old friend? Come on, Caj, its me-

Mariann." She was looking down at a pathetic figure sitting outside a small tavern. Mariann was here for Caj. He looked the same. A little older. Definitely drunk. But he was carrying things well. She was glad because what she heard about his drinking made her wonder what he would look like. She was so glad to see him. He was still so handsome.

"Mariann!"

God! his smile was just the same. Mariann melted at his smile. She kept that smile with her for all these years. She wondered about him, but could never bring herself to call. Until now. She wanted to be with him and decided it was the right time in her life. And there was that other matter, but that could wait. She had to get him home and sobered up. Then they could talk.

"Caj, I have a cab waiting here. Can you walk?"

He just nodded his head. He swayed back and forth; he didn't want to throw up.

"Stand up, Caj, and you can lean on me to the cab. OK?"

"Mariann." He mumbled this because he could barely talk. He was going to pass out again. Caj wanted to make sure it was somewhere soft, so he pushed himself up and into the arms of Mariann. "OK."

She felt his weight on her. He had put on some pounds and muscle since the last time she was with him. He felt good to her. She carried him to the cab, where he got into the back and promptly passed out. Mariann shut the door and climbed into the front seat with the waiting cabby.

"I guess you better bring us back to my hotel room. Where you picked me up."

He nodded and pulled out on to State Street. Mariann was content to watch Caj in the back seat, curled up and sleeping. All she could do was smile.

Ginny smiled as the cab pulled up with Nikki-D in it. She was excited to see her daughter again. Nikki-D sounded so up and happy over the phone. Ginny always listened to her daughter's moods. They connected so much at that level that Ginny could never understand why they got into so many arguments. Nick always said it was because they were so close, but Ginny thought of other reasons. Now wasn't the time to think about that; Nikki-D was home. That's all that mattered.

"Nick did you have her room cleaned and dusted like I said?"

"Yes, honey, it was all taken care of " Nick was used to his wife questioning whether he did something or not. He knew that it came from twenty years of not being able to rely on him when he was drinking. He didn't take it personally anymore. Ginny had become powerful at the bank in her own right and Nick was her second in command. They owned most of the stock of the bank through shrewd dealings on her part. They would be set for life, financially. Nick could only marvel at his wife's abilities when they were let loose. It made for a happy marriage and a happy life for him. He knew that some men couldn't handle their wives taking the lead, but it was a godsend to Nick. He was a team player and he liked it like that. "There she is!"

"I know that. Be sure and bring in her luggage and put it in her room." Ginny was nervous. She wanted this time with her daughter to be happy. She was gun-shy from all the bad things that happened over the years. She saw how sensitive Nikki-D was to events in her life. Ginny never thought Nikki-D would recover from Beau's death. So tragic. Ginny heard about the things Nikki-D was doing at the college. She closed her ears to the stories because even if they were true she knew her daughter was acting out and would revert back eventually.

Ginny watched Nikki-D get out of the cab. She was amazed; it wasn't her little girl that got out of the cab this time, but a woman. Her long, black hair flowed in the summer breeze, dark Cimmerian eyes confident and secure. Nikki-D was small like her mother, but Ginny could see the energy that she carried. Ginny saw her smile, dazzling and happy at the same time. Ginny felt a nagging fear stab at her for a second. Nikki-D came running up to Ginny; they wrapped their arms around each other and hugged and kissed on the cheeks. Ginny couldn't help but smile.

Nikki-D stood in front of the big bay windows, watching the sailboats float by. She loved this place. She knew that now. Home felt good to her. Her mother and father loved her and she loved them. She no longer wanted to fight. She was tired of trying to change the world. This last year brought some serenity and peace; especially with her past. It was time to move forward. In the process of moving on, she came to realize that she still had love inside her, a love that grew even as she stood there. It was hard to explain.

"Nikki-D, here's a large glass of Coke. Unless you want something else. Its hot today, so we can go out on the patio and enjoy the breeze." Ginny moved over and opened the glass door and walked through it. She set the drinks down on the table outside. Nick and Nikki-D walked out with her. They sat across from her with the sun facing them. Nikki-D reached over and took her drink. Ginny watched as she took a drink. She must have been thirsty because she gulped down half the drink before setting the glass back down on the table.

"You shouldn't drink cold drinks so fast. It will give you a headache. Nick, tell her that she shouldn't drink like that."

"She's right, honey. It will give you a headache. Besides, its not ladylike."

"I know. I know." Nikki-D tried to slow down because they were right: she was getting a headache from the cold drink.

"Do you want another?" Ginny and Nick knew something was coming up because Nikki-D always showed some abnormal behavior when she was nervous.

"OK."

Ginny got up to pour another glass for Nikki-D.

"Have you seen Jonny?"

Something in that question made Ginny nervous. She knew Nikki-D. In fact, she had seen Jonny all this week. They had been going to the new community building together to finish up on the grand opening of the building. Jonny was always with her to explain what the tribe wanted and then explain to the tribe what Ginny wanted. He was invaluable to them all. He had so much patience for such a young man. He still had that speech impediment and Ginny and the others had learned to wait for him because when he said something, it usually was helpful to whomever he was talking. She wanted to send him to a specialist herself, but he and Lois wouldn't have anything to do with that. They were too independent to allow her to pay for help. Yes, Jonny was a fine boy. He was becoming a fine man and a leader of the tribe.

Ginny wondered why Nikki-D asked about him. "I see him every day. He helps everyone on this new building. He is the link between the bank and the tribe. I think its great that someone that young works so hard for his people. Don't you, Nick?"

Nick looked over at his wife. She wanted Nick's support for some reason. He never understood how these two communicated with each other. A simple question lead them into unknown regions that would leave Nick shaking his head in confusion. "Yes, without Jonny I don't think they could have finished their new building. We should go down and take a look at it when you have time, Nikki-D." Nick thought he had given a good answer to his wife.

"Mom seemed to have a lot to do with getting that building built, too, Dad."

This stunned Nick. His daughter wanted him to recognized her mother's achievements. He was always left dazed and confused when speaking to either of his women. Nick felt the blood rise in his cheeks. They must have seen it, too. "I believe you're right, Nikki-D. I should have included your mother in my praise. She has become a great bank-owner and has instincts for loans that no one can match. I would say that in her work, she has really become the bank and the bank has become her. We are reaching new heights in financing and she is the leading force behind it. I'm sorry I left her out."

"Nick. Its all right. Nikki-D knows all of that nonsense." Ginny watched her husband sit back in his chair. She had to smile because she felt sorry for him when he tried to deal with her *and* Nikki-D. It was a no-win situation for him. Nikki-D's comment even threw Ginny for a loop. Nikki-D defending her mother? Something was up.

"What about Caj?"

"Oh now, Caj is a different story. I always thought he would be the one in that family who would make something of himself. But..."

"But what, Daddy?"

Ginny wanted to put an end to this. "Caj is a drunk. He came back from the war all crazy and ... you know ... crazy."

"Maybe he's the only sane one." It popped out of Nikki-D's mouth before she could stop. She didn't want to talk politics this time. She had more important things to discuss with her parents. She needed to talk about Jonny.

"Maybe, but he's sure a mess. Poor Lois tries to help him but she doesn't know what to do. If you ask me all he needs to do is grow up and stop thinking about the war. Its over for him. Soon it will be over for all of us. Nixon is bringing them all home. We need to move on from here."

Ginny and Nikki-D could hear the silent majority in Nick's voice; the pleading now to move on. The hard hats no longer wanted to send their boys over to be slaughtered in that war. They remained silent. They both knew that they had won against the hardheaded old men in power. There wasn't anything more to say.

"Well, Jonny's doing good. Why don't you go down after lunch and see him? I know Jonny is waiting to see you, since I told him you were coming home."

Nikki-D's ears perked up at this. Her heart raced. "Why did he say anything?"

Ginny gave Nikki-D a strange look. "No. He didn't say anything. You just talked to him last week. What's going on with you?"

"Nothing. I just thought he might have said something to you; like he was glad I was coming home. I suppose that's too much to ask from Jonny."

"Nikki-D!" Ginny didn't like her talking like that. "Jonny has always been there for you when you needed him. He is there for you now if you want him to be. You know that. You know he doesn't say much unless he has to. He shows you how much he cares in other ways."

"I know. I know. I just want him to say it this way once. You know."

Then it dawned on Ginny; Nikki-D wanted to know what Jonny felt about her. Ginny felt a rush of apprehension go through her. Oh no, after four terrible years away Nikki-D has come home to what she thinks will be her love. Ginny began to see her daughter again: Nikki-D, who wanted the world to be all her way, was walking into another wall that she built around love. Now Ginny knew that it was Jonny that Nikki-D had picked. She picked him because he was always there for her. He loved her unconditionally. Now she was going to test his love.

"Jonny has gown up and moved on since the last time you two were together."

Ginny saw Nikki-D flinch. She was right. Oh shit! Ginny would love to have Jonny and Nikki-D together but she knew from working with Jonny that there were obstacles. Ginny knew her daughter thought it was going to be easy as pie. Just walk up and tell Jonny that they loved each other and they were getting married and that was that.

Ginny and Lois knew that if anyone belonged together it was these two kids. Ginny saw the love between them. She also saw how the world was. She worked with Jonny and the other Indians. She could barely breathe. Her heart stopped and she wanted to tell Nikki-D to wait before she rushed into this. But she could say nothing. If Ginny said anything negative, then Nikki-D would blow it out of proportion and accuse her of interfering. No. Nikki-D would have to do this one on her own.

Jonny waited in front of the new building. It was huge. The community building stood on the edge of Battle Creek as it ran out into the bay. It was a beautiful site on the potlatch grounds. He walked in the doors and watched the final touches of carpet and paint being applied to the building. As you walked through the doors, the people's room was on the right; in the center was a new basketball court; and on the left were the new administrative offices for officers of the tribe.

Most all the tribal business would be conducted in this building. Jonny leaned against the doorway, touching the finished wood. Visions of his tribe rolled through his head. He saw the future of his people; he could see their growth over the years. Their poverty will fall by the wayside and they will become a rich tribe. Jonny could see that this building was just the beginning.

Jonny watched the people of his tribe come in and walk around the building. They couldn't believe that it was being built. He could see the pride in their faces. This made him feel good. He had worked with the elders of the tribe and the smokehouse people to get this building. The board members passed the motion to get money through whatever means available. That is what he did. Jonny knew that working with Ginny was the key to getting funds. She wanted the loan just as bad as he did. His mother talked to him every night about working with her. Ginny was demanding and had her ways about her but his mother would always talk him through it. The government matched the funding that the tribe had put up. It was hard during negotiations, but now it all seemed worth it. Jonny was excited today. This weekend was the grand opening. Then a new beginning would come to the tribe.

In his happiness, Jonny thought of Nikki-D. She was going to be home to see this. It was a triumph for Ginny, his mother and himself. They worked so hard for this. Nikki-D would see the results. Jonny wanted Nikki-D to see him in this ceremony. He knew that it would be something that would define him in her mind for the rest of her days. He wanted her there with him. She was his best friend.

Lois came walking up. Jonny walked over to his mother. "Mm..mm. Hi, Mom."

"Hi. How are things going?"

"Good. They will have ninety percent of the building done by time of the grand opening. It shouldn't cause any problems."

"You know that Nikki-D is back."

"Mm ... mm. Yes. I'm going to go up and see her when I get done."

"You don't have to. She's coming over. Ginny called. She said Nikki-D was asking about you."

Jonny was puzzled by this. "Mm ... mm. About me? I just talked to her last week. Is there something wrong?"

"I don't know; is there?" Ginny had said more than Lois let on.

"Mmmm ... not that I'm aware of "

Lois watched her son getting nervous. His speech always went south when he was nervous or unsure of himself. Any one that had been around him for long learned of his speech impediment. Lois had been around him the longest. She could almost feel it coming on before she heard it. She saw it now.

"She wants to talk to you. Ginny is wondering what its all about. If you know something, then you should try to let her know."

"Mmm-mm ... I don't know what Nikki-D wants to talk about. You know her; she always has a new cause that makes her go crazy. Mmmm ... maybe its something like that?"

"Well, she will be down here shortly. She's your best friend. She may need help. Ginny says she's acting different. You sure there wasn't anything that you talked about?"

"No. Nothing." Jonny was perplexed by this line of questioning from his mother. She must know something. Jonny was about to ask her what she knew but he got a call from Raymond Moses to come over.

"Mmmm ... I have to go. When will Nikki-D be down?"

"In about an hour or so. I will be around here too. We are cooking for the elders today. When she gets here, bring her over so I can say 'hi.'"

"OK. See you later."

It was later than Caj thought when he woke. It wasn't morning any more. He must have slept for hours. His mouth tasted bad. His eyes felt as if they were going to explode. He opened both eyes to find two pairs of dark eyes staring back at him. A little boy stood over him. They looked at each other before the boy became tired and moved on. Caj groaned.

Mariann walked in from the next room. " Caj, you're awake!"

Memory started coming back. He had thought it was a dream. Apparently it wasn't, because Mariann stood before him. She had a tall glass of something that looked cold and inviting. His shaking hand reached out and took the drink. Trembling lips sipped the ice-cold water. He was dehydrated and started to gulp down the water. Its coolness reached his brain, cooling down the pounding in his head. Soon the cup was empty and he lay back down and closed his eyes, his hand holding out the cup to Mariann. He needed more sleep.

The fog was lifting again. The night air was coming through the open window of the small rental unit where Mariann was staying. Caj was feeling like death when he opened his bloodshot eyes. Mariann was sitting in a tan, ragged chair. The cheap motel they were at must have been here since the Fifties. Nothing had changed from the first day they opened their doors. Caj looked at her some more. She was still slim and trim, with a lanky build that came from her people. It seemed like another life when he knew her. She was there in front of him, though, and he wondered why. She got up and came to him. He was about to find out.

"Caj, you want something to drink?"

"Yea," he croaked.

"OK. I'll get you some cold water."

"Water?" She was already out of the room. Caj closed his eyes and then pushed himself up to a sitting position. Whoa ... His head swam back and forth for a second. His stomach lurched a little. He grabbed the arm of the couch he was on and steadied himself. The room stopped spinning.

"Are you all right? I have your water." Mariann was standing in front of him again.

Caj jumped. Adrenaline went rushing through his head, making it hurt more. He wished she didn't do that; sneak up on him. It made him nervous. The water tasted good. It wasn't beer, but that wasn't what he needed right now. Caj watched her go over and sit down again.

"Its good to see you, Mariann. When did you get in?"

"Been here awhile. Came in from Oklahoma."

"Why?"

"To see you."

"Why?"

Mariann had been asking herself that question for a long time - what was it she wanted? Caj never wrote to her once since he left. That didn't deter her, though. She thought of him daily. Then when it became too much for her she had to take action. It wasn't as if she was leaving much behind. Welfare was the only income for her and her little boy. She skimped and saved a little at a time from her checks and when she felt she had enough money saved, she caught the bus to Washington. It was what she had to do.

"I wanted to see you."

Caj could see it in her eyes. The love. It was so strong that it scared him. He felt his defenses go up. This was something he could no longer handle. He wasn't ready for all this shit. Never was.

"Listen Caj. I know that you may not want to hear this. I can see it on your face. I've been around here long enough to know that you're in pretty bad shape. You drink all the time and don't work. I've heard this. I know you haven't been the same since coming back from the war. I've talked to someone about that."

Caj exploded. "What!"

Mariann was taken aback by this explosion. But the alcohol advisor guy told her to hold her ground. She never felt anger like this before: direct anger at her; his eyes turned into something that frightened her even more. It was as if he stared right through her. It scared her, but she had to remain strong or her plan wasn't going to work. More than anything, her plan was to be with Caj.

"Quiet down. Shhhh. You'll wake him." Mariann pointed to the bedroom.

Caj remembered that there was a little boy here before. It must have been her little boy. He didn't give a shit; it was nothing to him. Fuck her. What right did she have? He'd yell anytime he wanted and if she didn't like it she could kiss his ass.

"I think there's something wrong with you from the war, Caj. I talked to a man, Dick White, from the Evergreen Mental Health place. He said they are just looking into something called shock, or trauma. He says that's what may be happening to you. You were traumatized from the war. He says he would like to talk to you."

This caught Caj by surprise. His head started to hurt like it always did. The anger started to wane. "What do you mean there's something wrong with me? Like some chemical, you mean?" He rubbed his head, but it was his heart that hurt.

"I can't explain it; you have to go in and see this guy."

"Fuck that war. Its over for me. I don't need to see anyone."

"I want you to go."

Caj's anger flared again. "Who in the fuck are you? And why should I listen to what you have to say?"

"I love you, and if you can't do it for me, then do it for your son." Mariann didn't want to bring it up like this, but Caj had to know anyway. So it was time. She saw the stunned look on his face and thought that maybe she had gone too far. He didn't move or say anything for the longest time. She waited and waited until she couldn't take it anymore.

"Well! Did you hear what I said?"

"I heard." He was taken aback by her announcement and immediately thought that she must be mistaken. Then the thought entered his head that she was setting him up. How could he know if it was his son or not? She was probably saying that to get him to marry her. Just like women all over. "How do I know that he's mine?"

Now it was Mariann who was mad. She would have expected this from any one else, but not from Caj. Obviously he had changed from the boy she knew just a few years ago. The anger rose to her cheeks. "Forget it. Just forget it, Caj. If you have to ask me that, then you're not worth knowing. I don't need to marry any one. If you haven't noticed, you're not the best marrying material around. So just forget it."

Caj wasn't backing off. "Well, I may not be anyone else's marrying material, but you sure went through a lot of time and energy to find me."

"Get out! Right now! I want you out of here."

"Fine, I'm gone. Nice to see you, too."

Caj stormed out of the apartment without saying anything else.

Mariann heard small whimpers from the bedroom. The tears were rushing out of her eyes and she tried to stop them before going to her son. She grabbed a napkin from the desk and walked to her son. It was going to be harder than she expected.

Jonny stood on the front porch of his house, stunned. His mother was sitting in a chair in the corner. She wasn't saying anything. Nikki-D was standing in front of him. His mind was reeling from what she said; or asked. His face was hot with embarrassment from being caught off-guard. He heard Scout, behind him, snicker, and the little ones giggled.

"You girls hush up and go inside or go and play somewhere."

"But Mom..." They all yelled in unison.

"I said go!" Lois wasn't about to have them spoil this moment. She was happy, but kept it from her face. It was hard keeping a straight face. Ginny was coming down to pick up Nikki-D. She was right, of course; Nikki-D still went after what she wanted with no thought of the consequences. Now it was up to Jonny. They were so young and had so much going for them that Lois knew it would be a good union. She almost laughed at her young son because of the look on his face. He didn't have a clue. It was a shame.

Nikki-D stared at Jonny. She knew that telling Jonny they should marry caught him off-guard and he was trying to get back in control of himself before he answered. She wished he would hurry up. He'd been standing there for ten minutes now.

"Mmmm ... mm what did you say?"

"I said we should get married. We love each other, so we should be together."

Jonny was stuck. He looked at his mother for help but she sat there minding her own business. He saw that she was enjoying this, though, and a bit of anger hit him. His mind was racing, trying to figure out what to do, but nothing came readily to his mind except one lone statement. It stood there in front of his brain, flashing like a neon sign. Jonny wanted to ignore it but it wouldn't go away. It made him feel sick. He loved Nikki-D.

His stomach hurt.

"Mm ... mm. I can't marry you, Nikki-D," he lowered his head and looked at the ground, " you're not an Indian."

Nikki-D's face fell from the hurt. She couldn't think. This wasn't going the way she planned. Everything was falling apart. Her plan of marriage and love fell with her heart. What did he say? She wasn't Indian so he can't marry her? How could she know somebody so long and find out that she really didn't know him at all? The pain was too much and she moved away from Jonny.

"Jonny ... I, I have to go." Nikki-D ran down the steps of the porch. The tears came to her eyes. She moved fast down the road. She would have to go home and think. She needed a new plan. What did Jonny say? She wasn't Indian so ... A car went by. The bay was calm and a cool wind blew off the water. It was something Nikki-D needed: cold wind to wake her up. She had to go home. She needed a new plan.

"Jonny." Lois was mad. She heard those words come out of his mouth and she knew things were bad. Her heart went out to Nikki-D. The little girl who was so much a part of her son was now running down the bay road in tears, all because her son was too stupid to see beyond race. She was angry at Jonny. She thought she raised him better than that. A new car stopped and Nikki-D got in. It was Ginny, another mother with the burden of children. Ginny would have to be more tactful in talking to Nikki-D in the next few days. Just the thought of Nikki-D in pain again made Lois angrier. "Jonny, that was the stupidest thing that I ever heard you say. You broke that girl's heart. You love her, yet you say something like that! I want you to go. Go home. Go on."

Jonny's head was low. He couldn't bring himself to look at his mother. All he could do was leave. He had a knot in his throat. The pain was bad. There was nothing more for him to say.

31

FEELING

They were all lost. Nikki-D wasn't any different. She couldn't go back home; it was too painful still. Her degree in psychology would be given to her at the commencement next week. She wanted to get on with her life. The bitterness she felt was only a distant memory. She learned that broken hearts came and went, but memories were the final touch to life. In death, Nikki-D knew it was those memories that people hang onto for their journey. She was determined to use that attitude in her life. Through psychotherapy, she avoided the hard parts of her emotional state. It was a state of mind too remote for her to see at this time.

In the back of her mind, Nikki-D knew she was handling things wrong. She was smoking and taking drugs now. She had a type A personality and worked long hours during the week. She worked hard against the war. It was her real enemy. It took the only one she loved away from her.

She stopped...

A thought entered her mind; more like an image. It was of a young man. Not Beau. Her heart jumped at the image. The man came closer, almost as if he was walking to her. She was having more and more of these images. He was always too dark to make out. Just as in her dreams, he was there, always coming to her. She would run from him, but he kept coming. She tried to see who he was again. She strained to see. He was someone familiar. He kept coming to her. Then she saw him.

It was Jonny...

A large hairy hand came over her shoulder, found her breast and began to fondle her. The image disappeared.

Nikki-D was still in a drugged state, but she felt her nipple getting hard. She looked down to see her dark nipple extended between his fingers. She felt her whole breast flood with blood, pushing her nipple out. Nikki-D snuggled up to him with her naked behind, pushing her rear against his hardness.

Nikki-D opened her legs a little; letting him enter. She was wet. Sex was easy to her now. Not ugly, or morally wrong; it was just sex, meaningless except for the small pleasure that came once in a long while. She had been with many men over the past years. Annie called her all the time, trying to tell her to slow down. It was ironic that Annie wanted to help her.

The problem was, Nikki-D couldn't feel any emotions. She felt so lost and empty. Sex was about the only time she could feel anything. "Mmm..." She heard him behind her as he pushed himself deeper. Her breathing was becoming labored, too. An intense flush rushed through her head and she began to move up and down on him. She felt his legs against hers. Her left arm went back and she grabbed his tight buttocks and pulled him even closer. She was riding him now, her blood was flowing; Nikki-D began to feel something again. At least her body was alive. That was more than Beau could say.

Nikki-D stopped thinking. When she thought, she couldn't feel anything.

"Mom, Mom, I can't feel anything."

Lois watched Caj lying on the floor. He was drunk again. He's getting worse, she thought. Crying like a baby with big tears in his eyes; slobbering and weaving back and forth on his hands and knees. Lois wanted to help, but he was just like Franc now. All she could do was try to cope with Caj. Franc was easy since he began to get old, but Caj was new to this.

She sat in her favorite yellow chair that was worn with time. It faced the big window with a view of the bay. She loved sitting in it and watching the waves flow over the water onto the rocky beach. Lois looked around the room. Pictures hung on every wall. She looked at the handsome picture of Caj staring back at her. It was a big, "15x24" picture of him in his uniform. He looked so young then; too young to go off to war. His khaki green made his tan skin stand out. He still had the look of youth in his eyes, a swagger of immortality in the way he wore his bush hat on his head. Lois wished she had the boy back home again. In her heart she knew that he would never come home. He was lost like all the rest of the brave boys in that war. He was lost to her.

"I can't feel anything!" Caj tried to make her understand, but she couldn't see him. She couldn't see that his spirit ... his soul was broken. With blurred eyes, he watched his mother. Jonny said that she had an aura around her. He couldn't see it. Of course, he could barely see in front of him. His head swam and he felt like vomiting. Caj knew that he was broken.

"What, Caj? What can't you feel? I don't understand?" Lois couldn't stand to see her son this way. Her blood pressure was up and her cheeks showed it. Tension made her blood race. She wasn't feeling that well, and hadn't for some time now. She dismissed it, like all the other aches and pains that she thought came with age. She looked at her son again. She wanted to help him; take away whatever was in his head. Like all women, she could never see inside a man's head, not even when it was her son.

Caj saw both worlds. He saw the war, and the real world today. Neither one made any sense to him and he fought to keep his mind straight. Staying drunk was the only thing that really helped. He remembered getting so mad at his father for acting the same way. He wandered through the night just trying to figure things out. There was no confidence in him at all. The war took that away from him.

Still, he tried to get his mother to understand and would get angry with her frustration. It seemed so clear what was wrong with him; why couldn't she see it? How could she forgive him if she didn't even see what was wrong?

The world was spinning again. Thoughts came and went at hyperspeed. His mind ran from image to image. Caj was going to be sick; his stomach lurched for a second and settled down. Still on his knees, he threw out his arms to steady himself. His eyes were half-closed and the world spun around him.

"I feel sick."

It was too late for him now. He got up and staggered out of the house. The morning was cool and wet. The rain drizzled down from the sky. Caj looked up to the gray clouds and could see God peeing on him. God was only there to torment him now. He tried to get away but couldn't. God haunted Caj. He put on his shades; dark sunglasses he wore all the time. He wrapped his green field jacket around his ears. It was cold. He needed a drink. He thought of the bar at the Oriental Inn, down on State Street in Marysville. It opened early. There would be some excitement there; something to pick up his life, make him feel whole again. He staggered for a second and his head was dizzy; the clouds swayed in front of him. Caj lifted his head to the sky and let the rain hit his face. The rain mixed with his tears and trickled down his face. The Oriental Inn was waiting.

Lois limped to the window; her legs hurt. She watched Caj leave. He got into his little Volkswagen bug with its big wheels in the back and roared down the street. She realized that she couldn't help him if she didn't understand what was bothering him. That damn war! It destroyed them all. Lois was getting on in years now. She felt her weight as she moved to the kitchen. He hair was gray from a hard life. She had grandchildren that she could no longer take care of because it was too hard on her.

Dani had her little ones coming over today. Clair pulled up with her station wagon and got out. She carried little Deena in her arms. Clair was such a help to Lois nowadays: a real mother who would stay and help with the other ones. Dani would drop her kids off and head out to who knows where. She was still wild and ready to party. It was how they all escaped from the grinding poverty of the reservation.

Now Lois had to worry about Scout. She was a strong-headed girl who wasn't going to stay around for anyone. She fought with her father all the time. Lois couldn't talk to her without getting into a fight. She was just too strong at this point in their lives.

"Mom, Clair's here. I got to get going. You have any money?"
"No."
"But I need some for the dance tonight."
"I know, but we don't have any. I have to buy some food for the little ones."
"But what about me?"
"You're just going to have to find some money somewhere else. I can't give you any."

Lois was annoyed with Scout today. All of her kids seem to be going down the bad trail. The Res. was their life. They couldn't be accepted on the outside. The white people didn't even accept Lois, so how could she expect them to accept her half-breed children? She knew their lives were in their own hands and they were the ones who would have to make the world better for themselves. Or ... end up like Caj.

Katie, Alexcia and Shawn came barreling down from upstairs, running and laughing about something only they knew about. They were the young ones. They had to stay behind when the older ones were sent off to those boarding schools. Their laughter filled the house every day.

Why they laughed, Lois didn't know because they caught the full brunt of their father's drinking. The young girls always lifted her day.

Scout came out of the bathroom and stood there. She was dressed in jeans and a black, waist-length coat. She wore red lipstick; too much.

"You'd give Caj money if he asked."

"Not if I didn't have it."

"Yes, you would."

Katie stopped and looked at her older, bigger sister.

"Why don't you leave Mom alone? She said she didn't have any money."

"Shut up!" Scout moved toward Katie.

"You shut up!" Katie stood her ground as her two sisters watched.

"Stop it; both of you! Katie, take your sisters into the bedroom and play."

Lois didn't feel like arguing with Scout today. She was relentless in her stubbornness.

"All I need is five bucks. For tonight."

"All right. Let me see if I got any in my purse." Lois limped over and got her purse. Scout didn't notice her limp. She dug into it, pulling all of her things out one by one. It was a huge purse. Scout waited impatiently. Lois's whole arm was inside the purse; she grabbed hold of something and pulled it out. It was a cotton ball.

"Mom, I got to get going."

"I'm looking."

She dove back into the purse; again her whole arm disappeared, but this time she moved it from side to side. She lifted her purse almost all the way upside-down and then tilted it on one end. Nothing!

"There's nothing in here. I haven't any money."

"Shit."

"What did you say?"

"Nothing, what am I supposed to do now?"

"I don't know."

"I'm going to town."

"Be home early. I may need you."

"I said I'm going out to the dance."

"And I said to be home early."

Scout went into the kitchen. Lois watched her go. She was too tired to say anything else. Then she glanced out to the bay. The water was calm today. She thought about sitting in the yard and letting the wind blow against her. She liked the wind. It made her feel alive. Alive. It was so hard nowadays. The kids all had their problems. Now they had to contend with the grand-kids. Even though Lois loved all of her kids and grand-kids, it almost made her cry to think of solving problems that they all brought up. Still, they were a family. That made her feel good and the tiredness began to leave her. She knew she had a lot to do today. She always had a lot to do.

"Mom, I'm here." Clair came in with her little one. Deena was in her arms, waiting to be put down. Clair set Deena down on the old, worn couch and then went over and hugged Lois. She was the only one that did this. Lois always appreciated Clair. At least she stayed around and wanted to help.

For some odd reason, Lois felt tired again; and her hands were cold.

"You seem tired, Mom. Is everything all right?" Clair was concerned. She looked at the gray in her mother's hair. Her mother had put on so much weight. Lois wasn't a spring chicken and it was showing. But it was something else. Nothing to do with the body; her mother seemed tired all the time. Clair couldn't put her finger on it, but it concerned her.

"Was Caj here again?" Clair knew he was. She could still smell the alcohol in the room. He was in such a bad state, and getting worse. That fucking war. He was so distant and just ... just ... odd.

"Did you let him stay here again? You have to tell him to get his own place. He can't live like a vagabond for the rest of his life. He can't live like this, living in any room that one of the family puts up for him."

"He gave me some money." Lois knew that Clair was right, so she defended herself with that statement.

"Caj always gives you money. Where does he get it from?" Clair couldn't understand her brother. He always had money. If he didn't spend his money on booze and drugs, he would give it away. Like that. Clair resented him for it. The rest of them had to work hard just to make enough money for food and rent. To him it meant nothing. She would never understand him.

"What do you mean he gave you some money? What about me?" Scout yelled from the kitchen. She heard her mother and wanted to get in on some of this.

"Money for food." Lois wasn't going to argue over it and used her 'this is final' tone.

"Yea, right, its always money for food."

Scout walked by her mother as if she was going to run into her. Then she went to the front door and walked out, slamming the door behind her.

Clair went over and sat down.

"It looks like Scout is the same. Why don't you stop taking that crap from her?"

"She's just young and impatient."

"She's getting into trouble."

"That's what they said about you and Dani. Now nobody talks about you like that. You've become a young mother. Scout will do the same."

Clair looked at her mother with a look that asked if she could really believe that but she didn't pursue it any further.

"There's some coffee in the kitchen. I just got some from the thrift store with the rest of my commodities. I made some bread this morning and we have peanut butter and butter to put on it. Go and make yourself something. You're too skinny."

Clair laid Deena down on the floor and moved off to the kitchen. Lois moved over and watched her granddaughter crawl around. Deena crawled to her and spread her arms for Lois to pick her up. Lois bent over and a sharp pain ran through her. She sat there for a second just watching her granddaughter. The pain was growing. This alarmed her. She decided to just watch Deena crawl around. Her heart was pounding. Then the pain stopped and everything was all right. Lois shook her head. Age was going to be hard.

"Mom, do you want a cup?"

"Yes honey, with some brown sugar."

Little Deena wore a flowered dress that barely went around her bottom. She had chunky little brown legs and arms that bent when she tried to crawl. Lois smiled at her granddaughter and reached down and grabbed her two arms and slapped them together.

"How is Grandma's little lady?"

Deena smiled up at her. Clair came in with the coffee and set it down on the small coffee table next to her chair. Lois stopped playing with Deena and picked up the hot coffee and sipped it.

"Whew. Hot!"

"I know."

Clair sipped her own coffee. She was looking at her mother. The gray was coming out in her hair and she was putting on more weight. Even so, she seemed happier than Clair had ever seen her. This made Clair happy. She noticed her mom was wearing brighter colors and makeup. The change was dramatic but couldn't keep away the age. Her mother and her sister went out and did what they wanted now. Alice drove the Oldsmobile because Lois had never learned how. They were like two young women in their prime, checking out the world.

Both sisters had their big families. Now it was their time. Clair was the only one that understood this. She was there for her mother.

"When are Alice and Grandma coming over?"

"They should be here by now."

Soon as Lois said this, the old blue and white Oldsmobile drove up and parked in front of the house.

"Is there enough coffee made for them?"

"Mom! I made a huge pot of coffee. I can see that you plan to sit and talk for a while before you go. Where are you going anyway?"

"We thought we would go to the show today."

The two women got out of their car, both wearing brightly patterned dresses, like Lois. All three were having a second childhood. They where at an age where they could relate better than any other time in their lives. Lois could let go and not worry about every little thing. She was learning to let her grown kids take care of their own lives. Except for a couple of them, such as Caj, they were doing all right. Dani seemed to want to stay young a little longer than most, but she was the oldest and had the most in the beginning.

Lois always remembered her as the strong one of the family when things went wrong. The other kids would all fall in line with Dani and she never backed off her responsibility. It was just compensation for her now; at least Lois thought so. She knew Clair would always have a problem with it because she fought so much to be wanted like Dani. They were so different, her two oldest; all of her kids had such strong personalities in one area or another. Lois felt good about it.

"I'll go and get Grandma and Alice coffee. They're almost here."

"OK."

A strange tingling came over Lois. Her head began to swim. She reached for her coffee and picked it up to take a sip. Her arms started to shake. Suddenly her whole world began to move in slow motion. Blackness flooded the room. Then light. Blackness again. Fear struck her heart. She couldn't breathe. Lois tried to breathe; tried to get more air.

Her little granddaughter was watching her with a small child's curiosity. Lois tried to get up. She stumbled. "Clair! Clair, I need you!"

She fell where she stood. Her large body hit the floor with a final thud. Her eyes watched but could only see the final darkness as it surrounded her. The darkness brought a calmness with it. All of her worries left her. She remembered this feeling. It happened a long time before. When she was sick.

"Mommm ... ! Mom!" Clair came running out of the kitchen.

The remembering helped her.

The door opened and Alice came rushing in. Her mother was right behind. Clair was calling her name.

"Mom, its all right. Mom." Tears streaked down Clair's cheeks as she tried to help her mother.

"Lois ... can you hear me? Its Alice. Clair, go down and call the ambulance. Tell them to come as soon as possible."

"But Mom needs me. I can't leave her."

The little ones came out from the bedroom. Lois heard their screams as they all cried out her name. It was like before: the calm darkness and the last things she saw were her little girls and her family. It was OK.

She no longer fought to hold on.

"You girls go and get me some blankets." It was Lois's mother who told the girls what to do. She was holding on to Deena as Clair ran to get help. Funny – Lois never saw her mother hold a baby. It was always her who took care of the kids. They were her children. Her little girls brought blankets over and they covered her. So beautiful. Her children.

The warm darkness was like a blanket that kept out the cold thoughts.

Franc came in the back door. He ran over to her. "Get back!" She looked into his Indian-black eyes, the same warm eyes as when they first met so long ago. He was her first and only love. Life robbed him of so much. That's why God sent him into her life. She felt the love that was always there.

She could no longer feel her body. It didn't matter. She didn't need the pain. It was time to move on. Lois just lay there watching all the commotion going on around her. It didn't matter anymore. She let go.

The frantic sounds of her family who didn't want her to go seemed to be in the distance. The warm darkness invaded her soul. The heart that was her soul no longer pumped vital blood to her body. A great release came over her. Maybe it was the rush that Caj talked about? She only knew that it didn't hurt. It was a feeling that transcended the body and soul. A higher power. Her power.

Everyone was crying now. Katie sat with Alexcia and Shawn. The three girls just watched all the commotion go on around them. They knew it was bad. Clair was trying to get to her mother. The ambulance was on its way. She felt faint and sat down right on the floor where she stood. For everyone a feeling of helplessness engulfed them. Their mother, sister, daughter and wife lay dead on the floor and there was nothing they could do to change it.

Weee! Weee! Weee! Sad, sorrowful faces turned to the sound of the siren of the ambulance. Knowing it was already too late.

MOTHER

The clouds were dark and ominous, hanging over the potlatch grounds just as they hung over Jonny's dead heart. The pain was so hard and so deep that Jonny thought he would never be able to find the end to it. He was worn out from lack of sleep and from crying so much. His heart ached and his mind had all but shut down. He was glad it was all coming to an end.

The whole day seemed banal and dull; that's how much exhaustion everyone had. Jonny watched Dani; dressed in her black funeral dress, greet people at the front door. Jonny and Dani worked hard for the last few days trying to get everything done. Dani was in charge. It was her role as the oldest of the children. Jonny got his role by default. Gray, the oldest boy, was in Walla Walla Penitentiary and had to get a special pass to come to his mother's funeral. Caj was gone.

Jomy and the others looked all over for Caj. He disappeared the day of his mother's death. That was like Caj, though; he always disappeared for days on end, then he would show up at your doorstep. Franc was devastated by her death and it was unfair for him to be the one. Jonny was the only one left.

Dani saw Jonny looking at her and winked at him. She began to cry and he saw Loretta James come up to her and give her a hanky. She blew her nose and went on greeting people. She seemed so strong about all of this. The rest of the kids looked up to her to make the right decisions for them. There was no one else. It was their worst nightmare to bury their mother in the building that she worked so hard to get built. The building had brown cedar siding, and large evergreens stood around it. They built a parking lot that went down to the smokehouse and around the building. Cars were parking, filling up all the new spaces. They would have to park across the road because there were so many people. Jonny looked up the road to the totem poles that divided the road to Mission beach and Totem beach. Cars were still coming. He knew one thing: his mother was well-respected.

"Ooooohhh! Oooooohh!" The wailing went on and on. Ginny sat in the big gymnasium listening to the old and young as they cried over their loved one. Ginny's heart was in tears, too. She didn't have time to cry. Her friend needed her and she was strong for her friend. The past couple of days she had walked and talked with Dani and Jonny, making sure everything was being taken care of. She had to do this to keep herself from falling apart. Lois, her friend, was too young to die. Why did the good ones die so young? It wasn't fair.

Ginny sat behind the Esque family, who were in the front row. She just wanted to sit and rest, to think about her dear friend. Nick sat beside her, holding her hand. He was such a comfort. Ginny wore a black dress with a veiled hat. She reached under the netting with her hand to wipe away tears when they came up. There was so much movement in a funeral. The tribal people came in droves. She didn't know all of the families of the tribe, but could see that there was a distinct difference in each family. Some were tall, some short, or round. Some had long, black, Indian hair; some had curly hair. Ginny began to match some of them with family members she knew.

Most of the Esques family was sitting in front, with their off-shoot families in the back. The Madisons looked something like them: tall with light-tan skin. Everyone always talked about that strange group. All Ginny knew was they were always in some corner, always laughing. She might agree that they were a little strange. The Jones were dark and short, with beautiful Indian-black hair. The Henrys were another short, dark people, with big shoulders. Then there was the non-Indian family: the Bades; tall Swedish stock. Ginny looked at Lois's mother, whom she had met on numerous occasions. Stoic and composed most of the time, Ginny could see that she was being tested here. Ginny watched Lois's stepfather in tears. He cried so hard that it brought tears to her eyes. A heavy-hearted sigh came from her lips. She looked over at Alice. She was so pale. Alice was Lois's little sister. Lois and Alice were inseparable when they were young Knowles and that carried on into their adult lives. Alice was surrounded by her kids since her divorce and she was alone now. Ginny saw Ralph and Sherry and Gloria around their mother. Alice took her sister's death as well as you could expect. She would go up and give her comfort later. Alice had such a delicious sense of humor. There was no humor today.

The black emptiness went threw her like a knife, so deep and prevalent that only God could have thought of something like it. Ginny was afraid she was losing her composure. The darkness never left her and she felt like she was falling into the abyss. It was a black hole of timeless eternity that she and the Esque family had fallen into. It was the black hole of the heart.

Today was a colorless day. She was in a fog. Nick squeezed her hand. It was about to begin. She glanced around one more time - so many people, but not the one she wanted; not the one she needed. Nikki-D was not here.

"Cling! Cling! Cling!" The bells rang though the gymnasium, telling the people it was time to listen. "Cling! Cling! Cling!"

Jonny watched his sisters sitting in front. They were all beginning to break down. Their crying grew louder and louder as the old people sang over his mother's body. Scout was crying the hardest at the moment. Jonny knew he would have to keep an eye on her when they all brought the roses to be placed in the casket with his mother. God! it was getting hard.

"Oooohhhh! Oooohh! Mom! Mom!"

Everyone was in tears as the service went on. Leota Pablo was the speaker for the churches. She came to their house when she heard about their mother's death. She brought food and talked with Dani to let her know what to do. Dani was dazed and confused at first. She sat listening without saying a word. Leota came back the next day and talked to her again. Eventually she got through to Dani, and the service was coming off well.

"I would like to thank those who came here to comfort the family. Today we bury a mother, a wife, a sister, and a friend. The family need all the support they can get from you, their people. We all must come together to help the family. This is our way."

"Oooohh!" More and more people joined in their sorrow. Jonny felt himself crying and moaning along with them. The pain in his heart seemed to grow until he felt he was going to burst. He didn't want to see his sisters and father in such anguish. He wanted it to end. He wanted it to be three days ago, when his mother was alive. He wanted his mother back.

"Oh God! Oh God!" It was Claire's voice, rising above the rest. Jonny went over to her side. Her husband was trying to hold her, but she was beginning to go out. Jonny waited to see if she was going into a seizure. Her eyes were closing and opening while she moaned and leaned against her husband. Jonny saw that she was squeezing his hand hard and he was fighting not to wince at the pressure. "Oh God! Oh God! No, I don't want this to happen!"

Jonny put his hand on her shoulder and she looked up. Her eyes were glazed and red. She was on her pills, but Jonny could tell that she was with him. Their spirits merged and they both found strength with each other. He felt her body slow down. She stopped being so loud and she laid her head on her husband's shoulder and just moaned. Jonny knew that it was only the first sign of sorrow from his sister; there would be more.

Franc sat on the big, soft sofa with the young ones. He was so thin and drawn. His age was catching up with him from the drinking. Jonny saw that he had that blank stare in his eyes; that faraway look that he and Caj shared. His suit looked too big for his body, as though his body had shrunk. Katie was crying and holding on to Alexcia and little Shawn. Jonny could see how hard it was for them. They all had boyfriends, but not husbands. Katie's boyfriend Buck was standing at the edge of the sofa, trying to be supportive.

Jonny looked behind them and saw Joe and Jim watching his other sisters, so they all had someone to rely on. Jonny wasn't sure, but he went over to see how they were doing. The service was coming to a close and it was almost time to put the roses in the casket with their mother. He could see that they all held on to their red rose tightly as he had held his. It was a simple symbol of love.

Jonny saw Ginny sitting in the third row of chairs. He couldn't see her face very well through the veil, but he knew that she was crying, too. The sad emotions in the gym ran so high. He looked down at his rose, then back at Ginny. Only those people that were special to his mother had roses, but they were the immediate family. He left the front row and walked over to Ginny.

"Mmmm ... mm! Are you OK?" She cried so hard she couldn't answer him. Seeing this happen to Ginny brought up the tears in Jonny. He watched her lower her head as if she was in shame. All he could do to comfort her was offer her his rose.

"Mmm ... mm! Mmm ... mm! We're supposed to put these beside my mother before they close the casket." For a second he didn't think she would take it. Then her hand came up and she lightly plucked the rose from his hand; their eyes met, both looking into that black darkness of emptiness. Floating.

Jonny broke the connection when he caught a glimpse of someone at the door. He gave Ginny a final squeeze and moved on.

It was Caj. He was standing under the double door and he had Mariann with him. Jonny moved quickly.

Ginny and Nick watched Jonny go over to Caj. They watched as the boys hugged and then Jonny hugged the girl with Caj. Ginny was so happy that Caj finally came, because she knew his family was worried about him. They did not know what he might do at a time like this. He was always so depressed and drunk. The sight of him made Ginny look around again. She wished Nikki-D was here. They had left messages for her, but ever since that time with Jonny, she hadn't wanted to talk to anyone back here. A flash of anger came to Ginny. What did she expect? Jonny was caught off-guard, and didn't know what to say. Ginny watched the boys again.

"Caj is home." Nick nodded and squeezed her hand.

"Mmm ... mm! Caj, you're here! I thought you might not make it."

"I'm here. It looks like its starting. Where am I in the service?"

"You're the lead in the canoe ceremony."

"Who's speaking it?"

"Raymond Moses."

"Is the Inter-faith almost over?"

"Yea. Its getting emotional. Katie is taking care of the little ones. Scout is having a hard time. I don't know if Clair is gonna go out or not. Dani is taking care of everyone when she can. All of the husbands and boyfriends are at their side, so there hasn't been much to do."

"Is there a seat for Mariann and her son?"

"Right next to Ginny. All the family seats are taken."

Caj looked at Mariann with a quizzical look, wondering if that would be all right with her. She nodded her head and took her son's hand.

Caj leaned over and gave her a hug. It surprised Jonny that Caj showed affection in public. Mariann kissed Caj on the cheek. "It will be all right. Take us over there, Jonny."

Jonny looked at his brother and then took Mariann to her seat. Caj walked over to his family. Katie and Shawn were the first to see Caj. Then Scout saw him and jumped up and ran over to him. They both hugged for a second. Dani was crying. The family needed Caj there with them. He came up and hugged the little ones, then Franc, and

Clair.

Finally, he got to Dani. "How you doing sis? You're our mother now." He gave her a big hug.

They lined up on both sides of the casket. The pallbearers, Marlin Fryberg, Richard Jones, Marvin Jones, Dale Jones, BJ, and Buck, stood in front of the casket to help if needed. It was time to lay the roses inside with their mother and then bring her to her final resting place. Jonny stood waiting for the next move. Caj was crying with the others. Tears ran down Jonny's cheeks, too.

Raymond Moses came up in front and held out his hands for everyone to see. "I come to you with open hands and an open heart. I come not as a enemy but as a friend. The family wishes to thank all that came here to give their last respects to their mother. They thank all those families who came to them in their time of need. They thank those who volunteered their time to help, and those who worked in the kitchen: Uppy, Mary Stewart, Laverne and the others. They thank the tribe for its support. Now they will bring their dear, departed mother to her final resting place."

Raymond paused for a second and cleared his throat, thinking about what he wanted to say next.

"We will bring her out in a healing ceremony. The canoe ceremony comes from a dream a long time ago. The old ones used it to bring harmony back to our people. Today, the Esque family wants to use this ceremony to begin their healing in this building."

Raymond paused again.

"This building is new and will become part of our people. It is our future. We build our future from our past. Today we were going to dedicate this building to our children and their children. We start our future with this sad occasion and we must make amends. This ceremony will heal old wounds and bring us together again."

Everyone nodded their agreement, wondering what the ceremony would be like. People were shuffling around, waiting for Raymond to stop. Most of them were getting up and some were heading to the exits to get to their cars first and beat the rush to the grave-site.

"I come as a friend. The family thanks you." With that, Raymond raised his hands higher and turned to the casket.

It was time. Raymond went to the front of the casket. He would lead it out of the building. He and two drummers behind him were the lead singers. The pallbearers were on each side of the casket and more drummers followed the casket as they went out.

First the people would have their last chance to see Lois Esque. She lay in a state of death. The moaning began to get louder. Wailing came from women in the back. Emotions were rising again. It would be for the last time.

Everyone stood for the final prayer. Then it was the family's turn to view her and present the roses. There was more wailing; some people were weeping, and some screeched their sorrow.

"Nooooo! Nooooo!" The sobbing was loud and long. People filed by the cold body of Lois, looking down at her for the last time. Women, young and old, cried out their sorrow as their husbands and boyfriends walked by with heads down. The line of tribal members and non-members was long, reaching around the new gym. Jonny watched as his cousins the Madisons, walked by in anguish and remorse. They, too, lost a mother years ago. Jonny remembered it well.

They were an emotional family. Carol led her younger siblings by: Sandy, Steve and Michele, Guy and Richard, Karen and Margurite, and, finally, Kim and Ellene. They cried so hard that the whole place paused and watched them go by. It made Jonny's emotions come welling up. With tears in his eyes he watched as his other cousins from the Jones clan went by. They, too, wept hard at the sight of his mother. They had lost their beloved sister Juanita. The pain wasn't new to them, because it wasn't long ago when Juanita died.

Marvin and Richard Jones stood in front of his mother, almost like they were protecting her from any harm. Jonny remembered them doing the same thing for their brother Stomper when he died in the fire. And there was Marlin, whose daughter died in a tragic auto accident. And Mary Stewert's parents, Dolly and Teddy, who died on the water. The list went on and on: Gene Zackuse who's mother Pauline Comenote died recently, Duane Henry, whose brother Hanford was Caj's best friend and brother. It was an endless list that went back eons. This was the true reality of Indian life on the Res. They all were crying together. They all had their own reasons to cry.

The last of the people went by and now it was time for the Esques to get up and say their last good-bye. Most of the people were outside waiting. The white hearse was driven right up to the doors. They stood on both sides of the hearse, some smoking, most talking in hushed tones.

They were all impressed with the funeral. It was one of the most moving funerals that they could remember. That was what they talked about. A lot of respect was given today.

The line was gone and the only ones left were the family. Everyone was crying now. Except Caj. Jonny wondered how he could keep so much grief in when his mother was lying dead. Jonny cried just as hard as the others, but Caj just watched and tried to help when someone needed it. Jonny looked around with his tearful eyes and could see people wanting to watch the canoe ceremony. Most of them had never seen anything like this. Parts of the old way were coming back, slowly but surely.

Dani was the first to stand. The crying from the family rose as they all watched the oldest come over to Franc. He sat with his head down, in tears. Jonny noticed his father's age. Was he always that old or was it only when his wife died that age found him? Now Dani stood over him and put out her hand for her father to take. Franc's head came up with a lost look on his face. His hard, deep-seated black eyes, reddened by tears, searched his daughter's face for an answer. There was none.

"Its time, Dad." Dani could barely get the words out. She never wanted this responsibility but it was always thrust on her. The other kids resented her for this, but none of them could do what she could at this time. They all played the roles they were born to in the family. Dani was the oldest and she was expected to lead them past their mother. Dani cried. Her mother was dead. It hurt so bad that Dani didn't know how her heart could still beat. "Please, Dad."

Franc was immobilized. He barely heard Dani's words; like his mind shut down. Confusion crept into his heart and he didn't know what was going on. He could feel the pains of death seeking out his heart again; but he was on to them and shut them down to avoid the hurt. It was all he could do. He reached for the hand in front of him.

He didn't know if he could stand without assistance. The small hand was amazingly strong as his big hand wrapped around it. "Dani."

It was the longest walk that Dani ever made. She tried to be strong for her father but the tears wouldn't stop flowing. She began to cry harder the closer she got to the casket. The pallbearers stood along the back of the casket. They were all ready to begin the final funeral song that would come as they brought out the casket. Dani and Franc reached the casket and looked down.

Her mother's face was chalky-white. So pale. Franc and Dani pulled back for a second then came back to look at her for the last time.

"Dad, put the rose in the casket next to Mom." Dani took her father's shaking hand and brought it up to the casket. She brought her rose up, too, and then, with a last effort, they put the roses next to Lois. Dani could hear the others behind her as a loud wail came from her family. She thought she was going to be sick for a second but then composed herself. They need me to be strong. She was. She leaned over and kissed her mother for the last time.

When Dani and Frank were done, it was Clair's turn. She was completely out of it. Her senses had left her long ago in the funeral and now she could barely walk. Her voice was the loudest and what seemed like the most anguished. People watched as she slumped down, walking to her mother. Caj went over to her and he and her husband helped her walk the final way. When she lay her rose down, her head was hung down to her chest and she cried in desolation. She couldn't kiss her mother and Caj brought her arm back and led her over to the others. The pain was becoming too much for everyone.

"Clair, you all right?" Caj didn't want to get this involved with the funeral. Shit, it was the hardest thing for him to do. He looked over at Mariann. She was standing with a look of concern on her face. He nodded with his head for her to come over. He didn't think he could handle this too much longer. He flashed back for a second and thought about Vietnam. His anxiety was growing each minute and he felt like running from this room of death.

"Mariann, help hold on to Clair. The others need me," he whispered. She took Clair's arm and Caj went off to make sure the rest of his family was all right.

Katie and Alexcia held on to each other and put their roses in the casket. Shawn stood with them. It was always those three who supported each other. Katie worried about her younger sisters. They relied on her strength when all of the older kids were gone and it was no different now. She was the one they looked to, just like they looked to Dani in hard times. Katie and Alexcia went through the line. She saw her mother.

"Aaaaahh!" Shawn let out a cry behind them. Katie turned and put her arm around Shawn; Alexcia did the same thing. They were caught in their pain and had nowhere to hide. It hit all three of them at the same time. There was no escape.

"Katie, you have to go through this." It was Jonny, urging them on. He was there waiting behind them. Her bloodshot eyes tried to focus on him but everything was blurry. Katie pulled Shawn along and Alexcia went with them. They put their rose inside the casket and went over to the others.

Jonny stood with Ginny. She watched the young girls as they summoned the strength to see their mother in the casket, lying in a state of death. It was so sad to see them go through this; she wanted to help them but had nothing to offer. She was out of place here with the family. Jonny shouldn't have given her the rose. Despair hit her again and again.

"Mmm ... mm! Mrs. Thomas, its time." He moved one step to his mother. Truth was, he was scared. He never wanted this moment to come and now it was here. His heart was breaking from all the sorrow in the room. His mind reeled from the thought of his mother being dead. She was. That was the point of no return. She was dead.

"Are you all right, Jonny? Do you want me to do this for you?"

"Mmm ... mm! Mmm ... mm! No, I'm all right."

They both stepped up to the casket. God! she's so pale. Ginny couldn't believe her friend looked like that. Lois had put on weight over the years and Ginny always tried to get her to lose it, but Lois just laughed and dismissed her concern. Now Ginny wished she had pushed harder. Lois looked so peaceful lying there in state; it was something Ginny never expected. Life was so hard for her and these people; maybe that's why they have such beautiful funerals – because they can see the peaceful existence of death. Ginny didn't know. She put the rose in the casket alongside the others and waited for Jonny as he kissed his mother's forehead. He looks just like her, she realized.

Scout was screaming inside. She was unable to stand and bring her rose to her mother. Caj was called over. Scout wasn't doing well. Caj hated all the emotions coming from her. The sadness was overwhelming to him. He thought he was going to be sick. His head was pounding from the alcohol and lack of sleep. He couldn't stand any more death, but it always came to him. He almost broke down and cried with his sister, but then Scout tore from his arms and went to the casket, sobbing her heart out.

Jonny left Ginny when he saw Scout falling apart. Caj looked like he was about to crack from the strain, too, so Jonny went over to see if he could help. Caj had already gone over and put his arm around Scout and she slumped against him, no longer able to look at her mother's body. Jonny stopped and waited.

"Scout. You have to put the rose in the casket."

"I can't ... I can't." She sobbed harder.

"Here, let me help you. You have to do it. Mom would want you to."

Caj lifted her arm while his sister's face remained buried in his shoulder and then she dropped the last rose in the casket. It was over. Caj waited for the tears, but none came. He looked at his mother for the last time. She looked so cold and ... and dead. The aura and warmth were gone. She was just another body now. That thought is what kept Caj sane. It was his sanity that he had to hold on to. It was what he had to control.

"Come on, Scout. They want to begin the ceremony to the grave."

With that, they walked over and joined the rest of the family.

Raymond was standing in front with a red bandanna tied on the side of his head. He began to drum, the mournful sound came from his mouth, and he beat the drum again. The other drummers and singers behind him began their soulful song, beating their drums along with Raymond. The pallbearers lifted the closed casket like they raised a canoe. They moved back and forth with the sound of the drums. More drummers followed the casket as it moved off. Then the family was behind them. Then the others.

The casket was brought around the gym. People came back in as the singing began. They sang the deep, plaintive Indian songs from long ago. The men wore their traditional shirts with their streamers running from the chest down to the bottom of the shirt. All wore red bandannas, tied on the side. The drummers were like the paddles on the canoe, while the casket was the canoe itself and the people behind it were the waves of the sea. They were sending her on her journey to the other side, where the ancestors lived. Most of the people watched this go on and those on the outside streamed back in to see, too.

They moved to the slow drum-beat, the line growing as they went by people who joined them. Raymond led them around one more time and then he led them out of the gym. He led them out of the emotional darkness and into the light of the day.

In the December drizzle of the Northwest, they all stood around the grave. It was cold, with the north wind coming off the bay. Some took pictures and some just stood around until the body was laid to rest. Then they all began to leave, either alone, or couples, and groups, until only the family stood around the grave.

Jonny looked up and saw some people pointing to the sky. He looked up and so did the rest of the family. A large spot floated in the sky, circling around and around. It was the Eagle.

All headed back to the new gym for the dinner; they would wait there until the family came in; then they would eat. It was the final function of the funeral, after which the people would go home. The family would get together later for the burning. They would offer food to the spirits of their ancestors and then to Lois's spirit, burning her things so she won't come back for anyone. The children will be watched closely until enough time went by to see that her spirit was indeed gone. It was the only way to be safe.

The long cafeteria tables were set end to end across the gym. Young girls put tablecloths on them and set the tables for the people when they came back from the grave-site. It was one o'clock and it was time to eat. The tables were full as families sat with each other to wait for the final speeches. Coffee mugs were placed up and down the tables and were filled by the young ones working in the kitchen. A prayer was given and the people sat down and began to eat. Most of them talked in hushed tones while they ate. Then the room became silent as the first speaker got up and went to the mike standing in front of the gymnasium. It was Raymond Moses.

"Hello. Hello." He tapped on the mike. It worked well. "My People. I'm so happy to see you come here to pay your last respects to this family. They welcome you. They open their hands to show you they have no enemies. We, the Snohomish people of Tulalip, must remember who we are. We must remember who has left us. She was a good woman."

Raymond finished his talk and then went to the family, shaking each of their hands. People waited. Dani had already gotten up and thanked everyone for their help. Franc said some words, too, but everyone was really waiting for Caj to stand up and say something. He was the one they expected to speak for the family. He didn't move.

It was getting uncomfortable and Jonny heard people shuffling in their chairs. Caj didn't move. Why didn't he get up and say something? Jonny felt the pressure of peoples' eyes on him. They waited for one of the men of the family to speak.

The room became hushed as Jonny stood and walked across the gym. People were pointing and talking to each other. They expected Caj to talk, not Jonny. His face was hot and he kept his head down as he walked to the podium. He had to say something - that was all he knew.

He looked out across the gym. Faces stared back at him. People waited. He looked at his family; they were all supportive of him, but waited for him to stutter and struggle to get his words out. He looked across the room to where his mother's casket lay just minutes ago. There was an empty space there. Like in his heart.

"Mmm ... mm. Mmm ... mm." The words wouldn't come out. He heard some chairs shuffle. It seemed like the sounds were loud and impatient.

"Mmm ... mm. Many people." He raised his head. "Mmm..mm. I mmust apologize to you beforehand because I can't pronounce words right. I hope you will understand and bear with me."

Jonny looked around and took another big breath. His mind began to clear and words and images came to him. He began to speak.

"Mm ... mm. My people Mm ... We would like to offer our thanks to those who came to us and gave us their help. Mmm..mm. My family is grateful to those who worked in the kitchen. Those who woke early these past days to labor in the hot kitchen to cook all this good food. We thank the hunters and fisherman who have gone out and brought back the meat and fish for the family to serve to you. Mm ... We thank the young people who have taken time out of their day to place the food on the tables you now sit at. It is all we can ask for."

Jonny noticed the kitchen help come out and listen to him. This didn't embarrass him and he felt stronger. He looked across the gym again. People were beginning to take notice of him. His presence grew. Jonny could feel the dark area where his mother's casket used to be and the hole in his heart grew. She was no longer there and she meant so much. Jonny searched for the words. He searched for the vision.

"MM ... mm. Mmm ... mm. Mmm ... mm."

People leaned forward, waiting and wishing they could say the words that Jonny struggled with. He felt his face heat up.

"Mmm ... mm. To those people who don't know or never met my mother, I offer my condolences. It is you who have been deprived and now you will never know what it is to know a truly wonderful person."

Most of those people Jonny referred to stole a look at each other, wondering what he meant by his statement.

Marvin and Richard Jones sat with their families. Jonny saw them, and others like them, that his mother would take in and care for. The glimmers of his mother stood before him. He could feel himself get stronger.

"Mm ... mm. To those like Marvin and Richard Jones. who my mother brought in and accepted and loved as her own, I offer my family's acceptance, also. We have grown to love you as our brothers and sisters, just as my mother did. You will always be a part of my family."

Their faces fell. Jonny saw the pain and their sorrow. Marvin's head hung low in grief. Jonny was looking beyond Marvin. A light started to glow where his mother's casket had stood. It had a warmth to it and Jonny knew it was the aura of his mother's spirit. It was familiar to him, because he always saw it around his mother. Tears and emotions overcame him as he watched what no others could see: his mother.

The room grew silent except for some crying. It was random, as people were showing their grief. Tears began to flow again. Jonny wasn't sure he could go on, but knew he had to. He touched the peoples' hearts and they wanted him to go on. They waited for him to compose himself and when he was ready they became silent.

One woman sat straight up, watching him. Her prim and proper bearing propelled Jonny to go on.

"Mm ... mm. To my mmother's friend, Ginny Thomas who is sitting at my family's table, I offer our friendship and understanding. She is the one person my mother confided in with total trust. They became inseparable in their desire to see that the Res. and its people receive what is just and right. It is partly because of them that this new building was finally built. Mm ... mm. Over the years, my family got to see a true bonding of women that can only be described as true sisterly love. A love that goes beyond friendship. I know you will miss her."

Ginny was listening to this young man as he spoke of love and sisterhood. She knew he was right. It was what she always sought in life; to be a part of that. Ginny couldn't cry here, but later, in the privacy of her home, alone with Nick, she would finally let go. She knew that she'd cry the tears of a lifetime. Ginny was not like Nikki-D, who cried over the smallest things, but held her life close to her. Lois, her sister, had died and now Ginny must face her own life. She looked back at the remarkable young man at the podium. He saw things in simple terms and then spoke them ... just like his mother.

Jonny looked beyond Ginny. The aura grew larger. It seemed the more he talked, the more he was in touch with his mother. He wanted to say so much. He needed to go on. Jonny waited for the next words to come to him. His eyes surveyed the gym, stopping at the door. A woman was standing there and Jonny thought it was Nikki-D for a second. His heart jumped to his throat. Then he looked again. It was a young Indian girl – not Nikki-D. It was just a hopeful wish.

Jonny was ready to speak again.

"Mmm ... mm. Mmm ... mm. To Grandpa and Grandma and Aunt Alice I offer my envy because you have spent the longest time with my mother. You have planted a seed that you saw grow into a beautiful and magnificent flower. A flower that took nourishment from those around her and, with elegance and grace, made the world beautiful. And you were there to see it. For this, we envy you."

Jonny stopped talking for a second because they were crying so hard. He watched as his grandfather got up and left the hall. He was broken by the death of his daughter.

Dani and Clair went over to their grandmother and Alice. Jonny waited for a signal from them. His face was so hot because he didn't know if he had gone too far in his speech. Dani looked up and gave him a nod to go on. He tried to arrange his thoughts again.

"Mmm ... mm. ... mm. I'm sorry if my words hurt."

Dani left her grandmother and came up to Jonny. She whispered in his ear.

"Go on, Jonny. We want you to speak. Everyone will be fine." She gave his elbow a squeeze and went back to her table.

Jonny knew the hard part had come. His family was waiting for him to speak to them. It was time.

"Mmm ... mm. Mmm. To my sister Dani, I offer our family's strength and support because you have become the mother now." Jonny saw heads nod up and down. Dani's wasn't one of them. "Mmm. You are the first-born and I know that you haven't had time to grieve because of all the responsibility of the funeral. You are Mom's favorite, so you have lost the most by her death. You have been given our mother's blanket to keep. Some will resent you for this, but it is right. I hope it gives you some comfort."

Dani held her mother's blanket to her face. People came up to her and gave her words of comfort and then squeezed her shoulder and moved on. She was alone and she understood what Jonny said. He was one of the strengths that helped her get through the funeral. She would need them all down the road. They already had learned to rely on her; she was the new mother.

"Mmm ... mm. To my sister, Clair, who always sought our mother's love. Who worked hard to be good and do things right. Clair, who was always there at the hard times and the bad times; always a comfort during those times. Clair was there when my mother died. She is here now. To Clair, who wanted her mother's love so bad, I offer the love of your family. You have always been there for us and we are there for you now."

Jonny's heart hurt bad. He wished he had someone, too. Nikki-D was always there for him at these times but she wasn't here now. That hurt more than anything. It compounded the pain in his heart. He realized that he loved her with all his heart. He looked at the entrance again. There was no one there. He was alone.

Ginny ached for Jonny. She caught his eyes searching and knew he was looking for her daughter. She saw his pain when he couldn't find her. Ginny was angry herself and hurt that Nikki-D didn't come. She thought she taught her better than that. Ginny sighed.

"Mmm ... mm. Mmm ... mm. To my brother, Gray, I offer hope. We all have lost you to the system. And the system will take you back after this funeral. I have no idea what lies ahead for you, but we all offer our love and prayers for you."

There was nothing else to say. Gray was a product of the prison system and had to go through that process. He came to the funeral in chains and would leave in chains. He was close to his parole and the family had petitioned the court to allow him to go free. It looked good for him.

"Mmmmm. To my sister, Morgan-Mckenzi, the silent one, who lived in the shadow of others in the family, whose life is hidden to us because of the years living in Oklahoma, I offer our recognition. Mom seemed to understand you and supported you when you left and decided to stay away. She understood that you were smart and willing to sacrifice to reach your goals. You are independent and strong. Mom wanted you to be that way. She was very proud of you. You are a woman with vision and will be invaluable to this tribe. We are very proud of you."

Jonny looked at his sister, but she was crying with her head held up. She nodded her head to him.

The hole in Jonny's heart was growing again. His pain was overwhelming now. He couldn't think anymore and didn't know if he could go on. He tried to see words, or images, or anything, but his mind was shut down. Fear climbed up his spine. He was stuck with nowhere to go.

He looked to his mother's light. Something was happening and the light moved across the room. Jonny could see it. He knew that people must have thought he was nuts. His eyes never wavered as they watched the light. His mother's aura moved deliberately and settled down next to Caj.

Caj never cried or showed any grief unless he was super-drunk. The hole in him came from another source. Jonny and others wanted Caj to straighten up but he never did. Mariann came back into his life and there was a little improvement, but it never stopped them from worrying about him. Caj wanted his mother to forgive him but never said why. He sounded crazy some times when he came over drunk. Jonny missed the old Caj but knew that he would never be the same. He wished he could come back just this one time.

"Mmm ... mm. Mmmm ... mm. To my brother, Caj, I offer forgiveness. His soul has been lost." Caj looked up at Jonny in surprise. "He is tortured. He began life a giving and caring person. He thinks he is no longer capable of this and seeks redemption. At the same time he gives time and energy to just causes and gives his money freely. My family is lucky he is there for us, but are we there for him? His future is clouded and full of darkness. To him I offer my mother's love that she always gave me unconditionally. She is there beside you. She will always be there for you. She is within you. You must have faith and you will see."

Jonny watched his brother and then his mother's aura merged with Caj.

"Mmm ... mm. We love you and know that you must learn to love yourself again. You have seen things that we will never see and that keeps you from grieving for your own mother. I know you love her. I love her so much. Now she has left us. It hurts. I know you hurt."

He was right. Caj put his head into Mariann's neck. The pain was there. Caj was lost and wanted to be found. Tears fell from him.

Pain rushed through Jonny. He couldn't stand it anymore and he began to weep as he went on.

"Mmmm-mmm. Mmmmmmm. To my sister Scout I offer the stability of our family. She ran away when she was young and never came back. She was always protected by our mother. What will she do without her protector? Maybe now she will see that she is a strong young woman who can protect herself. If not, we are there for you."

Jonny wanted to finish now. He had to finish or he would break down.

"To my little sisters: Katie, you are now the core of the family. You have inherited all that is best in our mother. As the center of our family, we will gravitate toward you and rely on your understanding. You took a lot of taunting when you were younger but never backed away from it and faced it head on. It has made you stronger. To you I offer our mother's strength which you already carry. It is within you."

"To Alexcia, who lives in so much doubt: like Morgan-Mckenzi, you have talents that none of the others can match. To you I offer the foundation of the family. A foundation built on the love of our mother. With this you can achieve all that your abilities can produce."

"And to Shawn, the baby of the family." Jonny felt his heart heave. She was the last of the family who was their mother. Always wanting to be on her own to control her own world. "To you I offer our family's memories of a mother who has left you early. With these memories, maybe it will make your future easier to live through."

He saw his father Franc sitting there alone, knowing that he would have to pay for the past in the future. His wife of many years was buried. He was a part of her, but not a part of his children. Jonny saw a scared, lonely man. Maybe he was always that way. Jonny, who always wanted to be like his father; knew that he would never be. His brother Caj had ended up like him but hopefully he would change in time.

"Mm ... mm. And to my father Franc, who must live in loneliness and fear after his wife of thirty-two years has left him." Jonny saw his father's ashen face staring into the nothingness that was his wife. He wiped something from his open mouth. "To my father who must live without the woman who loved him for all these years." Jonny thought of her now from his heart and the tears ran freely. "Mm ... mm. To him I offer the love of his family. His children, who love him as much as they loved their mother. A love that held the demons and loneliness at bay. It is all that we have."

Jonny was at the end. The people in the big hall were all crying or waiting for his final words.

"Mm ... mm. Mm ... mm. And to my mother, who is now taking her final walk to the other side. We will miss you always because the pain of today will be with us. We will miss your soul that now walks in spirit form. We will miss your beauty and your wisdom. You were our mother and teacher, who taught us that the world is made up of good and decent people, as you were good and decent."

Jonny was crying hard along with everyone in the hall. Through the tears he felt more than saw the gray wolf walking across the floor. Fear rushed him. He thought his spirit was leaving with his mother. It was moving so slow, its head down swaying from side to side. Jonny stopped and watched the gray wolf walking to the entrance.

Then it sat next to someone at the door. Jonny could barely breathe as he saw her standing there. It was Nikki-D. Her dark, black eyes watched him from the entrance. Her long, black hair hid some of her face. The tears hid the rest. People looked where Jonny stared. Then he saw Ginny get up and go to her. Mother and daughter hugged and cried. Jonny saw Alexcia point to Nikki-D and he knew everything would be all right and he gained strength.

"Mm ... mm. And to my mother I offer the love and respect of an entire community. It is the people you have left behind who are better off from meeting you than they ever could be on their own. These are the people who are your legacy."

Jonny could barely go on.

"Mmmmm ... mm. Mmmmm.mm. To my mother I offer the love of your family.

We are your life and limb. We are left behind in tears as you walk into the next life. We wish you safe journey. There you will meet those that went before you and you will give them our love that you carry with you. That is good. To you, our mother, as you walk into the darkness of our hearts you offer the light of the future. It is all that we have left."

Jonny's head was down and he lifted it to see the people.

"Mmmm.mm. Mmm .... mm. To my mother, we say good-bye." Jonny stared into the darkness.

His final whisper;
                    "I love you."

The Wolf Guided him through the Pines to the Medicine Lake. Jumping Mouse Drank the Water from the Lake. The Wolf Described the Beauty to him.

"I must Leave you here," said Wolf, "for I must Return so that I may Guide Others, but I will Remain with you as long as you Like."

"Thank you, my Brother, said Jumping Mouse. "But although I am Frightened to be Alone, I Know you must Go so that you may Show Others the Way to this Place."

Jumping Mouse Sat there Trembling in Fear. It was no use running, for he was Blind, but he Knew an Eagle would Find him Here. He Felt a shadow on his Back and heard the Sound the Eagles Make. He Braced himself for the Shock. And the Eagle Hit! Jumping Mouse went to Sleep.

Then he Woke Up. The surprise of being Alive was Great, but Now he could See! Everything was Blurry, but the Colors were Beautiful.

"I can See! I can See! said Jumping Mouse over again and again.

A blurry Shape Came toward Jumping Mouse. Jumping Mouse Squinted hard but the Shape Remained a Blur.

"Hello, Brother," a Voice said. "Do you Want some Medicine?"

"Some Medicine for me? asked Jumping Mouse. "Yes! Yes!"

"Then Crouch down as Low as you Can," the Voice said, "and Jump as High as you Can."

Jumping Mouse did as he was Instructed. He Crouched as Low as he Could and Jumped! The Wind Caught him and Carried him Higher.

"Do not be Afraid," the Voice called to him. "Hang on to the Wind and Trust!"

Jumping Mouse did. He Closed his Eyes and Hung on to the Wind and it Carried him Higher and Higher. Jumping Mouse Opened his Eyes and they were Clear, and the Higher he Went the Clearer they Became. Jumping Mouse Saw his Old Friend upon a Lily Pad on the Beautiful Medicine Lake. It was the Frog.

"You have a New Name," Called the Frog. "You are Eagle!"

SISTERS

Part two in this moving trilogy comes from the perspective of the Esque women – the sisters as they fight for the future of the Tribe and themselves.

A story of growing up in a male dominated reservation system, in a home of silent chaos, and overcoming adversity in a continually harsh environment.

A story of triumph over impossible odds to maintain ones identity and be treated as deserved.

To order *"The Res"* directly
or other M² publications contact:

M² PUBLISHING COMPANY
6025 Lois Madison Drive
Marysville, WA 98271
(360) 651-0967
FAX: 651-0960
e-mail: m2write@aol.com